THE MIRROR OF NAPLES

BY THE SAME AUTHOR

The Pearl of France
The Queen's Spy
The Fair Maid of Kent
An Illegitimate Affair
The Epiphany Betrayal
The Making of a Tudor
Fire and Fleet and Candlelight
The Woodville Conspiracy

THE MIRROR OF NAPLES

CAROLINE NEWARK

Copyright © 2024 Caroline Newark

The moral right of the author has been asserted.

Apart from any fair dealing for the purposes of research or private study, or criticism or review, as permitted under the Copyright, Designs and Patents Act 1988, this publication may only be reproduced, stored or transmitted, in any form or by any means, with the prior permission in writing of the publishers, or in the case of reprographic reproduction in accordance with the terms of licences issued by the Copyright Licensing Agency. Enquiries concerning reproduction outside those terms should be sent to the publishers.

This is a work of fiction. Names, characters, businesses, places, events and incidents are either the products of the author's imagination or used in a fictitious manner. Any resemblance to actual persons, living or dead, or actual events is purely coincidental.

Troubador Publishing Ltd
Unit E2 Airfield Business Park,
Harrison Road, Market Harborough,
Leicestershire LE16 7UL
Tel: 0116 279 2299
Email: books@troubador.co.uk
Web: www.troubador.co.uk

ISBN 978 1805144 052

British Library Cataloguing in Publication Data.
A catalogue record for this book is available from the British Library.

Printed and bound in the UK by TJ Books Limited, Padstow, Cornwall
Typeset in 11pt Minion Pro by Troubador Publishing Ltd, Leicester, UK

*In memory of my mother,
Kathleen Mary Newark
who sailed across the sea to live in
the island below the horizon.*

THE FAMILY TREE
(SO FAR)

Edward the First, King of England, married Marguerite of France, and had by her issue, Edmund of Woodstock

♥

Edmund of Woodstock, Earl of Kent, married Margaret, daughter of Lord John Wake, and had by her issue, Joan of Kent

♥

Joan of Kent in her own right Countess of Kent, married Sir Thomas Holand, to whom she bore issue, Thomas Holand

♥

Thomas Holand married Alys, daughter of Richard Fitzalan, Earl of Arundel, by Eleanor of Lancaster, and had by her issue, Eleanor Holand

♥

Eleanor Holand married Thomas Montagu, Earl of Salisbury, to whom she bore, issue Alice Montagu

♥

Alice Montagu, in her own right Countess of Salisbury, married Sir Richard Nevill, to whom she bore issue, Kathryn Nevill

♥

Kathryn Nevill, daughter of Richard Nevill, Earl of Salisbury, married William Bonville, Lord Harington, to whom she bore issue, Cecily Bonville

♥

Cecily Bonville, in her own right Baroness Harington, married Sir Thomas Grey, Marquess of Dorset, to whom she bore issue, Elizabeth Grey

CAST OF MAIN CHARACTERS

Elizabeth Grey	daughter of the late Marquess of Dorset
Cecily Grey	one of her many sisters
Thomas Grey	her eldest brother, "the Marquess"
Leonard Grey	the second of her four brothers
Their mother	the dowager Lady Marquess
Their stepfather	Henry Stafford, Earl of Wiltshire
Meg Wooton	Thomas Grey's wife
The king	Henry VIII
The queen	Katherine of Aragon
Princess Mary	the king's sister
Charles Brandon	Duke of Suffolk, the king's friend
Thomas Wolsey	Archbishop of York, the king's advisor
The Emperor	Maximilian I
The Prince of Castile	Charles, grandson and heir of Maximilian
The Archduchess	Margaret, daughter of Maximilian
Jane Bourchier	a friend to Elizabeth
Lizzie Bryan	Jane's cousin
Francis Bryan	Lizzie's brother
Louis XII	the French king
The Duke of Valois	François d'Angoulême, Louis's heir
Madame Claude	Louis's daughter, wife of François
Madame Louise	mother of François
Mary Boleyn	daughter of Sir Thomas Boleyn

Anne Boleyn	Mary Boleyn's younger sister
Lord Norfolk	Duke of Norfolk
Thomas Howard	Earl of Surrey, Lord Norfolk's son
Lord Kildare	Gerald Fitzgerald, Earl of Kildare
Lady Gertrude	Countess of Devon
Alice	one of Lord Kildare's daughters
Tom (Thomas)	Lord Kildare's son and heir
Walter Delahide	Steward at Maynooth
Janet Eustace	Walter's wife
Piers Butler	claimant to the earldom of Ormonde
Thomas Cromwell	Wolsey's protégé, later principal secretary to Henry VIII

PROLOGUE

APRIL 1509

It took more than a week for the message to reach the hands of the king's lord deputy in Ireland. A whole page of official language was required to impart the sad news but nothing was said of the dying man's agonised pleading with God and the bargains he'd offered to save his immortal soul.

Once he'd digested the contents of the letter, the lord deputy sent for his son.

'Tudor's dead.'

The young man winced, crossed himself and murmured what onlookers assumed was a prayer.

'What's the boy like?' growled his father, more than ever aware of the frailty of man's existence. Born a year before the Tudor he'd somehow imagined God would have them both live forever.

'Henry? Seventeen, tall, good-looking, bit of a show-off. He's clever, mind you. A great student of the Bible.'

'Women?'

His son laughed. 'I doubt Henry knows what to do with a woman. He was ten when Arthur died. Afterwards, the old man never let him out of his sight. Losing one son was a calamity; to lose two would have killed him.'

'Any word of a wife? Breed another little Tudor.'

'There was some talk of Arthur's widow, the Spanish

princess, Katherine, but neither side could agree on the dowry.'

Speaking of Arthur brought back painful memories of that God-awful day at Worcester when they'd buried his friend; when the heavens wept a ceaseless torrent of rain. The hope of Tudor England, the king's elder son, just fifteen years of age and six months married – dead.

He'd been the same age as Arthur. Tears had poured down his cheeks as he rode up the nave astride the dead prince's courser and he was not alone in his grief; even the bishop could barely speak for weeping.

His friends in England said the court had become a dismal place full of grey-faced old men anxious for their futures with the Tudor coughing and creaking his way to the grave. Yet here they were in a new regime with a young king: dashing, vital, golden and handsome; and, thanks to the old man's careful hoarding of the nation's taxes, solvent. Twenty-four years since Bosworth and Henry, the eighth of that name, would inherit a kingdom at peace – more or less.

1

THE DOWAGER LADY MARQUESS
SPRING 1514

A muffled whispering at the far end of the room was followed by the patter of footsteps. One of the senior ladies stepped up to the dais and murmured into the queen's ear.

I laid my sewing neatly in my lap, wondering what could have happened: a maid fallen into a faint; a royal beast on the loose in the palace grounds; an armed insurrection?

The queen's gaze travelled slowly over the assembled company.

'Lady Elizabeth Grey.'

My heart leapt. I set aside my sewing, rose from my seat and curtsied.

'Your Majesty.'

'Lady Elizabeth, it seems the dowager lady marquess, your mother, is anxious to see you. I trust nothing is amiss.'

She paused just long enough for me to consider the multiple calamities that might have befallen my mother and reject them all. My mother was far too careful of her person to fall victim to some random accident or illness.

The queen smiled serenely. 'The dowager lady marquess has arranged an escort to take you to Holborn.'

Holborn! What was my mother doing at Holborn? She was supposed to be in the country. She was always in the country after Easter.

The queen continued. 'Naturally we shall be sad to lose you this afternoon, Lady Elizabeth, but a daughter's duty must come first, must it not. We shall expect you at supper.'

'Yes, Your Majesty.'

Queen Katherine might be genuinely sad to lose me but not as sad as I was at the prospect of seeing my mother.

As I hurried towards the Greenwich landing stage I spied the Dorset barge down on the river and, at the top of the steps, the unwelcome sight of my eldest brother.

Thomas was old enough to be my father, an unsettling man prone to the slamming of doors. I could tell he was annoyed by the way he was brushing imaginary pieces of fluff from the sleeves of his doublet, muttering about the waste of his valuable time. Doubtless he'd anticipated an enjoyable afternoon at the butts showing off his talents to the younger gentlemen. As the acknowledged head of the Grey family he resented being ordered about by our mother.

'You're late,' he hissed, under cover of giving me a courtly incline of his head. 'I do not expect to be kept waiting.'

I murmured an apology rather than argue that I'd come as soon as I'd received our mother's summons and could hardly leave the queen's rooms without her permission. Thomas expected subservience from his sisters so it was wise to say as little as possible. He was already acting as if this expedition was of my making and I'd no wish to anger him further.

My mother's residence was situated well outside the city walls, far from the noise and stink of the streets. It was one of her lesser houses, used on the rare occasions she deigned to visit London during the winter season. After Easter she spent her time at Astley so I presumed her presence here today meant a crisis was brewing. In my experience, which I had to admit was not vast, my mother enjoyed a good crisis. She reminded me of those old women who gain pleasure from watching a man choke to death at the end of a rope.

The last time I visited Holborn the house was considerably smaller but this past year the original humble dwelling of a wealthy gentleman had been refaced in red brick and enlarged to something more resembling a royal palace. The old house had sprouted two new wings, slightly lower than the main part which boasted a huge arched entrance complete with columns. The windows were tall and evenly spaced, pleasing to my mother's orderly mind but which my sisters said gave the house a strange foreign look. As none of them had travelled further than Dover and had no notion of what glories lay beyond our shores, I suspected their comments were meant to impress their listeners.

My mother's steward bowed a welcome while vainly trying to keep one pace ahead as Thomas strode into the house, through the hall and up the staircase, radiating fury with every footstep. I followed meekly behind, hoping to remain invisible.

My mother was sitting at her table, surrounded by piles of scrolled documents. It was hard to tell how old she was. There was pouching under her chin, partially hidden by the high collar of her black gown; a few creases across her brow and furrows of discontent down the sides of her mouth. She had a fine web of lines at the corners of her eyes but her eyesight was as keen as ever despite the constant squinting at figures in her ledgers.

When I was younger I once asked why she did not employ a man to oversee her accounts. I was told that men were inherently untrustworthy in matters of money and would cheat you unless they were watched. She had a vast household to do her bidding: a steward to attend to her domestic arrangements and supervise the indoor servants, a receiver, a lawyer, a secretary and an army of clerks to help in the management of her wealth, which my sisters said was considerable. Yet the passing years had not changed her opinion of men.

She laid down her quill and fixed us with a penetrating gaze. I sensed a familiar lurch in my belly as if I'd been skewered with a long silver needle.

'Is it true, what I'm hearing?' she said, having offered us no greeting.

My brother shifted his feet, expecting an invitation to sit and clearly annoyed that one was not forthcoming.

'That depends on what tittle-tattle you've heard, madam,' he said stiffly.

I looked from one to the other, recognising the familiar opening salvoes in their personal war of attrition.

'Distressing news from Spain.' Her voice was as smooth as honey with no sign yet of the sting of a bee.

'From whom?'

My mother lifted her black silk-clad shoulders in the slightest of shrugs. 'That I cannot say. My source prefers he remain anonymous. But he speaks of the queen's father and his words are not complimentary.'

I pricked up my ears at the mention of Queen Katherine's father.

According to my sisters, King Ferdinand had allowed his daughter to descend into near poverty in a disagreement with our late king over Katherine's dowry. They said the quarrel was a disgrace.

My mother smiled as if what she had to say was giving her pleasure.

'My source believes Ferdinand is not as steadfast as he once was, that promises made in the heat of last summer's triumphs have dissolved in the harsh light of a Spanish winter. So I ask again – is it true?'

My brother's eyes narrowed as well they might. Two years ago his reputation had suffered when King Ferdinand reneged on a promise to provide support for the military expedition commanded by my brother. I did not think steadfast was a word Thomas would use in connection with the queen's father.

'Since you ask, madam, King Henry has been apprised of a certain unfortunate development. Our envoys tell us that Ferdinand has been talking with the French.'

My mother seemed unsurprised that King Ferdinand would converse with his bitterest enemy.

'And?'

'Our intelligence is that their discussion concerned a truce.'

'Oh, a mere discussion, nothing more. So there is no need for Henry to worry.'

My brother clenched and unclenched his fists, a sure sign of mounting annoyance. 'What does it matter if it was a discussion or an advanced plan for a peace treaty. It is a betrayal of trust.'

My mother gave a glimmer of a smile as if she found the betrayal of our king's trust amusing.

'Henry did not know?'

'The king is a Christian prince who keeps his word and expects others to do likewise. He suspected nothing. Ferdinand protests his good faith and continues to assure the king of his support for their planned war against France.'

'Ah yes, the war against France.'

My brother cleared his throat as if to remind our mother he'd been offered no refreshment and that as her late husband's heir did not expect to be kept standing in front of her like an errant schoolboy about to be chastised.

'Naturally we had our suspicions,' he said. 'The queen's father is known as a slippery customer. His behaviour over the queen's dowry was not what the king's late father expected of a brother monarch, and his behaviour two years ago was nothing short of outrageous. This new move merely confirms his tendency to perfidy.'

'Henry is angry.'

'He is furious. He blames the queen.'

My mother gave a short laugh. 'Of course he does. Who else can he blame but his beloved wife, daughter of the faithless Ferdinand? It is not in Henry's nature to blame himself for being taken in by a sly old fox, well-versed in the art of treachery. An experienced man, or perhaps I should say one who was better advised, would have been more careful.'

I'd been in the queen's apartments when the king had first heard of his father-in-law's latest deceit. I'd looked up from my sewing to see him striding towards the dais where his wife sat with Princess Mary. Being taller than other men and possessing what my mother called a majestic body, Henry was always going to look imposing, but dressed in deep crimson with jewels glittering on his black velvet cap and a heavy gold chain around his neck, he was the epitome of princely magnificence. Everyone said he was the handsomest prince ever seen, a man whose heart was so full, his desires so virtuous and his nature so inclined to friendliness, that no Christian king would ever surpass him in glory. But that morning he'd looked far from friendly. He was scowling and shouting that he'd been betrayed.

My mother tapped the table. 'And what is being said in Mary's chamber?'

Mary was my cousin; I'd been her companion since I first came to court at the age of seven.

My brother was disparaging. 'Ferdinand is hardly the concern of the Princess Mary.'

My mother sat back in her chair and regarded my brother with dislike. 'What a fool you are, sir. I suppose you dismiss any information we women receive as false rumour and thus pay no heed.'

'What else have you heard?' My brother raised his voice. 'I demand you tell me.'

'Demand?' My mother pretended to cower in her chair, raising her hands in a parody of trembling surrender. 'Are you to use thumbscrews on your own mother, a poor frail elderly lady?'

This war between my mother and my eldest brother usually manifested itself in barbed insults delivered under the guise of exquisite politeness but this time I feared I was about to witness one of their occasional explosions into outright hostility.

My mother bided her time, watching my brother carefully. Eventually, tired of baiting him, she said, 'It is, of course, only tittle-tattle, but there are those who say the planned marriage with the queen's nephew will not go ahead.'

I gasped in disbelief. This was impossible! Cousin Mary had been betrothed to the queen's nephew for six years. It was a wonderful match. Charles, Prince of Castile, was heir to half Europe, the half that wasn't France. He was heir to his maternal grandfather, King Ferdinand, ruler of Aragon, and to his paternal grandfather, Emperor Maximilian, the Hapsburg ruler of the many Germanys, Burgundy, Austria and the Netherlands. One day Charles would be the wealthiest and most powerful ruler in Europe, a weighty counterbalance to the might of France. It was impossible that the marriage would not go ahead.

'Arrangements have been made,' I protested.

'Arrangements can be unmade,' my mother said drily. 'Promises can be broken. Hearts can be broken. Great men pay no heed to promises or heartbreak.'

'Mary has been in correspondence with the archduchess,' I said weakly, as if letters to the young man's aunt conferred a seal of validity on the proposed marriage.

'For what reason?' my mother enquired serenely.

'To ensure the design of her wedding gown meets with the archduchess's favour, Mary has promised to introduce Flemish fashion to all her English ladies.'

'How obliging.'

'And a list of Mary's attendants has been approved

by the archduchess. We've been told preparations for our arrival in Calais are complete.'

My mother sniffed. 'On the contrary, I hear excuses have been made.'

'Yes, yes,' my brother said irritably. 'They say Calais is infested with plague, which it is not. They want the wedding moved to Antwerp.'

'I also hear they're saying Mary is too old for the boy.'

'That is ridiculous! Four years is nothing in a marriage. Look at the gap between Lord Suffolk and his latest betrothed – twenty years if it's a day!'

'Ah, but the Duke of Suffolk is a man,' my mother said, moistening her lips as if savouring thoughts of the handsome duke's manhood.

'He's a jumped-up nobody,' my brother said crossly, dismissing the king's close friend as a man of no importance which was demonstrably untrue.

'I also hear the prince has been sick.'

'Charles is often sick. His constitution is feeble. What he needs is a wife.'

My mother demurred. 'Sounds as if he's in more need of a nurse.'

'They are suspicious,' my brother said firmly. 'Charles is a boy of the utmost importance to Maximilian. In the circumstances it is only natural he sees hazards.'

'And you, sir, should remember what happens when a ruler becomes suspicious.'

At that, my brother paled and looked decidedly sick. It was only five years since he'd found himself imprisoned in Calais in a purge ordered by Henry's late father, a man who saw imaginary threats to his rule at every turn. My sisters said our brother would have paid the ultimate penalty as a traitor but was saved from the scaffold by the old king's timely demise. Henry, in a gesture of goodwill, had Thomas released. Despite his lucky escape I reckoned my brother still lived in fear of the icy touch of an executioner's axe on the back of his neck.

'You cannot possibly understand,' my brother said, dismissing my mother's comments with a display of deliberate arrogance. 'These little difficulties are expected in an alliance of this importance. It is commonplace.'

'Ah, but is what is being said about the emperor also commonplace?'

'What have you heard?' My brother's voice was sharp.

'Oh just women's tittle-tattle. Nothing that would interest you.'

My brother's face was turning an alarming shade of puce. 'I warn you, madam, withholding information from the king is tantamount to treason. You'd do well to tell me what you know.'

My mother smiled sweetly, her painted lips curving in the smallest of smiles as the lines around her mouth crinkled.

'Maximilian is talking to the French. A treaty of peace is in the air.'

'That is impossible!'

'Entirely possible. Maximilian is fully aware of the vulnerability of his borders. He's been flirting with King Louis for years. Perhaps, like a nervous bride, he feels now is the time to consummate their relationship.'

My brother was not yet ready for defeat. 'It is a ruse. The emperor is trying to squeeze more money out of Henry, that's all.'

'But Louis is rich; he can offer more.'

'You know nothing of the king's closeness to the emperor. After we took Thérouanne and Tournai last summer I remember him dancing till dawn.'

My mother smiled and remarked, 'Means nothing. Henry enjoys dancing.'

'On the contrary, it's a sign of friendship. And I would remind you, madam, that Maximilian is bound to us by the treaty.'

'Is that the same treaty we agreed with the queen's father?' my mother asked, innocently fingering the papers on her table.

'God Almighty!' My brother clapped his hand to his forehead in despair.

'Poor Henry!' my mother soothed. 'Deceived in every direction. A lamb in a den of lions. Everyone using him for their own ends. If his father had paid more attention to his education in matters of state, he'd have known better.'

'Is this what you summoned me for, to boast of your superior spy system?' my brother said, seething with fury that our mother had known more than him; more even, it seemed, than Henry and his advisors.

'No, no, I have no wish to talk of Henry's woes. What matters is what this means for our family.' She nodded at me. 'How this will affect Elizabeth.'

My brother regarded me sourly. He did not consider me much of an asset to the Grey family, more a burden. I was yet another sister who would someday contract a marriage and the husband would expect a dowry commensurate with my brother's rank.

'I thought her inclusion in Mary's train would attract

an offer,' he said wearily, 'but as, according to your secret information, there will be no wedding, we shall have to look elsewhere.'

My mother peered at me. 'She's not unpleasing to look at. Mouth a little wide perhaps.'

'She is the king's cousin. That's all that matters.'

'A half-blood kinship.'

This was another familiar argument which had grown over the years. My father had been half-brother to Henry's mother and my brother liked to talk up his royal kinship. But if you brushed away the gloss of our paternal grandmother's second marriage to King Edward, my mother's lineage was more exalted than my father's.

'I'd not want to waste her on some impecunious gentleman,' my brother grumbled. 'God's truth, there's enough of them scrambling for places at court; all claiming kinship to some ancient lord you've never heard of, cluttering up the palace with their bags and their boys and their dogs, pissing against the walls like a bunch of peasants.'

My mother moved her gaze to the window. 'Of course we do not yet know how Henry will react when he learns of the emperor's betrayal, which of his advisors he will blame. I doubt he'll blame the queen even though Charles is her nephew; the boy is too young to have had any influence on his grandfather.'

'He cannot blame me,' Thomas said quickly. 'I only ever followed his lead in these matters.'

'He'll not blame Mary. She has no hand in this. Many would say she is more sinned against than Henry but he'll not see it that way. He'll take this setback personally as he always does.' My mother sighed. 'A man's vanity is truly a tender flower, so easily bruised. Woe betide the fool who destroys the image a man sees of himself when he looks in his mirror.'

We all knew what Henry saw in his mirror: himself at the head of a grand alliance with the mighty emperor and the ruler of Spain; their aim, to contain and destroy the power of France which threatened all their interests.

Cousin Mary said Henry was considering other marriages to bind the emperor closer: her elder sister Margaret, the widowed Queen of Scotland, as a new wife for Maximilian, and Henry's friend, Charles Brandon, Duke of Suffolk, as a husband for the emperor's daughter, the archduchess. Although that last must surely be a jest as Charles Brandon was not of noble stock as well as being betrothed to his ward – the girl twenty years younger than the duke. But if the emperor now preferred closeness to King Louis, none of these proposed marriages would take place.

The prospect was dismal. In the years ahead the great powers of Europe would be aligned against England and might gobble us up just as once we had tried to gobble up France.

I took a deep breath. 'Surely the king will make another match for Princess Mary – a better one.'

My brother gave a derisive laugh. 'There is no better match than with the emperor's heir. Who do you envisage – some petty foreign count?'

My mother eyed me speculatively, as if I'd said something clever. 'There's always Louis.'

I gasped. 'But he's old.'

'He is King of France and a widower; his age is immaterial.'

'Louis is our enemy,' my brother said firmly. 'Henry would never agree.'

'He could be persuaded,' my mother murmured. 'A clever man might point out how advantageous such a match would be in the circumstances and how angry it would make those who'd betrayed him.'

My brother was adamant. 'It would take a brave man to put France on the table.'

'And you, sir, are not brave.'

'It is not my place to advise the king on such matters,' my brother said loftily.

'Of course it is not, but you should remember that revenge is a dish much enjoyed by those who feel slighted. Once Henry is informed of the emperor's betrayal I think he might relish the prospect.'

'And in France we might find a suitor for your daughter.'

'Your sister,' my mother said, aiming the first shot in a new war over the payment of my dowry.

'I wager, he'll let us die spinsters,' my sister Cecily had whispered the last time we met. 'He says there's no money for dowries.'

Whoever she married, Cousin Mary would have a splendid dowry, one fit for the younger sister of the king of England. But for the Grey sisters, there'd be no such inducements for a potential husband. I feared we'd have to rely on our wits.

2

MARY, PRINCESS OF CASTILE
SPRING 1514

On my return to Greenwich I found my friend, Jane Bourchier, waiting for me outside Mary's rooms. Jane was a tall, serious young woman whose one failing was to believe everything she was told. In Jane's mind there was no careful sieving of information, no difference between the highly probable and the utterly impossible.

'Such news!' she said, her large brown eyes shining with excitement.

'What have you heard?' I asked warily.

'The beloved is enamoured with another.'

The beloved was the name used between ourselves for Mary's betrothed, the emperor's grandson, Charles, Prince of Castile.

'Are you certain?' I wondered where Jane had picked up this particular piece of unlikely gossip. 'Do we have a name for his new inamorata?'

'She's a young lady at the Flemish court. They say he cannot leave her alone.'

'My mother says he's taken to his bed.'

'Lovesickness,' Jane pronounced firmly. 'The doctors say it's a fever brought on by the moon but word is the beloved believes Princess Mary is wavering in her affections so has turned his attentions elsewhere.'

'Does Mary know?'

'She received a letter from him this morning, swearing undying devotion to his good wife. But I cannot believe he is sincere. He writes in such a chilly fashion as if addressing a block of stone.'

'Perhaps the archduchess tells him what to write.'

Jane eyes widened in horror. 'I'd not have my aunt dictate my love letters.'

'Do you write love letters? You didn't tell me.'

She gave me one of her rare secretive smiles. 'Perhaps I forgot.'

I thought it unlikely Jane was involved with some gentleman at court. We were seldom without supervision and even if Mary was, at times, a careless mistress, the queen could be relied on to keep an eye on the younger ladies. Her Spanish upbringing had been strict and she expected the highest standards. In the privacy of Mary's rooms we younger ones might laugh and romp and make teasing remarks but in the presence of the queen, our behaviour was of the highest order.

I put my mouth close to Jane's ear so that no-one else could hear a word. 'My mother believes the marriage will not go ahead. She says the emperor is talking to the French.'

Jane gasped. 'The Judas!'

'She says King Henry should marry Mary to the French king.'

Jane's eyes widened in shock. 'But that would mean breaking her sacred word. She swore to take the beloved as her husband. They're as good as wed.'

'If the emperor and his council are mired in treachery,

then she'd be justified. Not even the pope would find fault.'

'Should we tell her?' said Jane.

I shook my head. 'I think not. The king will make his wishes known when he has come to a decision. In the meantime we say nothing.'

All through the Mayday revels, the jousts, the feasts and the dancing, the continual round of entertainments organised for the king's benefit, we said nothing. Nobody spoke of an impending crisis or a change in the king's settled policy towards the great powers of Europe; nobody wanted to be the harbinger of bad news and destroy the fun and the jollity. Ballads were sung, the king composed another piece of music to universal acclaim and a competition to be adjudged by the queen was set for the cleverest piece of verse.

People spoke of how magnificently gowned the queen was and what a beautiful young woman the king's sister had become but nobody remarked on a particularly well-dressed French gentleman amongst those present. The man seemed ill at ease, spending part of the early evening in conversation with the Duke of Longueville.

The duke was one of a group of French noblemen captured at Thérouanne the previous summer, idling away their time at the English court waiting to be ransomed. They flirted outrageously with any English lady foolish enough to look their way and played cards with the king's friends but were known to cheat. This particular Frenchman was different, slipping carefully between the revellers, never stopping too long in any one place.

Next morning I was summoned to Mary's private room, where she went to be alone, to pray or talk with her confessor. I knocked at the door and when I entered, gave a small curtsy.

'Princess, you asked for me,' I said.

'I did, Cousin Elizabeth.' She indicated a chair next to her. 'Come, sit. I need some advice and I cannot ask Henry.'

I sat down, wondering what was so secret that Mary could not ask the one person to whom she usually poured out her heart.

'If I can help, naturally, I will.'

Mary was blessed with a rare beauty: an oval face, fair skin, high forehead, blue eyes and an abundance of red-gold hair. But this morning a small frown marred her perfect features.

She chewed her lip as if uncertain where to begin.

'Oh Cousin Elizabeth, I am not ignorant of the rumours about my forthcoming marriage to the emperor's grandson but I cannot believe they are true. The archduchess writes such warm words and Charles himself – you have seen what he says.'

She reached for the small carved wooden coffer on the table and picked out a bundle of letters, tied with blue ribbon.

'We've been writing to each other for six years, increasingly loving letters. I've kept every one. He says he cannot wait to see me, to make me his own. He has heard so much about me and believes I shall make him a perfect wife. Those are surely the words of a young man in love. But now I fear something is wrong.'

She proffered the latest. 'Please read it.'

I bent my head and quickly scanned the page. It was short, beautifully composed but written without feeling, as if the young man knew what he should say but had no warmth, no emotion, no sentiment for the lady to whom he was writing. As Jane had said, it was a cold letter, a little stilted and utterly devoid of passion.

'Perhaps he is shy, Princess. He is only fourteen.'

'Yes, I grant you he is young but Henry says that at fourteen he would have been eager to marry someone like me.'

I smiled. 'The king is very kind.'

'He is but I'd not want him to think I mistrust his judgement. That is why I cannot ask him about the Frenchman at yesterday evening's celebrations. You must have noticed him. Who was he? Why was he here? Was it to do with my marriage to Charles? People are saying King Louis is interested in taking me for his wife. They say a French marriage would be better for England. But I have given my word to Charles.'

I hesitated, wondering who had told her about a possible marriage with King Louis.

'Princess, I believe the man you saw might be an agent of the French king but I think he would be bargaining for the release of the Duke of Longueville. There's no reason to think there was anything sinister about him.'

She clapped her hands together. 'You're right, Cousin Elizabeth. Why did I not think of that. The duke has been with us for so long, he's become a fixed star in our midst. I sometimes forget he must surely wish to return home to France.'

Since his enforced arrival, the Duke of Longueville had become a great favourite amongst the ladies. Despite the existence of a wife, he was rumoured to be having an affair with the elegant Frenchwoman who'd taught Mary and her sister to speak French. Under the circumstances, perhaps he was in no hurry to be ransomed, especially as Henry enjoyed his company at the card table. If that was true, who was the mysterious stranger and what was he doing here?

Mary replaced the letter in the coffer but hesitated before closing the lid.

'Cousin Elizabeth, are you frightened at the thought of leaving England?'

I thought of the miles of sea between us and Calais, the unknown people we would meet at the archduchess's court at Malines, the thrill of another wedding, a proper one this time, unlike the proxy wedding of six years ago. But mixed with this excitement was a feeling of imminent loss, of leaving my sisters and my friends at the English court, those who would not be coming with us. Sometimes I wanted nothing to change, at others I longed for something new.

'A little but it is a great honour to be chosen to accompany you. No young woman of sense would prefer being left behind.'

She gave a sad little smile. 'Now the hour is almost upon me, I fear never seeing England or my brother again. Henry is dearer to me than anyone in the whole world. After I lost my brother Arthur and my mother, when my sister, Margaret, was sent away to marry the King of the Scots, Henry was all I had. Often I would cling to him for comfort.' She put up her hand to wipe away an imaginary tear. 'Sometimes I think it will be impossible to love another man as I love Henry.'

'Princess, the love a woman has for a husband must surely be different to the love she feels for a brother, no matter how dear that brother might be. The king will not abandon you; he loves you.'

Her face brightened. 'He does.' Then the frown returned. 'But what if my husband should make war on England? What if I am forbidden to write to my brother? What if Henry thinks of me as his enemy?'

I recognised the familiar signs of Mary developing one of her hysterias: her heart was beating faster, she was panic-stricken at imaginary disasters of the most unlikely kind. Soon there'd be trembling and shortness of breath until, at last, the weeping would begin. On several occasions I had witnessed these upsets and knew I must try to calm her.

I laid my hand on hers and spoke soothingly. 'Princess, your husband will wish to please you. He's already shown himself caring of your welfare so I'm certain he'll do nothing to cause you distress. You need not fear feeling alone; you'll have your ladies to keep you company and I shall be there.'

'What if he should dismiss my ladies. What if he sends them back to England. I'd lose you; I'd lose everyone. Don't tell me it couldn't happen because I know it could. Oh, Cousin Elizabeth, the thought of being left alone in a foreign land is more than I can bear.'

'The prince is not a monster, Princess.'

'How do you know? Perhaps his loving letters are nothing but a sham, a pretence. Perhaps he wishes to keep me prisoner for his own amusement. Perhaps he will hurt me.'

By the time I left, an hour later, thoroughly exhausted with calming Mary, I'd begun to consider the difficulties which lay ahead and wondered if my cousin's fragile constitution would crumble under the strain of having her dreams dashed. Whoever she married, be it the Prince of Castile, or King Louis, or someone else, no flesh and blood man could match up to the man of her dreams. She had woven a fantasy and on her wedding day would come face to face with reality. She was accustomed to being cosseted: the youngest child, the pretty indulged princess, the king's beloved sister. If matters turned out badly, I feared what she'd do. Like Henry she did not take kindly to disappointment.

With mid-summer fast approaching, rumours of a rapprochement with King Louis were flying around the palace like a whirlwind yet no-one was privy to Henry's mind on the matter. Would he continue to support Mary's marriage to the emperor's heir or look elsewhere for an alliance. Shadowy corners of the palace were thick with intrigue. Women whispered into the ears of friends, passing on titbits they'd heard from their menfolk. Gentlemen paid servants for information and laid bets on the outcome. Despite this flurry of activity, no-one was any the wiser.

The king's anger with the queen had passed like a brief summer storm but King Ferdinand's betrayal of Henry's trust was not so easily forgotten. Although the archduchess still wrote Mary encouraging letters, no further date had been set for the wedding and arrangements for our journey to Calais had come to a halt.

Even Mary now believed it unlikely she'd marry Charles. Her magnificent wardrobe, designed in the Flemish fashion to please her betrothed's family, lay untouched; her mirrors, her jewel cases, her gold plate, her china, her silver, her cushions and her tapestries – all waiting for the summons which never came. In the privacy of her inner chamber she shed tears at the loss of the young man she'd wanted as a husband, the recipient of those long loving letters written with such care, the prince she'd never met except in her dreams.

Now a different future beckoned: the prospect of marriage to a pock-ridden, gouty old man. This was hardly appealing to a young woman if the man in question had not been King Louis. She was conflicted. She had waited six long years to marry Charles, he was her perfect chevalier, but the thought of being Queen of France was like the taste of strong wine: sweet on the tongue, thrilling, intoxicating.

In the middle of the month, the king announced a surprise expedition. The whole court would accompany him downriver to Erith for the launch of his new warship. While other princes might find enjoyment in intrigue or the conquest of women, Henry's greatest delight was the machinery of war.

It was a beautiful morning when we set out, sunlight sparkling silver on the water and a slight breeze to keep us cool. The oarsmen in their green and white striped tunics kept perfect time to the beat of a drum and, with the tide in our favour, the barges sped merrily through the water like a mighty flotilla.

'Doesn't the king look magnificent,' Jane sighed.

I glanced across at the royal barge where the king and queen sat on their gilded chairs beneath a gold canopy. As befitted the supreme commander of the navy, Henry was dressed in a vest and breeches of cloth-of-gold, scarlet hose, with a whistle on a gold chain hung round his neck. None of the foreign ambassadors, muffled up in their furs against what they called "your despicable English weather", could mistake him for anyone other than a mighty ruler.

The queen sat at Henry's side, gazing proudly at her husband. She was not a great beauty, being small and inclined to plumpness, but in her cloth-of-silver gown with sleeves slashed with crimson satin and her hair covered by a richly embroidered Venetian cap, she looked every inch a queen.

Jane leant close and whispered in my ear. 'Cousin Lizzie says the queen is with child.'

'Are you sure?' I whispered back, thinking I'd not trust a word that Lizzie Bryan said. Her position in the queen's chamber was very lowly, hardly a young woman privy to her mistress's intimate secrets.

'One of the maids says she's missed her course. Twice!'

'Has she told the king?' I asked, wondering if the queen's news accounted for Henry's good humour this morning.

'Not yet but Lizzie says we can expect the birth of a prince in the New Year.'

I sat back and thought what joy that would bring to

the queen. Of all the women I knew, she was the most deserving of a healthy child. She'd been sadly disappointed since her marriage, first by the death of the infant prince born three years ago and then again last autumn with a dead baby. I admired her greatly. She was a truly pious woman, a steadying influence on Henry who, though perfect in every other way, could be inclined to wildness. But as my brother Leonard said, the king was still a young man and all men are entitled to some wildness in their youth, otherwise what was the point in being young; you might as well be born ancient and sober. Leonard was certainly not a sober young man unlike our brother Thomas who, I suspected, had been born a greybeard.

Erith was little more than a few humble houses built around a small harbour on the estuary of the River Thames but one of the king's gentleman who was in our barge, said the new royal dockyard would transform the place. Certainly Erith was busy with the kind of activity I was well-used to. As my mother's daughter I'd spent my childhood surrounded by the noise of masons and carpenters and roofers while our houses were pulled apart and rebuilt in extensive and costly renovations,

We disembarked from the state barges to the accompanying sound of trumpets and wild cheers from a crowd of onlookers. I took care not to miss my footing and fall into the river as nothing would be more shaming than to be hauled, dripping wet, out of the water by a couple of boatmen while everyone laughed.

Henry's new vessel was impressive, looming over us like a malevolent monster. There was a forecastle consisting of four decks, and a smaller aft-castle, seven tops and more than two hundred bronze and iron cannons. One of the king's gentlemen told me how the ship had been built at Woolwich by the royal shipbuilders but was brought here to Erith to be fitted out.

'She's to be called the Henry Grace á Dieu.'

'Great Harry, more like,' I replied, smiling at him because he was a pleasant young man and it did no harm to flirt a little.

'Will Princess Mary sail in her to Calais for her wedding?' Jane asked, blinking in the bright sunlight.

'Hush!' I said, digging her with my elbow.

Sometimes Jane was horribly indiscreet. She should have known better than to mention Mary's marriage plans to a man who was virtually a stranger. He seemed unperturbed, said he did not know and with a promise to see us later on board the vessel, hurried off to join the crowd of gentlemen jostling for a favoured position near the king.

'Look!' Jane said, nudging me. 'It's your mother.'

I could hardly miss my mother. She was dressed like an empress in tawny brocade, embroidered with gold and silver thread, trimmed with what looked suspiciously like egret's down, worn over a black kirtle. On her head was a magnificent crimson velvet hood. Her hand rested possessively on the green satin sleeve of my stepfather, Henry Stafford, Earl of Wiltshire.

Henry Stafford was some twenty years younger than my mother. He had dark hair, a florid complexion and was well fitted out, bulging in the middle rather like the king's vessel. My father died when I was four years old and

Henry Stafford was the only father I had known. But to see him with my mother was unusual for their marital paths seldom crossed.

'Did they marry for love?' sighed Jane, who was incurably romantic.

'I hardly think so,' I replied, smiling at the thought of my mother loving anyone other than herself.

'I suppose it was your stepfather being brother to the Duke of Buckingham.'

'My mother has far too high an opinion of her position as the dowager lady marquess to crave a connection with Buckingham.'

'But the duke is practically royal,' Jane protested.

'So is my brother, although he'd be hard put to explain exactly how.'

'Perhaps it was money. My aunt says the earl needed to make a good marriage.'

'He certainly succeeded. My mother is an extremely wealthy woman.'

'Bessie Blount says it was lust.'

I put my hand over my mouth to prevent myself from laughing out loud.

'Bessie would.'

'No, truly. Bessie says older women are insatiable, quite unable to leave their husbands alone.'

'Most of the older women I know seem only too glad to be apart from their husbands,' I remarked, thinking Jane would do better to avoid a girl like Bessie Blount.

Bessie was one of those young women about court, ever eager to please, always on the arm of some gentleman or other. She served as one of the queen's maids but oddly that did not impede her upward progress. She was a merry little thing, a superb dancer, light on her feet, often partnered by Henry or by his friend, Charles Brandon, Duke of Suffolk. But there were whispers that Bessie's favours extended to more than just dancing. Beneath the merriment she was gaining a reputation for wanton behaviour.

'Your mother must have married your stepfather for some reason,' Jane persisted. 'It wasn't as if she needed to remarry.'

'My sisters think she did it to spite my brother.'

'Truly?' Jane gasped in horror.

'Yes. In the early years of their marriage she spent so much money showering my stepfather with gifts that my brother complained to the king. He said she was wasting his inheritance.'

Fortunately, before Jane could delve further into the murky depths of my mother's feud with my brother over her relationship with Henry Stafford, the queue of people in front of us started to move forward. Soon we were being ushered up a flight of makeshift wooden steps to the deck of the king's new pride and joy.

Once on board, the slight movement of the ship beneath my feet made me unsure of my balance, but after listening to two Masses sung to bless the vessel, I forgot my fears. As soon as the archbishop had finished, we were taken on a guided tour by the king. He spent a long time explaining the need for hundreds of gun ports and how a tidal almanac was an essential tool when navigating French waters. It soon became clear that Henry was an expert on the intricacies of naval warfare especially the use of cannon in destroying enemy ships.

'How do they work?' said Jane, peering at the huge bronze pipes.

'They're for firing broadsides,' the lady next to us said, preening herself as if the king's words had been just for her.

'What's a broadside?' Jane whispered.

'I don't know,' I said, thinking how alien the world of men was, all these strange words they used. To add to their skill on horseback with lance and sword, they now had to master the firing of cannon. Perhaps when I had a husband he would explain the particulars to me, provided he wasn't too old, pock-marked and gouty to bother with naval warfare.

By the middle of July everyone knew of the emperor's betrayal yet Mary's contract of marriage with his heir had still not been formally broken. It was expedient for Henry to postpone the final breach with his treacherous ally and pretend that England was wholly committed to the alliance; that Mary would soon be united in body as well as in spirit with the emperor's grandson. Each time we poked our noses out of our rooms we would see Henry's chief advisor, Thomas Wolsey, followed by his secretary and a dozen underlings, hurrying importantly along the gallery to the king's private rooms.

Rumour was rife that a special peace was brewing between England and France. It was said the king had demanded one million, five hundred thousand gold crowns in addition to Thérouanne, Boulogne and St Quentin as the price for the hand of his beautiful sister. Alternatively, he would accept one hundred thousand gold crowns annually if Louis was willing to take Henry's other sister, Margaret, the widowed queen of Scotland.

'Used goods,' whispered Jane.

'It is the English connection they want,' I whispered back.

'The king is convinced of the rightness of his conduct,' Mary informed us, her voice a little unsteady. 'God guides him in this as in all things. As a loving sister, it is my duty to obey.'

'He'll make her repudiate the contract with the beloved,' Jane whispered.

'Not until he has Louis's agreement signed in his own blood.'

Haggling over the terms of the agreement dragged on. Tournai was added to the list of English demands. It appeared that Mary's sister, Margaret, was willing to co-operate in the matter of her marriage but the French believed her to be stout and coarse-featured; they wanted Mary. Arbitration by the pope was suggested and even Mary was beginning to doubt King Louis's appetite for a new bride.

But by the end of the month Henry was triumphant. One million gold crowns; Tournai and Thérounne to be retained by the English; Scotland to be included in the peace and the king of England's younger sister Princess Mary was to marry Louis, King of France.

3

A PROXY MARRIAGE
AUGUST 1514

We were at the royal manor of Wansted in Essex where Mary was preparing to make the final break with the emperor's heir. For her, this was a moment of great sadness, the end of a long road which she'd once imagined would lead to a lifetime of dutiful obedience and personal happiness. But it was not to be. Charles, Prince of Castile was to be cast aside. Better that, I told her, than the humiliation of being cast aside by him on the orders of his grandfather.

Together we selected a sober gown, one suitable for an occasion which was not joyful but forced upon her. The maids straightened her skirts while I made last minute adjustments to her lovely hair which she wanted left loose like the bride she should have been. She looked fragile, almost broken by her betrothed's faithlessness.

Members of the council, led by Lord Norfolk and the recently ennobled Duke of Suffolk, were waiting in the great hall. Mary gripped my hands as if wanting my strength which I feared was unequal to the task. We both knew where we were heading and it was no longer the archduchess's court at Malines but the royal court of King Louis in Paris.

She was very brave, keeping her chin tilted up so the men in the hall could hear her words.

'I charge my husband, Charles, Prince of Castile, with a breach of faith, and hereby renounce my wedding vows,' she said in a clear high voice which trembled only a little. 'Evil counsel and malicious gossip have turned him against me. I have been humiliated and am resolved never to keep my part of the bargain we made. The contract we agreed is null and void.' At this point she stumbled over the carefully rehearsed speech but a glance at the sympathetic faces of her brother's advisers gave her courage and she carried on. 'I no longer have any wifely affection for the prince and the severing of the nuptial yoke is entirely of my own volition.'

She then asked for King Henry's forgiveness, saying that in all things she was ever ready to obey his good pleasure.

It was a charming speech, striking a necessary balance between womanly pathos and Tudor determination.

'It brought tears to my eyes,' Jane sniffed as we trooped back to Mary's chamber, leaving members of the council to carry the news to the king that his will had been done.

Later that evening I went back to the room I shared with Jane. I found her sprawled on the bed, tallying up something on her fingers.

'What are you doing?'

'Counting my virtues.'

I raised my eyebrows. 'Why?'

'To see if I have enough for someone to want to marry me.'

'Jane! You're a Bourchier. Of course you have.'

'My father's views on marriage are not encouraging.'

Jane's father, Lord Berners, was a renowned scholar, a solemn, clever man, much in demand by the king.

'What does your father say?'

'That all a man needs for contentment in marriage is sufficient money for books and a wife who holds her tongue.'

I laughed. 'Does your mother agree?'

Jane shrugged. 'My mother is a Howard and likes to argue a point. I wish I had a brother like the marquess. He is bound to find a good match for you.'

'I'm not sure I agree. Did you see the way he was watching me today?'

'No.'

'Every move I make is scrutinised and if he thinks I'm too merry or too dull, he summons me to his room and tells me to mend my behaviour. He chastised me yesterday for smiling at Charles Brandon.'

'Mary smiles at Charles Brandon.'

'Of course she does. He's the king's friend and an entertaining companion. I like him.'

'So does Mary.'

'Oh Jane, it hardly matters if Mary likes Charles Brandon or not. She is going to marry King Louis. And it's you who should be smiling.'

'Why?'

'Because, you fool, when Mary marries King Louis she'll need at least a dozen ladies. Surely your father will get you a place.'

Jane's eyes widened. 'France!'

'Paris,' I said, tempting her further.

She sighed with happiness at the thought of Paris, forgetting about those all-important virtues.

Seven days later, peace with France was declared. There were no bonfires, no cannon bursts, no great feasts, yet the news spread like a lightning flash from London to Paris, to Malines and Vienna, telling everyone that the king of England and the king of France were as one and that King Henry was pleased to give his sister's hand in marriage to King Louis.

'Cousin Elizabeth, did you hear what Charles did when he heard I'd broken our compact?' Mary said.

I shook my head. 'No Princess, what did he do?'

I detected no hint of sadness when she spoke of the young man she'd never seen and who had now passed out of her life.

'He called for a young hawk. Once he had it in his hands he plucked its feathers while the bird was still alive.'

'*Sainte Vierge!* That is vile. Why would he do such a thing?'

'He told his councillors they had plucked him at their good pleasure because he was young and knew not how to complain, but they should bear in mind that, in the future, he would pluck them.'

'That is terrible.'

She smiled a little sadly. 'He was angry because he thought I was chained to his wrist but found I was not so easily tamed. His words were false and his sentiments insincere. My brother says I am well rid of him. He says Louis is the better match.'

I forbore to say that marriage to the French king was certainly the better match provided the gouty old man lived to see his wedding day.

A week later we gathered in the great banqueting hall at Greenwich to celebrate the proxy marriage of Louis, King of France, to Mary, younger sister of Henry, King of England.

All around the hall an arras of gold laced with an embroidered frieze of the royal arms of France and England, dazzled the spectators, but by the time the royal party arrived, the English lords in their silks and satins were tired of admiring their surroundings. They'd been waiting for three hours and I took a perverse delight in imagining how irritated my brother, Thomas, must be.

As our procession advanced down the stairs I noticed Queen Katherine presented quite a belly beneath her silver satin gown. Lizzie Bryan had been right in her prediction. Henry had a distinct swagger in his step as well he might: a wife carrying his unborn son and a sister marrying the king of the richest and most powerful country in Europe. A triumph for his diplomacy. Naturally in Henry's mind, his advisor Thomas Wolsey had played the lesser part in bringing negotiations to a successful conclusion, merely obeying his master's instructions. That was the nature of our king – generous, but only up to a point.

Mary looked beautiful. She was wearing a purple and gold chequered gown designed to match the robes of the Duke of Longueville who was not her husband but who, for one day, we would treat as if he was. The duke led the French delegation and had been chosen to stand in King Louis's place for this wedding. He was aided by two of Louis's ministers, men who'd helped finalise the peace negotiations and were probably thinking what a costly Queen of France, the English king's sister was proving to be.

The ceremony began with a lengthy address in Latin by Archbishop Wareham, to which one of the ministers replied that his master, the Most Christian King, was desirous of taking the Lady Mary to wife. Once the French authorisation for the marriage had been read out, the Duke of Longueville took Mary's right hand in his and spoke Louis's vows in French. Mary replied, also in French, after which the duke placed the ring on her finger, the kiss was given and the marriage contract signed. I heard Jane Bourchier sigh with satisfaction while my kinswoman, Lady Hastings, sniffed loudly. As Lady Hastings wept on every ceremonial occasion, I took no notice but kept my gaze fixed firmly on Mary who looked much too pale for my liking.

After the formal ceremony there was a Nuptial Mass sung in the palace chapel, followed by a wedding feast where we were entertained with music from the king's minstrels. Later Henry and the Duke of Buckingham cast aside their robes and danced for two hours dressed only in doublet and hose. Even the sedate Venetian ambassador admitted he was tempted to join in the revelry but in the end declined, due, he said, to his advancing years.

At last it was time for Mary to enact the final part of her symbolic wedding. Together with the maids of honour, I helped her change into her nightgown, a wonderful creation of ivory silk, blue satin and Florentine lace, designed especially for this occasion. We walked in procession into the chamber where the marriage bed had been prepared and helped Mary lie on the embroidered cover. Carefully, I lifted the hem of her nightgown, baring her left leg up to the thigh. None of the assembled company said a word but I could sense a hundred indrawn breaths from men witnessing the nakedness of the new Queen of France.

The Duke of Longueville's valet untied and then slowly removed the duke's red hose, leaving him bare-legged. I have to admit, the duke's knotted sinews and scarred knees were not such an alluring sight as the pale smooth length of Mary's limbs, but that was unsurprising. With a little difficulty the duke climbed onto the bed and lay down beside his queen, moving his right leg so that it just touched her left one. This was to represent the act of marriage, the joining together of their two bodies, transforming word into deed into irrevocable union blessed by the Church. Once bare skin had touched bare skin, Archbishop Wareham hastily declared the marriage consummated. The ceremony was complete. I was weary beyond belief but Cousin Mary was no longer a princess – she was officially Queen of France.

Mary was showered with letters of congratulations from across Europe and our days were punctuated by visits from ambassadors bearing gifts, all wishing to be on good terms with the wife of King Louis. Everyone knew how influential a beautiful young wife could be, particularly when the husband was old.

My favourite offering was a cup from the Milanese court, which sparkled with so many jewels Mary said it threatened to blind the drinker. But nothing the ambassadors brought could surpass the gifts presented by the Sieur de Marigny who had arrived to serve as a special attendant to his new queen. His role was to familiarise

Mary with the manners and customs of the French court. With him he brought a handsome white horse bearing Louis's gifts which showed the measure of the king's happiness: two coffers of plate, seals and devices and a cornucopia of wonderful jewels.

'My husband must love me a great deal,' Mary murmured.

'How could he not, Your Grace.'

'Oh look, Cousin Elizabeth! Is this not the most magnificent jewel you have ever seen.'

She held up a dazzling bejewelled diamond as wide as a man's finger. Every facet glittered like a burst of sunlight on a winter's day. Suspended below the diamond was a huge teardrop pearl, the size of a pigeon's egg, luminous and mysterious. I'd never seen so intricate a piece of craftsmanship nor anything so lovely.

There was silence in the room. Mary was not the only one lost for words.

'The Sieur de Marigny says the jewel is called the Mirror of Naples,' I said quietly. 'It is the most prized jewel in the king's possession.'

'And he sent it to me,' breathed Mary.

'He'll have wanted to show everyone how much you are valued.'

She gazed longingly at the necklace as I replaced it on its blue velvet bed. I could tell she wanted to snatch it back, press it to her bosom, luxuriate in knowing it was hers, but realised such behaviour would be considered unseemly.

'Cousin Elizabeth, I know King Louis had at least two wives before me. Whoever these women were, even if they were not valued so highly by the king, convention would have dictated a gift of some kind. Do you know what jewels he sent them?'

I'd no intention of upsetting Mary with gossip. It was better she knew nothing of King Louis' former wives. My sisters said jealousy had no place in a marriage and there were rumours the French king had been besotted with his last wife.

'Naturally he will have given them gifts, your grace. As you say, it would be expected. But I wager he never gave them anything as fine as the Mirror of Naples. It is a jewel which comes straight from the heart, showing he is already in love with you. As his queen, he wishes you to be the most wonderfully bejewelled woman in the courts of Europe.'

Mary smiled happily. 'I must ask the Sieur de Marigny to convey my thanks to my husband.'

And so it continued – little sparks of jealousy every so often, betraying how nervous Mary was at the thought of marrying an older man who must have loved other women.

It was late. I was thinking longingly of my bed as I stumbled back through the now empty rooms. When I reached the top of the stairs I found a well-dressed young man blocking my way. He was standing outside the door to the room I shared with Jane, leaning his shoulder against the wall. As I approached, he tossed a coin in the air, caught it smartly and then slapped it against the back of his hand. He glanced down at the coin and laughed.

'Are you waiting for someone?' I enquired politely.

He looked up, removed his cap and flashed a smile,

not a polite courtier's smile but a crooked one, a glimpse of white teeth against a sun-tanned skin.

'If I were, it would be my good fortune to have a pretty young woman like you come along for then surely my waiting would not be in vain.'

He was a gentleman, that much I gathered from his clothes and the way he spoke, but I had no idea who he was. He was not handsome but had another quality, one which might be described as dangerous – an allure.

'Sir, I do not know you,' I began.

He took a step towards me. 'Is that not the point of an encounter like this, to extend our knowledge, to discover what we can about the other, to explore what might be between us. I observe the effect of my opening gambit, whereas you, I surmise, are testing your defences and finding them sadly weakened.'

'I do not...'

'Not yet, Lady Elizabeth, but you will.'

'Sir, if you know my name, the least you can do is tell me yours.'

'Why? Will it please you to have a name to whisper to yourself when I am gone? And when all is said and done, what is a name but a distillation of the essence which is human. I see in you, not a solemn and dutiful Elizabeth, but a wild, untamed Isolde, betrothed to one man but secretly loving another, always at the mercy of her illicit passions.'

I opened my mouth to reply but no words came out. I was speechless at his audacity.

He came even closer. His voice was seductive and he spoke fast as if there was no time to lose. 'So much can be read in a woman's eyes; a message passed in the way she lowers her gaze, attempting to hide what she feels, her heart racing, those delicious inner tremblings which betray her desire.'

There were certainly inner tremblings but they owed more to anger than desire. He was insufferably rude. But I refused to retreat. He was the intruder, not I.

'My brother, the marquess,' I began.

'Oh, we need not worry about the marquess, he'll not bother us tonight. He has his own problems.'

'What problems?' I gasped, by now, thoroughly alarmed.

He grinned. 'The marquess has yet to learn the art of playing cards with Henry. Odd because he's not a stupid man. Perhaps it is greed, which would not surprise me. He has the eyes of a man who wants more than he has. You see, Lady Elizabeth, when a man plays with Henry he may lead in the game but must always allow the king to win, preferably by a margin within his means. The marquess is discovering that being the victor may fill his purse but a disgruntled monarch is a dangerous enemy. He should have known better.'

'It is only a game.'

'Life is a game. Love is a game. And what is this between us, if not a game. Are games to your taste, Lady Elizabeth? It would be my pleasure to teach you some more moves. What d'you say?'

At that moment the door opened and there was Lizzie Bryan framed in the doorway.

'Thank the Lord! I thought you'd abandoned me, Francis.'

My tormentor turned round lazily and said, 'Not I. Would you add faithlessness to my list of sins?'

Lizzie saw me and bobbed a little curtsey. 'Lady Elizabeth! Forgive me, I didn't notice you there. I see my brother has been entertaining you while Jane and I were talking.'

So the man was Lizzie's brother: Francis Bryan, a gentleman in Henry's chamber.

'Is that what you've been doing in there, Sister?' he said. 'I thought you were indulging in the kind of behaviour which might make a bishop blush.'

Lizzie ignored her brother's rudeness and apologised if she'd kept me waiting but she'd been eager to tell Jane the good news.

'What was the good news?' I asked as I helped Jane into her nightshift.

'My father has been appointed Mary's chamberlain. He will be going to France.'

'Oh Jane, how wonderful! And you?'

'I shall pray nightly that he'll get me a place.'

'I'm certain he will. And when we're in Paris it will be Mary I'll be helping into her nightshift, not you.'

'The Duke of Longueville"s legs were exceedingly hairy,' Jane said thoughtfully. 'Do you think King Louis has hairy legs?'

I placed her nightcap on her head, tucking in the last wisps of hair and tying the ribbon under her chin.

'There you are! And you don't need to worry about the French king's legs because I doubt you'll be sharing the royal bed.'

Jane smiled. 'If he asked me, I'd not mind if he had legs like a shaggy pony.'

'Jane Bourchier!' I said in mock horror. 'What would your father say?'

'Not a thing. He'd have his nose in a book.'

4

MEG WOOTON
LATE AUGUST 1514

As I turned in at the gate of my mother's house I saw an army of men in the gardens, clipping and sweeping and snipping dead heads from an array of late summer flowers. I was surprised any flower dared violate my mother's orders for perfection but, of course, even she could not halt the onset of decrepitude and death. Which brought me to uncomfortable memories of Francis Bryan.

I had been trained from the cradle to be ordered and obedient, yet he had seen me as wild and untamed. Surely no man wanted an untamed woman for a wife. But what if the outwardly docile young woman he married nurtured a desire not to submit, not to be tamed, a disobedient nature hidden from view. What then?

Wearily, I put thoughts of dark-eyed young men to one side and dismounted. I was uncertain why I'd been summoned or why my mother was still here but I'd dressed carefully, putting on my best green velvet riding habit and a pair of low-heeled black boots. My mother had sent a mounted escort to bring me to Holborn for which I was grateful as, not only was I kept safe in the streets but was spared another uncomfortable journey with my brother.

Inside, the house was cold and I found myself shivering. I was welcomed by a soft-footed menial who informed me that the dowager lady marquess wished to see me in her chamber and please to follow him. We climbed the wide flight of stairs and along an impressive gallery where windows overlooked the gardens. At the door of my mother's receiving chamber, I was announced by another soft-footed menial. I wondered how many of these men lurked in the nether regions of this vast house: dozens certainly, perhaps hundreds as I never saw the same one twice.

The room was hung with impressive tapestries, ones my mother had acquired this past year: huge sweeping depictions of hunting scenes, men and women mounted on sleek dark horses while deer peeped shyly from behind trees and hounds ran riot across the flower-strewn grass. More servants lined the room which indicated this was not a friendly family gathering. My mother meant business.

'Ah! It is Elizabeth.'

The voice was that of my sister-in-law, Meg Wooton. Meg was Thomas's wife and mother of their three small girls. She was seated near my mother, or as near as my mother permitted anyone to sit. Even though this was an early afternoon visit, Meg was dressed as if for a banquet in a gown of rich dark brocade edged with copious amounts of fur and wearing an unflattering Flemish-style headdress. She was twelve years my senior but insisted on behaving as if she was my grandmother, finding fault with my behaviour and complaining to my brother about the cost of finding me a husband.

I curtsied to my mother, who beckoned me closer and, surprisingly, proffered her cheek for me to kiss. Her skin was thick with rouge paste, the smell of dead roses mingling unpleasantly with the rich cloying perfume she habitually wore. As I stepped back I noticed a new gold chain around her neck, a double loop with diamonds and rubies glittering on her solid black satin bosom.

'What do you think?' she said, turning to Meg.

My sister-in-law peered at me as if I was an interesting specimen, a rare flower she'd found in her garden at Bradgate.

'She's of a good height but the colour does not suit. She would look better in ash-grey.'

'I thought crimson,' my mother said firmly.

'Really?' Meg gave the tiniest shrug to show that she disagreed but was loath to provoke my mother by saying so. 'A deep red would certainly suit her pale skin. But Elizabeth already has a plentiful wardrobe and my mother says young women become greedy if given too much finery.'

'I do not think Lady Wooton's opinion is required,' my mother said frostily. 'And if you're thinking of those gowns styled for the court at Malines, they will not do. The cut is completely wrong and the French consider a Flemish headdress unflattering. By next year they'll be quite out of fashion.'

Meg touched her own headdress, doubtless made for the now defunct bridal celebrations in Malines.

'Oh, do you think so?'

'Yes,' my mother said, driving the knife a little deeper. 'They do nothing to enhance a woman's looks. The Venetian cap is to be preferred for older women like yourself.'

'Mary is to have a new wardrobe,' I said brightly, not wishing to see my poor sister-in-law further filleted by my mother.

'Indeed!' remarked my mother, looking at me with interest. 'How many ladies will she have in her train this time?'

'At least twenty.'

'You will accompany me,' said my sister-in-law, exerting her authority over a mere lady attendant.

'My daughter will accompany the Queen of France,' said my mother, unwilling to yield an inch of ground to Meg Wooton.

'As will I.'

'As my son's wife.'

Meg acknowledged defeat. 'Naturally, as the Lady Marquess of Dorset. With my husband.'

But my mother was not finished. 'I trust my son will be generous.'

'In what way?' Meg asked suspiciously.

'Elizabeth must be properly fitted out. No expense spared. The French court is sophisticated, much more so than here. Of course Bocton is a rather mean place so perhaps you have no understanding of what is required.'

Meg flushed at my mother's intended insult. Bocton was the home of Meg's family and as my brother's marriage had not been of my mother's choosing, she enjoyed emphasising the lowly status of the Wootons – although, to my mother, everyone was lowly even, I suspected, the royal family. My sisters once told me that having flourished at court as the wife of the York queen's eldest son, my mother regarded the Tudors as rank outsiders – even, dare the word be whispered, usurpers.

'My husband said…'

'Yes, daughter-in-law. What did my son say?'

Meg was mean with money and wanted to win this battle. Doubtless Thomas, equally tight-fisted, had instructed his wife not to give way.

'The marquess considers the cost of your daughter's wardrobe should be furnished by yourself, my lady,' she said.

My mother's lips twitched in a momentary smile. 'I disagree. It is his responsibility. It is he who will reap the benefits of an advantageous marriage for his sister, not I.'

I decided to intervene to avoid bloodshed. 'My gowns for Malines could be cut up and altered. That would save some expense.'

However this was not an exercise in thrift, it was a battle for supremacy.

'The patterns are completely unsuitable for the French court,' my mother snapped. 'You will need a whole new wardrobe.'

'Yes, Lady Mother,' I replied meekly.

'How many gowns will the French queen have?'

'Thirty, I believe; sixteen in the French fashion.'

'And the others?'

'Six Milanese and seven English.'

'And for the wedding day in Abbeville?'

'A French gown.'

My mother turned to Meg. 'I trust you see how essential it is for Elizabeth to be lavishly dressed for her appearance at the French court. We cannot afford for her to be outshone by Frenchwomen who will be dressed to put us at a disadvantage. Of course Englishwomen are much prettier. You only have to look at my daughter to see that.'

Meg sniffed. 'I grant you Elizabeth is pretty but her mouth is considered a little wide.'

My mother smiled in the way an executioner smiles when approaching his victim on the scaffold. 'A man prefers a generous mouth on a wife, or have you not noticed. In marriage are mouths not used for kissing. But perhaps you have no experience in such matters. My son has ever been a cold fish where women are concerned.'

I gave an involuntary gasp.

Meg flushed and decided to yield. 'Very well, I shall do as you bid and inform my husband that Elizabeth will need three new gowns.'

'Six gowns should suffice.' My mother swept on as if Meg had not spoken. 'No English cloth, the colours are poor. Brocades from Brussels. My silk merchant will provide a selection of Florentine silks. Then there will be sleeves and kirtles to go with the gowns; chemises and stockings; at least six pairs of shoes, two nightshifts and a velvet nightgown trimmed with fur. Three headdresses in the latest French style, adorned with pearls; two velvet riding habits and four hats, one with a feather. Also she will need sufficient in the way of necklaces and bracelets for ornamentation. For the journey my son must ensure she has a good quality horse of her own, complete with trappings, a new saddle and, of course, a pair of elegant new riding boots.'

There was silence while Meg, overwhelmed by the vast expense, was doubtless debating whether a further objection would achieve anything or if she should wait for Thomas to bring up reinforcements.

My mother solved Meg's difficulty by consolidating her position whilst retaining the spoils.

'I know you are anxious to return to Bradgate to supervise my grand-daughters' care,' she said in her most unctuous tone, 'so I shall not detain you further, dearest daughter-in-law. Give greetings to my son and tell him if he wishes to see me I shall be at home on Thursday next.'

Meg made a timid farewell but was completely ignored by my mother who had turned her attention to me.

'Come!' she ordered, rising stiffly from her chair.

'Yes, Lady Mother,' I said, wondering where we were going.

I followed in her stately wake to an inner chamber, her private one, thinking of poor Meg Wooton slinking away in defeat, forced to tell my brother that yet more money must be found for his sister. "It is for the family", was a cantillation repeated time and again during my growing up years. Nothing was for the self, everything was to advance the family. If I made an advantageous marriage it was not for *my* benefit but to assist the progress of my brothers and sisters. I was to be the candle that drew moths to the flame, nothing more. My brother would choose who I would marry and it would not be a gentleman on the make like the disturbing, dark-eyed Francis Bryan.

'My jewel box!' my mother demanded as she sat down heavily in her chair.

Her maid, who'd been hovering by the door, scuttled over to a chest and retrieved my mother's casket of jewels but then hesitated, uncertain of what to do next.

'Well! Go on, woman, put it down!'

As gently as she could, the maidservant placed the casket on the table. My mother swatted her away, then lifted the lid. She rummaged about amongst the various jewels until she found what she wanted: a small dark green velvet bag.

She pushed it towards me. 'Open it!'

I did as I was told. Inside was a ring. The gold band was simple, the setting unpretentious and somewhat old-fashioned, but the stone was magnificent; a ruby nearly the size of the pearl on Mary's Mirror of Naples. I held my breath, barely able to believe the ring might be for me.

'I have often wondered which of my daughters should have this.' She paused as if still undecided. I kept silent. One ill-considered remark from my lips might lose me this prize. 'A jewel like this will get you noticed at the French court. A good investment if it catches you a wealthy husband.'

'But Lady Mother, why me? Surely Cecily or…'

'Don't be a fool! You must learn to accept a gift with good grace. You've seen how I deal with irritating women only after my money. Do me the honour of behaving like my daughter. This ring belonged to your grandmother – not that foolish, lowborn Woodville woman – your Nevill grandmother. She had it from *her* mother who was Countess of Salisbury and a great-granddaughter of the Princess of Wales.'

I slipped the ring on my finger. It fitted perfectly. My mother nodded approvingly.

'People say you resemble your Woodville grandmother. It is the colour of your hair. But they're wrong. You are like my mother. She was a Nevill.'

I remembered my Nevill grandmother. It was wintertime with snow on the ground. I was five years old, my eyes on a level with the old lady lying in the tapestried bed. As I watched, a bony hand emerged, clutching a piece of shiny blue ribbon. The colour gleamed in the candlelight. One finger beckoned me closer and a voice whispered, "It is for thee." My eyes widened in wonder as my hand crept across the bedcover to retrieve the ribbon. She smiled and her face collapsed into a web of wrinkled skin. "Come tomorrow, sweeting, and I'll give thee my knife."

But there had been no tomorrow and I never saw my Nevill grandmother again. Rough hands pulled at my shoulders and bundled me away. When I asked my nursemaid about the knife, she slapped my face for telling lies.

My mother closed the lid of her casket and turned her full attention to me. As always, I felt nervous under her scrutiny, certain I must have committed some fearful misdemeanour. When I was little I would sob when our nursemaid put Cecily and me into our best gowns and took us to see our mother. Now I was older I would not allow myself to weep.

'Hmm,' she said, running her gaze from the top of my head to the toes of my best black riding boots, stitching every failing into her memory. 'Your stepfather tells me you are much admired by Henry's gentlemen.'

'Me!' I said, surprised to be the subject of my mother's rare conversations with Henry Stafford.

'It is nothing to be proud of. Any young woman will attract men if she dresses well. I trust you do not encourage their attentions.'

An inward flutter of fear as I thought of dark-eyed Francis Bryan who needed no encouragement to take liberties.

I shook my head. 'No, Lady Mother. I behave as you would wish.'

'I should hope so. Remember, a young woman's reputation is all she has and, once lost, it is lost forever.'

Holy Mary! Had someone seen me. All I'd done was speak plainly to an impertinent man. Nonetheless, people talked.

My mother waited and when I said nothing she carried on. 'Tell me what you know of the French court.'

'I know very little. The Sieur de Marigny has explained its customs to Cousin Mary so that she will feel comfortable but I've not been privy to all their conversations.'

'I thought as much. Your brother would have you ignorant but he is a fool. So listen well. There are three things you should know. First: the French court is a dangerous place. Beneath the glitter lies real evil so you must always be on your guard. Trust no-one. Second: Frenchmen will take advantage of your innocence. To them, seduction is a game and the deflowering of an innocent young English woman the greatest of games, a rare triumph, something to be boasted of. Thirdly: French women will be jealous. They will seek to blacken your name in any way they can. You should be particularly careful of Madame Louise.'

'Who is Madame Louise?' I asked cautiously.

'Louise of Savoy, mother of François d'Angoulême, Duke of Valois. I trust you have heard of him.'

I shook my head, denying any knowledge of François d'Angoulême. My mother tutted at my ignorance.

'The French king has no sons. François d'Angoulême is his cousin and his heir. The young man is also Madame Louise's passion, her Caesar.'

'Has the French king no daughters?'

'Two. François d'Angoulême is married to the elder. But do not be deceived into thinking she has any influence because she does not. Madame Claude is a poor misshapen little thing. It is Madame Louise who is all-powerful. She will not be amused at having her position usurped by Henry's sister; nor will she delight in a deluge of English women at court.'

'I understand,' I said, unsure if I did.

'Indeed!' said my mother with a lift of one eyebrow. 'Well, let us see if you do. What does Madame Louise fear most?'

I thought for a moment, imagining the unknown Madame Louise eyeing the throne of France with her greedy eyes.

'That Mary gives the French king a son.'

'Exactly! If the gouty old lecher gets Mary with child, Madame Louise's plans for her beloved François will be in jeopardy and if the child should be a boy, her dreams will crumble to dust. If that happens, Mary and the child will be in the gravest of danger.'

'But why? She would be the mother of the heir to the French throne. Surely no-one would harm her.'

'Don't be naive. When a throne is at stake, a woman's life counts for very little, and that of a child, nothing at all.'

I understood now what my mother meant when she said evil lurked beneath a veneer of splendour at King Louis's court. We would be entering a world where Mary's life and that of any child she might have, could be in real danger. I swallowed twice, wondering if I would be safe.

'What should I do, Lady Mother?'

'Mary's safety will depend on you so be sure not to fail her. See she is protected day and night. Her food must be tasted. Remember, your success is tied to Mary's success. She must not be left alone and do not allow yourself to be sent away.'

'Who would send me away?'

'It is what kings do. They wish for mastery over their wives. Louis will want to send Mary's ladies back to England. Madame Louise will persuade him to surround Mary with French ladies who are loyal.'

'Loyal to Madame Louise.'

'Naturally.'

'I thought I would remain in France,' I said miserably, seeing my exciting new life ebbing away.

'It is what I plan for but if there is trouble, urge Mary to write to Henry – or to Wolsey.' She paused. 'Although I am your mother and should not need to say this: guard your virtue.'

I nodded vigorously, thinking how unappetising the French court now sounded.

'Lady Mother, have you been to Paris?'

She wrinkled up her nose as if a foul smell had wafted into the room.

'No, I have not. Your father was invited there once when he was a young man. He was tempted by stories of a fabled city of myriad delights but instead found the food disgusting, the women immoral and their habits, filthy. Let us hope matters have improved since those days, but I doubt it.'

She held out her hand for me to help her rise, leaning heavily on my arm.

'When do you leave for France?'

'Within the month.'

'Then I shall not see you again. I am for Astley once I have dealt with my son. Remember what I've told you and I pray God keep you safe.'

5

THE ROAD TO ABBEVILLE
AUTUMN 1514

Summer was over. It was already past Michaelmas, the last day nominated for our departure from England yet here we were, still in Dover. Doubtless the French king was beginning to wonder the whereabouts of his bride. Perhaps he feared a last-minute crisis of nerves with Mary unwilling to entrust herself to a husband she'd never met. His advisors might whisper, that in the peculiar way of English women, she preferred to remain where she was. How foolish when she could be enjoying the glories of the greatest realm in Christendom.

In my experience men did not take kindly to being kept waiting, and kings, above all, expected their wives to be punctual.

The room was chilly. There was no sign of light in the sky yet despite the hour I was out of bed and dressed in my warmest clothes. We'd been warned that sea travel could be unpleasant no matter the time of year and I was not prepared to risk freezing to death for the sake of vanity. Last night we'd received instructions from a bossy young man. "Rise well before dawn, ladies," he'd informed us. "Our ships must catch the early tide. There'll be no mercy for latecomers, whatever their rank. Those who ignore this order will be left behind."

I surveyed my travelling companions. Near the door the elderly Lady Mounteagle sat bolt upright, her eyes half-closed, ignoring Anne Jerningham who was whispering in her ear, the two of them encircled by a clutch of snivelling maidservants. The Duchess of Norfolk and her daughter, the young Countess of Oxford, both bleary-eyed from lack of sleep, looked as if they'd give anything to crawl back into bed, while the Fiennes girl, yet another of Jane's cousins, couldn't stop yawning. My sister-in-law, Meg, eyed me suspiciously as if early rising had been my idea before turning her attention to a huddle of young women in the far corner who were whispering to each other and trying not to giggle.

My stockings clung uncomfortably to my legs. Despite the best efforts of my maid in draping my garments over racks near the fire, none of my clothes felt properly dry. Contrary to Jane's romantic belief, ancient stone castles were disagreeable places to live. They might be stout defenders of enemy invasion but were easy prey to the ingress of damp. If we looked behind the wall hangings I was certain we'd find foul-smelling moulds, not to mention spiders.

The procession to Dover had been vast, the most splendid event of the season, so everyone said. It had been a magnificent sight: the king and Mary riding side by side, Queen Katherine following in the royal litter, four hundred lords and knights and barons all with retainers and personal servants, two hundred gentlemen and esquires with wives, damsels and equipage; a thousand palfreys and a hundred wagons carrying great ladies splendidly dressed in woven gold. The only person absent, was the Spanish ambassador.

'He's sulking,' Mary had said with a smile, as if the ambassador's master was of no importance now that she was Queen of France.

But even the Queen of France could not command the weather.

For twelve days we'd been immured in Dover Castle facing the full fury of an autumn storm and for twelve days our ships had been confined to harbour.

'The king is angry,' Jane whispered, shivering in the cold.

'The king is bored,' I replied. 'He's been starved of entertainment. Dover hardly offers the delights he's accustomed to.'

It was true. No hawking, no hunting, no bowling greens, no tennis courts and hardly enough room for a decent evening's dancing – not that anyone had felt in the mood for dancing. Outside in the sodden fields surrounding the castle, not a single sign remained of the thousands of merchants and pedlars and other hangers-on who'd attached themselves to our procession through Kent. Even if we ventured outside there'd be nothing to buy. Through a veil of rain I'd seen them dismantle their makeshift shelters and slink off with their carts and their packs, cursing the storm for spoiling what should have been a few days of profitable business.

Now, apart from some muffled sniffs and a few low murmurings, everything was quiet. The creaks and groans, our constant companions from the day we arrived, had finally ceased. Wind no longer howled around the walls, buffeting shutters and ripping tiles off roofs. Even the relentless gushing and splashing of rainwater had stopped.

Soon the call would come and we'd set off in procession down to the quay where our ships awaited and where final farewells would be exchanged. I had no farewells to make as most of my brothers were travelling with the royal party to France and my sisters were so jealous of my position in Mary's retinue they'd vowed they had better things to do than trail after me to Dover.

Mary would be accompanied to the waterside by Henry, a last opportunity for her to be with her brother.

'We've never been apart,' she whispered, conveniently forgetting Henry's foray into France the previous year. 'How shall I bear our separation?'

'You will be a queen,' I reminded her as I fastened the clasp on the front of her cloak, thinking that even if yesterday's gales returned, she should be warm enough. The cloak was lined with egret's down and, if needs be, was large enough to wrap twice round her slender body. Lady Guildford, who had cared for Mary as a child, fussed that her charge would be at the mercy of bitter winds blowing up from the south-west. She wanted Mary to wear her comfortable old cloak with lambswool sewn between two layers of cloth. But Mary needed to look her best when disembarking in France and had wisely chosen the egret's down.

But even egret's down with its extravagant warmth could not save the new Queen of France from a soaking. We'd covered barely half our sea journey when the storm returned with a vengeance, roaring through the top sails and battering the wooden walls of our cabin. Each time a wave crashed against the side of the ship, the vessel heaved, timbers shuddered, the forecastle shook, and seawater poured under the door. We were tossed about like a twig caught in a maelstrom, a piece of flotsam in danger of being sucked into the deep. While Mary's maids crouched, sobbing on the floor and their mistress lay retching into a basin, I clutched my locket with its picture of Our Lady and prayed for deliverance.

Just when I thought my prayers had been in vain and we were all going to die, the ship came to a juddering halt. A man, wrapped in a sodden cape and hat, dripping water everywhere, poked his head into the cabin to inform us that the captain was unable to get any closer to Boulogne. The winds were too wild and the waves too high. But we'd no need to fear. The ship was grounded within sight of land, just inside the harbour. We'd be rowed ashore in a smaller boat. I was unsure if I wanted to entrust myself to a smaller boat, not if the winds were wild and the waves were high, but it seemed I had no choice.

Somehow we managed to get Mary up from her bed, wrapped her in her cloak and took her out on deck where I had my first sight of France: a flat grey blur, a miserable place seen through a curtain of rain. Not the glorious country I had expected. I took one look at the waves crashing onto the shore and was convinced we'd all be drowned. A tall man, enveloped in a vast cape with rainwater streaming down his face, assured me we'd be safe; the small boat attached to the ship's side was perfectly seaworthy. Watching the flimsy little craft pitch and toss in a sick-making parody of a dance, I was not so sure, but said nothing.

Two knights from Mary's retinue helped first Mary and then three more of us down into the little boat, their arms strong enough to prevent any mishaps. Mostly I kept my eyes shut rather than look at the waters below. Once we were seated, the heavy ropes attaching us to the ship were cast off by two of the oarsmen, cutting us adrift. The waves were enormous. We lurched and dipped and then rose again. Each time we wallowed in a trough, I lost sight of the shore and began to wish we'd stayed on board ship.

'Have faith, Lady Elizabeth,' Sir Christopher Garnish said, grinning at me. 'We're perfectly safe.'

'I believe you, Sir Christopher,' I replied, wiping a burst of spray from my face.

Mary moaned quietly and laid her head on my shoulder. She was a sorry sight: pale, forlorn, bedraggled and drenched to the bone, resembling more a half-drowned kitten pulled from a well than the magnificent Queen of France. One of the oarsmen shouted something to Sir Christopher, who leant towards me and said, 'He can't get any closer. We'll have to wade to the beach. I shall carry Her Grace. Can you manage, Lady Elizabeth, or shall I return for you?'

I stared at the narrow stretch of water separating us from safety and reckoned I'd faced worse challenges. I assured Sir Christopher I could manage but asked that if I should yell for help, he'd not abandon me to a watery grave.

As agile as a man half his age, he vaulted over the side of the boat, reached in and picked up Mary. With the Queen of France cradled in his arms, he strode through the water and carried her up the beach to a waiting deputation of Frenchmen who looked utterly stupefied at this display of English gallantry. Perhaps laying hands on a queen in this way was considered a treasonable offence in France. Rather than touch her they'd have allowed their queen to drown.

Remembering what I'd been taught in my childhood about wading through streams, I removed my boots, tied the laces together, looped them round my neck and gingerly clambered over the side. The boat tipped alarmingly as I lowered myself into the water. There was an immediate shock as my feet protested at being immersed in cold seawater but I persevered, taking small steps and holding up my skirts as far as I dared. I had no wish to expose my legs to every Frenchman in sight but nor did I want my skirts to be completely soaked. My efforts were wasted. By the time I was helped ashore by a couple of eager servants, sent to help the English ladies, I was wet through.

I looked back towards our ship and saw another boatload of women bobbing up and down on the waves, trusting in God and the oarsmen to ferry them to shore. Further out to sea, were three more ships from our fleet, making their way through the scudding rain towards the safety of the harbour at Boulogne.

All in all it was a sorry way to arrive in France.

Three days later with everyone safely ashore and our party all accounted for, we set out for the town of Abbeville where the royal marriage was to take place. We travelled slowly southwards along the coast road through a pretty little seaport village called Étaples to the town of Montreuil-sur-Mer where we were to stay for two nights. Everything was strange: the food, the clothes, the houses, the pointed towers, the smells and the odd way people spoke. Even the soil in the fields looked different. It was nothing like England.

The French party who welcomed us ashore might have been stiff and reserved but the country folk could not have been kinder. They turned out in their thousands to welcome their new queen. My French was not yet fluent but I understood enough to gather they found Mary beautiful and were overjoyed to have England and France at peace once more.

At intervals along the route there were songs praising the royal marriage, welcome speeches by officials, and pageants of the kind Mary most enjoyed: simple, often awkward, tributes from the common people. By the time we finally reached our lodgings at the house of a Madame de Moncaverel, I was exhausted but Mary said she could dance all night.

'Do you think my husband will come to greet me on the way to Abbeville?' she asked as I helped her to bed.

'I imagine it would not be permitted, Your Grace. The Duke of Longeville says court etiquette here is very strict.'

'But do you not think a husband would want to see the woman he is to marry?' She pouted as if Louis's failure to surprise her at Montreuil-sur-Mer was a sad disappointment.

'I'm sure he's in a fever of excitement, Your Grace.'

She smiled. 'Yes, you're right, Cousin Elizabeth. Of course he is.'

'You must be patient.'

She lay back against her pillow and gave a huge sigh. 'If he was a young man, he'd come in disguise. That is what Henry would do. Do you remember when he and his friends dressed as Robin Hood and his outlaws?' She giggled. 'They threatened to take us hostage.'

I hoped Mary did not expect her husband to be like her brother. Henry was young, handsome and energetic, whereas the French king was reportedly old, pock-marked and often too gouty to rise from his bed. In no way would he resemble Henry.

Since we'd arrived in France I'd heard whispers that in the marriage bed, King Louis might not be able to be a husband to Mary, that doing his duty by his young wife might be beyond him. When, in a great deal of embarrassment, I'd confessed my fears to Sir Christopher he assured me that these were vile lies spread by scandalmongers. Even if there was a grain of truth in them, the piquancy of a pretty young wife could do wonders for male ardour. He laughed at my blushing face and told me not to worry.

Two days later we set off again. From the first of the fifty esquires in their bright silks to the last of the two hundred archers in their blazing colours, our procession must have stretched for miles along the muddy road to Abbeville. In front of Mary were her heralds and trumpeters led by the Garter King-at-Arms, preceded by the lords and barons and ambassadors paired by rank, many in cloth-of-gold and velvet bonnets.

Mary rode a white palfrey, with two running footmen at her stirrup. She was dressed in cloth-of-gold and crimson with a hat of crimson silk, cocked daringly over one eye. Next came her ladies, headed by the Duchess of Norfolk and my sister-in-law, Meg, in her role as wife of the Marquess of Dorset. The two senior royals by rank present rode on either side of Mary: the elderly Duke of Norfolk, bony and dour-faced, and my brother, Thomas, who at every opportunity watched me over his shoulder. The gaily decorated carriages trundling behind us were filled with an assortment of excited young maids of honour, middle-aged wives and elderly dowagers too infirm to ride a horse.

The first sign that something was amiss came as we neared a leafy forested part of the countryside when the whole procession came to a halt. I craned my neck but could see nothing. Then suddenly I saw them, riding up the edge of the track: a small group of well-dressed men. Their leader was tall, dark-haired and handsome. He rode up to Mary and doffed his hat in an extravagant gesture, bowing low in the saddle. A whisper passed from woman to woman along the line – François d'Angoulême! The Duke of Valois!

There was no mistaking the son of Madame Louise, not with those hooded eyes and that dark penetrating gaze. His nose was long and slightly curved, the face fine-drawn with the predatory expression of an eagle surveying its prey. I doubted there was a single woman in that procession who did not inwardly tremble as he ran his gaze over what the English ladies had to offer in the way of diversion. I thought my mother's warnings would not suffice as much defence against someone like François d'Angoulême, a man clearly used to having what he wanted.

'How old is he?' the young Countess of Oxford whispered, her eyes unnaturally bright.

'Twenty, I believe,' I said quietly, hoping her mother

was taking her straight back to England after the wedding. The senior ladies were probably not at risk from a handsome dark-eyed seducer but silly young women like the countess were easily impressed, easily compromised and just as easily cast aside.

'Why has he come?'

'Perhaps to warn Lady Mary that her husband wishes to surprise her.'

The countess giggled. 'I'd rather be surprised by the messenger.'

'Countess, I shall pretend I did not hear that remark.'

She tossed her head and took up her reins as we set off. Before we'd gone half a mile we stopped again, this time for what I presumed was the royal hunting party, a pretence to allow King Louis to meet his bride as if by chance.

First came two hundred guardsmen riding ahead of a group of churchmen and nobles who surrounded a man who had to be the French king. Despite the sumptuous robes of cloth-of-gold and crimson, and the beautiful hunter caparisoned in gold and black, this was no François d'Angoulême;. This was an elderly gallant in his dotage pretending to be a joyful young bridegroom.

Forewarned, Mary made to dismount and make her obeisance but King Louis would have none of it. Instead she blew him a kiss which made those of us in the English party smile. But King Louis misunderstood our English custom and took this as an invitation for further intimacy. To everyone's surprise, including Mary's, he advanced and boldly threw his arms around her neck and kissed her. She was well-prepared and did not flinch as this pock-marked old man pulled her against his chest and greedily placed his mouth on hers. A cheer was raised after which husband and wife, in name if not yet in deed, talked quietly together while I heaved a sigh of relief that this first important meeting had passed off without incident.

The meeting, though satisfactory to all concerned, was not to be prolonged. After a short while the king bade his bride an extravagant farewell and rode off with just a few men as guards, leaving the rest of his huge entourage with François d'Angoulême. It was to be the handsome Duke of Valois who would accompany the bride's party into Abbeville.

Despite a deluge of rain which required a hasty change of clothes, our approach to Abbeville was conducted in fine style with Mary riding under a white satin canopy supported by four of the town's officials. As we passed through the gates we were greeted by loud bursts of cannon fire, troupes of musicians and several elaborate pageants, all taking place to the accompaniment of a persistent wetting drizzle.

There was no time to gain more than an impression of crowds of cheering people, dreary grey buildings, shrieking children in rags and occasional splashes of brightly coloured silks, before we were led into the Church of St Vulfran. It was necessary to pay homage to the town's patron saint, I was told in a whisper by an unidentified Frenchman who had attached himself to my side. Then it was out into the drizzle again and a short journey through the streets to an ancient palace called the Hôtel de la Gruthuse. This was where there was to be the formal reception and presentation to the French king's court.

The faces of the senior officials were strange, dignified, a few curious, all suitably gracious towards their king's choice of bride, but it was impossible to know what they really thought. Eventually, after a long and tiring day, the new queen and her English ladies were escorted to an apartment in the Rue St Giles by Madame Claude, the wife of François d'Angoulême.

Madame Claude was Louis's daughter: small, horribly plain and totally in awe of her new stepmother. She must have been three or four years younger than Mary and from the way she simpered and smiled, seemed prepared to worship at the slippered feet of her father's beautiful new wife.

'Do you think her husband loves her?' Jane Bourchier whispered, inclining her head towards Madame Claude.

'Love is not a requirement in a political marriage.'

I hoped the dashing François was kind to his plain little wife but I doubted it. At Henry's court I'd seen too many men like François d'Angoulême, men with a different young woman on their arm each week, charming men who seldom accorded their wives more than the most rudimentary courtesy. Wives like Madame Claude languished in the country with their children while their husbands roistered at court with the king, enjoying intimate favours from young women like Bessie Blount and Lizzie Bryan.

Although my brother was a cold man, not one for amorous dalliances of the kind pursued by the king's friend, Charles Brandon, Duke of Suffolk, he rarely brought Meg to court, preferring to keep her at Bradgate. It struck me as a dull life, surrounded by no-one but small children and servants. I prayed my brother did not have that sort of marriage in mind for me. Perhaps in France, I might find a congenial suitor, one who would treat his wife kindly. If I was clever and played my cards right, if I remembered to wear my mother's ring to attract the notice of a suitable man, I might even discover that most elusive of treasures, a good marriage with love at its heart.

Next morning I woke early to find Mary out of bed. She was standing by the window staring at the garden which separated us from the king's lodgings.

'It's not like Greenwich, is it,' she said wistfully.

I wrapped my nightgown round my shoulders and padded across the floor to join her.

For those of us used to the glorious splendour of Henry's royal palaces where no expense was spared, the garden of the Hôtel de la Gruthuse was a dismal sight. Yesterday's rain had left puddles on the paths and water dripping from the overhanging eaves. But it was more than that. There was no symmetry, no pattern to the greenery, no flowers, nothing but a few dull bushes laid out in rows. I knew the palace buildings were very ancient and doubtless the garden had been planted many years ago, long before low hedges and parterres in the Italian style became fashionable.

'Do you think all French gardens are like this?' Mary said with an edge to her voice.

'According to the Duke of Longueville, the gardens at the Château Amboise are very fine.'

She sighed and said, almost petulantly, 'Perhaps once we're married my husband will let us live there. I should not like to walk each day in a garden like this.'

'Cousin Mary, Majesty. You are the queen. You can ask King Louis to plant your gardens in any way you wish. He will want to please you. My sisters tell me that in the first flush of marital happiness a husband will agree to almost anything to please his bride.'

At that she gave a wan little smile.

'I shall write to Henry and ask him to send me one of his gardeners.'

'I think you will have to ask your husband if you wish to have English gardeners, but I'm sure he'll agree.'

She turned and seized my hands. 'He told me yesterday I was all he desired in a wife; his body was aflame to make me his.' For a moment the queenly facade cracked and she was a young woman alone in an unfamiliar land without the protection of her brother, about to embark on the most intimate of relationships with an old man she had only just met. 'Cousin Elizabeth, what if he cannot... will he blame me?'

It seemed she too had heard the rumours. But I was not the person she should have been asking. I knew only garbled stories of what went on in the marriage bed, snippets of information from my sisters or from other young women, equally ignorant. Mary would have done better to ask someone like Bessie Blount.

'He will not blame you for anything. How could he. He loves you.'

Fortunately at that moment we were disturbed by Lady Guildford bringing Mary's maids to help her dress for her wedding, forestalling any further private conversation regarding marital intimacy.

The wedding day was all that any young women could desire. Mary wore gold brocade trimmed with ermine, her jewelled coronet hiding none of her beautiful red-gold hair. She was accompanied by the elderly Duke of Norfolk with my brother, Thomas, in attendance. The king was clothed in gold and ermine to match his bride but was outshone by a couple of men who must have spent a fortune on their robes. The Sieur de Marigny once told us that in France it was the custom to measure a man's wealth by the value of his robes whereas an Englishman's wealth was measured by the value of his gold chain. If this was true, Louis's master of horse must be the wealthiest man at court.

After the marriage ceremony and the Nuptial Mass, Mary held a special banquet in her own chamber where we were introduced to the powerful Madame Louise, mother of François d'Angoulême. As I curtseyed politely, I felt her gaze pass over me like the lightest of veils, committing my features and faults to her memory. It was said that each evening she put everything she'd observed that day into her journal, though I doubted I was of interest to someone like Madame Louise.

'The cousin,' she murmured.

'Yes Madame,' I replied meekly, hoping she'd not pry further into my family's tangled kinship with the English king. Fortunately she moved on to study Lady Hastings whose connection to me through my mother was even more of a tangle.

With a full complement of French ladies requiring strict etiquette, the banquet lasted for several hours. Once we were sated and the formalities had been fully observed, we crossed the garden to rejoin the king and his intimates for more feasting and an evening of dancing with members of the French court.

Those hours in the Hôtel de la Gruthuse passed in a whirl of loud music, glitter and an endless babble of conversation, most of it completely unintelligible. A tall young Frenchman trapped me in a corner and spoke urgently into my ear, issuing an invitation which seemed to involve something my mother would not have allowed, but because he spoke rapidly and my French was not yet perfect, I was unsure if I'd understood his words correctly. An elderly lecher tried to run his hands down the back of my gown before I stepped smartly away, then a young woman in red hissed how she would scratch out my eyes if I looked at her husband again.

At eight o'clock we escorted Mary to the royal marriage bed. All I remember is Jane tripping over the hem of Lady Hastings's gown and my young French admirer suggesting I might like to accompany him into the garden. After that, the day ended in a merciful blur.

6

FRANÇOIS D'ANGOULÊME
OCTOBER 1514

Next morning I woke to a low persistent throb behind my eyes, a slight feeling of nausea and pain where I'd rubbed a blister on my right heel. Once I was fully awake, the symptoms were impossible to ignore and the causes only too obvious, even to one in my present befuddled state: too much wine, too much rich food and an excess of dancing in slippers that were far too tight. I tried to recall what had happened after the banquet in Mary's chamber but could remember very little.

Once out of bed I tried to concentrate on which of my six new gowns would be suitable for today's festivities. The deep crimson damask over the patterned plum-coloured kirtle would be my first choice but the neckline was perhaps a little low and might give rise to further unwelcome advances from my dashing young French admirer. In the end I threw caution to the wind and summoned a maid from her mending to lace me into the crimson damask and pin on the sleeves. Just as I was putting on my shoes, Jane came rushing into the room and grabbed my arm.

'What are you doing?' I protested as she tried to drag me through the doorway.

'You've got to come,' she said, her eyes wide with panic.

I disentangled myself from her grasp. 'Why?'

'We're being sent away.'

I smoothed my sleeve where she'd disturbed the lie of the cloth. 'Who is?' I said, wishing Jane would be more careful.

'We are. All of us. You, me, Lady Guildford – everyone.'

'Where are we being sent?' I hoped it was Paris, though I'd heard rumours the court was first moving to Beauvais.

'Home. England.'

'England?'

'Yes. We're being dismissed. Sent away!'

I was about to say that was impossible, then remembered what my mother had said.

'Who gave the order?'

Jane shook her head. 'I don't know. My father told me. He received word only this morning.'

'He must be mistaken. I know some of the senior ladies like the Duchess of Norfolk and my sister-in-law, the Lady Marquess, are returning home before Mary's coronation, but the rest of us are staying.'

'All Mary's English attendants are dismissed.'

'The gentlemen will stay.'

'They too have been dismissed.'

'Not your father, surely?'

'Yes, I told you. Everyone. The men and the women. We are all being sent back to England.'

If true, this was savage. Jane had to be mistaken. But if the information had come from Lord Berners, it must be true. He was a careful man, not one to repeat idle gossip.

'This order can only have come from the king. No-one else would dare issue such a command.'

'But the king loves the queen,' Jane protested. 'He told the Duke of Norfolk how much he loves his new wife.'

'He may love her but that doesn't mean he wants hundreds of English men and women cluttering up his court. Think of the expense.'

'Queen Mary needs us. You know how she depends on Lady Guildford. She cannot do without her.'

'Perhaps the king wishes his wife to depend on one of the French ladies. What if he thinks Lady Guildford has too much influence. You've seen how she hovers over Mary like a mother hen with its chick.'

'Lady Hastings says the king dislikes Lady Guildford,' Jane said, as we hurried down the stairs.

'I expect he wants time alone with his wife.'

'Then his wish has been granted. Lady Mounteagle says the queen has been sitting by his bedside all morning.'

As a proper wife should, I thought. But I did wonder at a husband who was lying abed at this hour when his wife was up and dressed.

'Is he unwell?'

'It would seem so.'

'And Lady Guildford?'

'Packing her things. She's to be escorted to Boulogne – the king's express orders.'

'Sainte Vierge!'

'We'll need more than the Virgin's help if we're not to follow in Lady Guildford's footsteps,' Jane said darkly.

Apart from Lady Guildford and the elderly Duchess of Norfolk and her frivolous little daughter, all Mary's English women attendants were gathered in the largest of our allocated rooms. Some were sobbing, a few muttering but most looking utterly stunned.

'What are we to do?' said my sister-in-law Meg, who'd been preparing to depart with the Duchess of Norfolk but had delayed on account of the crisis. Being the most senior lady present, she had taken charge.

'I cannot go home,' wept Mary Fiennes.

'If the king of France orders you to go, you'd be a fool to stay,' remarked a dark-haired young woman who'd have done better to be silent. She was about fourteen, far too young to be voicing her opinions in front of her elders and betters.

'Be quiet, Anne!' whispered the young woman at her elbow.

At the mention of the name I remembered who the pair were – the daughters of Sir Thomas Boleyn, one of Henry's up and coming gentlemen.

'I think we are all agreed the queen needs her English ladies,' Meg said. 'And without her gentlemen advisers she would be in a perilous position.'

'Cannot someone appeal to King Louis?' I suggested. 'Lord Norfolk perhaps?'

'My father says Lord Norfolk has already agreed to the dismissal,' Jane said miserably.

'The snake!' Lady Hastings spoke before she could stop herself. To voice criticism of one of England's senior nobles was unwise to the point of stupidity.

'It's said Lord Norfolk does King Louis's bidding in everything.' Mary Fiennes ventured, sniffing and dabbing at her nose.

'If that is so then maintaining good relations with the French must be more important to him than Queen Mary's welfare,' Lady Hastings said crossly.

'How about Lord Berners?' I said. 'Being the queen's chamberlain he is well placed to plead her case with the king.'

'My father has already tried and been refused an audience,' Jane said mournfully.

Meg frowned. 'There must be some person we can ask to intervene; someone who has influence with King Louis.'

It was difficult. At home we knew who had King Henry's ear and who did not, which of the courtiers we could trust. If any of us wanted a particular favour we knew who to ask. But here, hundreds of miles from everything that was familiar, we had yet to discover the intricate connections and rivalries in the French court.

'Perhaps a woman would be more successful than Lord Berners,' suggested Anne Jerningham.

A little hiss of fear ran through the room from those whose experience of trying to wheedle favours from fathers or brothers had been far from pleasant.

'Impossible!' said Lady Hastings firmly. 'For one of us to approach the French king would be…' Her voice trailed away to nothing.

Yes, I thought. No-one would dare approach King Louis without an invitation. Such behaviour would be considered a grave insult.

'Madame Claude,' Jane suggested. 'She is the king's daughter and very obliging.'

'Madame Claude has no influence,' I said. 'Besides, her husband would not let her approach the king on such a delicate matter.'

'Madame Louise?' Florence Hastings, who so far had said nothing, was another of my mother's many Hastings kinswomen.

'Madame Louise would like nothing better than to be rid of us,' I remarked, thinking of my mother's warnings.

For a moment there was silence.

'You could always try her son,' Anne Boleyn suggested, earning herself another dig in the ribs from her sister.

'François d'Angoulême!' Lady Hastings exclaimed.

'He'd not agree to see one of us,' Jane said. 'Why would he?'

Anne Boleyn gave an enigmatic little smile. 'Why would he not?'

We contemplated the enormity of approaching the heir to the throne, the dashing but dangerous François d'Angoulême, Duke of Valois. We'd not been in France a week when we began hearing stories about his exploits. He had a mistress whom we'd yet to set eyes on, but despite her presence in his bed, it was said he plucked women like flowers from a garden, discarding them after a single night. The thought of being close to such a man was thrilling and yet utterly terrifying.

'Well yes. I can see that might work. He is certainly influential and extremely close to the king. But who is to go?' Meg cast her gaze over us as if searching for a prize filly to take to the stallion.

'Not me,' said a chorus of voices.

When I said nothing, Anne Boleyn's dark eyes regarded me with interest. 'Lady Elizabeth should go,' she said.

'Why pray should it be Lady Elizabeth?' Meg sounded piqued that no-one had suggested her.

'Because she is the prettiest, my lady,' Anne Boleyn replied.

I was not vain but the compliment, even from a nobody

like the little Boleyn girl, was gratifying. Yet the thought of approaching a man like the Duke of Valois made me wish I'd no pretensions to beauty.

'Yes! Lady Elizabeth should go,' murmured a dozen relieved voices, as hands pushed me forwards until I was standing before my sister-in-law. She nodded her approval at my low-cut crimson gown.

'Very suitable.'

Suitable for what? I wondered, as my belly knotted in fear at the thought of asking a favour from François d'Angoulême. I didn't admit it, even to myself, but what really frightened me was not the asking, but the favour the handsome young duke might demand in return.

Trying to appear invisible to the crowds gathered outside the apartment of the Duke of Valois meant keeping my head meekly bowed, my gaze on the floor and moving aside so as not to inconvenience anyone. Men could barge and shove their way to the front but a woman must be submissive at all times. I felt so submissive I wanted to prostrate myself on the floor. Luckily I was of no interest to anyone, just another petitioner seeking justice from the heir to the throne.

Twice, my fear of what lay ahead grew to such a pitch I decided to run back to the others, but thoughts of my mother's lectures on cowardice made me remain where I was. Eventually, after what seemed like hours, one of the ushers beckoned me forward. I half-expected, indeed half-hoped, my request for an audience with the duke would be summarily dismissed but a few enquiries as to who I was and suddenly I found myself whisked through the door.

Once inside I was escorted by a liveried servant through one vast ante-chamber after another until I found myself in what had to be the duke's presence chamber.

One wall was hung floor to ceiling with startling images of battle: gaily caparisoned horses, men in full armour, unfurled flags, a forest of pikes, gnarled trees and in the foreground, wisps of grass and a single solitary flower. To my left, in front of a draped curtain, sat a lutenist plucking his instrument, the music soothing and pleasant.

An elderly merchant with two boys in tow, hurried past, carrying a chest of bright-coloured velvets followed by a goldsmith clutching his tray of offerings. I tried to ignore the churning fear in my belly and let my gaze turn to the far end of the chamber. There sat the man I had come to see. I stood rooted to the spot, too afraid to move until a quick nudge from behind told me I should approach.

Close to, the heir to the French throne was even more good-looking than at a distance. His height, his dark eyes, the fine lines of his cheekbones, long nose, the curve of a pair of sensual lips and the aura of confident masculinity, all combined to make him a man of tremendous allure. He was only a few years my senior yet I felt like a small girl hauled up in front of a powerful father for chastisement. But the amused way François d'Angoulême regarded me out of those hooded black eyes was far from fatherly.

I curtsied, copying the elegant way I'd seen the French ladies lower themselves, a graceful sweep to the floor with my skirts held wide. I waited until he motioned for me to rise, then slowly raised myself up with my back held straight. It was impolite to look straight into the face of a man who might one day be king, so I kept my eyes lowered, preferring to examine the fingers of his left hand where they rested on the tawny-gold skirt of his doublet. Oh *Sainte Vierge*! His legs! Apart from King Henry, I'd not seen a man with such beautifully shaped calves. They were clad in white silk hose, the finest and surely the costliest I'd ever seen, and I wondered, foolishly, what it might be like to touch them, Quickly I looked down at his feet: white shoes, soft kidskin, gold buckles; the kind to please any young woman.

'How pleasant!' he said, smiling.

'*Monseigneur?*' I murmured. Then blushed. The greeting was wrong. '*Votre Grâce?*'

He laughed, a low intimate sound from the back of his throat.

'How exquisite you English women are.'

I could feel a blush spreading down my neck and across my chest. I felt half-naked and cursed the low neckline, wishing I'd worn a black velvet partlet to cover myself.

He stood up, stepped forward and placed two of those elegant fingers under my chin. I gave a little shiver of fear or possibly of something more akin to desire as he turned my face up, forcing me to look into his eyes.

'Mmm! Quite delightful!'

I wanted to turn and flee but forced myself to stay where I was. If he'd been any other man, an upstart gentleman like Francis Bryan, I might have slapped him hard across the face for daring to touch me in such an intimate way without an invitation, but as he was who he was, I stayed perfectly still and said nothing.

'So, my little English rose, why is it you have you come to see me?'

I hesitated, mesmerised by the gold flecks in the depths of his eyes.

'My lord, I come to ask a favour.'

'A favour is it?' A flicker of disappointment and his gaze darkened. I had no idea what he'd expected but guessed few people approached Duke François without wanting something. 'For your husband?' he said coolly.

'No, my lord. I am not yet wed.'

'How remiss,' he murmured, a smile teasing the edges of his mouth. 'For your father perhaps?'

'No, my lord.'

The smile widened. 'For yourself?'

I felt something uncurl in my belly and leap into my throat at the way he said those words.

'I... I...'

His eyes narrowed. 'Who sent you? Was it the English Lord Nor-ferk?'

The question startled me out of my stammering silence.

'No, my lord.'

'Wolsey?'

'No, my lord. I have no dealings with the Archbishop.'

'So, my pretty English damoiselle?' He stepped closer. 'No dealings with Wolsey eh? Who *do* you spy for?'

My heart beat faster. 'My lord. I am no spy. Nor am I a damoiselle, I am the Lady Elizabeth...'

His eyes gleamed. 'An English lady.'

He spoke the words as if describing a succulent dish he had yet to taste. One which so far had been denied him.

'Yes, my lord. Lady Elizabeth Grey.'

'Grey?' He frowned.

'My brother is the Marquess of Dorset.'

His face cleared. 'Dorset? Ah yes! The fair-haired one who scowls at Lord Nor-ferk.'

I nodded thinking the description apt. 'Yes, my lord. That is my brother.'

'King Henry's cousin, so I hear. And it is your brother who has sent you. What does he want?'

'My brother wants nothing, my lord.'

With one hand he took hold of my wrist so I was held fast and could not run even if I wished.

'Nothing. Ah, if only that were true. Everyone wants something, even you, I think, Lady Elizabeth Grey.'

His grip tightened.

'My brother does not know I am here, my lord,' I said hastily. 'I doubt he'd approve of my visit.'

That made him laugh. He placed his other hand on the sleeve of my gown, rubbing the rich crimson brocade between his fingers in the way a merchant tests a sample of cloth. The touch was so unexpected, so intimate as if a prelude to the removal of my clothing, I thought I might faint.

'So, Lady Elizabeth, this is just a little game you wish to play, is that it? A secret from your brother? I have made the acquaintance of many young women who wished to keep secrets from their brothers. Say no more, *ma chérie*. I know exactly why you have come.'

'You do?'

'*Bien sûr!*'

He slid his hand under my elbow and adroitly steered me, unresisting, across the floor into a small side chamber. Someone must have opened the doors but I was oblivious to everyone and everything except for the man at my side: the warmth of his body, the scent of his skin, the very breath from his lips. I glanced around but the usual lines of servants standing against walls were nowhere to be seen and my mother's warnings echoed loud and strong in my ears as I heard the chamber door close. I felt a rush of panic. A smell of musky perfume hung in the air.

The chamber was beautifully furnished with several cushioned couches and a huge curtained bed hung with rich red velvet François d'Angoulême pushed me firmly onto one of the couches, then picked up a silver jug from a nearby table and poured wine into two goblets. He offered me one.

I murmured my thanks, trying to remain calm. 'My lord, I think you misunderstand the purpose of my visit.'

He smiled and I noticed how sharp his teeth were.

'I think not, Lady Elizabeth Grey. Now, taste the wine and tell me what you think.'

I took a small sip. The wine was heavy-bodied, smooth, sweet on the tongue, with a slight sharpness as it slid down my throat.

I gave a shy smile. 'A fine wine, my lord.'

I took another sip to give me courage. And then another. In no time, my goblet was empty and he poured me some more. He watched for a moment and then came and sat beside me, his legs touching my skirts, too close for politeness, too close to allow me a chance of escape and far too close for any further pretence.

Gently he removed my drink and placed it on the low table just within reach.

'Now, my English beauty, let us get better acquainted.'

He placed his fingers on the side of my neck and began stroking gently from my ears, down to the expanse of bare skin above my neckline. I froze. This was no gallant gesture, this was horribly intimate, the action of a husband or… or of a lover.

'So delicate,' he murmured, running one of his fingers just underneath the bodice of my crimson brocade, touching the swell of my breasts. 'So soft. So deliciously innocent. You have such freshness, *ma chérie*. I am overwhelmed by what I feel for you.'

I gulped. No man had ever spoken to me like this.

'My lord, I cannot do this,' I whispered. 'Truly, I cannot.'

He chuckled softly. 'That is what they all say, *ma chérie*. But you will, I promise. You will and you will enjoy it.'

I was rigid with fear as his fingers continued their intimate investigation of my bodice, brushing places where no man's hand had any right to be.

'I came to ask a favour for the queen,' I gasped, trying to ignore what he was doing.

'The queen?' he said, removing his exploring fingers and turning my face so that our eyes were only inches apart.

'Yes, my lord.'

'She sent you?'

'No, my lord. I came… I came because…'

'Yes?' he said, placing his mouth so close to mine that I could almost taste the wine on his breath.

I found myself experiencing the most unexpected of sensations as his lips brushed mine. It was the ultimate temptation, like drowning in honey, a cloying sweetness while always an awareness of danger from a will more powerful than my own. I knew that if I yielded my mouth to him, I'd be lost.

I struggled to twist my head away and managed to blurt out, 'The king is to send the queen's ladies home to England.'

He drew back a little and regarded me with interest.

I carried on trying to remember why I was here. 'My lord, the queen will suffer great distress if she has to part with us.'

He nodded. 'Ah yes, the queen's domestic arrangements! So that is what this is all about – a fuss in the hen coop. I'm surprised you come to me, my English beauty, unless of course there is another reason.'

I was finding it increasingly difficult to concentrate on what he was saying while one of his hands lingered on my neck, stroking gently, inching its way up into my hair.

'There is no other reason, my lord. I am not a spy. All I seek is your help.'

'Mmmm, is that so.' All the while he was talking, one hand was busy removing the pins which kept my hood in place. 'Men who seek my help usually offer me a little something in return. What are you offering, Lady Elizabeth Grey, sister of the great Englishman, the one they call the marquess?'

At this point he gave a satisfied sigh as he at last succeeded in removing my hood and the long pins which kept my hair in place. His fingers buried themselves in the tumbling weight of my hair as he pulled me closer.

'I have nothing to offer, my lord.'

'I beg to differ, *ma chérie*.'

'Nothing other then my gratitude, my lord,' I said trying to disentangle myself from his arms. 'If you were to intervene with the king in this matter, I would be truly grateful.'

He half-closed his eyes. 'Gratitude! I do not think an Englishwoman's gratitude will be of much value when set against the contempt of my king for interfering in his marriage?'

'It would be a Christian act, my lord; a kindness to a young woman who is most deserving.'

'I think I would need more than that,'

'I… I am not sure I understand you, my lord.'

He laughed. 'Oh, I think you do, Lady Elizabeth Grey. I think you understand me perfectly. If I were to do as you ask, I would need something from you in return for the favour.'

He raised me up and led me, unresisting, towards the bed. I fixed my gaze on the intricate carving on the bedhead, refusing to dwell on thoughts of what he might do next. I remembered my mother's advice and wondered should I scream. And if I did, would anyone come.

He bent down and murmured softly in my ear. 'You see this bed, *ma chérie*? Here I have made love to many beautiful women, though none as beautiful as you. You understand, I have the stamina of a conqueror.' He threw out his chest as if to prove to me just how strong and virile he was. Then he pressed on my shoulders, forcing me to sit on the edge of the bed.

As he towered over me I was tempted to close my eyes but some awareness of danger made me keep them open. He didn't push me backwards onto the covers as

I'd expected, instead he started talking in a low insistent voice. 'You have seen our king.'

'Yes, my lord,' I whispered.

'He boasts he crossed the river three times on his wedding night. Three times!'

'That is a great many, my lord.'

'Do we believe him? I for one, do not. I'd be surprised if he raised his standard once. For me, three times would be nothing. But our Most Christian Majesty is an old man, pretending to be a young gallant. He is riddled with gout and unlikely to see another summer.'

'My lord!'

'Save your horrified gasps for your English ladies, *ma chérie*, and listen carefully. Not a single whisper has come out of the royal marriage chamber. Those who attend on the king's person are silent on the matter. His doctor speaks not a word. No-one says anything. I need to know what happened. Is our fair and lovely queen still intact or has my cousin managed to make her his wife?'

'My lord! I cannot ask the queen such a question. It would be impossible.'

He smiled, this time showing all his fine white teeth. 'As impossible as it would be for me to suggest to my king that he show clemency in the matter of his wife's English ladies.'

Now the bargain was clear: I was to provide information as to the state of Mary's virginity in exchange for the duke's help in persuading the French king that dismissing his wife's English ladies was unwise. I'd been mistaken in thinking this man was nothing but a compulsive seducer; François d'Angoulême was first and foremost a political animal, navigating a careful route to power. He disliked Mary, not for herself but for the very real possibility that she might give King Louis a son.

He leant over me and whispered into my ear 'When you tell me what I wish to know, my English beauty, then we shall conclude our bargain.'

'Very well, my lord,' I murmured. 'I shall see what I can discover for you.'

'Do not be long, *ma chérie*. I am in a fever of impatience to see you again.'

He raised my hand to his lips and gently nipped the soft mound of flesh at the base of my thumb.

7

THE CORONATION
AUTUMN 1514

Once out of the ducal chambers my knees felt so weak I leant against a nearby wall for support. The sight of me doubled up in obvious distress, gasping for breath, caused much amusement to a group of passing gentlemen who sniggered, speaking rapidly to each other. I understood less than half the words they used but it was obvious what sort of woman they thought I was. Doubtless the sight of a young woman in a dishevelled state leaving the duke's apartments was common enough for a volley of coarse jokes rather than an offer of assistance.

As soon as my legs stopped trembling and I was no longer in danger of collapsing onto the floor, I gathered up my skirts and fled back though the painted rooms of the Hôtel de la Gruthuse to the queen's apartments.

One look was enough to send Jane rushing to my side.

'Sit here!' she said, holding my arm as I was lowered into a chair like an old lady.

'Chamomile!' Florence Hastings ordered, snapping her fingers at one of the maidservants.

'Valerian,' murmured a voice from behind me, followed by a chorus of shushing.

'There's no need to worry. I am perfectly alright.'

Jane disagreed. 'You look far from alright.'

'Did he?' My sister-in-law was unsure how to pose the question.

I shook my head. 'I am unharmed, truly, but on no account allow any of the younger ones to be alone with the duke.'

Glances were exchanged, everyone wanting to know exactly what had occurred behind the closed doors of François d'Angoulême's private rooms. What had he said? What had he done? Fortunately no-one had the gall to ask as I knew my behaviour was far from what it should have been. Despite his attractiveness and despite the requirements of my mission, I should have resisted his advances. Instead I had allowed him to draw me close, caress my body and kiss my mouth. I had permitted liberties which should belong only to a husband and there was no excuse, none whatsoever.

'Will he help?' Lady Hastings enquired.

I nodded. 'It's possible, but first I must see Queen Mary.'

Someone pressed into my hand, a cup of what smelled like an infusion of dried chamomile flowers. As I sipped the warm liquid, I realised how lucky I'd been to escape unscathed from my meeting with François d'Angoulême. My pride was bruised but no lasting harm was done. Perhaps the knowledge that in close proximity to a persuasive good-looking seducer I was as susceptible as any other young woman would serve me well in the future.

I recalled the evening before when I'd drunk too much wine and an attractive young Frenchman had invited me into the garden. If I'd listened to the words he was whispering in my ear and accepted his invitation to stroll amongst the bushes, I might easily have compromised myself. Perhaps, like the French ladies at court, he had a low opinion of English women, assuming all I needed was a little encouragement to raise my skirts. To my horror, I wondered were they right. My encounter with François d'Angoulême might have ended very differently if he'd not thought Mary would confide in me.

I very much feared the duke was wrong. Mary and I might be cousins, friends even; we might have lived in close proximity with each other for ten years, but her intimate relationship with her husband was not a subject for discussion. It was private, sacred even; not one to be mentioned to anyone other than her confessor. Nonetheless, I had to try.

As I approached the queen's chambers, I met Madame d'Aumont, a member of the illustrious Aumont family, one of the French ladies allocated to serve the king's new wife. I thought she'd pass by with nothing more than her usual haughty nod but this time she put out her hand to stop me. Looking down her aristocratic nose as if I smelt of something unpleasant, she said, 'You were seen.'

'Madame d'Aumont?' I said politely, hoping this was not what I feared.

'You are not fit to serve a queen of France,' she hissed.

'The queen is my cousin. King Louis personally approved my appointment.'

'Cousin! Oh *bien sûr*! But now our Most Christian Majesty has seen the kind of filth your English king sees fit to send him, he does not tolerate the insult. All you English are to leave. Our royal palace is defiled by the presence of you dirty Englishwomen and your foul habits. Go! Pack your gowns and do not dare to approach anyone else for no-one here will help you.'

I squared my shoulders ready for battle. '*Au contraire, Madame.* The Duke of Valois has been most helpful. Now, if you will excuse me, I must attend Her Majesty.'

I pushed her hand out of the way and walked towards the door of Mary's private room. To my surprise, the guards opened the door and within a moment I heard it close behind me, leaving an open-mouthed Madame d'Aumont outside, seething with impotent fury.

I knew Mary would be upset but was shocked at the sight of her tear-stained face. She was no longer the wonderfully fair English bride, praised for her demeanour and her tenderness towards an elderly husband. Instead I found a grief-stricken young woman with red-rimmed eyes and blotchy skin, whose once beautiful red-gold hair was dull and lank.

'What am I to do?' she sobbed. 'If you leave, I shall be alone with no-one I can trust.'

'Majesty, Cousin Mary, please, do not distress yourself. We shall find a way.'

'There is no way,' she cried, la picture of utter wretchedness.

'Perhaps if you were to plead with the king.'

'How can I do that? My duty as a wife is to be obedient to my husband's wishes. Whatever he decides, I must accept.'

By now she had collapsed into a heap on her bed, overcome by a fresh fit of sobbing.

Having experienced many of Mary's emotional upsets,

I let her weep until she was exhausted and lay gnawing her knuckles. This was the first sign of what always came next: a burning Tudor sense of injustice.

'Perhaps the king is not aware how distressed you are,' I ventured, sitting down on the bed.

She raised her head. 'Oh, it is not my husband who has decided this. It is those weasels on his council, those evil men. They have been against me from the start. They do not want me here.'

'I'm sure that is not true,' I said, knowing full well that many men on the council resented the appearance of this nubile young Englishwoman with her horde of foreign attendants.

Mary clutched at the bedcovers and pushed herself up, the better to nurse her current grievance. 'They think I don't understand what they say. They imagine just because I am English, I am stupid. But I *do* understand. I know they have persuaded the king to send away dearest Mother Guildford. My husband says it pleases him to keep me by his side but *they* fear I shall influence him. They wish to silence me. Cousin Elizabeth, I love Mother Guildford and cannot do without her. Can my husband not see how wise and honourable she is?'

'Perhaps the king fears she is indiscreet.'

'She is like a mother to me.'

I sensed the problem was not merely the dismissal of Lady Guildford; there was more to Mary's distress than the loss of her faithful old retainer. It was several years since Lady Guildford had retired from royal service, replaced in Mary's eyes by Henry who was always ready to take his sister's part. But now, deprived of her brother's love and support, she had turned once more to Lady Guildford only to suffer the indignity of her abrupt removal.

'Perhaps we should ask the Duke of Valois for help,' I said cautiously. 'People say he is a great favourite with the king.'

'François d'Angoulême! I spit on him. He will not lift a finger to help me.'

'He might. I could ask.'

'I forbid you to ask for his help. Have you not seen the way he looks at me.'

I thought François d'Angoulême looked at Mary in the same way he looked at every other pretty young woman, although in her case his lust was mixed with a contrary desire to strangle her.

'Cousin Mary, surely…'

'No; I have decided. I shall write to Henry. He will help me. He loves me. He will tell my husband that I cannot live without my dearest Mother Guildford. That is what I shall do.'

'Perhaps also a letter to Thomas Wolsey?' I suggested slyly.

'A good idea, Cousin Elizabeth. Everyone says Wolsey is a clever man.'

And one used to oiling the wheels of diplomacy. My bother, Leonard, said Mary's marriage to King Louis was Wolsey's triumph when many said the French would never agree to the alliance. I thought Thomas Wolsey would know exactly how to put Mary's case in the best light without creating offence – and all in his excellent French.

I was fast coming to realise that in this matter of the French queen's English attendants, King Louis was not the only person involved who must be approached with tact, Mary also required delicate handling.

'Perhaps if you were to be content with the dismissal of Lady Guildford, your husband might allow you to keep one or two of your other English ladies.' Mary opened her mouth to protest but I hurried on. 'Oh Cousin Mary, I know she is like a mother to you, but no man wishes to share his wife with her mother.'

Mary gave a small smile, perhaps at last beginning to understand the root cause of her husband's problem.

It took more than the week we spent at Abbeville to resolve the bedchamber crisis but by the time we arrived at the Basilica of Saint-Denis on the last day of October. Mary had acquiesced with good grace to the loss of Lady Guildford. The king was generous enough to permit his dutiful young wife to retain a dozen of her English gentlemen and a small clutch of junior ladies but we would be a sadly depleted gathering.

The list of those who were to remain included Mary's almoner, her master of horse, her physician and a couple of pages as well as a few of what the French called maids of the bedchamber: Jane and me, Mary Fiennes, Bess Grey of Wilton. a distant kinswoman of mine; Anne Devereux, Eliza Ferrers, Anne Jerningham and both Boleyn girls.

To my surprise, overnight I had become the senior Englishwoman in attendance on the queen, a position which gave me an odd feeling of vulnerability in a court dominated by French men and women who took exception to our presence. We were interlopers, our countrymen the enemy, who a year ago had besieged their towns and killed their brothers. They eyed us with increasing suspicion and would have turned us out without a second thought if they'd not been afraid of offending their king.

'Madame d'Aumont is in charge of the maids of the bedchamber,' Jane reported gloomily, 'and the queen is to have Madame Claude as a companion as well as Madame Louse's daughter, Duchess Marguerite.'

'It will be Madame Louise making decisions about Mary's household,' I said bluntly. 'Madame Claude is very sweet but no match for her mother-in-law. She shrivels in her presence. Doubtless the duchess will do as she's told by her mother.'

'My father says the duchess has a pair of wonderful violet-blue eyes.'

I laughed. 'Your father said that! The man who never take his nose out of a book!'

Jane giggled. 'I think he was attracted by her learning, not her looks. She is said to be tremendously clever.'

I peered in the mirror, wondering if I might try a little rouge paste on my cheeks and if François d'Angoulême had received my note. I'd spent a long time planning what to say, explaining why I need trouble him no further, but was uncertain if I'd struck the right tone. It would not do to offend him no matter that he had greatly offended me. Where women were concerned I was sure he'd be a vindictive enemy. No man likes to be spurned and being spurned by an Englishwoman would make him doubly angry.

'Is the queen with the king?' I asked, deciding my cheeks were pink enough.

Jane sighed. 'They are discussing his proposed foray into Italy. He has promised to take her to Venice.'

I turned away from my unpromising reflection and thoughts of Duke François. 'Venice! Can you imagine anything more wonderful! I've heard such stories. I hope we're asked to accompany the queen.'

Jane leant forward and whispered, 'Is it true the king spent two nights in her bed on the way here?'

I nodded. 'Yes, it is true.'

'Do you think they...?'

I put my finger ton her lips. 'I do not think, I do not speculate and I say nothing. We must be careful. The queen has enemies here and if she's to remain safe, some matters should not be discussed, not even in private.'

At that moment, one of the French girls popped her head round the door and said Madame d'Aumont was waiting. She withdrew, muttering about lazy Englishwomen.

Custom dictated that an uncrowned Queen of France could not enter Paris, so Mary's coronation was to take place in the ancient abbey church of Saint-Denis, a few miles outside the city walls. A huge throng of ladies and gentlemen had ridden out from the city for the occasion, wanting a first glimpse of their new queen. To Mary's disappointment the only member of the English nobility who was to be present was the Earl of Worcester; everyone else had gone home after the wedding celebrations in Abbeville.

Before he left, Sir Christopher Garnish came to make his formal farewell to Mary. Afterwards, he seized my hand and drew me aside. 'I urge you to be vigilant, Lady Elizabeth. The waters here at the French court may look calm and pleasant but do not be deceived. There are dangerous currents. Beneath the surface lie hazards. I know you will serve our French queen well, for that is your nature, but I beg you to have a care for yourself. I should not like you to come to harm.'

I was immensely flattered by his words, assuring him I'd take the greatest of care, not just of our French queen but also of myself. For a moment I wondered if he was interested in me or merely being polite. He'd not mentioned a wife, not that my brother would even consider him as a potential husband. As Cecily had once said, the pool in which the Grey sisters were permitted to fish was horribly small. And to Thomas, Sir Christopher, for all his manly attraction, would merely be a minnow.

With Mary's coronation imminent, Sir Christopher's words and the absence of the great English lords, alerted me to the unwelcome realisation of how alone we were in France, how friendless, how unprotected if anything should go wrong. Mary's few gentlemen attendants would be no match for the combined ranks of the French nobility.

I expected the coronation to be magnificent but, to my dismay, the ceremony itself was simple with little of the grandeur which had accompanied the wedding at Abbeville. François d'Angoulême led Mary to the altar where she was anointed by the Cardinal Bishop of Bayeux and invested with the ring and sceptre and rod of justice before being crowned. The great matrimonial crown looked extraordinarily heavy but Duke François held it steady above Mary's head throughout the High Mass. I could see no hint of the anger he must have felt at the presence of this English woman who could deprive him of the throne. He must have heard about the royal couple's nocturnal closeness on the journey from Beauvais and I feared he might come looking for me to seek more information.

In the flickering candlelight of the church, Madame Louise's face was equally impassive as she watched her son's chance of becoming king slip quietly away, stolen by this young usurper who might even now be carrying the seed of his disinheritance.

8

THE HÔTEL DES TOURNELLES
WINTER 1514

Paris was not what I expected. We'd been told it was a world apart, the most beautiful city in Christendom, a cornucopia of delights to the human eye. But that was not what we found. Vast, noisy, dirty; crumbling walls and peeling paint; roadways littered with detritus and thousands of citizens, merchants, friars, apprentices, minstrels, thieves, and vagabonds crammed into narrow crooked alleyways, oblivious to the stinking piles of ordure. Animals and children scampered everywhere under foot, threatening the safety of our horses. The dwellings were tiny with women hanging out of their windows, shouting and screaming and waving ribbons. Overlaying everything, filling our nostrils, was the pervasive stench of mud.

But if I lifted my eyes from the filth, Paris was also supremely beautiful. Its palaces were magnificent and everyone of note wore silks, trailing their elegant robes across the mud. We'd been warned to beware of the *mauvais garçons* who terrorised the city streets should we be so foolish as to venture unaccompanied beyond the palace walls.

Our lodgings were at the Hôtel des Tournelles, so named for its many little towers. Despite the vast size of this beautiful palace, we Englishwomen found ourselves sharing a single bedchamber. The Boleyn sisters were relegated to a narrow cot while Jane and I took the bed nearest the window, and the other five slept in the two bigger beds by the back wall. It was reminiscent of my days in the nursery at Astley, sleeping under the watchful eye of a nursemaid, undisturbed by the terrifying presence of my mother.

With so many Frenchwomen now in attendance on Mary, I began to find their conversations tedious in the extreme: endless convoluted stories of courtiers I'd never met or the indiscretions of women whose names meant nothing. I longed for word of Queen Katherine's pregnancy which must be nearing its conclusion, or news of Lizzie Bryan who was due to marry Henry's young companion, Nicholas Carew. I'd not admit it but I'd have liked to know what Lizzie's brother, that dark-eyed charmer, Francis Bryan, was doing. However, no-one talked of England, everything was about France, our new home which felt most unlike anyone's home. It felt as alien as one of those new lands discovered by the Spanish, far across the Western Ocean.

Now that she was in control, Madame d'Aumont ensured we despised Englishwomen spent as little time as possible with Mary, inventing ridiculous excuses to exclude us from the queen's presence.

'The queen wishes for privacy this afternoon. She will sing for His Gracious Majesty who is soothed by the sound of her voice. She does not need you.'

'But Madame,' I began.

'It is decided,' she said firmly.

For three weeks the court partook in a continuous round of celebrations: music, feasting, dancing and display. Everyone commented on how there was complete harmony between the married couple. The king was a generous husband, lavishing gifts on his young wife, each day bringing a new collar or string of pearls, a bracelet or a piece made of diverse diamonds and rubies. None were as magnificent as the Mirror of Naples which he'd given her before their marriage but each one was wonderful in its own way.

I watched as Mary paid for her jewels with kisses and thought how pleasant it must be to be married. It was just as I'd been taught: an obedient wife can expect kindness from a satisfied husband; but if she should rail against him, be shrewish in her manner or kick against the traces, than she could expect nothing but beatings. Naturally the king of France would not beat his wife, there were far more subtle ways to demonstrate his displeasure.

Towards the end of November, a final banquet marked the end of the coronation festivities. The next day we repaired to the king's country residence at Saint-Germain-en-Laye where I expected King Louis to rest and take his ease. Yet from morning to night he seemed determined to please Mary in every way he could. He sat up late watching her dance, showered her with gifts and matched her appetite with his as dish after dish of the best confections the royal cooks could provide were set before them. Like all Frenchmen, his thirst for wine seemed unquenchable yet he remained sober – unlike one or two of the ladies who had to leave the table in great haste before they disgraced themselves.

The pace set by the court was punishing. Hunting in the king's forests around Saint-Germain-en-Laye was organised for the mornings with the added frisson of the promise of wild boar, while endless carousing each evening, was deemed essential.

'He can't keep this up,' I whispered to Jane.

'Duke François can,' she replied as we watched François d'Angoulême ease himself onto a stool beside Mary. He leant over and said something that made her smile. She repeated the duke's remark to the king, who laughed.

'What is he saying? I can't hear.'

'It's not what he's saying, it's who he's saying it to.'

Jane frowned. 'I don't understand.'

'Queen Mary is not used to a man like François d'Angoulême. He is remarkably attractive to women and she finds him disturbing.'

'He's not flirting with her under the king's nose, surely?'

I stifled a laugh. 'Not in the way you mean but he's clever with words. She doesn't know what he wants from her.'

'What does he want?'

'What do you think?'

Jane thought for a moment. 'I don't know.'

'Exactly. Neither does he, that's his problem. Think of him as a gambler. He's laying money on both sides so that whatever happens he'll be the winner.'

Jane's face cleared as she finally understood my meaning. 'You mean... Oh, but why not ask the maids. They'll be the first to know.'

'Madame Louise already has two in her pay.'

'Are you sure?'

'Queen Mary told me.'

Jane sighed. 'What if she's not?'

"Then François d'Angoulême must continue to placate the king until...'

Jane's eyes widened with fright as the probable destination of this part of our lives became clear to her. 'Holy Mother of Christ! What if...'

I put a hand on her sleeve to stop her from saying any more. 'Don't think about it. There's nothing any of us can do. Just be careful what you say. And keep your eyes on the queen.'

All too soon our rural idyll was over and we returned to Paris and the Hôtel des Tournelles for the winter season. Christmas came and went quietly. With the king finally retired to his sick bed, none of us expected rowdy festivities. Naturally the younger ones grumbled. Nativity celebrations in Henry's palaces had been joyous, an endless round of revelry and the subject of much excited preparation whereas in Paris all we talked about was our fear of what lay ahead.

Despite his waning energies, King Louis made gallant attempts to please Mary. His promises of future delights, delivered in a tired old voice were in marked contrast to the confident tones of François d'Angoulême who made it his business to spend much of his day with his cousin, which also meant being in the company of Mary. His marked attention to her and his reputation with women resulted in speculation at court that cuckoldry was afoot, that the handsome heir wanted Mary in his bed and she was not averse to his advances.

'Cousin Elizabeth, I'm frightened of him. The way he looks at me,' she said in a rare moment when we were alone together.

'Your Majesty, the duke flatters you with his attentions.'

'I grant you he's very charming but were anything to happen to the king, I would be at his mercy.'

'You are the queen.'

'But,' she lowered her voice to a whisper, 'if the king were to die, I would no longer be queen.'

'Then we must pray the king recovers.'

'Yes,' she said, immediately cheering up. 'His doctors say they've despaired many times but the king is a fighter, a man with marvellous powers of recovery.'

'This time will be no different,' I said, greatly afraid that my words were untrue.

'Cousin Elizabeth, what if he does not recover? He is very weak. Oh how I wish…'

I remembered my mother's advice.

'Your Majesty, if the worst should happen, your brother will help you.'

Her face darkened. 'You think so? I fear Henry won't help me unless it suits his plans. He'll leave me here, alone, where I have no friends.'

'I'm sure he'd not do that.'

'You don't know him like I do. He may love me but he cannot abide having his wishes overturned. He'll blame me. He'll say I exhausted my husband. "*Ces amoureuse noces*" is what François d'Angoulême calls it.'

She was right. The gossip at court was all of the insatiable appetites of the queen and the unsuitability of matching a sensual young women to a sick old man; how the king, in his desire to be a companion to his young wife, would die of his pleasures. "An old man in love, hugs death," they quipped. Worse, it was said that the king had been tricked by the English who'd sent a young filly to be his undoing and send him plunging to his grave. It would not take long for such stories to reach England.

'Perhaps if you were to approach the council,' I suggested. 'The duke of Longueville would surely help.'

Mary disagreed. 'The council have one eye on their futures. If anything should happen to my husband, I would be of no use to them. I'd be powerless.'

Gradually a change was taking place yet everything was exactly as it had been before with the same formalities which had governed our lives since we'd arrived in France, Perhaps it was my unfamiliarity with the French Court which failed to alert me to the more subtle signs of change, but by Christmas I'd noticed the beginnings of an insidious transformation.

In the early days, the Frenchwomen with whom we shared our duties mostly ignored us or satisfied themselves with occasional veiled barbs about the unsuitability of our clothing or our perceived lack of cleanliness. Now, one or two became overtly hostile. They turned their backs, gave us cold stares and "accidently" tipped boxes of powders over our shoes. One of the younger maids had her nightshift cut into shreds and Anne Devereux reported finding a bold-eyed French woman rummaging around in her chest.

I was asleep, when out of the darkness came a whisper. 'Lady Elizabeth!'

Instantly I was awake. The younger Boleyn sister, Anne, was standing in her nightgown at the side of the bed, her dark eyes gleaming in the candlelight.

'What is it, Anne?'

'The queen has been escorted back to her chamber. She is asking for you.'

I slipped out of bed and had Anne help me dress, all the time wondering what had happened.

I hurried as fast as I could through the darkened rooms to Mary's apartments where a guard held up a torch to examine my face before allowing servants to open the doors.

Mary was sitting on a gilded chair. Her face was pale, her eyes half-closed. She looked close to collapse. Beside her stood Madame d'Aumont with a full complement of French ladies and younger damsels, all immaculately turned out. It was Madame d'Aumont who spoke as Mary was clearly beyond speech.

'Lady Elizabeth, you have been summoned because the queen wishes you to know that a short while ago His Most Christian Majesty, King Louis, received the sacraments.' Her voice was crisp with no hint of distress.

Added to the notable absence of Madame Claude and Duchess Marguerite this must mean the king's death was imminent and the transfer of power had begun. Mary was a spent force unless…

'I shall remain with the queen,' I said firmly.

Madame d'Aumont gave a sorrowful smile. 'Her Majesty will spend the night in prayer, as you would expect of a dutiful wife. She has no need of you and under the circumstances, you understand, it is better that we are here to serve her.'

'I believe Her Majesty will be better served if one or two of her English ladies are in attendance on her at this sad time.'

'I regret that protocol forbids it.'

'Surely not.'

Lady Elizabeth, you and your friends are regarded as foreigners. Only those of us devoted to the cause of France may stay with the queen. Accordingly, I must ask you to leave.'

This made no sense but I had no wish to be bodily removed from Mary's presence so I retreated with my dignity in tact. 'I thank you for your care, Madame d'Aumont. I shall return in the morning.'

However, when morning came I was refused entry. Each time I returned the guards gave an apologetic French gesture but said no-one was to be admitted under any circumstances. They were very sorry but orders had been given.

In the late afternoon I became even more worried when a message came, ordering us to remain in our room. Servants arrived with food and drink but shrugged when I asked for news. They knew nothing, they said. Outside, wind and rain lashed against our window and, as darkness was approaching, I asked a passing servant to help with the shutters. He was a young fair-haired lad with a peasant's muscular body but the manners of a gentleman. Probably a young man with a kinsman in royal service who'd got him a position at court. He was anxious to be helpful and when I thanked him he smiled and said how pretty we English damoiselles were. After days of veiled rudeness it was pleasant to have someone, albeit a servant, pay me a compliment so, perhaps unwisely, I smiled back.

For the rest of the evening we sat and we prayed. We prayed the king would recover and that the queen was carrying a child, and we prayed the child would be a healthy son and that everything would be well because we all knew the fragility of baby princes. King Henry's son, welcomed four years ago with such joy, lived only fifty-two days. The child had died in his cradle at Richmond while the court was still celebrating his birth. For Queen Katherine, it had been a personal tragedy.

When we'd exhausted our prayers we sat in silence as there was little to say and none of us felt like playing games. If the king lived and Mary had a son, her future was secure as Louis's beloved wife and mother of a baby prince.

I wondered if a child would save Mary were the king to die. The long wait through the cold of a Parisian winter and the nights of a French spring until the height of the summer, the very air in her chamber poisoned by the insane jealousy of Madame Louise. And always the fear of an increasingly impatient François d'Angoulême. The perils of childbirth were well known and even if the baby survived it would be a simple matter for someone to put a pillow over the child's face. Nursemaids could be bought and afterwards easily disposed of.

I tried to marshal my thoughts in the way I'd been taught rather than let them run wild. What if the king should die?

If Mary's child was a boy, her place at court as mother of the king was assured although throughout the boy's childhood a careful eye would need to be kept on François d'Angoulême who would doubtless be made regent or protector or whatever the French called the man who governed the realm until the young king was of age.

If the child was a girl, she'd be of no use until she was old enough to be betrothed by which time Madame Claude could have given the new King François a dozen children whose marriages would be of far greater importance than a despised young princess of an unwanted English bride.

If there was no child, Mary would be sold by King François to the highest bidder in the marriage market unless Henry could retrieve his sister. None of these scenarios gave me any comfort.

At about seven o'clock we heard the first tolling of a bell. It came from the great Church of Notre Dame on the Île de la Cité. I crossed myself.

'What does it mean?' Eliza Ferrers looked scared.

'It means the king is dead. Listen! Can you not hear them – bells tolling from across the river.'

I wondered if François d'Angoulême had sent for his mother. After the coronation Madame Louise had retired to her estates at Romorantin, frustrated and angry at her son's hopes of the throne draining away. It was said she sought solace in the stars where the future might be written, presumably a future more to her liking. But with the king's death, she'd be certain to return. She'd want to oversee her son's ascent to the throne.

Unless Mary was carrying a son.

It showed how little we were regarded that the black cloth provided for our mourning gowns was of an inferior quality, thin and poorly made. We did our best with the unpromising material, spending the next day closeted in our chamber, stitching valiantly until our fingers were pricked and raw. The tedious work of seams and hemming was delegated to the maids, while the nine of us toiled in the fading light over embellishments, small details of embroidered sleeves and scalloped necklines and delicate bands of embroidery which would be scrutinised by Madame d'Aumont and every other Frenchwoman in the palace. Once we were suitably attired with thick black veils, stockings and shoes, I led us in procession to Mary's apartments.

The guard shrugged. 'I am sorry, damoiselle, the queen is unwell. She sees no-one.'

'Unwell?'

'*Oui, madame.*' He lowered his head and murmured quietly. '*La pauvre reine.* She faint when they tell her.'

'Then please tell Madame d'Aumont it is most important I see the queen.'

'It is the order of Madame d'Aumont herself. I dare not let you in.'

I remembered my mother's words – when a throne is at stake, a woman's life counts for little, and that of a child, nothing at all. Mary was in grave danger but I had no idea how to gain access or how to protect her. With Madame d'Aumont as gaoler, determined to deprive Mary of her English ladies, I had real fears as to what she intended for my cousin.

My mother once told me that for a throne to lie vacant was as perilous an interregnum as the white of pre-dawn. when men's eyes are fixed on the sun which is yet to appear above the horizon, when an unscrupulous man with enough courage may steal what is not his to take. If Mary was carrying a child, she was in the greatest of all dangers.

Every room in the Hôtel des Tournelles was draped from ceiling to floor in black and everyone from duke to the lowest kitchen knave was decked out with the glossy plumage of ravens. In the great hall, crowds queued to pay their last respects to a king whose embalmed body dressed in royal robes looked more regal in death than it had in life. The constant movement of people caused the draperies to billow and shift into some dreadful imagining of Hell, yet around the king's bier, one hundred beeswax candles burned steadily. In death the king was not alone, aided by the vigil of monks kneeling in constant prayer, giving hope of a speedy transition to paradise.

King Louis had left behind two daughters but had he also left behind a son, now growing in Mary's womb, a son who would ruin all François d'Angoulême's hopes of taking the throne? I did not know and, more importantly, neither did Madame Louise or her son. If Mary was with child and that child was a boy, Mary would have an important role as mother of the king. But if the child was a girl, she'd be of little interest to anyone, a third daughter ranking far behind Madame Claude and her sister, little Madame Renée.

Next day I made a further attempt to see Mary. I walked briskly along the gallery to the queen's apartments. When I arrived I found the door open and no guards on duty. To my horror I saw servants dismantling May's chamber. Four men up ladders were removing heavy tapestries and lowering them to others whose job was to roll them up and carry the costly hangings down to the store rooms. Dozens of men were sweeping up the detritus of two weeks occupation, corners which had not been properly cleaned during the daily attention of the servants, little items dropped on the floor and dust which had mysteriously accumulated under tables and chairs.

'Where is the queen?'

Nobody knew or else nobody was telling. A palace in deep mourning with constant Requiem Masses being said for the soul of the late king, was no place for asking questions.

Amidst the comings and goings we soon discovered that our needs were of no particular interest to anyone. What frightened me most was that Mary's English usher and her three pages were idling about with no occupation, her master of horse was complaining about lack of orders while none of the other gentlemen knew anything. The only person unaccounted for was Maître Guillaume, Mary's physician. Nobody knew where he was.

9

THE HÔTEL DE CLUNY
JANUARY 1515

It took me a week to discover Mary's whereabouts and when I did it was entirely due to the linguistic skills of the younger Boleyn sister, Anne.

'How did you find out?'

She gave a small shrug. 'I listened. I asked questions. The Frenchwomen are only too happy to talk to me, they think I'm one of them.'

This was no surprise. Anne's French was excellent. She spoke like a high-born French lady who'd spent the whole of her young life moving in the exclusive circles of the French aristocracy.

'Where is the Hôtel de Cluny?'

She smiled at my ignorance. 'On the Rue des Mathurins St Jacques on the other side of the river.'

'Why the secrecy? Why were we not told?'

She spread her hands in a particularly French gesture. 'It is the custom. Queen Mary is now *La Reine Blanche*, the White Queen. She must remain in seclusion at the Hôtel de Cluny as a precaution.'

'A precaution against what?' Jane should have known but was as ignorant of French traditions as most of Mary's English household.

I understood only too well. Madame Louise was

terrified of some treachery on the part of the English widow. She believed Mary capable of lying, of passing off a lover's child as a royal baby, of any kind of deception which would deny her beloved son the throne of France. As for François d'Angoulême himself, he could not ascend the throne until he knew for certain that Mary was not carrying King Louis's child. Not only was this a long-established convention, it would be an act of suicidal folly to do otherwise.

Throughout the day I made further discreet enquiries. I discovered that the mourning chamber at the Hôtel de Cluny was small, unheated, heavily curtained and airless. Etiquette demanded that *La Reine Blanche* was watched by two curators of the womb, women who would oversee her solitary existence, protecting her from harm and ensuring her days would pass in peaceful serenity. I feared for Mary in this situation, deprived of company and conversation, deprived of any kind of entertainment or diversion, all alone apart from those few French attendants approved by Madame Louise. From what I knew of the mother of François d'Angoulême, her appointees would be women instructed to watch *La Reine Blanche* carefully and be suspicious of her every action.

My mother had warned me of the potential danger to Mary in this very situation so I made up my mind that, convention or not, invited or not, dangerous or not, I must visit the Hôtel de Cluny. That was my plan but I reckoned without the obstinacy of the English gentlemen in Mary's household who were strongly opposed to any such move.

Bess Grey's brother, Sir Edward, who was the most senior of our little entourage told me that such an idea was out of the question, completely impossible and was amazed I thought it sensible. Until the matter of the succession was settled we must stay here within the walls of the Hôtel de Tournelles, comporting ourselves as King Henry would wish and do nothing which might cause offence. Besides, until the funeral, no-one was permitted to leave. He assured me the dowager queen was perfectly safe. We women should spend our time wisely, preferably at prayer.

As despised Englishwomen we had no part in the funeral procession through black-lined streets to the church of Notre Dame for the funeral eulogy, nor with the weeping crowds who watched the final journey of their king to the mausoleum at Saint-Denis where he was buried with a previous wife. Eleven days after Good King Louis, father of his people, drew his last breath, the staves of his household ministers were struck and with them the old reign was broken.

I expected a summons, either from Sir Edward or from Madame d'Aumont who would be with Mary at the Hôtel de Cluny, but nobody sent for us. We were given no instructions as to our future duties, whether we would remain with Mary in France or be sent back home like Lady Guildford and the others.

'Perhaps we've been forgotten,' Jane said.

'I think we're being watched.'

'How do you know?' she squealed, looking over her shoulder.

'Can you not feel it? The back of my neck prickles; men slide away rather than look at us; even Mary's pages are nowhere to be seen, which is odd.'

'What would anyone gain from watching us?' Jane said, picking up the chemise she'd been mending for the last three days.

'We're not trusted.'

'That is ridiculous. What danger could we possibly pose.'

'It's not us but Mary who is the danger.'

'She is the dowager queen!'

'Oh Jane. Think! What if she's carrying a child and that child is a boy.'

'Is she?'

I sighed in despair. 'If she is, she needs our protection. I must find a way to be with her.'

'Ask Sir Edward to arrange it.'

'He refuses. He says we should remain here.'

'I agree. Here is very pleasant. I for one am perfectly content.'

It was hard to feel oppressed when, even in the depths of winter, the Hôtel des Tournelles was designed with every delight a person could want. Within the vastness of its encircling walls there were halls and pleasure gardens to admire, an observatory in which to sit and watch the heavens, and a maze the men called "Dedalus". Not that I'd seen either of these latter two wonders. Like Jane, the others thought I was odd to want to leave such luxury.

I watched the main gates, noticing how people wishing to go out into the city streets were turned back by the guards. No-one in the palace was allowed to leave. In many ways we were little more than prisoners in this gilded cage and if I wished to see Mary, I would have to make a plan.

Late one afternoon when the usual young man came to close our shutters, I followed him outside the door, determined to engage him in conversation. At first he was hesitant because he should have been about his duties not loitering in the shadows with an English damoiselle. It might be against orders but I had judged him correctly as someone not averse to an idle flirtation with a pretty young woman and, like all young men, greedy for money. With a tentative smile and using as few words as possible I explained what I wanted. Immediately he was eager to help.

'You know the Rue des Mathurins St Jacques?'

'*Mais oui!*'

'The Hôtel de Cluny?'

'*Oui.*'

I beamed as if he'd said something amazingly clever. 'Oh, that is wonderful. But the guards on the gate, they will stop me. Is there another way?' I simpered. 'I should be very grateful.'

He grinned. '*Mais oui.* I show you. Is *dangereuse, damoiselle.*' He paused, embarrassed at raising the matter of a reward for his services. '*Et pour moi, l'argent?*'

I was slightly piqued that my charms on their own were insufficient and financial inducement was necessary. I told him how much I would pay. 'Half before we leave and half when you bring me safely back. Agreed?'

He grinned happily. '*D'accord.*'

As I expected, he took the opportunity to further our acquaintance with a kiss, but I said firmly, '*Pas maintenant.*' and, smiling sweetly, slipped out of his embrace and back into the room.

Jane looked up from her sewing. 'Your face is flushed. What have you been doing?'

'Making plans,' I said gaily, appalled at my behaviour. I could imagine how horrified my brother would be if he knew I'd been dallying with a servant.

An hour later a small boy came with a message which he repeated by rote, clearly not understanding a word. 'Six o'clock – he come.'

That night I barely slept, worrying I would oversleep and miss this precious opportunity. When eventually I slipped out of bed it was still dark. I woke the maid we shared who helped me dress in my oldest, warmest gown. I recalled Cecily, jealous as a stable cat, watching as I packed my chests. "Wonderful! Just the thing to wear when scrubbing the French king's floors!" I didn't care. This early, it would be cold outside and this gown would keep me warm

I pulled my heavy hooded cloak round my shoulders and fastened it with a clasp. I sighed at my odd appearance, thinking longingly of egret's down and my blue velvet cloak. Remembering tales of the *"mauvais garçons"* who frequented the city streets, I wrapped the money I had and the few jewels I habitually wore ,in a length of cloth. This I tied securely round my waist under my chemise. The bundle felt uncomfortable but, hidden beneath my clothing, it would be safe from thieves. I swore the maid to silence and sent her back to her straw pallet while I sat on a stool and waited.

When the bells rang for Prime I heard a scratch at the door. My accomplice was on time.

We slipped down the back stairs, through a maze of

tiny rooms and out through a door near the kitchens, meeting no-one other than a couple of sleepy boys. It was still dark but the young man had thought to bring a lantern so at least I could see where I was going and not trip over obstacles. He led me round the back of a row of buildings and through a small gate into a part of the pleasure gardens I'd not seen before. We skirted a stand of stately trees, their branches bare and dripping from last night's rain, until we reached a door in the wall, half hidden by a tangle of ivy. With a quick glance to make sure we'd not been followed, he slid the bolts and opened the door. I stepped out into darkness.

'*Suivez-moi,*' my guide whispered. '*Ne parlez pas.*'

We walked quickly down a long deserted alleyway where the high wall on our right separated us from the palace. Now that we were away from the perceived safety of the Hôtel des Tournelles, I was terrified who we might meet. I imagined murderers and robbers lurking in the shadows, cutthroats, assailants with clubs, men with daggers. Feeling even more frightened than during my encounter with François d'Angoulême, I squashed the urge to cling onto the young man's arm. It was disgraceful enough being out before dawn in the sole company of a male servant but intimacy of that kind would have had me shamed.

A dog barked as we reached a wider thoroughfare where there were signs of the city stirring into life. It was cold but the sky had paled a little so we had no further need of the lantern. Through the half-light I could just make out the outline of some large buildings on the other side of the street. A couple of wagons piled high with what looked like vegetables lumbered by followed closely by a dozen urchins dressed in rags who stuck out their tongues and jeered at the two of us stumbling along. The ground was filthy with puddles of what I hoped was rainwater but from the smell, was probably effluent. I tried to step to one side and nearly fell over a woman, asleep in a doorway.

'Is it far?' I whispered.

He shook his head and pointed. Through the pearly light of early dawn I could see the familiar sight of the great church of Notre Dame on the Île de la Cité. I turned my head to say how beautiful it was.

Suddenly out of nowhere, I was seized from behind by a pair of strong arms. A heavy cloth came over my head, blinding me.

I screamed.

My first instinct was to struggle but my arms were pinned tightly so I kicked out at my assailant, trying to free myself. There had to be at least two of them as a voice in front of me cursed and dealt me a stinging blow to the head. I screamed louder until another blow knocked me to the ground. This time my arms were twisted behind my back and my wrists tied. I tried to free them but the cord was too well-knotted The man who'd done this, knew what he was doing.

Since no-one had come to my aid, I assumed my companion had received the same treatment, though I'd not heard him shout, nothing but a sort of gurgle. Perhaps he'd been knocked down and left lying in the mud. Holy Mary! What if they'd killed him! I was sure that whoever our attackers were, it was me they wanted, not him. Who would want a mere servant.

'You scream, I slit throat,' said a voice in broken English. The man hissed the words through the suffocating cloth and, to back up his threat, pushed the pointed tip of a knife against my lower arm. I gave a little mew as a cold steel blade pierced my skin.

I lay there hearing the sound of wheels splashing through puddles, running footsteps and muttered conversation. Then I was lifted up like a sack and thrown bodily onto what felt like a solid wooden board. This jarred every bone in my body, causing me to give a muffled grunt of pain.

My legs were tied together despite my trying to kick whoever was grasping my ankles. Then some kind of rough sacking cloth was pulled over my body and someone rested their boots on my shoulder. Heavy boots. What I was lying on shifted and creaked and I realised I'd been put on a wagon. I wriggled, trying to free my head but that earned me a hefty kick in the ribs. After that I lay still and tried to think. What did these men want? Who were they? What were they after? And it wasn't long before I asked myself the other question – who sent them?

With a great lurch which threw me to one side, the wagon set off, swaying and bumping as it went. Over the rumbling and rattling of wheels I could hear the heavy clatter of horses hooves, the noise of wagons passing in the opposite direction and an occasional shouted greeting. After a while It began to rain, a pitter-patter hitting the sacking, and splashing which meant puddles. From inside my cloth and sacking prison I heard voices, some far away, others nearby, people calling, a man singing and some distant cheering, but it was impossible to distinguish any words.

At one stage in our journey I was certain we'd crossed the river because twice we rumbled over what I thought was a bridge. Trussed up in the dark, it was hard to estimate the passing of time but from the increase in noise outside in the streets I reckoned it must be full daylight. There were bells and the sound of children laughing but at no point could I say definitely where we were except that we were still within the city. As far as I could tell we'd not passed through any of the city gates.

Eventually the wagon halted with a judder and a creak, catapulting my head against something hard which made me cry out. By now every part of my body ached and the pain was almost worse than the terror. One ear hurt horribly where I'd been struck by a man's fist, my ankles and wrists throbbed from being bound too tightly and my ribs felt as if they'd been crushed, making it painful to breathe. There was more conversation conducted in the rapid Parisian way and, after what sounded like a heated argument, I was pulled unceremoniously from the wagon and half carried, half dragged up some steps and into a building. It was the cessation of noise and cold which told me we were inside. At this point someone slit the rope that bound my ankles and I was hauled upright.

'*Marche!*' ordered a man's voice as I was pushed from behind. I tried but my ankles were too weak and I fell over, sprawling onto a cold tiled floor and banging my forehead.

More arguing before someone pulled the cover off my head, leaving me blinking in the light. I'd been brought into a large hall where candles were lit. I recognised the kind of surroundings and knew my captors worked for someone of note.

This was no spur of the moment abduction for money or for something worse which my limited knowledge of what could happen to women was fortunately unable to imagine. Whoever wanted me and for what purpose, had planned this carefully. They had waited until I was away from the protection of the royal palace before they pounced. Or had they been waiting for someone else and I happened to come along and disturb their plans.

There was no time for more than an impression of wealth and splendour before I was dragged upright again. My wrists were untied but if I imagined this was a precursor to freedom I was to be sadly disappointed. Both my upper arms were firmly grasped and I was forcibly marched through a doorway, along a passageway, down some steps and into a low dark room.

'What is this place?'

'*Ici*,' said one of my captors. 'You stay.'

And with that they departed. If I'd harboured any doubts, the thud of the door followed by a rattle of chain and clank of a key, confirmed that I was not a privileged guest in this house. I was a prisoner. To begin with I could see nothing but as my eyes became accustomed to the gloom I realised there was nothing to see, just four bare walls. No window, no stool or chair, no table, no bed, no candle. If I wanted to sit it would have to be the floor which on closer inspection was none too clean. I squeezed myself into a corner using the two walls to support my aching back and waited.

After what must have been at least an hour or maybe longer, I heard footsteps and sounds of the lock being undone. The door opened and my two captors came in and without a word, pulled me up from my corner, manhandled me, protesting, through the door, up the steps and into yet another room. A well-dressed man in a dark brown doublet was sitting at a table with a pile of parchment scrolls at his side. He looked up and frowned, eyeing the three of us with a certain distaste.

'Has she a blade?' He spoke with none of the Parisian gutter speech of my captors.

The embarrassed silence was enough of an answer.

'Fools! ' He jerked his head. 'Gaston! Search her.'

The larger of my two captors grabbed my arms and quickly tied my wrists behind my back while the one called Gaston ripped off my cloak and placed his hands on the bodice of my gown. He groped and squeezed with undisguised enjoyment, examining the length of my sleeves and down the folds of my skirts. I shut my eyes, knowing he'd not stop and I was right. His horny fingers hoisted up my skirts and fumbled their way between my kirtle and my chemise and then up my legs, poking and prying with great interest until he reached the cache of treasure tied round my waist.

'Ha!' he cried.

I felt a great tug as the cloth bundle was ripped from beneath my chemise and brought out to be held up in triumph. Gaston was about to unwrap the bundle but brown doublet ordered him to put it on the table.

'Let us see what we have here.' He peeled back the cloth and stared at his find: two rings, my locket with the tiny picture of Our Lady, and a few coins.

'It seems we have a little thief,' he said, curling his lip.

'They are mine,' I said.

'Ah, *damoiselle*, so you have a voice.' Brown doublet picked up the locket and weighed it in his hand.

The brute Gaston licked his lips. '*Putain,*' he said, adding a disgusting remark as to what he'd like to do to me.

I knew the words and could not believe they'd mistaken me for a street whore.

'Where did you find her?' brown doublet said, eyeing me with growing interest.

'Where you said, master, back walls of Les Tournelles.'

'Any company?'

'A lad.'

Up went the eyebrows. 'Indeed! An accomplice. What did you do with him?'

The man grinned, drawing his finger across his throat.

I felt sick when I realised the fate of the young man. If I'd not asked him for help and he'd not been willing; if I'd been more sensible and he'd not been greedy, he'd still be alive, running around the royal palace making eyes at the maids and dreaming of his home in some village near Paris. Because of me he was dead.

Brown doublet rose from his chair, walked slowly round the table and stood in front of me.

'*Eh bien, damoiselle.*'

'Where am I?' I demanded, sounding braver than I felt.

'The Hôtel de Cluny? Did you not know?'

'How could I? Your brutes had me trussed and thrown in a wagon.'

'Is it not most convenient for you to arrive here?'

'I would have preferred to walk.'

'I think not.' His words were uncompromising, the tone hard. 'Who sent you?'

'Nobody.'

'I shall ask again. Who sent you?'

'And I shall tell you again – nobody. I am not the kind of woman you seem to imagine.' I suppressed a desire to spit in his eye.

'I imagine nothing. That is not my job. I follow orders and require to know who you are and who sent you.'

I set my lips firmly together and stared at him defiantly.

I thought I was winning our exchange when suddenly his fist shot out and punched me hard in the stomach. I gasped, doubled over and fell to the floor. The pain was overwhelming and it was all I could do not to cry out. His shiny dark boots were a few inches from my face and for a moment I thought he was going to kick me. I closed my eyes.

'Get up!' he ordered.

Slowly I struggled to my feet, using my shoulder against the edge of the table to keep my balance as my hands were still tied.

'*Bien*!' he said, ' You prefer I allow these men to spend an hour alone with you, or do you co-operate?'

I glared at him. 'You will regret striking me.'

He gave a thin smile. ''I think not, *damoiselle*. You are English. That much I know. Why protect your mistress. Be sensible. Tell me her name.'

With some difficulty I straightened my back, trying to ignore the agony. I would show this cur I was no underling.

'I am a cousin of *La Reine Blanche*,' I said in a clear clipped English voice but my little speech was spoiled by an involuntary groan as a spasm of pain shot through my body.

Brown doublet came closer and with his right hand took hold of my chin. 'You are a bad liar, *damoiselle*.'

'I am not lying.'

'*Damoiselle*, in no way do you resemble a cousin of *La Reine Blanche*. Look at yourself.'

I was only too aware of how I must look. My gown was mud-spattered and torn, my face bruised, I had lost my coif and my hair was tumbled over my shoulders.

''The attentions of your men,' I said coldly. 'I require the services of a maid. Hot water, a comb and a fresh gown. I am certain the lady of this house can provide me with something suitable.'

Brown doublet laughed but his eyes were hard. 'We do not have such luxuries here, not for women like you, damoiselle.'

Before he could say anything more, another man, tall and thin with a slight stoop, edged into the room, a senior servant judging from the shiny buttons on his tunic. He approached brown doublet and the two of them had a whispered conversation in which the only words I caught were "*Madame*" and "*tout de suite*". There was some disagreement and from the way the tall thin servant kept glancing my way I gathered it concerned me.

'*Eh bien, damoiselle*,' said brown doublet when their conversation ended. 'It is time. Untie her hands Gaston, I think she will not give us any further trouble.'

Gaston fiddled with the thin cord until my hands were free. I rubbed my wrists, noting livid red wheals where the cord had cut into my flesh, and had to curb an unladylike desire to kick the churl.

10

LA REINE BLANCHE
JANUARY 1514

Leaving my captors behind in the bowels of the house where they belonged, brown doublet and the tall thin servant took me up a wide flight of stairs, along a gallery, through a large chamber where benches were placed against the walls and into a further chamber where a door was guarded by two men in an unfamiliar livery.

After a whispered conversation the guards stood aside while a couple of men threw open the doors allowing me a view of the room beyond. Warmth, splendour, comfort and effortless good taste. On one side a display of magnificent tapestries, and on the other tall arched windows, curtained with heavy velvets in blue and gold to keep out the winter cold. Whoever inhabited these rooms knew exactly how to impress their visitors. A trio of musicians were playing quietly on their instruments while at the end of the room on a raised dais sat the woman I'd been brought to meet. I had no difficulty in recognising Madame Louise, mother of François d'Angoulême, heir to the throne of France.

I had no idea how old she was but Madame Louise was still a handsome woman with neat features and a fair complexion. It was said she had educated her son like an Italian prince, fostering in him a love of books and music. It had been her plan to make him heir to King Louis. To have achieved her aim meant she was not only blessed with good looks but was also a clever woman, not one to be underestimated.

With great difficulty I sank down into a curtsey. If nothing else, Madame Louise was a duchess and deference was due to her rank.

'Madame,' I murmured.

'Ah yes,' she said with a note of triumph. 'The cousin. I should have guessed it would be you, Lady Elizabeth. Few Englishwomen would be foolhardy enough to venture alone into the streets of Paris but my son tells me you have an impetuous nature.'

'Madame, I have no idea why I have been treated in this way.'

She smiled. 'Have you not? I credited you with more intelligence.'

'Your servants have treated me badly, as you see.'

'I see a young woman who should not have been out alone in the streets in the dark. No woman of breeding ventures into the city without an armed escort. Danger lurks everywhere especially when times are unsettled. People are like animals when they are fearful, They turn to violence. It is no wonder my men mistook you for one of the city's unfortunates, women who make a living by preying on others.'

I opened my mouth to protest but she cut me off and turning to the two men said, 'Maître Valery, you may go. I shall not forget your service and the way in which it was done.'

Her voice was as cold as ice and if I was brown doublet I'd have been fearful, not just for my position but for my head.

I stood there wishing in one way that I too could have been dismissed but Madame Louise had more to say.

'You intended to come here, to the Hôtel de Cluny *Pourquoi*? What was your purpose? What did you bring with you?'

'I brought nothing. I came to see Her Majesty, *La Reine Blanche*.'

She gave a hollow laugh. 'To see *La Reine Blanche* is impossible. She sees no-one. It is forbidden. You knew that so I ask again – why did you come?'

'Madame, *La Reine Blanche* is my cousin. I have known her since we were both children. If you keep her alone in the dark with no company and no diversions, she will wither like a flower denied sunlight. She has a fragile disposition. I merely wished to ensure her health was not suffering.'

'Is that so, Lady Elizabeth. From what you say it appears you have an intimate knowledge of *La Reine Blanche*. If that is so, I shall give you a little task – you will persuade her to tell me the truth. Then her suffering will be over.'

'The truth about what, Madame?'

She gripped the arm of her chair with both hands and leant forward.

'Do not play games with me, Lady Elizabeth. You know perfectly well what it is I wish to know.'

'Forgive me, Madame, but I am not privy to your thoughts.'

'The child! Is there a child? Is she *enceinte*? Does she carry Louis's seed?'

Of course that was what Madame Louise wanted to know. Nothing was more important to her than keeping the throne for her beloved François. A son born to the English *Reine Blanche* would ruin her plans

'What does *La Reine Blanche* say?'

She waved her hand as if Mary's words had no worth. 'My son has spoken with her. She tells him she is not *enceinte* but I do not believe her. She is an Englishwoman and like all your kind, well-versed in deceit. She uses lies to trick my son. She presents herself as an innocent. But I know her kind. She wishes to ensnare him.'

'What has she told you?'

'Nothing. She tells me nothing. She refuses to speak to me.'

'Perhaps there is nothing to say. *La Reine Blanche* would not lie on such a vital matter, not to you. She understands the situation. She knows the difficulties your son, the duke, faces. If she cannot say whether or not she is with child. Why would you disbelieve her?'

'Because it has been more than seventeen days and my women report her linen is still clean.'

Sainte Vierge! How I wished I knew more about the making of a child. My knowledge was the usual muddle of gossip and prurient observation but I knew Queen Katherine's maids were often asked about the state of her linen.

'Your women believe she is with child?'

'Yes. Yet *La Reine Blanche*, who must know the truth, says nothing.'

Madame Louise pursed her lips in a moue of irritation. 'She does not deceive me. I know her. If she cannot produce a legitimate child to show to the world, she will produce an adulterous one. This is why I have her watched.'

'Madame! Your thoughts do you no credit.'

'Do not look so shocked, Lady Elizabeth. You are well acquainted with the ways of women. A determined woman will go to any lengths to secure her position and when that prize is the most glittering one of all, a lie must seem such a small deceit.'

'*La Reine Blanche* would not lie.'

'You think not? Do you imagine that having once been considered the most important woman in France, lauded wherever she went, praised for her beauty, an Englishwoman would throw all that away?'

Madame Louise craved power. I could see the hunger reflected in her eyes like a kind of madness. The throne with its opportunities for greatness was tantalisingly close, so close she could almost touch it. But even now the prize might slip through her son's fingers and that thought had driven her into a wild insane jealousy of the English *Reine Blanche*.

'Madame, you know Queen Mary had neither the opportunity nor the inclination to contrive such a deceit. She was a true and loving wife to the king.'

'Pah! You are *imbécile* if you think that. She had Louis wrapped round her little finger. The old fool lusted after her but could not raise his standard. The maids say she used whore's tricks to make him perform but he was too old, too sick, a husk of a man. She was so desperate she even importuned my son. She asked him to cuckold the king, to give her a child. Oh, but she was clever. It is no wonder the English court is full of men raising other men's children.'

'Madame! I fear you are misinformed about the English court. Queen Katherine insists on the highest standards of modesty in her ladies.'

Madame Louise sat back in her chair and laughed. 'Would that your king and his friends did likewise. I hear they rut like stags in season.'

She beckoned me forward until I was a mere foot away from her skirts.

'You will go to her. You will discover the truth. Hold her down if necessary. Have them strip her naked. Use any means you like, but bring me proof.'

'If you wish, Madame, I shall see what my cousin says.'

'Now, go!'

I was hustled out of Madame Louise's presence and into a small room where I was provided with some items of clean clothing, a bowl of warm water and the services of a dumbstruck maid who was almost too frightened to touch me. Two hours later I was passed into the care of a well-dressed servant who escorted me to the mourning chamber of *La Reine Blanche*.

The room was handsomely appointed but airless, cold and depressingly dark. The windows were heavily curtained to keep out sunlight as custom decreed. The only illumination was a single flickering candle which cast eerie shadows on the black wall hangings. It was here that Mary had spent the last two weeks: silent, friendless and alone, attended by women sanctioned by Madame Louise. I suspected these servants had been ordered to watch Mary's every move, ensuring she received no messages and had no contact with the outside world. Madame Louise's suspicions had condemned Mary to a prison from which there was no escape. The putative child in her womb would keep her incarcerated here until, one way or another, the mother of Duke François could assure her son – "*La Reine Blanche* is not with child."

My sisters once told me of an old crone at Astley who, for a handsome fee, would provide a potion for ridding a woman of a child in the womb. They said it was dangerous and the woman sometimes died. I prayed Madame Louise had no access to such potions.

Mary was curled up like a small child, her plain white coif the only part of her visible in the gloom. I went swiftly to her side.

'Your Grace. Cousin Mary.'

Her head moved slightly on the pillow and she opened her eyes.

'Cousin Elizabeth.' Her voice was very weak and sounded as if she'd been weeping. 'Is it you?'

I put my hand on her cheek. 'Yes. It is me.'

'I was unsure. You see, I imagine things. I think my mother is here with me but then I remember she is dead so I wonder if I too am dead. I think I am wrapped in a shroud. I am awaiting burial. In the silence I hear prayers for the dead. Then I fear I have become a little mad.'

I gathered her up in my arms. She weighed no more than a bird and I could feel her bones beneath her thin white shift. 'Cousin Mary, do they bring you food?'

'Oh yes.' Her voice broke on a little laugh. 'They bring food but I do not eat. I fear they will poison me.' She grasped my sleeve. 'I have written to Henry. I have told him I am in despair and do not know what to do.'

'You must not despair. I am here now and I shall keep you company.'

She shook her head. 'She will send you away. She says I must endure this alone. But I cannot, I truly cannot.'

She closed her eyes but tears continued to seep from under her lashes, trickling down her cheeks and onto her plain white shift.

'This is not right,' I said. 'To deny you the company of your English ladies is very wrong. Even your late husband, God rest his soul, came to realise the importance of our presence.'

For a moment I thought she would not reply but eventually a small voice whispered, 'There is nothing you can do. You see, I am trapped. I fear I may die here, alone in the dark.'

'You know what they want.'

'Yes and I have told them I am not carrying a child but they do not believe me. She thinks I am lying. She believes I want to deny her son his throne. But I do not. All I want is to go home to England, to Henry, but she tells me that will not happen.'

'Why will it not happen?"

'She says her son will choose another husband for me, one friendly to the interests of France.'

This was something I'd feared. Even a widowed queen has value in the marriage market, as Henry's offer to Louis of his widowed sister, the Scot's Queen, had shown.

'I do not think Duke François will do that?'

'Who is to stop him?'

I thought for a moment. 'King Henry will not allow the duke to offer you to a man of his choosing in a marriage which would benefit France. Henry will insist only he has the right to decide your next husband.'

Mary gave a wan smile. 'Henry said I could choose my next husband.'

I thought this unlikely. As a widowed Queen of France Mary was a great marriage prize. Henry and François were both powerful man. In no way would either of them allow Mary to choose for herself. They would squabble over the spoils like a couple of angry curs. But how to tell Mary.

'Cousin Mary, when did your brother, the king, make this promise?'

'At Dover, by the waterside. He promised. He knew I was unhappy at marrying Louis. He said if I did my duty with a good and loving heart, next time he would let me please myself.'

I remembered Mary on the quayside at Dover, tears at that moment of parting, clinging to her brother, the urgent whispered pleas and the impatient frown on Henry's face. Henry hated scenes. He liked gaiety, joyous laughter, fun. He did not like weeping women asking for favours. I imagined him telling Mary what she wanted to hear. Of course he didn't mean it. He couldn't possibly have meant it. No king, and especially not a king like Henry, would allow such a valuable opportunity as his sister's remarriage to slip through his royal fingers.

'When you return to England your brother will certainly consider your wishes,' I said diplomatically.

At that Mary threw herself back against the pillows.

'There will be no return to England. François will keep me here. He says he will sell me to the Duke of Savoy.'

'When did he say that? Has he been to see you?'

'Yes.'

'Surely it is forbidden.'

Mary gave a hollow laugh. 'Nothing is forbidden. Not to him.'

Nothing is forbidden! *Sainte Vierge*! What had happened to Mary here in the Hôtel de Cluny alone in the dark with no-one to protect her.

'Cousin Mary, why did he come?'

'He did not say but he came late, when the servants were asleep in their chairs. He sat by my bed. He took my hand in his and behaved most lovingly towards me.'

'Lovingly?'

She had the grace to blush. 'He talked of private matters, matters which pertained to my person. He asked questions, oh so many questions. Once he asked was my bed soft enough, pleasing to my tastes. Last night he asked had I made any promises of marriage, in any place, to anyone. He was most insistent I open my heart, tell him everything. Oh Cousin Elizabeth, I do not understand what he wants from me.'

Of course she didn't. Mary was, in many ways, an innocent, possibly, for all I knew, still a maid. She had never said if King Louis's attempts to claim his rights as a husband were successful and I had never asked; yet it was on the result of those few precious nights after their marriage that her whole future depended. Could Duke François truly be trying to seduce *La Reine Blanche*, a widowed queen obeying the ancient custom of solitude designed to protect the throne of France? And if so, why? Did he intend to put poor little Madame Claude aside and marry Mary?

This was a conversation to be handled with great delicacy.

'Cousin Mary, forgive me, but has the duke behaved

improperly towards you? You understand what I am asking?'

She thought for a moment, doubtless deciding how much she was prepared to say about those late night trysts in the dark with the handsome François d'Angoulême.

'He said if he allows me to return to England, Henry will sell me to Emperor Maximilian. He says the emperor wants me for himself and has demanded a portrait.'

'It is possible,' I said, thinking the emperor must be even more ancient than King Louis. 'He would be a powerful ally for any king.'

'François says the Prince of Castile also wants me.'

'Cousin Mary, I do not see how that could happen. Only last summer you rejected the Prince. It was a very public rebuff and would surely poison any marriage. Think how a young man might take revenge on such a wife. Do not forget the story of the young hawk he plucked.'

Her fingers fluttered as she remembered the scene at Wansted, the renunciation of that long betrothal, the letters they'd exchanged, the months of preparation for a wedding that never happened and what the Prince of Castile had done when he heard the news. If Mary married him, she might be the one to be plucked, not the hawk.

'François says Queen Katherine is urging Henry to make the match and Henry wishes to please his wife.'

This was believable. With Louis dead and the French alliance in tatters, Henry might well prefer to salvage the Castile match and send Mary to Malines to wed Katherine's nephew.

But I was suspicious. 'The duke seems very certain of his facts.'

'He has spies. They tell him everything. One minute

he threatens to keep me here, the next he says if I return to England I shall be in danger. Cousin Elizabeth. you know what he is like, how frightening he can be when he is not being charming.'

Oh yes, I knew exactly what François d'Angoulême was like.

'I was afraid of what he might do to me so I told him.' She stopped. Put her hand in front of her mouth like a small child caught saying something she should not.

'Told him what?'

Her fingers began fiddling with the cuff of her nightshift pulling at the edges and screwing it up into a ball. I wondered was she was going to lie or would she tell me the truth. She peeped up through her lashes the way she did with Henry when trying to wheedle a favour.

'I told him I had made a promise, one that bound me.'

For once in my life, Mary shocked me. When a young woman speaks of a binding promise, it means a promise given as a prelude to marriage. Although Mary had numerous admirers since coming to France, courtiers who made pretty speeches and swore they would die for their queen, she'd not, to my knowledge, been alone with any man other than her husband and Duke François. To whom could she have given this promise?

'A promise?' I said cautiously.

'Yes but I cannot tell you what it was or to whom it was given. You see, I swore I'd keep it secret. I promised I'd not tell.'

'Yet you told Duke François.'

'Only because he was importuning me. I was frightened.'

'What did he say?'

She smiled. 'He was very kind, told me he would prove a true and loving friend and I need have no fear. But Cousin Elizabeth, I am afraid.'

Clearly Mary believed Duke François. But Mary had not been raised by a woman like my mother. Everyone said Mary's mother had been a queen of incomparable virtue, an attentive mother, a kind and loving woman, her sweetness reflected in Mary's own nature. My mother, on the other hand, saw treachery and betrayal at every turn, believing no-one should be trusted and the closer a person moved towards the levers of power, the more dangerous and duplicitous they became.

François d'Angoulême stood very close to those levers of power and Mary's word was the final obstacle between him and the throne, a fragile barrier which he was determined to breach, a citadel he might pay handsomely to have delivered into his hands.

According to my sisters, our mother's life had been lived to the accompaniment of rebellion and murder. When our father fled overseas with our eldest brother, he had left her facing the wrath of an angry king and years of loneliness and disgrace. My mother, as well as seeing her daughters were properly educated, ensured they were armed to deal with what she perceived as a dangerous world. Since coming to France I'd blessed her foresight.

Despite the years at her brother's court as a petted younger sister, Mary was remarkably ignorant about men. While the likes of Bessie Blount would flirt with Henry's courtiers, learning about gentlemen and their duplicitous ways, Mary's behaviour had to be above reproach. Not for her a light-hearted flirtation or easy dalliance; no man would risk the king's wrath by compromising his sister.

François d'Angoulême on the other hand was a practised seducer, a gracious and witty man who doubtless enjoyed Mary's dependence on him. I very much suspected there was no child in which case Mary must not make him her enemy. He would be the next king of France and could, if he chose, make her life intolerable. He could keep her short of money or place restrictions on her household. He might even have her exiled to Blois. And, most important of all, she would need his permission if she wished to return to England.

'Perhaps soon you will be able to give him your solemn assurance there is no child. Then you will be able to ask for the return of your English ladies. Tell him you will write to Henry saying how well you are being treated. Tell him that if he agrees, the way is clear – he will be free to arrange his coronation.'

That night I insisted on sleeping in Mary's chamber on the low pallet bed usually reserved for one of the senior ladies keeping vigil over *La Reine Blanche*. The air was chill and fetid and it took me a long time to fall asleep. When I did, the world became a dark and evil place full of ruffians and thugs intent on rape and murder.

I awoke to a scream.

'*Vite!*' The smaller of the two French women had hold of my arm and was trying to pull me out of my bed. I pushed her away and sat up.

'What is it?'

'*La Reine Blanche!*' She was jabbering away so fast I was unable to catch half the words but those I did hear had me out of bed and on my feet in a moment.

Mary was sitting on the edge of the bed wearing a white velvet nightgown. Her nightshift was lying in a heap on the floor at her feet. She was weeping.

'What has happened?' I said.

With a triumphant flourish worthy of the finest court entertainer, the Frenchwoman pulled back the sheets, revealing evidence of Mary's failure. There would be no royal heir for France from the body of the English *Reine Blanche*.

Within minutes, the room was full of women, quickly followed by the hurrying footsteps of Madame Louise and her attendants. The crowd of onlookers melted back in the face of their mistress's arrival, nudging each other and exchanging smiles. To them, the failure of the foreign queen was a joy.

Madame Louise looked at the blood-red stain on the sheet and smiled.

'At last we see you for what you are, Madame – a liar; nothing but a common little liar. You tried to trick me but you have failed. There is no child; there never was.' She stood over Mary with her hand upraised as if to lash out in fury. 'I warrant you're as untouched as the day you arrived at Abbeville.'

Mary looked up at her tormentor, her Tudor chin raised high.

'As you see, Madame, there is no child. You may tell the Duke of Valois he need delay no longer. He may claim the throne. It will be as he and I agreed – he shall be King of France and I shall return to England.'

Madame Louise drew back her lips. 'What a fool you are. Do you imagine my son will allow you to scuttle off back to your brother? There will be no return. You will stay here.'

'Madame,' I said quickly before Mary had a chance to reply. 'Since seclusion for the dowager queen is no longer necessary, I presume you have an apartment suitable for her position as a royal widow. I shall remain in attendance on her until her future is decided. In the mean time I shall send for her English ladies and the men of her household.'

Madame Louis smiled. turned her back and swept out of the room, followed by her ladies, allowing Mary and I a moment of quiet conversation together.

'They'll not let me go,' she whispered.

'Have faith. God will guide Duke François to mercy. Now he has what he wants, he will be kind.'

'Powerful men are seldom kind to women for whom they have a use.'

'Henry is not unkind.'

Mary's face softened at thoughts of her brother. 'I pray he will rescue me. I shall die if I cannot go home.'

'Cousin Mary, someone will come. It is not just your personal safety which is at stake. With a new regime in France, King Henry must secure his peace treaty.'

I'd not been privy to the details of the agreement which had given Louis the hand of Henry's younger sister, and Henry Tournai, Thérounne and a million gold crowns; nor to the inevitable haggling over the dowry. If Mary went back to England, which of the gifts she'd received as queen would she be allowed to take with her and what price would François d'Angoulême demand for letting her go. For Mary's sake, I prayed it was not more than Henry was prepared to pay.

11

THE ENGLISH ENVOYS
FEBRUARY 1515

In early February, a week after François d'Angoulême, Duke of Valois, was crowned King of France in the cathedral at Rheims, the expected English delegation arrived in Paris. There were three of them: Charles Brandon, Duke of Suffolk, Sir Richard Wingfield and Doctor Nicholas West.

As protocol required, they had already presented their credentials to King François at Senlis, condoling with him over the decease of his cousin and offering their congratulations upon his accession. As all parties were aware of the political crisis brought about by Louis's untimely death, they also assured King François of their master's wish to establish friendly relations.

We were still lodged in the Hôtel de Cluny when the English envoys came for their first meeting. The view from our window was of Paris bathed in early spring sunshine, damp streets glistening beneath an enamel blue sky, the kind of day to give a young woman hope.

I thought it a mark of the high regard in which Lord Suffolk was held by Henry that he'd been chosen to lead the English delegation as there were certainly more senior and more experienced men available. I'd been aware of Charles Brandon from the moment I'd come to court as a girl of seven. Bold and enterprising, a man built in Henry's image: tall, broad-shouldered, energetic, good-humoured, a lover of all kinds of sport, including the pursuit of women.

He'd been at Henry's side for as long as anyone could remember. His father had been killed at Bosworth, carrying the standard for Henry's father so when the time came, a place was found for the son in the household of young Prince Henry. The rumour was that Charles Brandon's marital affairs were tangled but, if so, it seemed not to impede his progress at court. My bother, Thomas, did not like him, regarding him as an upstart, a time-server of the worst kind; but Thomas liked few people.

I knew the other two envoys by reputation if not by sight. Sir Richard Wingfield had once been married to my stepfather's mother. He was an experienced diplomat who could be relied on to prevent Lord Suffolk from giving away too much in an excess of bonhomie. Doctor West was a cleric, a protégé of Bishop Fox and highly thought of by Thomas Wolsey who'd probably recommended him for this mission.

The meeting was held in private, Jane and I the only women in attendance. Mary's new rooms at Cluny were not large, and her private room gave us an illusion of closeness which I found not unpleasant after the draughty rooms at the Hôtel des Tournelles. To my surprise, Mary was gracious but not over-welcoming. She mostly kept her gaze lowered and seemed particularly ill at ease with Charles Brandon which was odd as he was her brother's friend and a man with whom she was well acquainted.

'Your Grace,' Sir Richard explained. 'Rest assured we have your best interests at heart.'

'You have come to escort me to England?' Mary asked eagerly.

'Eventually, Your Grace. Our orders are first to obtain possession of the gems and precious stones given to you by your late husband and to make an inventory of your English jewels, plate and other valuables so that we may secure full restitution of their value.'

'*Then* you will escort me home.'

Sir Richard gave a small cough. 'Your Grace, we must also have repayment of the cost of your transportation to France.'

Charles Brandon shifted unhappily in his chair. 'King François wants Tournai back. We'll use that to twist his arm.'

Mary turned to Sir Richard. 'But you *will* take me home. I cannot stay here.'

'Your Grace, these matters take time but we have every expectation of a satisfactory outcome to our negotiations.'

'I understand that, Sir Richard. How long do you anticipate these negotiations will last?'

Sir Richard smiled like a doting uncle hoping to placate an unhappy niece. 'Have no fear, Your Grace. His Majesty, your bother, is every bit as anxious to have you returned to him. To that end, there have already been preliminary talks, exploring areas where agreement will likely be forthcoming. We do not wish to be antagonistic, we wish to approach these negotiations in a spirit of friendship. For you this has been a tragedy and we must ensure we can salvage as much as we can.'

'My jewels are mine,' Mary said sharply, the Tudor acquisitiveness coming to the fore. 'They were gifts to me from my husband.'

Si Richard demurred. 'I doubt the French see it like that, Your Grace. To them there is a difference between the Queen of France and your most gracious person.'

'Sir Richard, in case you have forgotten, I *was* Queen of France.'

Sir Richard nodded sagely. 'Yes,' he said gently. 'But alas, no longer.'

At this point Charles Brandon roused himself to speak. 'Henry believes François intends to keep you here. He'll force you into a strategic marriage alliance, one which gives him political profit. He may claim to be the Most Christian King but he's not an honourable man. He'll toss you over to some foreign duke if it suits him. He's a slippery rogue for all his flattery.'

Sir Richard resumed his patient questioning. 'Has King François spoken to you of his plans for Your Grace?'

Mary lowered her gaze, refusing to look him in the eye. Unsurprisingly she was embarrassed to tell these men exactly what had happened to her in that dark, airless mourning chamber. There was no doubt in my mind that François d'Angoulême had taken outrageous liberties with a defenceless young woman, though exactly what he'd done, she steadfastly refused to say.

'He came to see me when I was in seclusion,' she said quietly. 'He made suggestions, said certain things about me and my relationship with my late husband. I did not know what to do. You must understand, Sir Richard, I had no one to advise me.'

'It would be helpful if you could elucidate a little more on your private conversation with the then Duke of Valois, Your Grace.' Sir Richard was pressing but I was certain

Mary would not divulge any secrets. If she'd not tell me she'd not likely tell Sir Richard.

The discussion advanced no further in the next half hour. Mary demanded to know when she would go home, Lord Suffolk said very little and Sir Richard said a great deal yet, when I thought about it later, managed to say nothing at all. Doctor West, like many a cleric, digested the conversation, scribbled one or two notes, but made no comment, merely looked sombre and inscrutable.

Eventually, defeated by an obstinate and tearful woman, the three men made their farewells, promised to return when they had more news and rose in a rustle of satin and velvet.

As they left the room, I hurried after them.

'Sir Richard! Is it true we are prisoners here?'

He nodded gravely. 'It is certainly true that you cannot leave without the express permission of King François.'

'And that gives the French leverage in your negotiations.'

'Are you in training to become a diplomat, Lady Elizabeth?' he said with a smile.

'No sir, but it seems to me I should prepare Her Grace for disappointment.'

He laughed. 'By no means. A wise man never comes empty handed to the table. There are certain things the French want from us.'

'Like Tournai.'

'Indeed, as Lord Suffolk said.'

'Sir, I have also heard that King François wishes to renew his war on Milan.'

Sir Richard laughed even louder. 'Say no more, Lady Elizabeth. Next time His Majesty gives me a commission

I shall ask if you may accompany me, as my aide. I think you will be invaluable.'

He strode off, chortling as he went, leaving me to pacify Mary who, by now, was convinced she'd be trapped in the Hôtel de Cluny until King François sold her in marriage to a man she did not want.

When we first came to Paris, petitioners would come daily to see Mary, hopeful the new English bride would intercede with the king on their behalf. But with Louis's death, everything changed. A childless, foreign-born royal widow had no power, no influence with the new king, no way to effect any change and everyone knew it. She might be entrancingly beautiful, she might be well endowed with property and jewels, but having failed in her sacred duty to provide France with a royal male heir, she was viewed as worthless, just another expensive mouth to feed.

Throughout the next week, messages passed between the envoys and the queen dowager with increasing frequency. Most mornings, Mary and her secretary were closeted together composing her replies but on two occasions she wrote the missives in her own hand and passed them privately to the messenger. I had no idea what she was writing but could imagine it only too well. She was becoming more and more frantic as the days went by, constantly turning over in her mind her previous conversations with François d'Angoulême.

'He said the Duke of Savoy was pressing his suit. And the Duke of Lorraine.'

I tried to look non-committal, wondering if King François was playing games with Mary, dangling illustrious suitors in front of her like imaginary sweetmeats, or was he in deadly earnest. Did he truly intend to marry her off to his own advantage or would he return her to Henry. It was impossible to say.

Every day I felt more and more gloomy about my own prospects. I could not desert Mary and feared King François would not permit her to leave. Even if he did and we returned to England what would Henry do? Mary might trust her brother implicitly but I knew all men were untrustworthy, especially brothers; and brothers who were kings, more than most. If we returned to England Mary might well find herself bundled off to Flanders, an unwilling pawn in Henry's ambitions for domination in the power games played by princes. I doubted he'd keep his promise, the one he'd made to Mary at the waterside in Dover.

'The king of Portugal has made a bid for his eldest son.' Mary sounded like a woman reciting a shopping list.

I would have laughed at the endless number of suitors but to princes, beauty, riches and closeness to power were always irresistible; Mary was truly a prize to be coveted.

'William of Bavaria,' Mary said, morosely. 'The mightiest prince in Christendom.'

'You will most certainly have your pick,' I said brightly, trying to raise a smile.

'I have already made my choice,' she said quietly.

We were back where we started with the mysterious man to whom Mary had made a promise, the one she'd mentioned to François d'Angoulême in a moment of weakness. I was unable to blame her. I, of all people, knew how charming he could be, how persuasive and how dangerous. Perhaps this mysterious man did not exist. Mary, like all young women, was quite capable of lying, although deceit was not usually in her nature.

As the most senior of Mary's English lady attendants I was expected to be by her side, always on hand to see she was well served and that the younger girls behaved. Once her period of seclusion ended, our days remained quiet with few visitors. Madame d'Aumont and the French ladies had mysteriously melted away with the winter snow, leaving behind just a couple of faded women from lesser families who'd been unable to get a place with Queen Claude.

I longed for something to break the tedium, a letter or a visit from the English envoys who were still negotiating our future and whom we'd not seen for a week. *Sainte Vierge!* Surely they had not abandoned us.

Two day's later we were sitting by the fire, talking quietly amongst ourselves when Mary's usher came in. The Duke of Suffolk had requested a private audience with Her Grace.

'I shall see him alone,' Mary announced.

The others rose and made to leave but the flush on Mary's cheeks was enough to alert me to danger.

'Your Grace,' I said quietly. 'You cannot be alone with Lord Suffolk. People will gossip. Someone will tell King François.'

She turned to me with a slight shrug of her slim shoulders. 'Oh very well, Cousin Elizabeth. If it bothers you, you may stay. It makes little difference.'

Lord Suffolk came in like a man on a mission and straightaway knelt in front of Mary. He pulled off his hat and was so intent on Mary, he didn't notice me sitting quietly in the corner. I was unable to see his face but I could see Mary's and knew immediately what I was witnessing. All pretence of diplomatic discussion was gone.

I had long suspected Mary's interest in Henry's friend but had dismissed it as a fancy, knowing it could lead nowhere. Charles Brandon might be Henry's closest friend and raised to a dukedom but nothing could disguise his low birth. Henry would never permit him to marry his sister – never. Princesses were not like ordinary young women, they could not wed where they chose. They were destined for great political marriages and until Henry had an heir, any son of Mary's might one day become King of England. Charles Brandon must realise that. For both their sakes, I hoped Mary did.

The two were as close as lovers, holding hands, whispering: Charles Brandon prevaricating, shaking his head, Mary wildly distressed, pleading, incoherent, weeping. I was not privy to the full extent of Mary's pleas but she was clearly frantic with fear and viewed Charles Brandon as her saviour. I'd no idea what she was asking him but suspected she wanted him to yield to the French in the negotiations so that she could go home. Mary had never been required to understand the political manoeuvring necessary to keep England safe from her mighty neighbours and I doubted Charles Brandon had the courage to tell her.

If Charles Brandon lacked courage, Mary certainly did not. I suddenly realised what it was she wanted from him. Not his negotiating skills, not his undying friendship, not his promises of rescue, but him. The man himself. She was like a desperate gambler risking everything on a final throw of the dice. She wanted him to marry her. Oh dear God! How had it come to this.

After a while the weeping ceased. At this point Mary became pliant, exhausted, easily persuaded to lie down and rest. Charles Brandon asked should he call Her Grace's physician, Master Guillame, giving me an apologetic smile from one conspirator to another. I thought that curing what ailed Mary was far outside Master Guillame's competence but agreed a draught to help her sleep might be sensible. I told him I would attend to everything but, if he would permit, might I have a private word.

'Lord Suffolk, please forgive me if you think I am impertinent.'

He grinned. 'Lady Elizabeth, in all the years you've been at court, I've not once known you be impertinent.' He leant a little closer. 'You are the soul of discretion.'

I eyed him carefully, thinking how easy it would be for a woman to forget discretion in the company of Charles Brandon. Like Francis Bryan he had that mysterious allure so disturbing to young women. I pinched the palm of my hand to remind myself who I was.

'My lord, the dowager queen is very fragile as you will have observed. She wishes to go home to England but it is not within our power to give her what she wants.'

He nodded his head. 'We are making progress.'

'I am certain you are but the dowager queen is impatient and I fear she will ask you for something else. Perhaps she has already done so.'

He looked at me with a puzzled frown. 'Have no fear, Lady Elizabeth, I never forget who I am.'

'Or, I trust, who she is.'

Lord Suffolk looked taken aback at my directness.

'Lady Elizabeth, the dowager queen is very dear to me.'

Yes, I thought, you have made that very plain.

'She is very dear to all of us, my lord, and in these difficult times we must all look to her safety.'

'I would never do anything to harm Her Grace,' he huffed, aggrieved at my insinuation that he was somehow careless of Mary's safety.

'I know you would never intentionally harm her, my lord, but you cannot be unaware of how much Her Grace is attracted to you.'

He smiled. 'So she tells me.'

How vain this man is, I thought, and with male vanity comes carelessness. The time had come to be even more direct.

'My lord, it cannot be. King Henry would not allow it.'

He grinned slyly, 'I know. Ordered me to behave myself.'

I raised an eyebrow. So Henry knew of his sister's attachment to Charles Brandon yet had sent his friend to retrieve her from France. Not something I would have done. Surely Henry knew the old adage *amor vincit omnia*. In certain circumstance love is stronger than the bonds of male friendship or those of family loyalty. And Mary believed she'd been given permission.

Once Mary was asleep I walked back along the narrow gallery to the room I shared with Jane. I now feared we had an even bigger crisis on our hands. I'd not forgotten that Mary was a Tudor and could be as stubborn as her brother. If King François could not be persuaded to let her go home I feared she would try to salvage from the wreck of these endless negotiations, her most precious treasure: marriage to the man she really wanted.

Jane was sitting on a stool trying to read by the light of a single candle. She held up a heavy book.

'My father writes that I must improve myself.'

'We all need improvement,' I said gloomily, sitting down on a stool to remove my shoes.

'Here, let me,' Jane said, unpinning my sleeves. 'Has something happened? You look worried.'

I turned round so that she could unlace my gown.

'Do you remember after Henry took Tournai when there was talk of a marriage between his sister, the widowed Scottish queen and Emperor Maximilian?'

'Yes, I remember,' said Jane's voice from behind me.

'And d'you remember there was talk that the archduchess greatly admired Charles Brandon and would consider him as a husband.'

Jane giggled. 'I heard she was tempted. You have to admit he is very attractive. I know I'd be tempted.'

'Tempted or nor, she did not do it. Why do you think that was?'

By now I was clad in only a chemise.

Jane thought for a moment, biting her lip. 'His low birth. He may have been a duke but that was not enough. My cousin Lizzie said once the archduchess heard Charles Brandon was not so very noble after all, despite the favour of the English king, she refused to discuss the matter.'

'In other words, she remembered who she was.'

Jane nodded. 'It was a foolish idea from the start.'

'Do you think Mary remembers who she is?'

'I would imagine...' Jane sopped mid-sentence and stared at me. 'Oh! You don't mean...Charles Brandon. Surely she cannot... he cannot intend marrying her?'

'He'd be a fool to try,' I replied, 'and she'd be a bigger fool to agree.'

'But if she loves him.'

'Jane Bourchier, have you learnt nothing since we came to France. Mary has been queen of the greatest country in Christendom, praised by everyone. She is now the most sought after young woman in Europe, desired by princes, her hand sought by every ruler for himself or his son. Do you think a woman with any sense would throw away those opportunities.'

'No, but...'

'And what do you think happens to a man who dares to marry a king's sister without his permission?'

Jane shook her head, perhaps starting to comprehend the enormity of the disaster looming.

'And to the sister? What would the king do to her?'

'Put like that, I think you should advise her against such a move.'

'I pray she will listen to me,' I said, wishing I had someone here to advise *me*.

We said our prayers and climbed into bed. As I was falling asleep, a voice whispered into the darkness, 'They cannot marry in Lent.'

True, I thought. We are safe until Easter by which time, hopefully we'll be home and the problem of what to do with Henry's wilful sister and his close friend, will no longer be mine.

The following morning I asked for an interview with Sir Edward Grey, the senior gentleman in Mary's household. Since my flouting of his instructions to remain at the Hôtel des Tournelles, he had watched me warily as if at any moment I might turn round and bite him. I walked into his room, thanked the page who had shown me the way and gave Sir Edward my sweetest smile.

'Sir Edward, I am worried about Her Grace, the dowager queen.'

He lowered the letter he'd been reading, holding it against his doublet as if for protection. 'In what way, Lady Elizabeth? Your actions in the past have shown you to be a little over-sensitive when it comes to matters concerning Her Grace. What concerns you this time?'

'I am not over-sensitive, Sir Edward. I am worried.'

'Lady Elizabeth, there is nothing for you to worry about. Our English envoys report good progress is being made in their negotiations with the French and it will not be long before we're all back home in England. I think it wiser to leave everything in their capable hands and not meddle in matters which do not concern you.'

'I think, Sir Edward, that this matter concerns you as much as it concerns me. While we are here in Paris, I am in charge of Her Grace's women attendants, you are in charge of the men. If something untoward should happen, King Henry will look to blame both of us.'

He looked startled. 'What do you mean – untoward?'

I took a deep breath and ploughed on. 'Her Grace and the Duke of Suffolk are becoming too close. They spend too much private time together.'

'Private?'

'Yes, just the two of them with myself the only lady permitted to be present. I sit in the shadows while they whisper to each other. And there is more. She is practically in his arms, Sir Edward. I fear Her Grace is about to commit an unforgivable folly.'

'Lady Elizabeth! Have you no shame! To make such an accusation.'

'It is not a matter of shame but of prudence. I care for Her Grace but I also have a care for my own skin and so should you.'

Sir Edward began to babble about outrageous effrontery, foul slander and foolish young women who'd been dragged up out of the gutter which I presumed must be a reference to my family. Eventually, having run out of spleen, he calmed down.

With a great sigh he subsided into a chair, placing the letter on the table. Waving a hand for me to be seated, he said, 'You'd better tell me the rest.'

So I told him with as much delicacy as I could about everything that had happened while Mary was in seclusion in the mourning chamber of *La Reine Blanche* and what I feared Mary and Charles Brandon were about to do.

'What of King François? Sir Richard tells me the French king plans to marry Her Grace to one of his cousins. That would prevent any nonsense.'

'Her Grace feels trapped. She does not wish to marry the French king's cousin nor does she know what King Henry has in mind for her future.'

'Dear God! I knew this position was a poisoned chalice. I wish I'd stayed in England as my brother advised.'

I smiled. 'Too late for wishing, Sir Edward.'

He put his head in his hands. 'Perhaps you should have a word with Her Grace, persuade her to wait until she is back in England.'

'She believes King François will not allow her to return.'

Sir Edward had a mind, quicker than that of Charles Brandon, and understood immediately how Mary planned to sever this particular Gordian knot. 'Marriage to Lord Suffolk would destroy her value to King François so there'd be no reason for him to prevent her leaving.'

I nodded in agreement. 'Unfortunately, marriage to Lord Suffolk would also destroy her value to King Henry. He would be furious.'

'And his fury would be directed at me. What a mess! What a bloody awful mess.'

'Sir Edward, could you perhaps have a word with Lord Suffolk, man to man. He might listen to you.'

'More like knock my head off.'

'What about one of the others – Sir Richard perhaps?'

'Lord Suffolk is the senior envoy. Sir Richard would not dare gainsay him on a matter of this nature.'

'But if he is harming King Henry's relations with the king of France, it would be a patriotic act to intervene.'

'Lady Elizabeth, if you want my advice – return to your post and pray. That is all you can do, all either of us can do.'

Deep in my heart, I feared he was right. Matters had gone too far and there was nothing we could do.

So I returned and I prayed.

12

THE SECRET MARRIAGE
FEBRUARY 1515

Two days later I was roused from my sleep by one of the maids. She said we were wanted by the dowager queen. Wearily I rose and dressed quickly, wondering what crisis had arisen since yesterday. Jane was still yawning as we stumbled along in the early dawn, bleary eyed from lack of sleep. Outside, the streets of Paris were waking to another day with the now familiar sounds of church bells, rumbling wagons and shouting.

In Mary's chamber, piles of clothes were strewn on top of chests, shoes littered the floor while Mary's maid was lacing her mistress into a dark red gown.

'Your Grace?' I enquired, wondering what was happening and why so early.

Mary held out her arms for the sleeves and then stood impatiently while the delicate hood with its double band of pearls was placed on her head.

She turned and smiled.

I should have known. Of course I should. I, who knew Mary better than anyone, should have realised long ago that this was no idle girlish fancy. In one way I had known but I'd not believed that the two people involved could be quite so reckless, so careless of each other's safety.

As we walked into the tiny chapel where the priest

stood waiting, the look on Mary's face said it all. For her, this was love, a lifelong passion to be nurtured and cherished until death.

Charles Brandon, Duke of Suffolk, charged with bringing King Henry's sister home to England, looked unruffled at having thrown caution to the wind.

'I know you disapprove, Lady Elizabeth,' he murmured.

'Lord Suffolk, it is not my place to disapprove.'

'But nonetheless, you *do* disapprove.'

I chose my words carefully. 'I fear the repercussions.'

'You mean Henry.'

I nodded. 'Yes. He will not like this marriage. You know that.'

'Henry knows of Mary's affection for me.'

'Lord Suffolk, I think we both know there is more to Her Grace's feelings for you than affection.'

He grinned. 'You're right. She says she loves me, swears she will have no-one other than me for a husband.'

I sighed, thinking of these frantic weeks with Mary panic-stricken at the thought of being married off to some foreign count and sent away by King François, the hours of weeping, the clinging, the gnawed knuckles.

'And you, my lord. Are you not frightened for your own skin?'

'Henry is my friend.'

'But, if you will forgive me for saying, there are many others who are not.'

The vultures at court: Lord Norfolk, my brother the Marquess, the old families who already thought Charles Brandon favoured too highly, men who resented the award of his dukedom, his interference in matters of state which they considered the province of better men. Charles Brandon had enemies at the council table. I feared that when they heard of this marriage they'd urge Henry to slap down the presumptuous Duke of Suffolk.

'Will the king protect you against a charge of treason?' I murmured.

'Do not fear, Lady Elizabeth. Wolsey will not let it come to that,' he said with great confidence.

I was not so sure. Unauthorised carnal knowledge of a royal princess was most definitely treason and Henry had not given Lord Suffolk permission to marry his sister. Far from it. Henry had expressly forbidden any commerce between them, ordered his friend not to make advances, apparently extracted a solemn promise from the duke before he left England. But as with most men, Henry had underestimated the woman in the matter.

In one way I did not blame Charles Brandon because this marriage was clearly Mary's idea and she could be most persuasive. Like many men, he was susceptible to a pretty weeping woman, and Mary must have convinced him that her brother would forgive them. Henry was a romantic man and she doubtless thought this demonstration of true love would appeal to him. I feared he'd take it as an insult. After all, what power does a king possess if he cannot control his own sister.

The wedding was conducted in the utmost secrecy with only a handful of witnesses and the priest, no-one of importance. Jane and I said nothing to the others but in the days that followed, with Mary keeping Lord Suffolk at her side, the inevitable happened and people began to talk.

'They're saying she's married him,' announced a wide-eyed Mary Boleyn. 'They say he shares her bed.'

'And what do you say?' I asked, thinking what a gossip the older Boleyn girl had become, always found where people were gathered, repeating whatever lewd bits of tittle-tattle she'd heard.

'I say, if not, she'd better be quick before...'

'Before what?'

She put her hand over her mouth to stifle a giggle, her eyes dancing with merriment. 'Lord Suffolk is a very lusty man, do you not think, Lady Elizabeth. I wager the maids will soon be busy unpicking seams.'

'And you, Mary Boleyn, should be busy with your duties.'

She gave a little bob and was off.

It was impossible to stem the tide of gossip. Within a week rumours were rife on every street corner in Paris that the English *Reine Blanche* had disgraced herself by marrying a servant. Someone informed King François who was said to have laughed, and Madame Louise was reported as writing the news in her journal. I began to wonder if this had been King François' plan from the outset: to destroy Mary's value to Henry by encouraging her marriage to Lord Suffolk.

The two other English envoys could no longer ignore the situation because soon the news would reach the ears of the English king,

'Cousin Mary, Your Grace. I urge you, have Lord Suffolk write to your brother.'

'Why?'

'Cousin Mary, you cannot be unaware of the rumours.'

She tossed her head in that particularly Tudor way. 'I do not care for rumours.'

'Your Grace, what is being said in Paris is bound to find its way to London. Lord Suffolk should plead your case to your brother before the king hears of it from others, men who would pour poison in his ear.'

Mary pouted. 'Henry knows my feelings for my husband. Besides, he said I could choose for myself.'

I sighed, thinking of that unwise promise given at the waterside, those few scant words held by Mary to be sacrosanct. She was convinced Henry would keep his word but I was less sure. Henry's hopes must have been dashed by Louis's early death. He knew the French king was not strong but had doubtless reckoned Mary's marriage would last a few years, time for him to strengthen the alliance and for Mary to bear a son. Events had not played out as Henry hoped and, as my mother said, when things went wrong for Henry, he looked for others to blame. I prayed he'd not blame me.

Days passed with the letter to Henry still not yet ready, the composition taking the beleaguered Duke of Suffolk a very long time. He was not a man given to expressing himself on paper, more a man of action, certainly not a poet. Then with the ink not yet dry on the latest version, disaster overtook the couple. Mary confessed to me she thought she was carrying a child.

'Is it not miraculous, Cousin Elizabeth? You are the first to know. Mother Guildford used to say a woman should wait until she feels the child move before telling her husband but I shall tell Brandon this evening. He will be overjoyed.'

Mary looked radiant but I, seeing disaster approaching, felt sick.

With Mary's news, delay was no longer possible. Perfected or not, Lord Suffolk's letter must be sent at once. After that it was a matter of waiting.

Waiting for a reply from England was like scanning the horizon for dust from an enemy army: a dull persistent throb of fear, not knowing exactly where or when disaster would strike yet knowing that, as surely as night followed day, it would come. Mary was bathed in a world of sunshine and roses but I sensed a nervousness, an unease, about Lord Suffolk as we passed our days in idleness.

When at last the letter came it wasn't from Henry but from the Archbishop of York, Thomas Wolsey, and the message conveyed to the Duke of Suffolk was stark. King Henry was furious. There was no hope of either approval or forgiveness due to the extreme gravity of the duke's offence in secretly marrying the king's sister. This was a matter that touched not only on the king's honour but also on the promise enacted by the duke's own hand at Eltham. The king wished the extent of his displeasure to be known to one whom he had, through blind affection, raised up to great honour.

'Wolsey says Brandon is in the greatest danger a man was ever in,' Mary wailed.

As I suspected, Mary and Brandon had, up to now, been oblivious to the magnitude of their offence. The duke said English affairs in France were in good order; François had approached their talks in a spirit of concession; they had banqueted together, jousted together, laid plans for a meeting between both kings. He was genuinely shocked by Wolsey's letter.

'Did the Archbishop of York suggest any remedy?' I asked delicately.

At this, Mary thrust the letter into my hand and burst into tears. 'He says I must give everything to Henry. My jewels! My income! Everything that is mine! I shall have nothing left. How can he be so cruel?'

I took the letter nearer to the light and scanned it quickly. It was a particularly harsh letter; easy to read but uncomfortable to digest. Wolsey was uncharacteristically blunt. He made great play of Henry's rage and sorrow at this betrayal of his friendship and the danger from those who would willingly send Lord Suffolk to the scaffold.

He suggested a remedy might be found if the couple were to offer to the king, all Mary's English plate and jewels, all the jewels given to her by King Louis after her marriage and also pay back Mary's entire marriage portion. This, Wolsey suggested, might conceivably appease the king.

He also rebuked Lord Suffolk for negligence and lack of perception as an ambassador, being too willing to make concessions. He advised him to have no further dealings in the matter of Tournai but to turn his attention to a satisfactory financial settlement with France concerning Mary's dowry and personal possessions. Clearly the Duke of Suffolk was in disgrace.

Once Mary calmed down I laid the letter back on the table and pulled up a stool.

'Why not send Henry a peace offering, the finest of your jewels. Tell him you are truly sorry to have offended him. Abase yourself. Place yourself at his mercy.'

'The finest?' Mary was clearly suspicious of what I was about to suggest.

'The Mirror of Naples.'

'No! Not that! It's my most treasured possession. I'll not give it up. It was a gift from King Louis.'

'Yes it was and it's a rare and beautiful jewel of inestimable value.'

'I cannot lose it. The Sieur de Marigny said it showed how much Louis loved me.'

'Cousin Mary, you have chosen to marry Lord Suffolk and Henry has made it plain that your choice comes at a cost.'

'But it's too much. He's being unfair.'

'Cousin Mary, Henry is the king and he is angry with you. You'd be wise not to antagonise him further.'

'He'll come round,' she said uncertainly. 'He loves me. He's always loved me. He'll not deprive me of my jewels.'

'It may be that, in time, he'll give it back.' I crossed my fingers against the lie. Henry was greedy for jewels. Once he got his hands on the magnificent Mirror of Naples, he'd never relinquish it. No prince would.

It took two days and a mixture of cajoling and explanations of what Henry might otherwise do, to part Mary from her prize. But, once reconciled to the loss, she followed my advice and added eighteen large pearls to the bundle of loot she sent secretly to Henry. Her letter was heartfelt and pleading, designed to melt the hardest of hearts and, where his younger sister, was concerned, I knew Henry's heart to be extremely tender.

Mary and Lord Suffolk also decided that a second wedding, conducted by a bishop, would settle any gossip about "sinful accompanying" and other allusions to the widowed queen's activities which were rife in the taverns and alleyways of Paris. On the last day of March, a Saturday, in the chapel in the Hôtel de Cluny, Mary again wed Charles Brandon, Duke of Suffolk, described by many French courtiers as a person of low estate. Now the news could flood out to every princely court in Europe, disappointing Mary's many suitors, causing astonishment and derision in equal measure and requiring diplomatic shifts to be made in councils from Ghent to Milan.

Just as I thought we were clear to leave Paris, a row blew up between the French and English representatives hammering out their agreement. The French required Mary to return the Mirror of Naples. The jewel was, the French explained, an heirloom of the Crown, not the personal possession of the queen and was traditionally hers only during her queenship. It was a star of great price, valued by the French chancellor at thirty thousand crowns. When Lord Suffolk confessed that the Mirror of Naples and some eighteen pearls had been sent by his wife to King Henry and she was unable to get them back, King François was not at all polite. He demanded their immediate return and accused the English of thievery.

Deprived of any advantage with King François, the English negotiators now found themselves outflanked. Lord Suffolk developed a haunted look, beset on all sides by demands and recriminations. It was perhaps only in the arms of his wife that he achieved some kind of respite, although with Mary asking daily when they might leave, I doubted even his discussions with her were peaceful.

In the end, King François's determination to retrieve Tournai was so great, a deal could still be done. Mary was to receive her jointure intact and be paid two hundred gold crowns as restitution for half her original marriage portion which included twenty thousands crowns for her travel expenses to Abbelville, a figure reached only after a great deal of haggling. Her gold plate and most of her jewels, save for twenty-two diamond, sixteen pearls, one ruby and a large emerald which she had already appropriated as her personal property – for these, Sir Richard informed her, and for the Mirror of Naples, she must tender a formal receipt.

'It is more than we expected, Your Grace,' said Sir Richard.

'And I am free to go?'

He smiled. 'The treaty of peace and amity has been signed, Your Grace. Full liberty of commerce and a peaceful settlement of all outstanding grievances.'

It sounded wonderful but I noted his disinclination to discuss various other matters which I knew had been raised: the planned meeting between Henry and François; the marriage alliance between Queen Claude's sister, little Reneé of France and the Prince of Castile; and the return of the Duke of Albany to Scotland, a move which threatened the rights of Henry's sister, the widowed Scottish queen. I thought relations with France might not be quite as rosy as Sir Richard pretended.

On 16th day of April, after the Easter festivities were complete, we left the walled city of Paris. Our party was accompanied by King François and a small contingent of

Frenchmen, doubtless glad to see the last of the extravagant English *Reine Blanche* and her not-so-beautiful ladies who'd done nothing for France but stir up trouble. At Saint-Denis, King François made his farewells. Never one to ignore any good-looking woman, he bent over my hand.

'*Au revoir*, my little English rose. I assure you, I have not forgotten the debt you owe me. Until we meet again, Lady Elizabeth Grey.'

I felt myself blush to the very roots of my hair.

'What did he say?' Jane whispered as our procession rode out of the little town along the road to Senlis.

'Nothing,' I replied. 'French gallantry, that's all.'

If anyone had cared to count, which I doubted they did, they'd have noticed that Mary had two less lady attendants in her train than she had the previous week. The Boleyn girls were to remain in France in the service of the French queen.

'On whose orders?' I asked when I realised Anne had not packed her chests.

'My father has found me a place serving Queen Claude,' she said smoothly.

'Why would he do that?'

'Because I asked him.'

'Do you not wish to return to England?'

'Not yet. Here I shall improve my education and be of more use to my family serving Queen Claude than if I...' She stopped, opened her brilliant black eyes wide and smiled. 'You are experienced in these matters, Lady Elizabeth. I'm sure you understand.'

Of course I understood. A position with the Queen of France was preferable to serving a royal widow going home in disgrace for having contrived a secret marriage against her brother's express orders. In the new French queen's household, Anne would improve her linguistic skills while learning the art of pleasing men with witty conversation and flirtatious allusions, important weapons in the armoury of any young woman who wished to make her mark. From what I had learnt of King François, he would preside over the most glittering court In Europe and little Anne Boleyn would become as French as any Frenchwoman. In a few years time, the clever Thomas Boleyn would summon his younger daughter home, having arranged a splendid marriage for her with a man who'd appreciate an educated wife.

I did not have a father to summon me home but It would be pleasant if my brother spent as much time as other men in arranging splendid marriages for the young women in their family.

'What of your sister?' I asked, thinking it might better if Sir Thomas Boleyn called his elder daughter home before her reputation was ruined. Far too pretty, far too free and easy with her favours, every month young Mary Boleyn acquired another French admirer. So far the presence of the English ladies had kept her in check but I feared what might happen once we were gone.

'My sister will stay. She has no desire to go home.' She gave me a knowing smile. 'Soon our father will find her a husband. Then she'll have to behave.'

We lingered for two weeks in Calais, exploring the walls and winding streets of the little port town, watching ships sailing in and out of the harbour, the loading and unloading of goods on the quay and talking to the townswomen. It was liberating to be on English-held soil but I was nervous. We were still waiting for permission to return to England. It was like being one of those knights of old, banished from the kingdom to spend the rest of their lives wandering from court to court as exiles.

Now that our return was imminent, Mary was becoming increasingly distraught lest Henry's reception was not the merciful one she expected. What if he deprived her husband of his offices and property and banished him from court? What if he listened to Lord Suffolk's enemies round the council table, men who were calling for his imprisonment or his head? What if Henry forced her to renounce her marriage? What if he left them with no means at all?

'I have written another letter to Henry,' she confided, dabbing her eyes after another bout of weeping. 'I told him I will never give up the man I have chosen. I reminded him of the promise he made and said I would wait here in Calais, within his jurisdiction, for his forgiveness.'

From the high walls of Calais I looked out at the few short miles of sea which separated us from England and hoped that Henry's forgiveness would stretch this far. I wondered what Mary would do if it did not. Since our arrival we had been honourably entertained by the town but I'd no wish to spend the rest of my life here, waiting for Henry to decide on the required punishment for his erring sister and his faithless friend.

'He will be merciful.' I assured her, wondering who Henry would blame for this whole miserable disaster.

'Do you think he'll be kind to my husband?' she asked.

Thomas Wolsey's most recent letters had been less than hopeful. The Duke of Suffolk's rivals on the council were working on the king to have the duke put to death, or if the king could not stomach having his friend executed, then thrown into prison.

At Montreuil, Charles Brandon had addressed one last desperate appeal to Henry. Composing the letter had taken him a full day, assuring Henry that he was "my sovereign lord and master who has brought me up out of nothing" – I urged that particular phrase as by now the duke was in such a state he was unable to find the words he needed and had appealed for help. The letter contained many references to his humble heart and how "he yielded himself to Henry to do with his poor body your most gracious pleasure, not fearing the malice of others." From Wolsey's letters, it was made clear that malice abounded in certain factions at court. It was no wonder Mary reported her husband was unable to sleep at night.

The future looked particularly ominous.

But Henry could always surprise you and on the day following May Day, permission was received to set sail for Dover.

We had been away from England for exactly seven months. It felt like a lifetime.

13

THE ROYAL PALACE OF GREENWICH
MAY 1515

It was a beautiful May morning when the court gathered at Greenwich for the wedding of the king's sister, Mary, and Charles Brandon, Duke of Suffolk, sometime close friend of the king.

At a private meeting with the couple, Henry had made plain his extreme displeasure at their actions, but swayed by his love for them both was more generous than they'd hoped or, some said, deserved. The financial penalties were savage and would severely impact on the way they lived but, other than that, Henry was prepared to be merciful. Mary wept tears of joy on my shoulder and whispered she'd secretly feared the worst.

The irregular nature of Mary's previous weddings to Lord Suffolk in Paris had given rise to much criticism: they were secret, conducted during the Lenten season, entered into without the customary banns being called and with no records kept. Such a situation caused people to gossip and some might question the legitimacy of any children they would have. Hence the third wedding.

'My mother says the king is making the best of a bad job,' Jane whispered as we walked behind the now indisputably married Duchess of Suffolk.

'Every time the Duke of Norfolk sees Lord Suffolk he growls about sow's ears and silk purses,' I replied.

'And your brother?'

'Just growling.'

As we swept along the gallery, all of us dressed in our glamorous French fashions, much envied by the other women at court, Jane glanced out of the window.

'Hardly any people outside.'

'No spontaneous public demonstrations of pleasure?'

'Not a single one.'

'Maybe the people do not approve.'

We rounded the corner and began our descent down the wide staircase to the great banqueting hall where the whole court awaited.

'Will they stay at court?' Jane murmured.

'If the king permits. And if they can afford to.'

'Anne Jerningham says Lord Suffolk has a house in Southwark. She boasts she is to accompany his duchess.'

'And you?'

Jane hesitated. 'My father has arranged a marriage for me.'

'Oh Jane! Who?'

'Edmund Knyvett, Sir Thomas Knyvett's younger brother.'

I trawled through my memory. The name was familiar. Then I remembered.

'He is a very large man.'

That was all I knew about Edmund Knyvett, sergeant porter to the king. A broad-shouldered, broad-chested giant of a man with a jutting jaw and fists like hams. Breaking up fights between courtiers and denying entry to the king's palaces to ruffians and scum from the streets, were matters that required a large man so he'd hardly be thin and ferrety like Lord Norfolk's son, Thomas Howard.

Jane looked apprehensive. 'I am quite tall.'

'Oh I think, Edmund Knyvett will manage to carry you off with ease, Jane Bourchier.'

'Where would he carry me to?'

Jane was delightfully easy to tease but I wanted her to be happy in her marriage. 'Somewhere lovely. My sisters say large men are gentle with their wives. Men like Edmund Knyvett have nothing to prove so treat their women like delicate pieces of Venetian glass.'

Jane gave me a wan little smile. 'My father says he will settle his property at Ashwellthorpe on us when we are wed. Do you think I shall like living in Norfolk?'

Norfolk? My brother, Leonard once told me the county was chilly, like the duke; winds blowing from the east.

'I think you will be very content in your house at Ashwellthorpe. Perhaps Lord Norfolk will visit.'

We both laughed at the ridiculous thought of the mighty duke coming to visit Jane in her little manor house. But as her father's sole heir, Jane had good prospects. Edmund Knyvett had done well for himself.

'What of you?' said Jane as we took our places on the benches.

'Cousin Mary says she and Lord Suffolk are to spend the summer at Tattershall,' I whispered. 'I shall go there.'

Although I had hopes of staying with Mary, I was yet to discover my place in my brother's plans. I'd not seen Thomas in private since our return from France but was under orders to come to his rooms after the wedding banquet, not an interview I was relishing.

Thomas Grey, Marquess of Dorset was in, what my sisters called, "full Marquess mode". Still dressed in his impressive blue velvet banqueting robes, he stood behind a large table glaring at me.

When faced with my brother, I sometimes wished our father was still alive. According to my eldest sister, Dorothy, he'd been a kind man, treated badly by Henry's father and hounded to death by his enemies.

'You are a disgrace to our family.' Thomas's voice was cold, his shoulders rigid, eyes narrowed, a stray hair catching a gleam of candlelight.

'In what way, my lord?' I said humbly. As a young girl I'd learnt the hard way that it was best to overdo the boot-licking in situations like this. I wondered should I kneel.

'Gross impropriety!'

I searched for the focus of his fury and decided it must be my visit to François d'Angoulême's rooms on the morning after Mary's wedding. Someone must have told him. Probably Meg.

'I took the advice of your wife, my lord. She approved what I should say and what I should wear.'

His face flushed red, a vein in his temple throbbing dangerously. 'How dare you involve my wife in your improper dealings with men,' he shouted. 'Of all my sisters I thought you knew how to behave. But the moment you're out of my sight you dishonour our family name.'

'My lord, I have done nothing of which I am ashamed.'

'Do you deny meeting privately with François d'Angoulême; offering yourself to him.'

'I did not offer myself to him.'

'Call it what you will; to be alone with such a man invites censure.'

'He is King of France,' I reminded Thomas.

'He is a man with only one use for a woman. You knew that, yet allowed yourself to be compromised.'

'Nothing happened.'

'Liar!' he hissed.

'I swear to you, my lord, I am as chaste as the day I left England.'

He turned his back on me and stared out of the window at the evening dusk. After a prolonged silence in which the room vibrated with anger, his words were slow and deliberate.

'There are more ways than one to undo a young woman's virtue. A man has no need to risk all.'

I wondered did his knowledge come from experience or from lewd jokes amongst acquaintances at court. If rumours were to be believed, Lord Suffolk knew exactly how to undo a young woman's virtue and was said not to hesitate at the gate but venture deep into the undergrowth, risking more than a scratch from a thorn bush. My sisters said Thomas was a cold fish and much too careful to risk the king's displeasure to play games with the likes of Bessie Blount and Lizzie Bryan.

'I do not know what you mean, my lord,' I said to his back, wondering how much Meg had told him of that day in Abbeville and what I'd said about my meeting with François d'Angoulême.

'Don't take me for a fool, Elizabeth. Close acquaintance with the ladies of the French court can hardly have left you ignorant of such practices. Can you swear he never laid a finger on you?'

I thought of François d'Angoulême, removing the pins from my hair and sliding his fingers beneath the neckline of my bodice.

'My duty was to help Cousin Mary.'

'Your duty was to your family.'

'Mary was in trouble. I approached Duke François to ask him to intercede with King Louis.'

'And did he?'

I shook my head. 'He was unwilling.'

'So your quest failed.'

I hung my head and tried to look repentant.

'What of your unauthorised visit to the Hôtel de Cluny. Sir Edward tells me you were ordered to remain at the Hôtel des Tournelles, yet you were seen out in the streets before dawn with a man.'

'He was a servant.'

'A servant indeed! What were you doing with this servant?'

'Nothing. He was guiding me to the Hôtel de Cluny.'

'You do not deny disobeying Sir Edward.'

'No,' I said wearily. 'I do not deny it. Sir Edward was wrong. Cousin Mary was in danger.'

'How dare you question Sir Edward's right to give you orders. The question of whether or not there was danger was not one for you to judge, was it?'

'No, but…'

'It seems you were partially unclothed when interviewed by Madame Louise.'

'My lord! Whoever told you that is lying. I was attacked by some brutes in the street. My gown was torn. That is all.'

'Torn? How torn?'

I sighed. Thomas, clearly imagining serious misbehaviour on my part, was determined to wring every last drop of my disobedience from this degrading incident.

'My sleeve. A maid was summoned with needle and thread.'

'There was no interference with your person.'

'No.'

I thought it best not to tell Thomas of the interference I'd suffered at the hands of brown doublet's henchmen or the humiliating search carried out by Gaston.

'Where else did you go with this young man?'

'Nowhere. I've told you. The same brutes who attacked me, killed him. I believe they dumped his body in the river.'

'What did they want with you?'

'They didn't say. When a man throws a sack over your head, he rarely stops to explain. I thought I was being abducted, but they took me to the Hôtel de Cluny.'

Thomas sat down, rested his left elbow on the table and began rubbing the side of his nose.

'When I think of the money I wasted on you: those gowns, the cost of that saddle. And for what? Your reputation is ruined. No man will want you now.'

'I shall remain with Cousin Mary.'

'You will not. I'll not have you dragged down by a woman seduced by an arriviste. She has thrown away all her advantages of birth – and for what?'

'Love,' I suggested.

Thomas stared at me, as if the word was disgusting.

'Love! Is that what you call it. There's a better word for it but I'll not lower myself to utter it in the presence of a woman. I am sending you to Astley, to our mother. Ask her to tell you about love. And while you're there you can spend time on your knees, praying for forgiveness.'

'Am I to remain at Astley?' I asked timidly, appalled at the thought of being immured with my mother.

'When the king returns from his summer progress, you are to join the queen's household. I have secured a place for you where you will be properly supervised.'

I breathed a little more easily. It could have been worse. He could have chosen a convent.'

'Thank you, my lord,' I said,

'And Elizabeth.'

'Yes, my lord.'

'Do not waste this opportunity. There will not be another.'

I crept away, not daring to speak, leaving Thomas standing at the window, satisfied that a just punishment had been firmly administered.

Next day I was escorted back to Astley, the scene of my childhood, where my mother was far from pleased to see me. She treated me to a lengthy interview where my sins were picked apart and laid out in a row like so many dead rats. The stench in the room was unbearable.

14

LORD LEONARD GREY
FEBRUARY 1520

One cold bright morning in February, while waiting at the landing stage at Greenwich, I spied the Norfolk barge. It was a relatively modest affair with discreet gilding and a small canopy. Lord Norfolk knew better than most not to cause offence to his royal master. Only my stepfather's brother, the mighty Duke of Buckingham chose to rival the splendour of the royal barge, but he was known as a proud man, fully aware of his royal pedigree and unwilling to concede an inch to lesser mortals.

As the barge nosed alongside the long wooden pier a pair of liveried watermen moved forward to secure the ropes. Three men stepped out. I recognised the narrow frame and scowling face of Lord Norfolk's son, Thomas Howard, Earl of Surrey, but not his dark-haired companion with whom he was having a furious argument. The third man, to my great surprise, was Francis Bryan.

'Lady Elizabeth,' he said coming over to greet me. 'How kind of you to form a welcoming party.'

'Slim pickings, sir. Only me and I'm here to meet with my brother.'

'The marquess?'

I wrinkled my nose. 'No, Lord Leonard.'

'Still not forgiven?' He cocked his head to one side, eyeing me with amusement.

'I have no idea what you mean.'

He moved closer and spoke in a confidential undertone. 'Lady Elizabeth, I have been to Paris. I have visited the French court. I know what is said about you there.'

'And I, sir, know what is being said here in the English court about you and your visit to Paris.'

I was certain that after five years, no-one at the French court remembered my transgressions. Memory fades as newer, juicier gossip overtakes the misdeeds of previous years. Young women disappear from view and are quickly forgotten. I doubted even Madame d'Aumont remembered me. But the diplomatic mission to Paris where Francis Bryan and his friends had publicly disgraced themselves by throwing eggs and stones at people in the street, horrified Queen Katherine's ladies. We were not surprised when, on their return to England, the young men were dismissed from Henry's privy chamber and sent away from court. That was Cardinal Wolsey's doing, or so I was told.

Francis Bryan laughed. 'We are two sinners, you and I. Perhaps we should sin some more. What d'you say, Lady Elizabeth? A tryst by the garden stairs? A little dalliance à deux. You can divulge your secrets and I shall whisper mine in your ear.'

'You, sir, are a rogue. Besides, it is too cold for dalliance in the garden and I have no secrets to tell.'

He grinned. 'That is not what I hear.'

I'd spent five years trying to forget my behaviour of that winter in France and model myself on the perfection of Queen Katherine. I had no wish to discuss my past indiscretions with Francis Bryan. I decided to steer the conversation in a different direction.

'Who is Thomas Howard's companion?'

'Lord Kildare. Now there's a thought. Yet another sinner.'

'Lord Kildare? Why, what has he done?'

'Offended Henry. Never wise. A man should always strive for royal favour like our mutual friend, Thomas Howard.'

'I barely know Thomas Howard.'

'You barely know Lord Kildare yet I notice a gleam in your eye. Do I sense a little interest stirring?'

'You do not.'

'Think of it, Lady Elizabeth. Kildare is a fine man. Tall, strong-limbed, the kind to appreciate a mettlesome young woman like yourself pulling on the bridle.' He ran a single finger down my sleeve. 'Does the thought not make your heart beat faster, your pulses race, your knees grow weak? It brings a blush to your lovely cheeks, I see. Think what a man like Kildare could offer you. I hear they dine daily on brains of roasted ox in his castles; and you know what that does to a man's desire. It is said the Kildare menfolk bed as frequently as they piss and when they bed, they breed mighty sons. More steadfast a man than lean and hungry François I hazard.'

'Go away, Francis Bryan or I shall tell my brother you were making improper suggestions to me. You'd best run after your friends for they're about to disappear.'

He laughed, pulled his hat back on, bowed and whispered into my ear in perfect French, 'À *bientôt, ma chérie.*' Then he ran lightly up the steps to join the others who were already at the door to the palace, still arguing.

I gazed after him, wondering how Francis Bryan would fare with Henry now that a more sober court prevailed. It had been ushered in by Cardinal Wolsey whose presence, both real and ephemeral, was felt everywhere, from the king's privy rooms to the council chamber to the heat of the royal kitchens. When Bessie Blount gave birth to Henry's son last summer, it was Thomas Wolsey who stood godfather and organised a princely household for the child and it was Thomas Wolsey who would arrange a suitably discreet marriage for the mother. She would not be returning to court to resume her affair with the king.

Everyone could see Henry doted on his newborn son as much as he doted on his daughter, four-year-old Princess Mary, a clever child with her mother's colouring. For the queen, the birth of little Henry Fitzroy must have been a bitter blow, a public demonstration of her husband's infidelity and a distressing reminder that a single healthy daughter and a trail of tiny coffins was all she had to show for ten years of marriage. But Katherine was a daughter of Spain and had been trained in a hard school. Whatever her private grief, which I could only imagine, she made no comment and like the rest of us, had attended the festivities arranged by the king to celebrate the birth of his son.

'Surely not Thomas Howard?' said a voice in my ear.

I spun round and was caught in an embrace by my favourite brother. Leonard was a few years older than me, a military man to the metal toecaps of his long leather boots, a man rising fast in royal favour as Henry liked nothing better than a good fighter who enjoyed gambling at cards.

'Never,' I laughed. 'Besides, he is married to Buckingham's daughter. One treads lightly near the royal duke.'

'Was that Kildare, I saw?'

'Apparently so but I never trust anything Francis Bryan tells me. Who is he?'

'Kildare? Lord deputy in Ireland.'

'I was not aware Henry needed a lord deputy.'

'To keep order in Ireland, a king needs a host of lord deputies.'

'So why is Lord Kildare here at court and not in Ireland?'

'He's come seeking a new wife.'

'He seems more interested in quarrelling than in wooing'

Leonard laughed. 'You're right. His quarrel with Piers Butler has not pleased Henry.'

I knew nothing of Ireland and had no idea who Piers Butler was. I had more important things on my mind.

'Did you bring it?'

Leonard handed over a carefully wrapped package. 'I trust it is what you wanted.'

'It's for Cousin Mary's new daughter. She's to be called Eleanor.'

'A good enough name. Have you seen Cousin Mary?'

I shook my head. 'No, she's been at Westhorpe this past year.'

'Ah, the joys of country living: soft green pastures, mossy dells, milk warm from the cow. Brandon will make a dairymaid of her yet.'

'Don't be unkind. She's been unwell and you know how Henry dislikes sickness of any sort.'

'And Brandon?'

'With Henry. Poor Mary; she misses her husband.'

'Perhaps Henry will soon have a use for her. Have you heard about Wolsey's proposed jaunt?'

It was cold standing by the river so I took Leonard's arm and steered him away from the landing stage and the busy river.

'What jaunt? I thought the cardinal wished to keep Henry away from idle pleasures.'

'He does but this is no idle pleasure. It is a meeting of kings: Henry and François. A splendid affair. Feasting, jousting, dancing; an opportunity for dazzling display.'

This sounded far more to Henry's taste than depriving him of the disgraceful presence of Francis Bryan.

'To what purpose?'

Leonard gave a crooked smile. 'Increase the bond of friendship. Brotherly love between fellow monarchs. Everlasting peace between our two nations. That is what we're meant to think.'

'But?'

'Henry is curious. He wants to see for himself what kind of man François is.'

'I could tell him that,' I said sourly.

The only person I'd told about what had happened to me in France was Cousin Mary and even she did not know the whole truth. Thomas had his suspicions from his conversations with the senior men in Mary's household but I'd told the others nothing. My sisters would have wanted to know every sordid little detail, my mother would have called me a stupid harlot and the queen would have been shocked to the core.

'Shall we take a walk?' Leonard suggested. At this time of the morning the gardens at Greenwich were peaceful. Leonard held the gate open and we strolled through into a magical world where rows of frosted trees glinted in the weak winter sunshine like a bejewelled army.

'D'you know who I met today? Mary Boleyn,' I said watching my breath drift upwards in the cold morning air.

'A sprig off the Boleyn tree.'

'The elder daughter. One of Mary's maids of honour in France. She tells me she is to marry William Carey.'

I would not tell Leonard what else Mary Boleyn had confided to me. She'd only spoken because we'd been together in France, but even so I was shocked. She looked so innocent with her soft fair hair and sweet smile but, if I'd understood her correctly, she was far from innocent and worried in case her husband would know.

I gave a deep sigh.

Leonard put an arm round my shoulder and gave me a quick squeeze. 'What's the matter?'

'Cecily! She says she's to marry soon.'

There had been a great deal of crowing from my sister over her forthcoming marriage to the Dudley heir: she would marry before me; what a mistake they'd made sending me to France not her; look at the money Thomas had wasted; it was all very well waiting to catch an earl or a duke but what if one never came along, what then? I'd be a dried-up old spinster and shouldn't look to Cecily for help, she'd be much to busy with her new husband.

This one-way exchange was typical of sisters more

inclined to be rivals than friends, squabbling in childhood over whatever crumbs of affection came our way. Although we were both grown women, we were still fighting our nursery battles. I loved her because she was my sister, but mostly hated the woman she'd become.

'Elizabeth,' Leonard said, 'Thomas would never waste you on a fool like Lord Dudley's son. He has bigger plans in mind.'

'So I'm always being told but there's never a husband for me at the end of Thomas's plans.'

'Be patient.'

'I am. But even Bessie Blount is to have a husband.'

With his arm draped round my shoulder it was impossible to miss how Leonard stiffened, an involuntary tightening of his muscles, a rigidity of his jaw.

'Is something the matter?'

He sighed. 'I suppose I can tell you but you must keep it a secret. I went to see Wolsey yesterday. Offered myself.'

'Offered yourself? In what way?'

'As a husband for Bessie.'

I made the mistake of laughing. 'You want to marry Bessie Blount?'

My brother rarely surprised me but I'd not expected this. I'd no idea he even knew Bessie, except in the way we all knew her as a young woman about court whose natural grace and desire to please a man had caught the king's roving eye. Unlike Henry, Leonard was not a man given to romantic sentiments. I doubted he'd ever written a verse to a young woman yet here he was sighing over Bessie Blount like a lovelorn swain. It was unbelievable.

'I can think of nothing more pleasant than to be

married to someone like Bessie,' he said mournfully.

I arranged my face so as not to betray my feelings. 'What did Wolsey say?'

Leonard grimaced. 'Read me a little homily about abstinence and how a young man with ability and ambition who wished to rise in the king's estimation, should look higher than his royal master's leavings. Advised me to consult the marquess if I wanted a wife.'

I giggled. 'Did you?'

'No. Can you imagine what Thomas would say.'

'I doubt Thomas rates marriage highly but it's different for you, you're his brother. For his sisters, marriage is a costly business. Do you know if Cecily's dowry is settled?'

'Thomas says he is going to Astley.'

We smiled at each other knowing what a visit to Astley entailed – another angry encounter with our mother, arguments over money, insults hurled and nothing resolved.

'And you? What will *you* do?' I asked.

'Nurse my broken heart. Return to the joust.'

'Henry rates you highly.'

My brother smiled. 'I think I shall go and be pleasant to Thomas Howard.'

'Is there a reason?'

'Wolsey favours diplomacy but Thomas Howard values war for the honour and glory and rewards it brings. If a man cannot love, he must fight.'

Leonard looked so tragic I wanted to kiss him.

'What of you?' he said.

'Back to the queen's rooms.'

'What do you women do there all day?'

'Pray, sew, read, sing, dance, practice our instruments and gossip about you men.'

He laughed. 'Give my humble greetings to Queen Katherine.'

I gave him a sisterly hug, hoping a meeting with Thomas Howard would lift his spirits and stop him brooding over the unattainable Bessie Blount.

I went into the palace by the side entrance and hurried up the stairs to the queen's rooms. As usual, her chamber was suffused with the kind of calm only achieved by a well-ordered household overseen by a loving mistress. One of the Spanish ladies was reading aloud while the others sat dutifully with their fine embroidery in their laps, stitching industriously. Queen Katherine noticed me slip into my place but said nothing. Once Inez had finished her reading, I was summoned,

'Your Grace,' I said politely, giving a little curtsey.

'Did you find your brother, Lady Elizabeth?'

'I did Your Grace. He asked to be remembered to you.'

She smiled, inclining her head. She looked tired. 'Lord Leonard is a pleasant young man. It is time he found himself a wife.'

I did not tell her about Leonard's visit to Cardinal Wolsey. In the queen's rooms, the less said about the desirable Bessie Blount, mother of the king's bastard son, the better.

'I saw the Earl of Surrey down at the landing stage, Your Grace. He arrived with Lord Kildare.'

The queen nodded. 'The king tells me he has summoned Lord Kildare. It is a wise prince who is aware of what is being done in his name.'

'Yes, Your Grace.'

'When I was a young girl, my mother and father rode from one end of Spain to the other to watch over their kingdom. They regarded it as their duty. My nephew, Charles, has an even greater burden.'

A year ago, old Emperor Maximilian had finally died and in the summer, Cousin Mary's "Beloved", Charles, Prince of Castile, was handed the imperial crown. Word was that King François had wanted it and laid out vast sums in gold in his bid to be elected. But it was the queen's nephew who was chosen and the imperial ambitions of France had come to naught.

Unsurprisingly, both Henry and Katherine were pleased: Henry, because he mistrusted François, the queen because Charles was part of her Spanish family and she could not help but want him to succeed. She yearned to bring her husband and nephew closer. Although she never interfered, I knew she favoured an alliance with the young emperor rather than Wolsey's planned rapprochement with France.

That May, the vast royal procession making its slow way to Canterbury eclipsed even the great cavalcade which accompanied Mary, the year she married King Louis. In the queen's rooms we'd been making preparations for this "jaunt" for months. Lengths of cloth-of-gold, satin, velvet and damask were purchased for the queen's robes, and exhausted seamstresses stitched daily until the light faded and then continued their duties by candlelight. Goldsmiths and silk women were in constant attendance and the maids were so overwhelmed with work, one or two fainted and had to be sent home.

Daily instructions were issued by the cardinal's office, informing every man of the number of servants and horses and carts he was permitted to bring: too many and there'd not be enough ships to transport us all, too few and we risked being seen as a laughing stock. To my amusement, Henry decided to re-grow his beard in honour of the king of France. Sadly this did not please the queen who preferred her husband clean shaven.

I was considered fortunate to be chosen as one of the queen's attendants and to my delight had a whole new wardrobe for the occasion, paid for by my brother who complained that Cardinal Wolsey was bringing three hundred servants while he was restricted to fifty. I'd not expected to be part of the event and in many ways would rather have stayed in England, safe from what I perceived as the dangerous court of King François.

I was a very lowly member of the queen's retinue which numbered more than a thousand and included the Earl of Derby, the Bishop of Rochester, the Duchess of Buckingham, six countesses, twelve baronesses and all their servants. Sir Thomas Boleyn was organising the cardinal's plans in the Pale of Calais so it was unsurprising to see Mary Boleyn, now Lady Carey, as one of our number although, naturally, she was of even less importance than me. I wondered if her husband had discovered she was not the innocent young maid he'd been led to believe but was unsure if a man could know such a thing.

The royal party left Greenwich accompanied by over a hundred peers and princes of the Church, and by the end of the third week in May we had reached Leeds

Castle where we stayed one night before moving on to Canterbury. To look at the queen you'd not have guessed how excited she was. After years of waiting she was about to meet her nephew, her sister's Juana's son, Charles, the newly elected holder of the imperial crown and Cousin Mary's one time betrothed.

By a stroke of good fortune the young emperor was returning from his new Spanish kingdom and had been persuaded to break his journey to meet with Henry. As our departure to Calais could not be delayed, the queen was anxious lest her nephew's ships should not arrive in time. We all knew how contrary winds could be, even at this more placid time of year. But to the queen's joy, the wind stayed in the south-west, blowing the imperial ships steadily towards Dover.

I tucked my stockinged feet under my skirts where I sat curled up on the settle in Cousin Mary's room in the archbishop's palace. It was late, the evening's banquet was over but Henry was still celebrating and Queen Katherine was most unwilling to leave while her nephew was still awake.

Mary was weary and had retired to her rooms. She sat in a chair in her nightgown and shawl, her beautiful red-gold hair gleaming in the candlelight as it streamed over her narrow shoulders. To my eyes, she looked far too thin, like one of those nuns who starve themselves of food, the better to serve God.

'Was he as you expected?' I asked, thinking of the cold-eyed young man who'd sat near Mary at the high table.

She gave me a sideways smile. 'How odd to think

I might have married him. He was very respectful. I imagined him to be more imposing, less subservient.'

'He certainly says very little but he's watchful. It's as if he cannot quite decide if he wants to be our friend.'

I thought him far too serious a man to have been a husband for Mary. Despite his age, King Louis had a spark of gaiety about him, a glimpse of the merry young man he'd once been, while Charles Brandon was lively and full of enthusiasms. He enjoyed snowball fights as much as he enjoyed jousting – just like Henry. The emperor, on the other hand, was a man born prematurely old, too neat in his habits to frisk about like Brandon, a man who would make no decisions without careful consideration of the facts. In truth I thought him a trifle dull.

'He refused to dance, said it was not a pastime at which he excelled,' Mary said, amazed that any man would not wish to take to the floor. At Mary's proxy wedding to Louis even the elderly Venetian ambassador had wanted to dance.

'You danced with Henry.'

She smiled. 'Henry is a truly magnificent dancer.'

'Better than your husband?'

She giggled. 'Much better. I tell Brandon he needs lessons. I offered to teach him.'

I smiled. 'Cousin Mary, I think you know there is nothing the noble Lord Suffolk needs to learn.'

She frowned. 'Did you notice how Henry was watching Buckingham?'

I yawned, thinking bed would be a blessing. 'The feast was so crowded it was hard to watch everyone.'

'Henry is suspicious.'

'Of the Duke of Buckingham?'

'And others, but mainly Buckingham.'

'Why?'

Mary lay back against he pillow and sighed. 'People are beginning to ask, what if Katherine cannot give Henry a son.'

Of course they were. I was. It was a question of the greatest importance.

'There is still time. My sisters say many women conceive when they are older than the queen.'

'Brandon says Henry fears Buckingham is eyeing the throne.'

I wondered if this was true. Certainly the duke was a proud man with an all too powerful awareness of his ancient lineage. Henry's father had taken the crown, not by right of inheritance but by victory on the battlefield of Bosworth. The Tudors lack of legitimacy was a running sore through the ranks of those with Yorkist blood and the noble Duke of Buckingham's blood was thicker and a darker crimson than most. But surely he'd not challenge Henry. That would be supreme folly.

'Henry has a daughter.'

Mary gave an indulgent smile.

'I love my niece but men do not like the idea of being ruled by a woman and any man the princess married would rule England.'

'What does the queen say?'

'She is convinced she will have a son.'

No-ne wanted a prince for England more than the queen. If she could, Katherine would pray one into existence. I thought of the hundreds of women nightly praying they'd conceive a son and for some reason remembered something Francis Bryan had said – "the Kildare menfolk bed as frequently as they piss and when they bed, they breed mighty sons."

What if there were no mighty sons for Henry. I resolved to pray harder that the queen would have a healthy son, one who would live.

'Enough of this,' I said briskly. 'Let us think of our new adventure. Are you nervous – going back?'

Mary frowned. 'A little. It was a long time ago, yet it sometimes feels like yesterday. And of course, François is an unreliable man. He does not mean what he says.'

I laughed. 'Cousin Mary, no ruler speaks the truth. You know that.'

She gave a shiver. 'Behind the smiles and kisses, the courtesies and the offers of friendship, he frightens me.'

'He cannot touch you. Lord Suffolk. would break him in two. So would Henry. You are their Helen. They'd raze Troy to the ground to protect you.'

'She shook her head. 'Henry must be seen as magnanimous. He cannot afford to offend François.'

I thought that where King François was concerned it was I who had more to worry about than Mary. I had offended him badly and, although nearly six years had passed, he struck me as a man who did not forgive those who slighted him, nor did he forget who they were. I could only hope that amongst the duchesses and countesses and baronesses, I'd he hidden from view and not be anywhere near him.

Perhaps, if fortune smiled on me, I might find a husband on this jaunt. It was dispiriting to have reached the age of twenty-three without a single offer of marriage. Like most of the younger ladies at court I'd received offers but they were not the kind a sensible young woman should consider. I'd no wish for a secret assignation in a gentleman's room or an afternoon's dalliance amongst the bushes. Such liaisons led nowhere and no matter what Thomas believed, I did have a care for my reputation.

15

THE FIELD OF THE CLOTH OF GOLD
SUMMER 1520

It was the Feast Day of Corpus Christi and the sound of cannon fire could be heard booming across the plains of northern France. Out from the castle of Guisnes rode the king of England, accompanied by a host of his courtiers. Henry was dressed in cloth-of-gold and silver, so bejewelled he glittered like the sun and on his head he wore a black hat with a huge feather.

The king sat astride a mighty bay whose harness jingled with golden bells, while at his side, in the role of attendant squire, rode the cardinal on a docile white mule. In the distance, away to the south-east, we could hear cannon fire sounding from the headquarters of King François at Ardres. Both men were bound for what people here called the Golden Valley, half way between the two castles. It lay outside the English Pale of Calais but for this occasion was designated as a place of peace in the kingdom of France.

'I wish we could see them meet,' Cousin Mary sighed.

'They say King François has a pavilion of gold damask lined with blue velvet embroidered with fleur-de-lys,' the Countess of Surrey remarked.

'I hear it is guarded by a statue of St Michael the Archangel.' The Countess of Oxford gave a little flounce as if she knew better than anyone what the French king had to offer. I remembered the way she'd looked at him on the road to Abbeville, as if she'd like to do more than eye the handsome François d'Angoulême at a distance.

There was a very definite air of anticipation as we waited in our rooms at the castle at Guisnes. Every woman wanted to see and be seen, eager to gaze at the wonders we'd only heard about. But for those of us who'd endured the dark days of King Louis's last illness and the anxious months of not knowing if we'd be allowed home to England, there was also fear, a deep-seated, stomach-churning fear.

Today was the meeting of the two kings when Henry and François would doff their bonnets, embrace each other and spend time in François's golden pavilion sipping hippocras. I wondered what they'd make of each other, if reality would live up to their ambassador's reports. I'd seen both men and knew Henry to be more handsome, fairer skinned, kinder, probably stronger and certainly more trustworthy. François was as slippery as a bag of eels; good-looking but with a face that five years ago had already begun to show signs of over-indulgence. He was lean and angular while Henry was more robust. I thought François was hungrier and if Henry had asked my advice, which of course he'd not because who wanted the opinion of a woman, I'd have told him not to trust François, not even one tiny single inch.

'Do you think they'll remember us?' asked a wistful voice at my elbow. It was Mary Boleyn, Lady Carey of four months standing.

'I doubt it,' I replied, devoutly hoping it was true.

'Queen Claude made me a gift of a pair of gloves when

I left her service. King François used to call me his English beauty. He was very gallant.'

Mary Boleyn had been a pretty young girl at the French court, light on her feet, willing to please; and François was persuasive. Naturally she'd have been overawed at the attention, easy prey for a lecherous king. Perhaps it was as well her father had summoned her home for marriage with William Carey.

'What of your sister?'

'Anne is with Queen Claude. My brother says she will come home soon. Our father is arranging a marriage for her with an important Irish lord.'

So Anne Boleyn was destined for Lord Kildare. Sir Thomas Boleyn had certainly aimed high for his younger daughter. I remembered Anne as a clever young women, well-educated, determined and considerably more circumspect than her sister.

Cardinal Wolsey had arranged matters with scrupulous attention to detail. There was to be no advantage to either side. Even the ground where the pavilions were pitched must be of equal elevation. No-one should be able to look down on their enemy.

There was to be feasting and jousting and dancing and midsummer games, all arranged with perfect symmetry. The tournaments were organised by Lord Suffolk and Admiral Bonnivet with rules decided by a committee of French and English knights. An equal number of contestants was to be selected for each side so neither would have the upper hand.

The same equality applied to feasting. If Henry was to

host an intimate supper for the French king, then François must repay the compliment in his pavilion; and if Henry was to visit the French queen for a banquet with her ladies, then François must visit the English queen.

Queen Katherine's banquet was to take place in the huge palace which stood on the plain before the castle at Guisnes. Overnight, a magician had conjured up this magnificent edifice with walls of stone and a leaded roof which shimmered and glittered under the hot summer sun.

Yet it was a illusion, not what an observer might think. These were not real stones but timber, cleverly painted by a team of artists employed by the cardinal; and the roof was not real lead but specially oiled canvas. At each corner were vast towers topped by statues of the king's royal beasts and the archway to the interior of the palace was surmounted by the king's coat of arms and guarded by four golden lions. Outside on the green was a fountain with an antique gold Bacchus spewing wine and a Cupid whose bow was drawn, ready to strike unwary young people to love.

But these wonders were nothing compared to the gilded interior with its great glass windows. The inner court was so light it was like being outside in the open air. The upper rooms with their beautiful tapestries and gold ornaments, which a visitor might think would be dark, were bathed in colour from the sun's rays streaming through dozens of painted windows.

Every lady in the queen's train was required to be present at the banquet, all of us wearing our most exquisite gowns and hoods. There were rumours that the French considered their women more elegantly dressed than us while our men said the clothes worn by the French women were too revealing and singularly unfit for the chaste.

'Are there any chaste women at the French court?' the Countess of Oxford enquired pertly.

'Hush, Countess,' I said. 'King François is due any moment. This is neither the time nor the place for such an observation.'

'Of course you would know, wouldn't you, Lady Elizabeth. I've heard you were a great favourite at the French court.'

Before I could reply we heard trumpets sounding for the arrival of the French king.

Queen Katherine, clothed in garments covered in precious jewels and pearls, with an ornamented hood in the Spanish style covering her lovely abundant hair, played her part to perfection. She sat under an embroidered canopy opposite King François, with Cardinal Wolsey at one end of the table and Cousin Mary at the other.

The banquet was lengthy, the air stifling, the food rich and the wine plentiful. The cardinal had seen to it that the French king would be astonished at the sophistication of the English court. We were served a meat called turkey, which I'd not tasted before, and asparagus in a butter sauce, both novelties designed to impress. There were sweet wines from Anjou which were soothingly familiar. Queen Katherine was polite, the French king equally, almost disdainfully, courteous but conversation was minimal as we were entertained during the feasting by the choristers of the Chapel Royal .

When the last dishes were removed, King François, to

my horror, asked if he might have the honour of meeting the queen's English ladies. We had been warned this was a possibility but I'd prayed it would not happen. He'd have forgotten me and our encounter of that winter. He'd remember Mary, he'd spent many hours in her company but I was surely insignificant.

One by one, in order of precedence, we were ushered in front of the French king, our names announced by the Earl of Derby, leader of the queen's retinue.

First came the two duchesses, Mary as Duchess of Suffolk and Eleanor, Duchess of Buckingham. François spent several minutes talking to Mary and ended by kissing her lovingly on her lips. The middle-aged Duchess of Buckingham was treated to a few words, an incline of the royal head and a peck on the cheek.

On it went. A line of noble ladies, shimmering, curtseying, murmuring, blushing and in most cases treated to something more than mere politeness when it came to the royal kiss. The countesses and baronesses had drawn to one side, a few of them quite overcome by the closeness of their encounter with the handsome King of France.

'The Lady Elizabeth Grey,' announced Lord Derby, glancing at his list. 'Sister of Thomas Grey, Marquess of Dorset.'

I stepped forward and curtseyed. Then the royal hand indicated that I should rise. I kept my gaze lowered, praying he'd not remember. But my prayers were in vain.

'We meet again, Lady Elizabeth,' the royal voice said softly.

'Your Grace.'

He took my hand and drew me closer. I felt his hot breath on my cheek as he leant forward.

'Our bargain, it was not complete.'

I said nothing.

'I do not care to be insulted, my little English rose.'

'No, Your Grace.'

He kissed my lips softly, then murmured.' I shall send for you.'

I was like a woman in a trance as I backed away. What did he mean? How could he send for me? I was not his to command. I was under the protection of the English king. My heart was thumping and my mouth felt dry.

'What did he say?' the Countess of Oxford said eagerly.

'Nothing.'

'He told me I was an ornament to my husband's house.' She almost wriggled with pleasure at the memory. I guessed she received few kind words from her husband, who my sisters said was a wastrel.

I watched her whisper to the others while I tried to suppress the panic, the feeling of utter helplessness in the face of this imminent punishment for my sins. For punishment was clearly what King François had in mind and I knew exactly what form his retribution would take. He would call it the pleasurable seduction of a chaste young English lady but it would not be a seduction, it would be a violation for I would not be willing, not this time.

After King François and his immediate entourage had left, we retired to Guisnes. When designing this event the cardinal decided it was wiser for the ladies not to sleep on French soil so the vast Palace of Illusions had no bedchambers. For the gentlemen there were two dozen brightly coloured tents pitched on the plain but, like the queen and her ladies, the king and those closest to him retired at night to the castle. A covered walkway of rich red cloth embroidered with golden birds had been erected to allow us to pass safely from the palace to Guisnes although it was whispered there was also a secret tunnel, dug in case of French treachery.

For all the outward signs of friendship I knew nobody trusted the French. At their first meeting, Henry had worn a breastplate under his robes in case of some deceit by François. It was said the two kings cordially hated each other in spite of the elaborate politeness. There had been a difficult moment when one of Henry's heralds read out a proclamation beginning in the usual fashion, "I, Henry, by the Grace of God, King of England and France," – but trouble was averted when Henry, with his usual courtesy, said that for the duration of our visit he would be simply Henry, King of England.

The days passed and I began to relax my guard. Nobody would come for me, no minion would slide in with an invitation to meet with the French king, no French servant would come requesting my attendance at King François's golden pavilion. With Mary constantly in attendance on Queen Katherine there was no-one in whom I could confide my fears and it wasn't long before some of the others began to wonder why I was loath to venture outside. I excused myself saying the wind had blown dust in my eyes or the sun was too strong.

'Hotter than St Peter's in Rome,' Lady Carey announced.

'Twice yesterday I had to change my gown because of the dust,' the Countess of Oxford complained. 'You'd think they'd have chosen somewhere more sheltered. Why does the cardinal not pray for the wind to die down?'

The Duchess of Buckingham threw her a malevolent look as if criticism of the cardinal was a direct criticism of God.

'There is another tournament in the tiltyard,' said Lady Gertrude, the young Countess of Devon whose prominent blue eyes gave her the appearance of a startled fawn.

'The king will ride today. Queen Katherine has said we shall all attend and that means you too, Lady Elizabeth.' The stern-faced Duchess of Buckingham was looking at me.

The crowds surrounding the lists were the largest I'd seen. Not only were hundreds of English and French courtiers present but also thousands of servants, as well as people from nearby villages who'd come to view the fun. Nothing like this had been seen for as long as they could remember.

We sat with Queen Katherine in the English viewing gallery while opposite us was the tiny figure of Queen Claude, surrounded by her French ladies. The noise was tremendous and, because of the dust, it was not always possible to see what was happening. On a rise at the end of the lists were two huge trees of honour for the challengers' shields, one bearing Henry's emblem of the hawthorn and the other François's raspberry leaf.

A whisper rippled through our ranks that the French king had lost his golden pavilion last night, blown away by the wind. A sign from God, it was agreed, but exactly what it signified, nobody knew.

Courtesy and wisdom dictated that the two kings would not joust against each other but instead would each run the same number of courses. Some of the men were having difficulty in couching their lances because of the strong gusts of wind but, as if in obedience to some unheard royal command, the wind died as Henry took to the field. Six times he raced and six times he was successful, the combat so fast and furious that sparks flew off his armour. On the seventh run, he appeared to hurt his hand and had to retire.

'Did you know,' Lady Carey whispered, 'King François has a black eye.' She giggled as if the thought of the handsome King François so disfigured was a joke.

The day wore on until the final course was run and Lord Suffolk was announced winner for the afternoon. Now there would be feasting and dancing until the sun went down.

The dancing that night took place in a wonderful pavilion of red cloth where the two queens could sit side by side. Neither danced. Queen Katherine preferred to watch and Queen Claude was too near her time to dance, her belly proudly displayed beneath her gown as another symbol of King François's potency. She had already given him two boys, a feather in the cap of the French king and a poignant reminder to Queen Katherine of her own failure to give Henry a son.

In the strange summer twilight of northern France where night was held at bay by a pearly luminescence, no-one wanted the dancing to stop. But Queen Claude looked weary so Queen Katherine kindly suggested the queens should retire. This meant the ladies must also retire. I smiled and thanked my last partner, a rather exuberant Frenchman who could have done with some of Cousin Mary's dancing lessons, then took my place in the queen's procession behind Baroness Audley. Beside me was Lady Carey. She was flushed and looked a trifle disordered as if she'd been doing more than dancing.

Very slowly our procession moved past rows of bowing gentlemen, a phalanx of satin and brocade and velvet, fit to match our glittering gowns. As we made our way towards the covered walk which led to the castle, the cheering crowds, drunk on free wine, pushed forward enthusiastically, wanting a closer view of "Les Anglaises" and, if possible, a touch of a silk skirt. The guards had their hands full trying to keep the hordes of common people at bay and those of us at the tail end of the procession were in danger of being overwhelmed.

I was deafened by the roars of the crowd as a woman barged into us and Lady Carey stumbled. A man seized my arm and pulled me to one side. At first I thought he was trying to prevent me being crushed by the mob but as soon as he spoke I realised my mistake.

He had come for me.

There were two of them, both wearing the French king's livery. They'd not come to issue a polite invitation but were prepared to use force. I'd experienced brutal treatment at the hands of their sort before, in the bowels of the Hôtel de Cluny.

A large woman thrust herself in front of the smaller man and for a second he let go of my arm to steady himself.

"Run!" screamed a voice from my childhood. "Run!".

We were playing a game of tag in the fields at Astley and Cecily and I were being chased.

A gap opened up in front of me and without thinking, I dived through it, pushing aside anyone who got in my way.

I had no idea where I was or in which direction I was running. I just knew that if I didn't run I'd be caught. Two small pavilions loomed up on my left. I veered away from them, scared they might be part of the French king's domain. I was borne along by a moving mass of people, held up by shoulders and arms, caught between the coats of those in front and the press of people at my back. A large coarse-faced woman flashed me a grin. A small boy wriggled past my legs and to one side I heard the sound of singing, a lusty ballad, sung at the tops of people's voices.

After a couple of minutes the crowd thinned and I risked a glance behind me. Neither of my would-be captors were there. But a woman on her own in this company was at risk of the horrors we'd been warned about by our governesses – the voracious appetites of men! A florid-faced French gentleman decided I was an easy woman and made a grab for me saying something unrepeatable. I twisted away from his leering face and grasping hands and ran panting towards what I thought was Henry's Palace of Illusions. But I was mistaken. It was a large pavilion where a large number of Frenchmen were drinking themselves into a stupor. One of them was doubled up, vomiting onto the grass while his friends hooted with laughter. In front of me, barring my way, was a line of young women with skirts hoisted up round their thighs, singing and dancing. I tried pushing my way through but got kicked for my pains. By now I was exhausted, lost and frightened. In the melee, my skirts had become covered in mud, I'd lost my hood and, with no cap, my hair had come loose.

In the dark it was impossible to know where I was and there was no-one I dared ask. I wanted to weep but told myself to be brave. A group of young Frenchmen nursing a keg of beer as if it was a trophy, called out for me to join them, they could offer me some fun. Eager to get away, I tripped over two young women lying sprawled on the grass, laughing. I scrambled up, wiped my hands on my skirts and fled.

Nowhere could I hear an English voice just a babble of coarse French voices, shouting singing and uttering curses. A dog ran yelping through the crowd, chased by a horde of bare-footed boys carrying sticks. Someone was singing a bawdy French song I remembered from our days in Paris. Paris! I panicked in terror and ran the other way.

'Hé!'

Sainte Vierge! My pursuers! They shoved their way though the crowd and were almost on top of me.

I turned, ran, my heart thumping painfully, not caring where I was going and bumped straight into a solid figure in dark velvet. I tried to dodge round him but he put out both hands and grabbed me by the shoulders. I struggled, fighting as best I could, trying to pull away, but he had me held tight.

'You're quite safe, Lady Elizabeth,' said an unfamiliar voice.

'Those men!' I gasped, turning my head in the direction of my pursuers.

'They'll not harm you. Not with me and my men here.'

In my relief at hearing an English voice I collapsed against him. He was real. He was one of us. I was safe.

I would have wept over the front of his doublet had I not heard echoes of my mother's voice in my ear – a young lady never gives way to displays of unseemly emotion in front of a gentleman. Relief quickly gave way to embarrassment. I tried to move backwards but he refused to let me go, instead wrapping his arms tightly around me as one might a small child. I was pathetically grateful if not a little surprised.

'Who were they?' my rescuer enquired, releasing his grip.

'Servants of the French king,' I replied in a low voice.

'Indeed! And what did these servants of the French king want with you?'

I said nothing because I'd just realised this man had called me by my name. I glanced up at a vaguely familiar face. I'd seen him somewhere but that was unsurprising. Everyone of note from the English court was here at Guisnes and his clothes, if nothing else, marked him out as someone of means. Yet I was unable to put a name to the face.

'Forgive me, sir. You know my name but we've not been introduced so I do not know yours.'

He gave a short laugh. 'Kildare. Gerald Fitzgerald, Earl of Kildare.'

Now I remembered. The landing stage at Greenwich. January, when I was waiting for Leonard.

'Your pursuers?' he enquired.

'King François wishes to see me.'

A raised eyebrow. 'Does he indeed. An odd way to issue an invitation. I take it you do not wish to see him.'

'No, I do not.'

'May I ask why?'

I hesitated. 'It's complicated.'

He smiled as if my admission was amusing. 'Most things are, Lady Elizabeth.'

He looked at me as if waiting for an explanation.

'It's a very long story,' I said, reluctantly.

He looked around into the growing dusk where the flaming torches caused great pools of darkness between wavering circles of light. In the far distance I could just make out the outline of a castle.

'It's a long walk back to the safety of Guisnes. Perhaps a long story is what we need, Lady Elizabeth. In my experience a story is preferable to an awkward silence.'

I tried brushing bits of grass and dry mud from the front of my skirt but achieved little and my rescuer seemed uninterested in the state of my clothing.

'I broke a promise.'

'To King François?'

'Yes.'

He gave a throaty chuckle. 'Unwise.'

'I suppose it was.'

'May I ask what it was you had promised him or is that too private a matter for a lady to divulge?'

I was glad of the darkness because he was unable to see the blush staining my cheeks. Each time I thought of that encounter with François d'Angoulême, I squirmed with embarrassment; ashamed and puzzled at what I'd done. How could I have been so foolish, behaved so wantonly. I was not an empty-headed ninny like Bessie Blount, I was a well-educated young lady from one of the greatest families in the land.

'It was nothing really,' I said in a low voice. 'Just a business deal.'

'Hmm. It seems I have been away from court for too long. Were you buying or, if it is not too vulgar a word, selling?'

I flushed, wondering if he thought I'd been bargaining with François d'Angoulême for my virtue. Looking back at what had happened, even I wondered.

'He wanted me to acquire a piece of information for him. In return he would do me a favour.'

He had the good manners not to enquire as to the exact nature of either the business deal or the favour but I thought him the kind of man who might well cause a woman to forget herself and say more than was wise.

'You reneged on the deal.'

'I promised to return but did not.'

'And this was when?'

'Five, six years ago.'

For a minute he said nothing. I was aware of the half-dozen men in blue and green livery who walked at our side, booted, cloaked and, I suspected, discretely armed, a reminder of the underlying dangers in this vast gathering.

'An old grievance, then,' Lord Kildare said.

'From a past I thought gone forever.'

'Ah, Lady Elizabeth, the past is always with us. It consumes us and it seems His Most Christian Majesty has been nursing this grievance for a long time.'

'It was when I served my cousin, Mary, when she was Queen of France. Before King Louis died.'

'So you have a vast experience of the French court.'

'No, not vast. We were there for less than seven months although it felt much longer.'

We passed through the town gate into a steep winding street. There were houses on both sides, shuttered and silent; dusty cobbles hard beneath my feet. Ahead of us was the yawning entrance to the castle. To my surprise, I felt a pang of regret as if this solid representation of safety had arrived too soon, like a traveller interrupted before the tale of his adventures is told, a feast whipped away before I'd had time to sit down.

Lord Kildare was apparently not in a hurry. As we ambled slowly up towards the castle, his men dropped behind, matching their pace to their master's. I could hear their footsteps and the breathing of this man at my side. The noisy revellers in the Golden Valley sounded very far away.

He took my hand in his to help me up the steps. I was struck again how strong he was. At the sight of Kildare livery, the guards stepped back and the great wooden gates of the castle swung open.

'When two people talk they learn about each other. It is much like a business deal. I have learnt a great deal about you, Lady Elizabeth but have told you nothing about myself. It hardly seems fair. Is there anything you wish to know about me, any question you would like to ask?'

I thought of the thousand questions I might like to ask but in the end blurted out, 'Do you know about cannon and naval warfare, Lord Kildare?'

There was momentary hesitation as if he could not quite believe I'd asked such an odd question. Then he grinned.

'Are you thinking of starting a war?'

In the final two days of feasting and dancing, I kept close to the other ladies. I saw nothing more of Lord Kildare, not that I had a particular wish to meet him again but it would have been polite to express my thanks once more. On the Saturday, a solemn Mass was celebrated by Cardinal Wolsey. He was assisted by five fellow cardinals and twenty bishops with singing from choristers of both royal chapels. The kings embraced, the queens kissed and to my profound relief, after one more day of feasting, mumming and dancing, it was time to leave.

Our huge procession wound its slow way back to Calais where, in a series of meetings, Henry undid every agreement he'd made with King François. All the swearing of eternal friendship, of a lifetime of peace between England and France, counted for nothing and the betrothal of Henry's daughter to François's son was swiftly forgotten in the forging of a new accord with the queen's nephew. Little Princess Mary would marry her cousin, the emperor, notwithstanding that she was only four years old and he a young man of twenty. From now on we were to be allies of the emperor.

As I'd told Cousin Mary, kings are not be trusted because no ruler tells the truth.

16

BRADGATE MANOR
NOVEMBER 1520

Cecily might have wished for a bright spring morning on her wedding day. She might have wished to be marrying a young man high in the king's favour and I knew for a fact she'd dreamt of a wedding in the presence of their royal majesties. But none of this was hers to choose. Instead, a gloomy November morning with rain threatening was all that was on offer when we gathered at Bradgate for my sister's wedding to the Dudley heir.

Cecily's betrothal had been arranged long ago when Thomas saw an advantage in marrying his sister into the Dudley family. When a new king and a new regime rendered the connection less valuable, my brother found that Lord Dudley had sewn up the betrothal contract with unbreakable thread. My brother was not pleased.

In a new gown, smiling demurely and with a gentle blush on her cheeks, Cecily made an enchanting bride. Her husband was dressed like one of Henry's peacocks, his outfit rivalling those seen on the noble Duke of Buckingham. I reckoned at this rate he'd run through Cecily's dowry before the next Dudley heir was tucked up safe in his cradle.

During the celebrations everyone behaved as if the match was all they could have wanted. Even my mother had opened her purse and provided a suitably valuable wedding gift for the couple. But it was impossible to miss the costly pearl buttons on our stepfather's new embroidered satin doublet or the heavy gold chain on his shoulders, both recently purchased for him by my mother.

Queen Katherine had given me three weeks absence for my sister's wedding, aware of how tiresome journeying could be in November with short days and early dusks. Time had rushed by and now there was only one day left before I must leave.

'You're wanted!'

A voice disturbed my contemplation of a long slow journey back down the muddy roads to London. It was my brother, John.

'Who wants me?'

He grinned. 'Thomas. There's to be a family conference.'

'What for?' I called after him as he loped away but got no reply.

Out of habit I made the usual check: hair, face, gown, shoes, all clean and in good order. Then I hurried to Thomas's room where to my surprise two sturdy liveried servants stood guard at the door like a pair of hounds protecting a meaty bone.

The door was opened and I saw my mother sitting at the head of a table surrounded by a full complement of male Greys. Today she was no less grandly dressed than she'd been at the marriage celebrations, wearing embroidered crimson velvet with white satin billowing where the sleeves were slashed. Beside her, drab in an unbecoming ash-grey gown with black sleeves, sat Meg

Wooton who, in contrast to my mother, resembled a tame hooded crow waiting for crumbs. I was somewhat surprised to see Meg as Thomas tended to disregard his wife where family matters were concerned. Her position on a stool next to my mother indicated a rise in her status since giving my brother a son and heir.

Thomas stood near the hearth where he had a commanding view of everyone. He was still wearing his best clothes, the one's he'd worn at yesterday's ceremony which made me wonder if he'd been to bed or had he spent the night planning what to say. Family conferences were rare events, Thomas preferring to select his victims for evisceration one at a time with no witnesses and no impertinent supporters for the accused.

I glanced round but there was nowhere for me to sit so concluded I was expected to stand. Thomas looked slightly drunk but perhaps it was only firelight colouring his cheeks, he'd hardly need wine for courage, not when facing his family.

'I have received certain information,' he began.

My stomach lurched as I remembered my last encounter with Francis Bryan shortly after our return from Calais. Like all my encounters with the dangerous Sir Francis, there had been an undercurrent of flirtatiousness and a certain amount of teasing innuendo which a couple of times had bordered on rudeness so extreme I'd had to administer a sharp rebuke. This had encouraged him to suggest something so utterly disgusting that I'd walked away. Had somebody seen us and told my brother?

My mother looked completely unruffled but I'd become used to her being privy to everything I did and if Thomas had secrets to reveal, she probably knew them already. I doubted even Wolsey had a spy network to rival my mother's and we all knew Wolsey was all-seeing and all-knowing, the better to further his master's concerns.

'Are we to know more?' my mother enquired. 'Or must we guess?'

'The Earl of Kildare has made me an offer,' Thomas said pompously as if he'd just been offered the papacy.

At the name of my rescuer from Guisnes I raised my head. What did Lord Kildare want with my brother.

'What kind of offer?' John said, fiddling with the buttons on his jacket.

'He wishes to ally himself to our family. He sees my support in the council as invaluable.'

'Money?' John was permanently short of ready cash.

Thomas looked as if raising the question of money was in bad taste. 'Marriage,' he said coldly. 'He wishes to marry Elizabeth.'

This time my heart leapt. An offer!

'Garret Og,' my mother remarked.

'What in God's name are you talking about, old woman?' Thomas was easily irritated by my mother.

'It's what the Irish call him,' Leonard explained. 'Gerald the younger. The father was Garret Mor, the great earl.'

Thomas frowned at Leonard. 'It's unimportant what he's called by the bog Irish. What matters is, do we wish to risk involving ourselves with Kildare?'

'Too big a risk for a small man,' my mother mused, half to herself.

'What do we know of him?' John asked.

'Lord deputy in Ireland,' Leonard replied.

Thomas hated being interrupted yet none of my brothers was frightened of him the way my sisters and I were.

'For the moment Kildare is lord deputy in Ireland but I happen to know the king is minded to replace him.'

'Won't work,' said my mother.

Thomas, glared at her. 'The king has sent Thomas Howard to Ireland as Lord Lieutenant. The Irish are to be persuaded to peace.'

My mother snorted. 'Peace!. Since when was a Howard in favour of peace. All they know is fighting.'

I remembered the furious row between Lord Kildare and Thomas Howard on the landing stage at Greenwich and agreed with her, though I'd not dare say so.

'Thomas Howard has taken more than a thousand men.' Leonard's conversations with Lord Norfolk's heir had clearly been of use.

John whistled through his teeth. 'By St George! That's some army.'

My mother chuckled. 'Henry should learn the lessons of the past.'

Thomas bent over and hissed at her, 'Mind your tongue old woman or you'll find yourself in Wolsey's sights. He's got his eyes on Buckingham. We don't want him questioning your loyalties.'

'The Irish are said to be a quarrelsome race,' Dickon remarked, opening his mouth for the first time.

John gave his younger brother a well-aimed kick. 'How would you know?'

Thomas glared at both of them. 'The king is said to retain a fondness for Kildare from his youth. They were friends.'

'Nonsense!' my mother said. 'Kildare was Arthur's friend.'

There was silence at the mention of Henry's brother, the prince who died, the young man who would have been king and who'd been married to Queen Katherine.

'Henry favoured him,' Thomas said firmly. 'The question is, does he favour him now? We cannot have our family name hitched to a falling star.'

Lord Kildare had not struck me as a man who would tumble from the heavens but I knew nothing of what went on in the king's council and less than nothing about the cardinal's plans for Ireland or anywhere else. All I knew was that agreements were made by kings only to be broken, and betrothals of young women were bartered away for a more promising prospect. But still – it *was* an offer.

'What is Kildare accused of?' John asked.

'Maladministration; usurping royal authority.'

'King of Ireland,' my mother said, smiling. 'That's what they called the old earl.'

'Yes,' Thomas hissed. 'It landed him in the Tower.'

'It did,' my mother said equably, 'until Henry's father found he couldn't manage Ireland without the old man. Tried to bind his hands. Didn't work. Never does.'

Thomas chose to ignore my mother. 'Kildare has just been released from the Tower.'

My heart bumped again. I felt peculiarly distressed at the thought of Lord Kildare shut in the Tower.

'What was the charge?' John enquired.

'Making trouble for Thomas Howard,' Leonard told him.

Thomas frowned. 'Kildare is anxious to find friends at court. If there's trouble again, he'll need support.'

'Why should there be trouble?' Dickon was unable to follow the threads of the conversation.

Leonard smiled. 'Oh, how ill-informed you are, little brother. Kildare is suspected of sending messages to his men in Ireland. He is trying to undermine Thomas Howard and, when the king finds out, he'll not be best pleased.'

'He should make Henry laugh,' my mother said. 'That's what the old earl did, made Henry's father laugh. Found himself reinstated as lord deputy in no time at all. Tell Lord Kildare to make Henry laugh.'

Thomas glared at my mother. 'Don't be ridiculous.'

My mother's eyes sparkled with malice the way they did when she managed to rile Thomas. 'There are some men who have no sense of humour, who fail to be amused in any way, who cannot even see how foolish they are themselves. Perhaps they are the greatest fools of all.'

'Has Kildare spoken to Elizabeth?' Leonard asked, changing the subject as he noted the danger signs of a full scale battle between our mother and her eldest son.

All of them turned to look at me.

'Well! Has he?' Thomas said.

I bit my lip, wondering what, if anything, he knew of my ordeal last summer in France.

'I have only met Lord Kildare once,' I said quietly. 'At Guisnes. He said nothing.'

The suspicion in my mother's eyes was unmistakeable. She knew there was more to my encounter with this Garret Og than I'd said but she kept her own counsel and said not a word.

'He made no mention of marriage?' Thomas persisted.

'No, but...'

'But what?'

I hesitated, unsure if Mary Boleyn's foolish prattling was worth sharing, then decided that Thomas had a right to know. 'Lady Carey says Lord Kildare is to marry her sister.'

Dickon looked bewildered. 'Who is Lady Carey?'

'William Carey's wife,' John said with a leer. 'Very obliging!'

'She is Sir Thomas Boleyn's elder daughter,' I replied.

'Kildare has no use for a Boleyn daughter,' Thomas said firmly.

Leonard sucked his teeth, clearly knowing more than he was prepared to say.

Thomas's gaze moved round the room. 'Well, what shall we do? Is the risk too great? Wolsey claims Kildare has overstepped the bounds of his governance and the council may well agree. There have been plenty of complaints coming out of Dublin these past few years. Kildare is seen as a useful man who has the support of both the Irish and the great lords but the king is not in the mood to forgive anyone who trespasses on his royal authority.'

'Brandon says the king mistrusts everyone.' Leonard had made it his business to befriend Lord Suffolk which was a wise move as Henry confided in his friend.

'Brandon should watch his own back,' Thomas growled. 'He's an ass. Henry has not forgotten his disobedience in marrying his sister.'

Leonard disagreed. 'Their bond is deep. Henry loves him and Brandon will not step out of line again.'

Thomas, as always, was irritated at being contradicted.

'Nonetheless, we must be careful. I've warned our stepfather to keep his distance from his brother. Buckingham is treading a dangerous path and we cannot afford to be associated with him in any way.' He glared straight at my mother. 'An unfortunate match, would you not say, madam?'

My mother smiled sweetly. 'A match which gives me a great deal of pleasure but then you are a cold man, Thomas, and know nothing of the warmth that a good man can bring to a woman of mature years.'

My eyes darted from one to the other. All those lectures on how marriage was for the benefit of family, that a woman's feelings were of no importance; yet here she was hinting that she'd married for marital warmth.

Warmth was far from Thomas's mind as he tried to calculate the benefit of having Lord Kildare as a brother-in-law.

'What d'you say, Leonard?'

'I say we go ahead. Kildare is clever. He'll worm his way back into Henry's favour.'

'John?'

'I agree. It's worth the risk.'

'Dickon?'

'Yes.'

'We shall have to obtain Henry's permission for the marriage and money will need to be laid out, but if we're prepared to wait for the rewards of the connection, then I'll speak with Lord Kildare when I return to London. In the meantime we must be careful what we say.'

'And Elizabeth?' my mother enquired.

'What of Elizabeth?'

'Should she not make the acquaintance of the man she is to marry.'

'She has already met him.'

My mother sighed. 'You are obtuse, my lord marquess. A man must be kept interested unless you want your fish to wriggle off the hook.'

'I'd let the lovely Lady Carey wriggle on my hook anytime she likes,' John murmured to Dickon with a grin.

Thomas glared at John 'It is not Elizabeth who is bait for Lord Kildare, it is our family name and our help in his troubles with Wolsey.'

'All the more reason for them to become acquainted,' my mother said. 'Or do you doubt your sister's ability to catch and keep a man.'

Every eye on the room was turned to me.

'She's remarkably pretty,' said Dickon warmly, earning himself a sisterly smile.

'Takes more than looks to keep a man interested,' John said with a smirk.

I'd have done better to ignore his rudeness but I was tired of being belittled by John. 'What would you have me do, brother – offer him favours?'

'Elizabeth!' my mother snapped. 'Be silent! And you, John, mind your tongue.'

'I shall arrange a meeting,' Thomas sighed wearily as if the chore was really too much trouble. 'Christmas will soon be here. Nobody will notice.'

I was unsure why this meeting had to be secret and why my mother considered a man who had offered to marry me needed to be kept interested, as if our family name was insufficient.

My mother swept past me in a waft of perfume from the folds of her skirts. At the doorway she turned and beckoned.

'Elizabeth. I need to speak with you.'

Obediently I followed, walking at her heels through one sumptuous room after another until we reached her apartments which were some of the finest at Bradgate.

I waited quietly while she sent her servants out of the room and then settled herself in the large carved chair with broad arms which had once belonged to my father. My mother complained that Bradgate was cold and my brother mean with his logs but I thought her room stuffy and overheated with a huge fire burning merrily in the hearth.

She watched me carefully for a minute before speaking. 'You should not fear your big fish will swim into deep waters and be swept away. I remember him as a boy: steadfast, never one to break his word, loyalty once given was constant. If he has made an offer for you, he will abide by it.'

'I thought him kind.'

My mother gave a wintry smile. 'Kind or not, makes no difference. Your brother has decided you shall marry him so you must be prepared.'

I imagined a wardrobe of gowns and rooms of gold plate, like the ones Cousin Mary had made ready for the wedding in Calais and the betrothal which Henry ordered her to break.

'Might he change his mind?'

'Your brother or Lord Kildare?'

'My brother,' I said quietly.

'No. He lacks imagination. He has one prey in sight. For him that is sufficient.'

Did Lord Kildare also have only one prey in his sights. Everything had been decided before I'd been aware there was a decision to make. I wondered if our meeting in Guisnes had decided him or if his plan to ally himself to our family had been made earlier. Was I part of the bargain or would any of my sisters have done as well. It was foolish in the extreme to think I was of importance. Vanity, Cecily would have said. Yet every young woman likes to think her betrothed a little in love with her and Gerald Fitzgerald, Earl of Kildare might well prove worthy of the investment.

'You remember I waned you what could happen in France,' said my mother, watching me as if she could read every thought which ran through my mind.

'Yes, Lady Mother, and you were right.'

Her lips twitched. 'Naturally I was right. So listen carefully to what I shall tell you now.'

She indicated that I should sit on the stool at her feet which was a mark of favour. Usually I was expected to stand during these interviews.

'You have seen the king's beasts?'

Henry had a wonderful collection of wild beasts in the Tower, given by foreign princes seeking to lure the English king to their side with impressive and unusual gifts.

'I went with Cousin Mary when I was first at court. We saw a lion, and a tiger with stripes on its skin.'

My mother nodded. 'So you know of their savagery, the sharp teeth and cruel claws which can rip a person apart. Men like to pretend they are civilised but they are more like the king's beasts than you can imagine. I have known five kings and none of them was more civilised, more princely, more magnificent than Henry and none was more dangerous.'

'Mother!'

She gave a short laugh. 'You think I am mistaken. You think my wits addled because I am old and faded. You are wrong. Henry is a young beast who is discovering his power. He is beginning to sees danger everywhere and when a beast sees danger, it lashes out. The years of the merry king are coming to an end and it is a wise woman who takes her future into her own hands.

'What should I do?'

'Embrace this marriage. Let Lord Kildare take you to Ireland away from Henry's court. And do not come back.'

'Never?'

'Listen to me. When I married your father I thought I'd be safe for the rest of my life. My stepfather was the York king's greatest friend and my husband was the York queen's eldest son. I was an heiress, a young woman to be envied. We kept close to the royal court so that your father could progress. But the days of glory did not last. Men proved treacherous. The Tudor invaded and took the throne from the last of the sons of York and we were no longer safe.'

'That was a long time ago, Lady Mother.'

'It was yesterday,' she said bitterly.

She sat staring at the logs which had crumbled to ash as if the answers to our problems could be found somewhere in the white-hot depths of the fire.

17

GERALD FITZGERALD, EARL OF KILDARE
CHRISTMAS 1520

The meeting that Thomas had arranged with such care took place in the middle of the Nativity festivities at Windsor. My sister-n-law Meg acted as chaperone because Thomas feared a maidservant gossiping about a private conversation. After an hour's increasingly panicked deliberation, I wore a low-cut green gown with furred oversleeves turned back almost to he shoulder. Meg said my plain white kirtle with tight sleeves gathered at the wrist in a pleated frill, was an inspired choice, making me look younger than my years.

'Should you not wear a French hood?'

'The queen prefers her ladies to wear the Spanish hood,' I replied, wondering if Meg was right and was there time to run back to my room and change.

'You look lovely in either,' she said generously.

I sat in the window embrasure with a book in my lap, the image of a dutiful, educated young woman, though in truth I had no idea what I was reading. Meg had given me the book to hold, telling me the sight his betrothed industriously studying was sure to impress Lord Kildare. A weak winter sun, low in the sky, filtered through the small glass panes of the window, painting the floor with lozenges of glittering gold.

'Lady Elizabeth!'

He was standing in front of me. I glanced up, then immediately lowered my gaze to my lap.

'May I join you?' His voice was as I remembered: deep and measured with a slight accent that marked him as a man who'd stayed a long time away from England.

I moved slightly to one side and indicated where he might sit.

He was a large man, not bulky like Charles Brandon but not slender like Francis Bryan. When seated he was a solid bulwark at my side, a comforting presence if I'd not been so nervous. Being careful not to stare, I noted a plain black doublet, a hint of white linen shirt at neck and wrist and a narrow gold chain over a pair of broad shoulders.

'I understand you have been informed of my offer.' His voice was neutral, betraying nothing of his feelings.

'I have,' I replied, thinking perhaps I should say more. Cecily would certainly have said more.

'Do you find the offer to your liking?'

I gave a small smile. 'Lord Kildare, I do not know you so I cannot say. My brother has expressed his wish that I marry you and I am a dutiful sister.'

He looked somewhat taken aback at my reply. Perhaps he'd expected a flood of gratitude.

'Lady Elizabeth, forgive me. I am sadly out of practice at this. It is many years since I courted a young lady.'

'Were you successful when you went a-courting? Was the lady agreeable?'

He smiled a little ruefully. 'We were both young and awkward with each other. Neither of us had a choice in the matter of our betrothal. It was arranged by the old king. But yes, we made a good enough pretence of courtship.'

'You married her?'

'She was my wife for fourteen years and we were happy enough. She died three years ago.'

'And now you seek a new wife.'

'As a man must.'

I thought of the courtships I'd observed over the years: idle flirtations between the king's gentlemen and young women at court; the stiffness of young couples with no particular liking for each other but forced by their families to marry; the pursuit of foolish girls by men with no thought of marriage, and, in Paris, the passionate courtship of Cousin Mary and Charles Brandon.

'You have more experience in the matter of wooing than me, Lord Kildare. All I know is what I see at court. A man writes verses to a young women he likes, he praises her eyes, her smile, her wit. He flirts a little. Is that courtship?'

'Alas Lady Elizabeth, I have no skill with the pen.'

'You cannot write?' My eyes flew wide open in surprise.

He laughed. 'I expressed myself badly. I mean I have no skill to write verse.'

I smiled in return. 'And I no desire to read what foolish young men care to write.'

He frowned. 'Do many young men send you verses?'

'One or two. Also small gifts. But I send them back. You need not fear that I have compromised myself.'

'Lady Elizabeth, I know exactly how far you have compromised yourself. You told me so at Guisnes.'

I felt my cheeks grow hot. I'd no wish to discuss my indiscretions with this man or with anyone else. They belonged in the past, a past I would rather forget. I thought quickly to ask him a question.

'My brother has told me nothing of you, Lord Kildare: your worth, your ancestry, your place at court. These are not considered matters of concern to a young woman; but I should like to know about your family. Where did they come from?'

'Not from the forests and bogs of Ireland if that's what's worrying you,' he said with a grin.

'You are not Irish?'

'The Fitzgeralds are descended from a Norman lord and a Welsh princess. We are distant kin to the Tudors.'

'Distant kin?'

'Like yourself, Lady Elizabeth; not as royal we might like to be.'

I flushed, embarrassed at the way Thomas presumed a close kinship to Henry when we were only half-blood kin.

'And the Norman lord?'

'His name was Gerald. He came with Strongbow.'

'Who was Strongbow?'

'The de Clare earl of Pembroke who conquered Ireland for the second Henry.'

'That was a very long time ago.'

'We Fitzgeralds like to remember our origins, not hide them. I have rhymers in my hall who tell stories of our glorious past so the young do not forget. '

I imagined a vast gathering like the ones at Windsor when Henry ordered stories sung by his minstrels.

'You have children?'

'Five – four girls and a boy.'

'And you seek a mother for them?'

'I seek a wife.'

He was so direct I felt flustered.

'Do your children not wish for a mother?'

'They do, especially the girls.'

'And you?'

'I want you, Lady Elizabeth. Forgive me if you find me plain-spoken but I think it wise to be blunt in these matters. It is a long time since I was in England and I have few pretty manners any more. There are several women who I'm sure would make admirable mothers for my children but only one woman I wish to marry.'

'Lord Kildare, you do not know me. How can you be certain?'

'Oh, I am certain.'

My sisters said I had no need to worry as my brother would ensure I was well provided for and properly protected but I feared my dowry would feature more prominently in Thomas's mind than anything else. At Guisnes Lord Kildare was surrounded by his men but I had no idea how wealthy he was or if he could mount a suitable guard for his wife.

'Do you keep an army, Lord Kildare?'

My question caused him a great deal of amusement. When he finished laughing, he said, 'My house in Dublin has a guard of musketeers and I have enough cannon to blow down the castles of my enemies. Does that satisfy you, Lady Elizabeth?'

'Do you have many enemies?'

'There is not a man in Ireland without enemies and

the greater the man, the greater the number of enemies he acquires.'

'My brothers tell me that in Ireland you are a great lord.'

'I am.'

So no false modesty. I liked him all the more for that little flash of pride for why should a man not be proud of his achievements. I thought of Thomas Howard gone to Ireland with an army, of the musketeers and cannon, and of Lord Kildare's enemies conspiring to pull him down in his absence.

'Forgive me but I know little of Ireland. I hear it is a long way away.'

He smiled. '*Terra Incognita.* An island below the distant horizon. Further than Paris, as far away as Cologne and a foul journeying. Not even the king's council know much of Ireland. Why should they? To them it is of no importance.'

'But it is important to you.'

'It is home.'

'And the people?'

'As here – friends and enemies.'

'Should a great man not make peace with his enemies or does he crush them beneath the heel of his boot?'

He smiled. 'You're a very bloodthirsty young woman, Lady Elizabeth. No other woman talks to me of battle other than my daughter Alice. She would be a soldier if she could.'

His voice softened as he spoke of this child of his.

'How old is Alice?'

'She is ten years old.'

'And your other children?'

'My eldest Cathleen is eleven and my two younger girls are five and six. Tom, my son is eight.'

'You would wish me to be a mother to them.'

'If it pleases you. I know it would please them, although Tom, like all small boys, believes he has no need of a mother. He was four when my wife died. Children of four wall up their grief.'

'Do you have brothers and sisters?'

'More than you, I think. I have five brothers and four sisters.'

Now it was my turn to smile. 'You are mistaken, sir. I have four brothers and six sisters.'

'How fortunate we both are, surrounded by family to keep us warm when the chill winds blow.'

Lord Kildare's family might provide him with warmth and comfort but mine were mostly cold, distant or openly hostile.

'Do your brothers live in Ireland?'

'They do.'

'And your sisters?'

'Yes. You must understand how it is for the Fitzgeralds. My father married his daughters carefully, some to important Gaelic chiefs like the McCarthy and the great O'Neill of Ulster, others to lords like us who look to England.'

'There are other great lords in Ireland?'

'There are, but not as great as the Fitzgeralds of Kildare. There are the Desmond Fitzgeralds who are kin and Piers Butler of Polestown who is married to one of my sisters and hopes to be Earl of Ormonde.'

'I believe I have heard of Piers Butler.'

'A thorn in my side, like all Butlers.'

'Why a thorn? He is your sister's husband. Or do you quarrel for fun?'

'No, not for fun. There has been enmity between Fitzgeralds and Butlers since before I was born. The marriage was made to heal the rift.'

'Like my cousin Mary's marriage to King Louis, designed to keep peace between old enemies.'

'Indeed, we are old enemies. It is a familiar story. We Fitzgeralds were supporters of the White Rose, the sons of the Duke of York, while the Butlers supported the Lancastrian king. There was no common ground between us and when Henry Tudor took the throne my father would not give up the fight. He supported a young man he believed was the rightful king and many of our men paid with their lives for what some said was an act of folly.'

'That was a long time ago.'

'It was yesterday,' he said in an echo of my mother's words.

'And that is why you quarrel with your brother-in-law.'

'Partly, but just now it is more complicated and not something you need to know.'

'Lord Kildare, I trust that if we marry you will confide in me, else you would find me of very little use.'

'Lay Elizabeth, if I had my way I would marry you this minute but I cannot ask you to join yourself to an exile.'

My heart jumped in a most odd way. I told myself this was only a preliminary meeting, not yet a binding contract, no matter his eagerness for me to commit.

'Exile?' I said, hoping he'd not notice how my voice faltered.

'I cannot return to Ireland until Henry allows me to resume my office as lord deputy. Until he does, I have no power and my enemies will try to tear me apart.'

'Will the king be magnanimous?'

He grinned. 'I may have to endure a few more spells in the Tower until he sees reason.'

'You make the Tower sound something to be feared.'

'It is. I was twelve years old when I saw the young earl of Warwick brought out from the Tower and beheaded on the orders of Henry's father. And it was Henry himself who had Edmund de la Pole executed. Edmund had spent seven years in the Tower. So yes, it is a fearsome place.'

'Were you kept in a dungeon?' I was curious as I knew little of the Tower other than as a royal residence we occasionally visited.

He laughed. 'No Lady Elizabeth. My accommodation was eminently suitable for a man of my rank. I had books and pen and paper, and a servant to bring me meals and a change of linen. And there was a fine view from the window of the green where they execute traitors.'

I sensed he was not being completely truthful. Knowing the fate of other men, he must have had slivers of doubt; gut-churning moments when he feared a short walk down the winding stone stairs and onto the green might be his last.

'If you do not think the question too intrusive, may I ask what misdeed deserved such a severe punishment?'

'I sent a few letters, stirred up a bit of trouble, nothing much.'

'What kind of trouble?'

'The kind that Thomas Howard does not like. He has

taken a thousand men to Ireland but will find it is not enough so will ask for more.'

'Is that what you want?'

He laughed again. 'Yes! Henry will refuse. He will not agree to Thomas Howard's demands because he has more than one eye on France. He will not commit his men to an Irish war they cannot win against an army he does not understand. He is cautious when it comes to Ireland. It is a problem he has not encountered before. The old king discovered he could not govern Ireland without my father and Henry will find the country can only be governed by me. The Fitzgeralds are the most powerful force in Ireland. We have more supporters, more men under our command, more lords who have sworn vassalage to us. No Englishman issuing orders from a castle in Dublin will succeed in keeping peace without us on his side.' He smiled. 'My price for co-operation is high.'

'Oh.'

'Lady Elizabeth, forgive me, I did not mean to speak to you of insurrection and my sojourn in the Tower. I believe young ladies prefer gentler talk. Shall I tell you about my home which I hope one day soon will be your home?'

I smiled at his assumption that I was a fragile young lady who needed gentle handling. 'That would be very pleasant.'

'You will find in my house at Maynooth the kind of home you are well used to. I have many servants and my children stay there because it is safe. I have a library of books and old manuscripts and am building a college. I see you enjoy reading. Though,' he reached out and took the book from my lap and turned it round, 'I think if you hold your book this way up you will find the words make more sense.'

I glanced up to find him laughing at me. He knew perfectly well the book was a prop in a pretty tableau designed for his benefit. He had not for one moment been deceived. I bit my lip and lowered my gaze to the offending book, hoping the heat in my cheeks did not betray me.

'I have something else you may like, Lady Elizabeth. I have the finest stable in the whole of Ireland. When you come to Maynooth you shall choose a mount for yourself.' He leant closer. 'I would not say this to the king but I wager my horses are finer than any he keeps in the royal stables.'

I smiled, remembering how proud the keen horseman Henry, was of his favourite, a sprightly bay named Governatore.

'Perhaps you should send the king a gift of one of your best horses.'

We talked a little longer about the pleasures of his home, then he rose to make his farewell.

'One thing more, Lady Elizabeth,' he said, taking my hand and speaking in a low voice. 'If you are tempted by a young man who writes pretty verses, whose words make your heart beat faster and your pulses race; if his touch should make your eyes grow hazy with desire, then I pray you will let me know.'

I looked up somewhat startled out of the pleasant reverie his words had evoked. 'Why? What would you do?'

'Throw you up on my saddle and ride off with you to *Tir na nÓg*.'

'Is that another of your castles?'

He grinned. 'To the Irish, *Tir na nÓg* is a paradise, the

land of everlasting youth where bloom is on every bough and the air is heavy with the sweetness of orchards.'

'Like Utopia.'

'Utopia is more rooted in Thomas More's own ideas and leaves little to a man's imagination.'

'Your imagination, sir, would earn you another spell in the Tower.'

'Oh but Lady Elizabeth, it would be worth it.'

Despite his assertion that he was no versifier, I thought Gerald Fitzgerald, Lord of Kildare, a man well able to conjure words out of the air to sprinkle in the lap of a young woman and thus capture her unsuspecting heart.

18

WESTTHORPE MANOR
WINTER 1521

I saw nothing more of my erstwhile suitor throughout the cold days of January, when frost nipped at my toes and there was little to entertain us. When the queen announced she would make a pilgrimage to Walsingham, I thought it nothing more than another wearisome diversion. Then I remembered that Lord Suffolk's house at Westhorpe was only a few miles from our route through Bury St Edmunds, so I asked if I might make the short journey to see the Duchess of Suffolk. I could, the queen said kindly, stay for a week or so if I wished. I quickly penned a note to Cousin Mary asking if I might visit, hoping the intrusion would not be inconvenient.

It was an uncomfortable five days jogging along winter roads in Queen Katherine's train, accompanied by a small group of shivering women, all wondering why the queen had chosen January to fulfil her holy vow to pray for a son at the shrine of Our Lady at Walsingham. We were greeted each morning by a cold red sun peeping over the horizon and a queen's guard who looked as if they'd prefer a return to the warmth and camaraderie of Greenwich.

We travelled up the Great North Road to St Albans, then very slowly on to Baldock and Cambridge and lastly to Bury St Edmunds where I made my farewells to the queen and received her blessing. The others wished me safe from all ills, a sour note of envy creeping into their voices. My journey would end before the day was out in the comfort of Westhorpe whereas they had to endure four more days of misery on the road before reaching Walsingham.

I'd been to Lord Suffolk's grand house at Southwark many times but this was my first visit to Westhorpe. My small escort and I clattered over a three-arched bridge which spanned the moat and rode slowly up to the house. I climbed gingerly down from my horse and passed the reins to one of the Westhorpe grooms, gazing with undisguised curiosity at Mary's country home. It was a stately enough house, set low amidst the rolling landscape of Suffolk but nothing like the royal palaces where Mary and I had lived together. It was certainly not Greenwich and in no way did it resemble the Hôtel des Tournelles in Paris. It was a house for a woman who was no longer an English princess or a French queen, a house which reminded me disconcertingly of Bradgate.

As I climbed up the steps, the door opened and there in the hall waiting to greet me was Mary accompanied by her two stepdaughters. Charles Brandon had placed his daughters from his first marriage into Mary's care and the arrangement had worked well. The young women had a mother to guide them and Mary had companionship when her husband was away at court, which seemed to be most of the time. The elder must be sixteen or so, quite old enough to be a friend to Mary, the younger about ten.

After we'd dined, the young women offered to fetch the little ones and ran off gleefully to the nursery.

'I cannot imagine life here without them.' Mary said tenderly, watching her stepdaughters laughing together as they hurried out of the room.

'You have your own children now.'

'Yes, but they are young and there is not much conversation to be had with a five-year-old.'

The three small Brandons were shown off like a trio of performing dogs, reciting words they'd been taught or, in the case of two-year-old Eleanor, demonstrating her newly acquired skill of bobbing a curtsy. Harry, the eldest, was a shy slender boy of six with an unhealthy pallor but the middle child Frances was sturdy and intelligent, a five-year-old quite capable of holding a conversation. She said she'd wished to go to court with her father but her mother could not spare her. 'It is a shame for I should do very well,' she confided.

Once the children had been returned to the nursery and Mary's stepdaughters, with great reluctance, departed to attend to their duties, Mary and I settled down to exchange our news. Hers was mainly domestic, the small everyday doings of a wife left in the country with her children, though she was more entertaining than Meg Wooton who enjoyed leading you through every detail of a daily conversation with her steward.

'Do you not miss your life at court?' I asked.

'Sometimes, but I am content here and Henry invites me to court for grand occasions.'

'You do not regret your marriage, the life you might have lived as the wife of some great prince?'

She smiled. 'Not for one moment do I regret marrying Brandon.'

'Even though it cost you your jewels, your plate and your place at Henry's side; even though it might have cost your husband his titles or his life.'

She shivered. 'We knew the risk.'

'Yet you went ahead.'

'I thought they meant to kill me. That horrible little room and those women with their hard cold eyes. I refused food for fear of poison but they said I must eat to nourish my unborn child. When I said there was no child, they laughed. Madame Louise would not leave me alone. She whispered the foulest of words in my ear until I wanted to scream. Brandon saved me.

'And it is enough?'

'Yes. But…'

I waited for some expression of regret. 'But?'

'I wish he were at Westhorpe more.'

'Does he not wish to come?'

'He does but knows it would be unwise to offend Henry. We owe everything to Henry. If he withdrew his favour I do not know what would become of us.'

I watched her, wondering where Henry's dazzling little sister had gone: the brave young princess who publicly broke her betrothal to the Emperor's heir, the bride who cocked her hat and blew a kiss to the king of France. Instead there was this woman, faded, powerless, resigned to her small estate and the absence of the man she professed to love.

'How can you bear it? The solitude, the smallness of everything.'

She looked surprised. 'You think it small?'

'I do.'

She smiled a little sadly. 'Perhaps, like all wives, I have become accustomed.'

In that moment I promised myself that no matter who I married, I would refuse to accept a life like this, with no company other than a houseful of servants and small children; my horizons limited to the surrounding woods and fields.

'Now,' said Mary, 'tell me your news.'

I told her about Lord Kildare and my brother's hope that a marriage might follow.

'You sound unsure? Is the marriage not to your liking?'

I hardly dared admit to myself how much it was to my liking, how fascinating I found Lord Kildare, how my heart thudded painfully whenever I thought of him.

'I fear he may not win back Henry's favour.'

'I know nothing of Ireland. Is the position of lord deputy an important one?'

'When his father was lord deputy they called him King of Ireland.'

Mary giggled. 'Oh Cousin Elizabeth, do not tell Henry.'

'I have told no-one but you.'

'How do they live? Has he a castle?'

'A fine one. Maynooth.'

She smiled at the unfamiliar name. 'Do they speak English or shall you have to learn Irish?'

'Gaelic. And no, at Maynooth people speak English.'

'Has he family?'

'Five children from his first wife and a string of brothers and sisters and cousins and nephews. He does not lack kin.'

'And when he is at court his children will be company for you as my stepdaughters are for me.'

'There is no court in Ireland unless it is where the lord deputy is,' I said firmly.

I refused to imagine a life where my husband would enjoy the pleasures of court while I languished in the country. I had no desire to be like my sister-in-law or like Cousin Mary. If my husband went to court, I would go too.

'Who is lord deputy now, if it is not Lord Kildare?'

'Thomas Howard is the king's lieutenant.'

Mary wrinkled her nose. 'I have no love for the Howards. Thomas Howard and his father urged Henry to have Brandon executed for treason for marrying me.'

'I thank God they did not succeed.'

'Amen,' Mary said devoutly.

I spent three weeks at Westhorpe, weeks in which we did very little other than gossip about times past or play with the children. On Sundays we walked to church and sat in the Brandon family pew and Mary promised that if only I would stay a little longer we would go to Bury St Edmunds for the Easter Fair where she would hold court in a tent of cloth-of-gold.

I remembered the day she rode out with Henry at Guisnes to dine with the French king in his magnificent golden pavilion, a dazzling figure in white satin with a flowing veil, the most beautiful lady in the land. I suspected the gentlefolk of Suffolk would settle for something less splendid: green brocade perhaps with a neat little French hood decorated with pearls.

When word arrived that it was time for me to make my way to rejoin the queen's train, I was sad to say farewell to Mary but more than ready to leave the stultifying boredom of country life where whole days passed when nothing happened, and Mary often repeated an anecdote she'd told me the day before. As I rode up the lane from Westhorpe towards Bury on that Thursday in the middle of February I gulped in great gasps of cold air as if finally I was free and able to breathe again. I smiled to myself and began to sing and soon the whole of my escort was singing with me. It was joyful but somehow I had a nagging feeling of sadness as if in leaving Mary, nothing would ever be the same again.

No sooner had I arrived back at Greenwich Palace than I was waylaid by Leonard. He scowled when he saw me.

'Where have you been? I've been looking everywhere.'

'At Westhorpe with Cousin Mary.'

My explanation was received with a frown. 'Next time you decide to absent yourself from court, you'd best let me know. Thomas is furious.'

'Why?'

'Lord Kildare has been ordered to appear before Star Chamber at Easter. We've had to lay out ten thousand marks on his promise.'

For a moment I wondered if that was what Lord Kildare's pursuit of me was all about – his need for ten thousand marks.

'That is a great deal of money.'

'A vast amount so you can imagine what it did to Thomas's temper to find you'd taken yourself off somewhere.'

'Why? I have no money.'

'Kildare has been ordered not to leave London and not send messages into Ireland without permission. Thomas expects you to ensure he does not slip away.'

'And how exactly would I stop him?'

'By being sweet and obliging.'

'You wish me to sit in a window in Southwark exposing my wares for all to see,' I said sharply. 'I am not a whore, Leonard, and will not be used as one to save Thomas's skin.'

Leonard laughed. 'Not his skin – his money. In no way would Thomas have agreed to support Kildare if he thought there was the slightest risk to his neck. He's far too careful. He felt the edge of the executioner's axe in Calais and once was enough. None of us expect you play the whore, Elizabeth, just talk sweetly and keep Kildare on the hook.'

Next day found me back in Thomas's room with one of my mother's elderly women as chaperone. Meg had apparently returned to the rural domesticity of Bradgate.

'Here we are again, Lady Elizabeth.'

My fish looked very much as he had at Christmas, a good solid man. His forthcoming appearance in front of the whole council did not seem to worry him unduly or else he was adept at concealing his fears.

I gave him an encouraging smile and settled down to charm him. It was remarkably easy as he was only too eager to succumb to my attempts at being the most delightful of young women at Henry's court.'

'Tell me about your first wife, Lord Kildare.'

He smiled, ready to be equally charming. 'She was a kinswoman of the old king, the daughter of Sir John

Zouche of Codnor, a little younger than me. It was an excellent match and she was a pleasant young woman. I like to think I was a good husband; certainly she made no complaints. I was sad when she died and had her buried beside my mother which would, I believe, have pleased them both. I loved my mother, but do not all sons love their mothers.'

The sentiments were conventional except I detected a note of real warmth in his voice when he spoke of his mother. She must have been much loved.

'I do not think the marquess loves our mother and I believe she has no liking for him.'

'And you?'

I was guarded in my reply lest he repeat what I said. 'I respect both my mother and my brother. I would be an ungrateful daughter and sister to do otherwise.'

He smiled as if hearing the truth behind my careful words. 'My mother was a good woman. She died when my father and I were kept in England. Some said it was from a broken heart.'

'Losing a mother is a great loss,' I said quietly, thinking of Cousin Mary's sorrow when Queen Elizabeth died.

My fish agreed. 'When I said farewell to my children I asked what they would like me to bring back from England. My daughter Alice, she must have been eight years old at the time, said she wanted a mother. When I asked did she have any particular advice because it was hard for a man to know what kind of mother she wanted, she said, a pretty one.'

I blushed at this back-handed compliment.

'Did you spend much time with your wife?'

'As much as most men.'

'Most men of my acquaintance spend very little time with their wives,' I said, thinking of Cousin Mary languishing at Westhorpe.

'Lady Elizabeth, you are not ignorant of the ways of the world. You understand that men have duties and often those duties keep them apart from their wives.'

'I would hope to be at my husband's side whenever possible.'

'In battle?'

'Perhaps not,' I conceded, 'but I would polish his armour.'

He took my hand in his. 'I shall teach you to fire a musket.'

'And a cannon?'

'I do not think you would like that. The exercise is filthy, noisy and dangerous.'

'When you were summoned to England, did...'

'My wife accompanied me to England.'

'I would not be left behind.'

'You would not.'

Amongst Henry's New Year gifts that year was a magnificent wine goblet in the latest fashion, engraved "With humble, true heart", given by my stepfather's brother, the duke of Buckingham.

'What does it mean?' I asked Leonard.

'Not what it seems.'

'Do you doubt the duke?'

'Wolsey does. He says Buckingham is gathering troops.'

I thought no more about what Leonard said and forgot our exchange until one day, soon after Easter, I heard the duke of Buckingham had been arrested. He had been on his way to Windsor and was now languishing in the Tower where he'd been charged with imagining and compassing the death of the king.

The shocking news spread like a chill wind through the palace, from the warmth of the queen's privy chamber to the claustrophobic rooms of young gentleman to the heat of the royal kitchens. People were scared, tiptoeing about as if walking on broken glass, avoiding anyone they feared might have had dealings with the noble duke, constantly alert for the sound of marching feet and the appearance of the royal guard.

Our family's close connection to the duke was a continuing worry and I was summoned by my brother and cautioned to be careful how I conducted myself.

Thomas indicated a man standing in the shadows by the hearth.

'Lord Kildare wishes to meet with you again. I have said you may walk together in the inner privy garden. You will be in full view of others so there can be no suggestion of anything untoward or any impropriety.'

'Thank you, brother,' I said politely.

Lord Kildare stood back while I walked through the side door into the sunshine. It was too early for roses which were barely in bud, but the air was sweet with the unmistakeable smell of springtime.'

'The marquess is very careful,' my suitor remarked. 'Very correct.'

'He has reason to be.'

'Calais?'

'Yes. And Buckingham. As I'm sure you know, the duke is close kin to our stepfather.'

'Buckingham's a fool. He should have been a friend to the king instead of insulting him. Henry is an easy man to befriend but a dangerous enemy.'

'I was told your late father befriended the old king and made him laugh.'

Lord Kildare smiled. 'When accused by the Archbishop of Cashel of burning down his cathedral, my father replied he should not have done such an act of sacrilege but he'd been told the archbishop was inside.'

'The king found this amusing?'

'He did.'

'I trust you do not make a habit of burning down God's houses.'

'Only when necessary.'

His answer did not come as a surprise. Leonard painted Ireland as a violent place where strong men kept the peace and squabbled with each other over the spoils.

'Who says what is necessary?'

'I do.'

'You aim to control everyone, even the Church.'

'Lady Elizabeth, Henry will have his coffers filled more readily if he allows me free rein.'

'Should you not consider the desires of your overlord? Is it not risky to do otherwise?'

'Lady Elizabeth, you told me yourself you have taken risks, behaved in ways other young women might consider disgraceful. There are not many ladies who would approach the heir to the French throne, a man with a formidable reputation where women were concerned, and venture unaccompanied into his chamber.'

'I did not say I was unaccompanied.'

'But you were.'

'It was necessary,' I protested, realising how neatly he'd trapped me.

'What of your adventure in the streets of Paris, in the dark, all alone?'

'Who told you about that?'

He laughed at my indignation. 'Hush, Lady Elizabeth. Some men would be shocked but I am intrigued. You are like a draught of strong ale and suit me better than one of those pale-faced young women who inhabit the queen's chamber.'

We walked a little further round the tiny garden, avoiding other courtiers out taking the air and when I asked about his appearance in front of the council for which my family had laid out good money, he waved away the experience as if it was unimportant.

'Wolsey called me "King of Kildare", his usual insult. There were complaints of maladministration and encouraging my friends to make trouble, but nothing to worry you. And see! Your brother is coming to rescue you.' He looked at me with a sideways smile. 'Or perhaps he is coming to rescue me.'

19

THE BOLEYN SISTERS
AUTUMN 1521

The execution of the duke of Buckingham was a terrible sight, not something I'd ever envisaged. Nearly the whole court was present on the green: nervous, breath held, unsure if at the last moment there'd be a reprieve. One or two women held handkerchiefs to their mouths while others were murmuring prayers. My brother Thomas, who'd supported Lord Norfolk at the trial, had a prominent position but Henry himself was absent. I thought most likely he was looking out of a Tower window wanting to ensure that justice was publicly seen to be done. I closed my eyes as the axe fell. There was a moment of utter silence before the duke's severed head was held aloft.

Sitting beside me in the barge on our way back to Greenwich was Lady Carey, white-faced and trembling.

'I though him too great a man?' she whispered.

'No-one is too great,' I replied, thinking of Lord Kildare whose father had once been called "King of Ireland".

'Was he truly a traitor?'

'He was tried and found guilty.'

Her eyes grew wider and her mouth formed a little gasp. 'I wish Anne was here.'

'Is your sister still in France?'

'Yes, but she will come home soon. Our father has settled her marriage.'

My heart contracted painfully as I suddenly remembered what she'd told me at Guisnes, that Anne Boleyn was to marry into Ireland. In the excitement of the past few months I had completely forgotten.

'Is it to be Ireland?'

'Yes. Poor Anne.'

'Indeed,' I said bleakly. 'Poor Anne.'

After Buckingham's execution the court was very subdued. It was not a matter of sympathy for the duke, a man considered deserving of his fate; it was more a realisation of the powerful grip the king had on people's lives. Henry might still be the cheerful, affable monarch he'd always been but the execution of his kinsman showed us his ruthless side. The queen's friend, Lady Salisbury, with her connections to the York kings, was in disgrace, and the Grey family kept particularly quiet as our connection with Buckingham through our stepfather made us uniquely vulnerable.

Thomas, who professed total loyalty to the king, was awarded three of Buckingham's manors but I was sunk in despair, fearing my marriage hopes would come to nothing. I had the example of Cousin Mary's betrothals to show me the folly of pinning all my hopes on one man. There would be others, I told myself, but somehow that did nothing to lift the gloom.

It was early autumn when I had another encounter with Lord Kildare. We met by accident in the gardens at

Greenwich. Like all the other men at court he had cut his hair short to echo the king. It made him look younger than at Guisnes when he'd sported a head of long dark hair beneath his cap and a full beard, now he was cleanshaven. To be truthful I rather liked how he looked – until I remembered what he'd done.

'Lady Elizabeth.'

'Lord Kildare.'

'Will you walk with me?'

I looked around but all my friends were watching the gentlemen play bowls and I was not quick enough to think of an excuse.

'If it is your wish,' I said coolly.

We walked slowly side by side. I could think of nothing to say to him. Lady Carey had brought her sister to Queen Katherine's rooms that morning and I'd seen how much Anne Boleyn was admired for her French gowns and her French manners. She was more poised and witty than when I'd known her in France. I had to admit she would make a wonderful wife for an ambitious man, a man who needed contacts at Henry's court. And her mother was Thomas Howard's sister, another valuable connection.

'Lady Elizabeth, forgive me, I'd not realised how chilly it was out here. May I offer you warmth?'

He made to remove his cape but stopped when I shook my head.

'I thank you but no, I'm not cold.'

He looked at me closely. 'Are you angry with me?'

'Should I be?'

'Not to my knowledge but with women one never knows.'

'It seems that with men one never knows either,' I said sharply.

He blinked. 'I *have* offended you.'

I stopped and turned to face him. 'Lord Kildare, I do not care to be a made to look a fool.'

Just then, the patter of feet announced the arrival of Lady Carey running down the path towards us clutching the queen's shawl. Seeing us she gave me a complicit little smile, bobbed a curtsey and hurried on.

Lord Kildare looked at me and raised his eyebrows.

'A friend?'

'Lady Carey,' I said shortly. 'Sir Thomas Boleyn's daughter.'

He nodded. 'Ah yes. A pretty young woman.'

'So people say.'

'You know her?'

'She and her sister served my cousin when she was Queen of France.'

'And is the sister also pretty?'

I thought of dark-haired Anne Boleyn with her olive skin and black eyes. 'She is clever and amusing but not pretty, a polished pebble made to resemble a jewel.'

'You do not like her.'

'Lord Kildare, I neither like nor dislike Anne Boleyn. She is nothing to me.'

'D'you think she'll be happy living in Ireland?'

The remark was like a knife driven into my heart. So it was true. He'd been trifling with me, leading me to believe we might have a life together, fooling my brother into laying out money, while all the time he'd been talking to the Boleyns. It made no sense. Our family must be worth ten times what Thomas Boleyn was worth. It was important I did not lose my dignity. My heart might be breaking in two, my rosy future vanishing in a tissue of lies and deceit, but he would never know.

'Happiness has nothing to do with anything,' I said sadly.

He frowned. Lady Elizabeth, forgive me but at our meeting after Easter I thought our marriage was to your liking.'

I turned my head and looked straight into his eyes. 'At our last meeting I thought you a better man, not like other men. But I have been proved wrong. If you will excuse me, I should like to go inside. I no longer wish for company.'

With that frosty remark I turned on my heel and left him standing in the garden while I hurried back to my room before I gave myself away by weeping. A woman in tears for a love which had been nothing but a figment of her imagination is an object of pity and I refused to be pitied.

Twice in the following month I saw Lord Kildare deep in conversation with Sir Thomas Boleyn and congratulated myself at having extricated myself from an embarrassing situation. I had no idea what they were discussing but doubtless it concerned his forthcoming marriage. Christmas came and went and I saw nothing more of him at the celebrations and my brothers made no comment on his absence. Perhaps he had gone back to Ireland or perhaps – my heart caught uncomfortably – he'd been returned to the Tower.

In February I saw Thomas Howard walking along the gallery towards the king's apartments which was odd as I'd thought him in Ireland. The only person who would know and might tell me was Leonard but he was difficult to find. I could not go running around the palace looking for him and a few tentative enquiries elicited no information, until I happened to meet a familiar figure strolling from the direction of the queen's rooms.

'Francis Bryan.' I stopped, smiled and inclined my head.

He gave an extravagant bow and came up smiling. 'Still here, sweet lady? I thought you'd deserted us, run off to the bogs of Ireland. I hear you were at Westhorpe. What have you been plotting? Will our lovely French queen desert our friend Brandon and return to the embrace of he who rules half Christendom and plans to rule the other half. What a blow that would be for our dear queen.'

'Why so?'

'She wants him for her midget daughter.'

'I see your tongue is as foul as ever, Francis Bryan.'

'Ah Lady Elizabeth, you could sweeten it if you would only let me place it between your lips in a kiss.'

I would have walked away from his outrageous presumption but Francis Bryan was a man who knew everyone's whereabouts.

'I am looking for my brother, Lord Leonard. Have you seen him?'

'I may have done but I rarely give out information for free. What are you willing to pay?'

'Nothing you would want.'

'Come with me to Brittany.'

'Why Brittany?'

'Thomas Howard is taking an army and there is a noticeable lack of lovely women in our train. I hear you have a taste for rough wooing. I cannot offer you dancing or dicing but imagine us encamped beneath the stars with the enemy at our gates. Imagine the blood coursing through your veins as I make you mine.'

'Will your wife accompany us to Brittany? I hear you are to marry.'

'When did the bonds of matrimony prevent true love.'

'Francis Bryan, if you do not know where my brother is I have no further use for you and bid you good day.'

With only a week to go, preparations for the Easter masque were well advanced and in the queen's rooms there was a suppressed feeling of excitement. Every day we watched those who were to perform, perfecting their steps. To my surprise, both Boleyn girls had been chosen for the masque as well as their brother's betrothed, Jane Parker, and their Howard cousin Meg Shelton. Cousin Mary was to be "Beauty" while Lady Carey was "Kindness" and her sister, "Perseverance".

'I have heard,' whispered Lady Gertrude who was to play "Honour", 'that young Lady Carey is a mite too kind.'

'What do you mean?' I reckoned Lady Gertrude's observations were markedly more barbed since she'd become a countess.

'Too free with her favours.'

'Lady Gertrude!'

'Of course where the king is involved one does not wish to pass judgement.'

I had closed my eyes these past weeks in the same way the queen must have been doing. It was impossible not to notice how often Henry chose to sit with Lady Carey; how frequently they danced together, shared a dish of sweetmeats, their fingers touching; how she blushed whenever he came near. I had hoped this was just another idle flirtation.

'You are certain?'

'Oh yes. Servants always know what is going on. Of course it is unsurprising. The queen has failed him. He's a man and needs to prove himself.'

'He loves the queen.'

'Lady Elizabeth, she cannot give him a son.'

'He respects her.'

'I'm sure he does but without a son he is bound seek consolation elsewhere. And afterwards – who knows.'

'Lady Gertrude, you are in danger of talking yourself into a treason.'

It was all true. Watching Lady Carey dance gracefully, her yellow gown shimmering seductively in the candlelight, I realised her new position made a Boleyn marriage all the more attractive for Lord Kildare. To have your sister-in-law, mistress to the king, placed you in a powerful position. It was well known that favours given between the royal sheets quickly transferred into favours granted to the woman's family, and Lady Carey was just the sort of young woman a man like Henry would want to please.

There was only one young woman who might have stolen the prize from Lady Carey that day – her sister. Anne Boleyn, with her French ways, was the most elegant of the dancers and drew the eye. But because of Henry's new flirtation with the emperor, no-one had a good word to say about the French. I recalled my brother Leonard once saying if he had a drop of French blood in his body he would cut himself open to be rid of it. His companions had agreed. It seemed Lord Kildare was the only man eager to embrace a young woman who, in many ways, appeared more French than English.

20

THE ORMONDE INHERITANCE
SUMMER 1522

As if to emphasise Henry's rearrangement of his own political map, we were treated to the excitement of another imperial visit. In June, Emperor Charles arrived with two thousand courtiers and a thousand horse. He was rowed up the Thames from his lodgings in Bridewell Place to Greenwich where the whole court turned out to welcome him. At the doors of the palace he knelt to Queen Katherine asking for her blessing: a dutiful nephew and a loving aunt. The queen was overjoyed, not just because of their close family tie but also because one day he would marry her beloved daughter, little Princess Mary.

I was hurrying along the path to join the queen and the other ladies who were watching the gentlemen play bowls when I almost ran into Lord Kildare. He must have seen me coming but did not step aside.

'Lady Elizabeth, how delightful!'

To my annoyance I could feel myself blushing. His pleasure seemed genuine but of course he was a practiced deceiver.

'Lord Kildare,' I said, wishing he would move out of my way.

'It has been a long time. Are you well?'

'Perfectly I thank you.' I kept my head lowered, refusing to look at him.

'Have you forgiven me yet?'

I bit my bottom lip and tried to think of something clever to say. 'I was not aware you wished for forgiveness, Lord Kildare.'

'Lady Elizabeth, it is difficult for a man when he is unsure what he has done to offend a lady but over these last few months I have concluded I must have done something. So, I beg for your forgiveness, a general pardon for any offence I may have committed.'

I looked up, which was, of course, a mistake. 'You lied to me.'

'Not to you, never to you.'

'You were playing with me, pretending.'

'No.'

'You never intended marriage.'

'I intend marrying you. I told you.'

'What of Sir Thomas Boleyn's daughter?'

He raised his eyebrows. 'What of her?'

'Do you deny you are going to marry her?'

'Lady Carey is already married.'

'Anne, her sister.'

'Ah, the pebble polished to resemble a jewel.'

'Do you deny it?'

He grasped my hand before I could stop him. 'Lady Elizabeth, there is only one woman I intend to marry and that is you. If we were not in full view of the court I would pull you into my arms and kiss you as I have longed to do every time I've been in your company.'

My stomach lurched, assailed by a sudden sliver of doubt.

'You are not going to marry Anne Boleyn?'

'I am not.'

'Then why do people say you are.'

'People?'

'Lady Carey.'

'The pretty sister.'

'Sisters confide in each other so if anyone knows the truth, it is Lady Carey.'

He smiled. 'Come with me and I shall tell you a story.' He put his hand under my elbow and drew me towards a turf bench overlooking the bowling green where the court was cheering on the king.

I came with him reluctantly. 'I am not a child, Lord Kildare. I do not need stories.'

'I think you will find this one instructive.'

He took off his cape and spread it over the seat. Grudgingly I sat down. He settled himself beside me and, without asking permission, reached for my hand.

'This is a long story and, as we are not walking back to the castle at Guisnes, you must be patient.'

I gritted my teeth at his mention of that evening at Guisnes when I'd revealed more about myself than I intended, far more than was sensible for any young woman to tell a man.

'Are you ready?'

'Yes,' I said, wondering what lies he was about to tell me.

'About seven years ago the old Earl of Ormonde died. He was a wealthy man but had no son to inherit, only daughters.'

'That is not uncommon. But I have never heard of your Earl of Ormonde.'

'Patience, Lady Elizabeth. There were two claimants to the earldom: a grandson and a distant male cousin.'

I had no idea where his story was leading or why he thought I needed to know and I still mistrusted him. Men who lie once will usually lie again.

'Do I know any of these people?' I asked rudely.

'The cousin's name was Piers Butler.'

'Your brother-in-law?'

'The same.'

'And the grandson?'

'Sir Thomas Boleyn.'

'Oh!'

'I see I now have your attention, so listen carefully. The bulk of the Ormonde lands lie in Ireland and as his claim was through a direct male line, the Irish council in Dublin confirmed the earldom on Piers Butler. But King Henry decided he wanted it for Thomas Boleyn. He ordered me to facilitate the claim of Sir Thomas's mother to inherit.'

I frowned. 'Why Thomas Boleyn's mother? What has she to do with any of this?'

'She was one of the old earl's daughters.'

I shook my head, trying to understand the intricacies of the old Earl of Ormonde's family: a daughter who was mother to Sir Thomas Boleyn; a distant male cousin who was married to Lord Kildare's sister; and a king interfering with the laws of inheritance.

'Can the king do that?'

'Lady Elizabeth, there is very little a king cannot do. Inheritance is complicated. No-one knows if the Ormonde title can be passed through a female or if it must pass through an unbroken male line. The king has lawyers searching for proof. My brother-in-law, naturally, is displeased at the prospect of losing the earldom and has accused me of not supporting his claim. I am trapped. I cannot refuse the king's wishes but know my brother-in-law's revenge will be swift and brutal. My lands will be ravaged and I am not there to defend them.'

'The king has put you in an impossible position.'

'Indeed he has. But Wolsey has found a solution. My brother-in-law will keep the earldom and his son will marry Boleyn's younger daughter. In that way Thomas Boleyn's grandson will. in due course, inherit the earldom.'

And is Thomas Boleyn in agreement?'

'He is not happy but if it is the king's wish, he has little choice.'

'So it is not you who is to marry Thomas Boleyn's daughter.'

'No, it is not,' he said gently. 'It never was.'

It took a moment or two for me to accept this new reality, that what I had believed was true, was not; that Anne Boleyn's marriage into Ireland was to be the wife of Piers Butler's son.

'I have been remarkably foolish.'

He smiled. 'It is the nature of women to be foolish but you, Lady Elizabeth, are the least foolish woman I have ever encountered.'

'Will you forgive me for doubting you?' I asked.

'I would forgive you anything.'

I hesitated, almost afraid to ask. 'Our marriage?'

'Last minute delay with the dowry.'

I smiled. 'My mother and brother have been fighting over our dowries for the past six years, neither one prepared to give way. My sister Cecily despaired over her wedding to the Dudley heir. If that is all that prevents us from being married, I can wait.'

He leant closer and caught my other hand. 'Wolsey is to intervene. I promise you the matter will be resolved by the end of this summer.'

'And the position of lord deputy?'

He shrugged. 'The king has given it to Piers Butler. But I shall have it back. Do not doubt it.'

'Why would I doubt it. You always get what you want.'

He grinned. 'I do. And now, Lady Elizabeth, as we seem to be unobserved, perhaps you will allow me that kiss.'

We were married in November and immediately began making plans to travel to Ireland. The new lord deputy had urgently requested my husband's return as disorder amongst his kinsmen had become uncontrollable in his absence.

'He needs me,' laughed my husband.

'I need you,' I said thinking how much I enjoyed being a married woman. Not just our conjugal closeness which was every bit as gratifying as my sisters said it would be, but the additional respect shown me by others. I was now a countess which meant Cecily must curtsey every time she came into my presence.

One morning shortly before we departed I asked my husband's permission to pay a visit to Cardinal Wolsey.

'Seeking an annulment after only three weeks of marriage?' he asked, lazily fiddling with a lock of my hair.

I gave him a conspiratorial smile. 'Just making preparations; laying down a little goodwill.'

'Wolsey doesn't like me.'

'Maybe not but he has always been good to the Grey family.'

'He doesn't trust me.'

'Neither do I,' I said, skipping out of reach of his hand which was trying to pull me back into bed.

'You will be careful.'

'I shall be immensely careful,' I reassured him. 'This visit is for both our sakes.'

Cardinal Wolsey lived in great state, so great that a foreign visitor might mistake his establishment for the royal court. There were hundreds of servants, some wearing damask and velvet, one with a heavy gold chain hung around his neck. There was great formality, no sign of foolish young men lounging around, no card playing, no giggling behind closed doors or passing of secret notes, but everywhere the gleam of gold, heavy silver crosses and the deep, rich scent of power.

I was escorted into the cardinal's presence by one of the gentleman ushers who padded softly away to he back of the room once I'd been announced.

'Your eminence,' I said softly, lowering myself onto a chair placed in front of the cardinal's table.

'Lady Kildare,' said the smooth tones of an educated churchman. 'What may I do for you?'

'I come first to thank your eminence for intervening between my lady mother and my brother, the marquess, in the matter of my wedding money. I should not like my husband to have no profit by me as I find him as good and as kind to me as any men may be to a wife.'

The cardinal beamed in his avuncular way, settling himself more comfortably in his chair.

'I trust God will bless your marriage, Lady Kildare, and you will not find the mood in Ireland too rough for your delicate sensibilities.'

'I think my delicate sensibilities were well tested when I was in Paris with His Majesty's sister, my cousin, the French queen, your eminence.'

'Ah yes.' He lifted an orange pomander to his nostrils as if trying to rid himself of the stench of betrayal at the hands of the French. 'Paris,' The word rolled seductively off his tongue.

I wondered if, like me, he recalled the words he'd written to Charles Brandon that winter when none of knew if we were safe or if we would ever see England again; how he had manipulated people and events to his own purpose, placing both Cousin Mary and her husband in his everlasting debt. As my husband had said, it was wise to be careful when dealing with the cardinal.

'I came, your eminence, to ask a favour,' I said sweetly, 'to ask if you might advise me from time to time as I shall be far from those whose counsel I value. I fear Lord Kildare does not care to venture his accusations in the way others do. I thought if I kept you informed of developments in His Majesty's domain, you would be able to dismiss false reports sent by those who wish my husband harm. I am certain you have councillors in Dublin who advise you but it seems to me that my observations might be of some little use.'

He smiled at my naivety. 'By all means Lady Kildare. I shall be pleased to receive your reports and look forward to reading your evaluation of events.'

'Thank you, your eminence.'

'And Lady Kildare, take care. Ireland is a dangerous place for the unwary.'

Possibly he was right but I reckoned not as dangerous as the cardinal's rooms.

21

BEYOND THE DISTANT HORIZON
JANUARY 1523

We sailed into Dublin Bay on the darkest, coldest day of the year with low clouds scudding across the sky and a complete absence of sun. Even the gulls looked frozen, hovering hopefully for scraps from the ship's galley. A large crowd had gathered to watch us disembark, mostly just curious at the arrival of a great man and his retinue, but one or two come to welcome the earl of Kildare on his return to the land of his birth.

Dublin itself was an oddity, a small market town pretending to be a city. The pretence was so ingrained and of such long standing that Gerald said the inhabitants had built not one but two small churches which they pleased to call cathedrals. I felt awkward, knowing nobody and not understanding half of what was being said. Some people spoke English, I supposed the rest was Irish or as my husband kept reminding me, Gaelic. People's clothes were different: inferior, heavy cloths, no velvets or brocades and most of the poorer sort went barefoot. There seemed very little grandeur but of course ports were for trade, not for ostentatious display, that would be reserved for people's houses, not that I could see any I would care to inhabit.

The moment we set foot on Irish soil we acquired an escort of about twenty heavily armed men. They were fierce-looking warriors, bearded, clad in jackets of chain mail over long tunics and carrying huge two-bladed axes. Behind them trotted a horde of long-haired boys, laden with pikes and spears.

'Who are they?' I whispered to my husband.

'Horse-lads.'

'And those?'

'My galloglass.'

'Pray, what is a galloglass?'

Gerald laughed. 'My guard.'

'Do you need such a bloodthirsty looking crew?'

'I am a great man and great men need protection. Henry has his yeoman of the guard, I have my galloglass.'

I wondered if, now he was home, my husband imagined himself King of Ireland like his father.

'Is that where the lord deputy lives?' I enquired, seeing high stone walls surrounding a castle.

Gerald gave a smile. 'It is but I doubt you'll find him at dinner today. Knowing I was coming, Piers Butler will have scuttled back to Kilkenny to raise an army.'

'Why would he need an army? Surely you're not going to make trouble. We've only just arrived. I should like to see my home before my husband starts picking fights.'

Gerald leant closer. 'I am not the troublemaker here. Butler has announced his intention of defending his right to the Ormonde title by force.'

If Piers Butler was raising an army I now understood why my husband had summoned his galloglass.

'Does Henry know?'

Gerald laughed. 'He will when I write and tell him.'

I'd not thought to begin my new life composing letters

to pacify Henry but everything about life here in Ireland was not what I'd expected.

'If you write to Henry make sure you appeal to his vanity by being suitably humble. Allow him to think he is your benefactor. Henry likes to be generous but hates being disobeyed.'

Gerald raised his eyebrows. 'You seem to know our king very well.'

'I've been at court since I was seven years old. I've had time to study him.'

Gerald tucked my arm in his. 'What a good wife you are proving to be.'

'I am, aren't I,' I said, happy to have my husband's approval. 'Now I trust you will take me home.'

The journey to Maynooth with our escort took us along a muddy winding track hemmed in by trees where the going was easy if a trifle soft underfoot. I found myself enjoying my first glimpses of Ireland beyond the relative civilisation of Dublin. Unlike a ride with my brother where nothing and no-one was permitted to hinder the progress of the marquess on his great bay hunter, my husband found it necessary to stop at every settlement on the way, no matter how small. Men appeared from nowhere to surround our entourage, clamouring to have their good wishes heard, calling out greetings, cheering and waving, while their womenfolk looked on smiling, their arms folded across their chests in the way of poor women everywhere. Children and dogs ran behind us from village to village and at a river crossing we were joined by a young man on horseback who threw his arms around my husband.

'My brother, James,' Gerald called back to me.

The young man, eyed me curiously.

'My new wife, Lady Fitzgerald.'

The young man's face cleared and he gave me a bow from the saddle.

'You are most welcome, my lady, most welcome. I pray you had an easy ride and the Heavens did not once open. We had a terrible rain last night. The river, as you see, is in spate, but nothing a Fitzgerald cannot manage – unless my brother has become soft with his English living these past three years. If you would prefer, m'lady, I myself could lift you across.'

'Lay one finger on Lady Fitzgerald and you're a dead man,' laughed my husband. 'And call me soft again and I'll knock your head on the ground. Where are your brothers?'

James grinned. ' Richie's off chasing his woman, planning a Fitzgerald welcome for the husband; Olly's at Maynooth and the two striplings are on their way. You'll have a full house tonight.'

'Is that Maynooth?' I asked, spying a substantial castle high above where two rivers joined in a thunderous moil of churning water and spray.

James laughed. 'Nay lady, That's Leixlip. Edge of the Pale.'

'There be dragons,' I replied, recalling what I'd been told about the forests and bogs beyond the English Pale. 'I hear them already.

'Only those which roar where the king of England's writ does not run,' Gerald said, 'and I shall deal with them.'

'So I am safe?'

'Never safer than with a Fitzgerald,' he replied. 'Now

let's be on our way or we'll not reach Maynooth before nightfall.'

I was shocked at my first sight of Maynooth but had no wish to distress my husband so bit my lip, straightened my back and smiled. Maynooth looked less a pretty castle where a lord's family might take their ease, more a fortress. The huge stone towers of the gatehouse, the high walls and narrow slit windows, all showed that Maynooth had been built to keep the Fitzgeralds warm and safe within and their enemies outside in the cold and the rain. This was not a house designed for pleasure but a defensible stronghold created in time of war, and from everything I'd heard since landing in Ireland, war was still very much alive.

But there was no time for disappointment. Flags and banners festooned the upper walls and my ears were deafened by the sound of horns and bugles and drums. The track up to the gatehouse was lined with hordes of jostling, cheering people, all come to welcome their lord home. Boys had scrambled onto the tops of thatched roofs, onto gates, steps, the lower branches of tress, anywhere to get a better view of Gerald Fitzgerald, Earl of Kildare, coming back to his own.

We passed through the darkness of the gatehouse archway into a different world, the one my husband had described, where I could imagine beauty and comfort, time for all the pleasures of life. The castle itself looked sturdy but not forbidding like many I knew. This was no Bradgate or Astley, this was in many ways more refined, more desirable, designed by someone who treasured elegance but also learning. I chastised myself for being taken in by first appearances – Maynooth was perfect, if one could ignore the noisy mob at our heels.

Once inside, the crowd was no less clamorous: back-slapping, hugging, kissing, weeping and more cheering until my husband climbed on a table and called for quiet. After a few words of thanks he raised a cup thrust into his hand by a well-wisher and drank a toast to the Fitzgeralds and all their kin, friends and supporters. Then he extended his hand to me. I felt a pair of strong arms grip me from behind, glanced round to see James grinning with undisguised pleasure, and felt myself lifted bodily up to join my husband. He laced his fingers in mine and raised our joined hands in the air.

'Lady Elizabeth Fitzgerald! My wife. Honour her as you honour me for she is now one of our own.'

The cheering grew wilder as I blushed, quite unused to such public adulation.

He pulled me against him and kissed me on the mouth while the cheering grew to an almighty crescendo. Then, with a grin, he jumped down and put up his arms.

'My lady?'

I smiled and allowed him to help me down. Then he took my hand and the two of us walked through the hall and into a further room where more people were waiting. At the front was a well-dressed man in dark green wearing a black bonnet. He was older than my husband and bowed politely.

'Sir Walter!'

'Welcome home, my lord. A thousand welcomes! I've ordered a keg of ale to be served to our friends out there but I think we may need more.'

Having seen how fast my husband's friends could down their ale, I agreed.

Gerald drew me forward. 'This is Sir Walter Delahide, my steward, my right-hand at Maynooth. Walter this is my wife, Elizabeth, Lady Fitzgerald.'

Sir Walter bowed to me. 'Welcome my lady. We heard about your marriage. It was a matter of great wonder and celebration. May I offer my congratulations and hope that you will be happy here at Maynooth.'

'Thank you, Sir Walter. I'm sure I shall.'

My husband turned to a plump little woman standing to one side. 'This is Sir Walter's wife and my dearest kinswoman, Janet. She has care of the children.'

The woman shot me a curious look and curtsied.

'What have you done with them, Janet?' my husband. enquired. 'Shut them in a closet?'

She smiled at my husband the way everyone did, with open admiration. 'Nay my lord, I have them here.'

Standing at the back of the room was a line of five dark-haired children, the eldest clutching the hands of two little girls who could not have been long out of the nursery.

Sir Walter made a beckoning movement with his fingers and a boy stepped forward and bowed to my husband. He was a slender child, of about ten.

'Tom?'

'Yes, my lord.'

'Do you remember me?'

'Not really my lord.'

'I remember you,' piped up a voice.

'Hush, Alice,' Janet said reprovingly. 'Your father was not speaking to you.'

My husband looked ruefully at his children. 'I have been gone too long. Four years is an eternity for a child.'

'Cathleen remembers you well,' Janet said softly. 'We often talk of you.'

'And me!' piped up the voice again.

'I think you'd better let them off the leash,' my husband said with a grin.

She clapped her hands. 'Come and greet your father, girls.'

Suddenly Gerald was engulfed in a flurry of arms, long hair and flying skirts, Training and rules about greetings were lost in an excited outpouring of love. Even the little ones held on tight to their father's thighs as if afraid he'd run off and leave them again. Cathleen the eldest stayed close by his side, gently touching his jacket while Alice, she of the piping voice, tried to climb into his arms.

After a minute he set them aside and said, 'Now come and show Lady Fitzgerald you are not little savages but proper well-trained Fitzgeralds.'

The girls formed a line as they'd been taught and one after the other, curtsied and gave their names. They were very sweet but the effect was spoiled by Alice saying loudly, 'Is she to be our mother?'

'Would you like me to be your mother?' I enquired.

Alice looked at her father. 'She's very pretty.'

My husband smiled. 'She is, isn't she. It took a long time to find such a wife, one that was pretty enough for you.'

'Where did you find her?'

'In a field.'

There was a smothered giggle and the eyes of the

youngest Fitzgerald widened. 'In a fairy ring?' she whispered.

Her father ruffled her hair. 'No *macushla*, she was running away from two wicked men.'

'And you rescued her,' Alice exclaimed triumphantly.

My husband turned to me and grinned. 'Something like that.'

'He was very brave,' I told them.

After that the younger girls had a dozen more questions and even Cathleen, who was a tall girl on the verge of womanhood, said she was pleased I was to live with them.

'They are children to be proud of,' I told Janet as she led me up the stairs to my quarters. 'You have raised them well.'

She smiled sadly. 'Poor weans. Such a tragedy. The little ones barely remember their mother.'

'You have been a mother to them.'

'Oh aye. I've had young Tom in my care since he were a babe in arms.'

'He's a fine boy.'

'He could do with a brother.'

My sisters would have asked regularly if I had obliged my husband yet so I was not embarrassed by Janet's comment. It was natural for people to be curious and she'd only said what everyone else was thinking. From now on I must expect to be the object of daily scrutiny as the whole castle watched and waited for more little Fitzgeralds.

Looking around my beautifully appointed rooms on that chilly January day, I truly believed I could make a good life here with my husband and his children and his household.

I knew a great deal about men and their lust for power. As a girl I'd watched a young King Henry desire nothing more than pleasure, virtue, glory and immortality, all of which his advisors assured him was possible. In those early years Henry's sunny disposition shone on all of us. But when others took advantage of his friendliness and the betrayals began, his smiles turned to scowls and, like a baited bear nipped once too often, he became suspicious, bitter and full of rage.

As a young woman I'd watched an elderly King Louis despair as power slipped slowly away, while his ambitious cousin began openly whispering secrets into the ears of the young queen. As the year turned he resigned himself at last to death. Had he, in those final moments, prayed for a son to come after him or had his seed never been planted? None of us knew and Mary had never said.

I had seen clever men like François d'Angoulême scheme and plot to get what they wanted and lesser men like Charles Brandon and Francis Bryan trim their sails to survive. But none of that knowledge helped me when dealing with a man like Gerald Fitzgerald, Earl of Kildare.

In those early days, with me an eager pupil anxious to learn about my new home and enjoying the pleasures of love, our relationship was harmonious. Riding out together in the soft Irish springtime, he showed me the broad flat acres surrounding Maynooth, the miles of pasture and gorse rolling out in front of my eyes against a backdrop of thick woodland and faraway smoky blue hills. As promised, I was taken to see his prize horses, the ones he bred for pleasure and profit, and even I, ridiculously ignorant about horseflesh, could tell that these animals were special.

At home in Maynooth and occasionally at my husband's other castles at Kilkea or Portlester, we lived every bit as luxuriously as he had promised, certainly in finer state than my brother, the marquess. My jewel box overflowed, each gift reciprocated with a kiss and certainly Gerald was more desirable to embrace than pock-ridden old King Louis had been for Cousin Mary. I often thought of Mary, tucked away in her country house at Westhorpe and wondered at how blessed I was to have a husband who was not only generous and loving but also not at the beck and call of the king.

It took a twelvemonth for me to discover a side of my husband I had perhaps suspected but was unwilling to confront. We were enjoying our first Christmas together at Maynooth, a celebration reminiscent of Francis Bryan's description of wild gatherings to which court ladies were not invited, where men became roaring drunk, imported women from across the river, danced on tables and music drowned out conversation.

At Maynooth, Fitzgerald tradition meant that all women from the countess down to the lowest laundry girl took part in the fun. It was exhilarating. But my enjoyment came to a shuddering halt at the height of the festivities on Twelfth Night, when a messenger arrived with news from Kilkenny.

'James did what?' I spluttered, outraged at the sheer stupidity of such an act.

'It was sad to disturb their Christmas celebrations, but necessary,' Gerald said calmly.

I could barely speak I was so incensed. 'Your brother

has murdered the sheriff of Dublin and all you can say is that it was necessary.'

'The man was on his way to keep Christmas with my brother-in-law, the man who calls himself lord deputy.'

'Piers Butler *is* lord deputy,' I said firmly. 'Henry appointed him.'

'A grave mistake as I'm sure you agree.'

There was something in the way he spoke that made me instantly suspicious.

'Did you order the killing?'

He began removing the heavy chain from around his shoulders. 'I would certainly say it was convenient and naturally James knew the road the sheriff would take.'

'Because you told him.'

'There was no need, James has his own spies.'

I stood staring miserably at the fire. 'Will this blood-letting never end? I write letters to Wolsey for you, telling him what I think it wise he should know of your feuds, imploring him not to believe what others say. I urge him to favour your suits. I tell him your foray into Ulster with your army last summer was solely to defend your own lands and not meant with hostile intent to others. I advise you how to respond when you are called to the council in Dublin to answer complaints. And now you do this! Have you no sense?'

I was quivering with rage. All my careful work had been undone by him and his brother and their insatiable bloodlust.

'You are delightful when you lose your temper, Lady Fitzgerald,' he said, smiling. 'I thought you were used to our rough ways by now.'

'Not when you undo all the good I've done in soothing Wolsey these past twelve months. I sometimes think you forget you have an overlord.'

'I have a lady whom I would happily overlay,' he said provocatively, catching me round my waist and pulling me close. 'Might always wins.' He lowered his mouth to mine. 'And my armour is in sore need of polishing.'

To my annoyance, Gerald was proved right. In the summer, three commissioners arrived from England, ordered by Henry to settle the dispute between the Fitzgeralds and the Butlers. Once they had taken evidence from the principals and heard witnesses from both sides, my husband was reappointed lord deputy. Naturally he was triumphant. I pointed out that he'd given a solemn promise to observe the conditions of the agreement with his brother-in-law, but he brushed the bond aside as an irrelevance.

For a while there was peace but before the year was out, rival skirmishes began again.

By the time our first son was four months old, I was in despair.

'You cannot have done this. You promised.'

My husband peered at the baby who had just learnt to smile. 'A son needs a strong father.'

'Your son will have no father at all if you carry on like this. Henry will have you back in the Tower.'

'Elizabeth, the man murdered his bishop. What did you expect me to do?'

I shuddered. 'Not this.'

The public crucifixion of Maurice Kavanagh, Archdeacon of Leighlin, for the murder of Bishop Doran, was the culmination of five months of violence with both Fitzgeralds and Butlers urging their Gaelic supporters to raid the lands of their rivals. Ireland was in a virtual state of war and I blamed my husband.

'Would you care to tell me what you've done about the Earl of Desmond,' I said tartly.

'He is my kinsman.'

'I am aware of that but Henry will expect you to carry out his orders and arrest the earl, kinsman or not.'

'Only because he thinks Desmond is talking to King François.'

'Is he?'

My husband smiled. 'I do not ask.'

I sighed. 'Then you must write to Henry.'

'Again?'

'Yes, again. You will have to soothe him. Say you are bound to him, not just by allegiance but by your service in his youth.'

'You wish me to remind him of Arthur?'

'Jesu, no! Henry is sensitive on the subject of his brother. You surely remember how it was. Best leave sleeping dogs be.'

'What else?'

I thought for a moment. 'Tell him it is not just his good lordship you crave but because both your wives were his kinswomen.'

'And some flattery?'

'Tell him you cannot find it in your heart to do anything other than serve him before all the princes of the world because of his nobility and his prowess.'

'Does that not go too far?'

'Not for Henry. And tell him that you know that if you did otherwise it would lead to the destruction of you and your kin.'

'You're certain?'

'Yes. The words will please Henry. But I'm not sure what to do about Wolsey.'

'Flattery?'

'Doesn't work.'

'A bribe?'

'Perhaps a gift.'

'Same thing.'

'Not at all, Wolsey is mistrustful so your words must be chosen with care. I'll think of something.'

As I tried to guide my reckless husband away from the precipice of Henry's displeasure, I remembered my mother's warning not to return to England. If Gerald was to be kept safe he needed to remember he was being watched, not only by enemies like Piers Butler and his supporters on the Irish council in Dublin, but by Wolsey's spies.

The following winter, the Fitzgerald men and their allies moved against the O'Donnells, pushing further west through the woods and bogs into Connaught where fighting was fierce and casualties high. As expected, news of this renewal of violence found its way to the ears of the cardinal and in August my husband received an order for both him and his brother-in-law, Piers Butler, to present themselves at court. Henry had been told what was going on in the furthermost parts of his realm and was furious.

Unconcerned with offending Henry, Gerald delayed his return to England to do a little matchmaking. He said it was time to get the rest of his daughters wed. At the beginning of the year we'd celebrated Cathleen's marriage to young Viscount Gormanston and now it was Mari's turn. Her betrothed, Brian O'Connor, was the kind of man any young woman would want: dashingly handsome with a wicked twinkle in his dark brown eyes. At Henry's court I'd known many handsome young men with wicked twinkles in their eyes and they seldom made satisfactory husbands.

'Will he treat her well?'

Gerald smiled at my concern for his daughter. 'It's a good match. O'Connor is loyal to the Fitzgeralds and will care for her as I care for you.'

'And Alice? Will she also be cared for?'

A year previously, in a moment of generosity, Henry had given Gerald the wardship and marriage of James Fleming, the young heir to the Slane lordship, a gesture which my husband promptly turned to his advantage by betrothing the boy to Alice.

He gave me a sideways look and took my hand. 'God has designed the world so that a man is master in his marriage, and rightly so, but I think James Fleming may struggle. I do not worry for Alice.'

'And your youngest?'

'A match with the favourite son of Mulroney the Great.'

'The O'Carroll boy?'

He nodded. 'I destroyed the old man's castle a while back. The boy and I have been friends ever since.'

I found the shifting allegiances and the way these men resolved their quarrels, utterly baffling. Sons fought against fathers and murdered their brothers, attacked their sworn enemies then married their daughters in an extravagant display of mutual amity. I sometimes felt I was living in the midst of a full scale war where the protagonists changed sides at will.

By early September we were ready to leave Maynooth but at the last moment our removal was delayed when Gerald decided the newly married Lady Slane should accompany us to London.

'She will be company for you,' he said firmly. 'Besides, it is time she experienced court life.'

'Gerald, your daughter is seventeen. She is only just married and will make her home at Slane. A taste of Henry's court is hardly necessary. Besides, what will her husband think of you whisking his bride away?'

'He understands I have need of her.'

'I thought it was I who was supposed to have need of her,' I said suspiciously.

He smiled and took me in his arms, the way he did when I needed persuading to his way of thinking. '*Macushla*, the babe is already moving and I understand enough of the dangers of childbirth to know you will need someone you trust at your side. Janet cannot be there; she must stay here with the little ones and you'd not wish her elsewhere.'

'No,' I agreed grudgingly, thinking of our son, still so small and so vulnerable. 'But I shall have my English family.'

My husband laughed uproariously. 'Sweetheart, I have great faith in your lady mother, as you well know, but I doubt even you would want her in your birthing chamber.'

He was right, of course. Our second child would be born some time this coming winter and without Janet I would feel alone and very far from home. She had been at my side as the midwife toiled to deliver my son and when young Gerry had given his first cry it was Janet who had wrapped the child in a shawl and carried him out of the room to present to his father.

We were to travel to England with a full complement of servants and at least three priests, but Janet would remain at Maynooth. it would be hard to leave my son who had just started walking and could already master a few words but I consoled myself with the thought that it would not be for long – a year at most. We'd be back at Maynooth by next summer.

22

THE CITY OF LONDON
AUTUMN 1526

It was a cool morning in early October when we rode into London at the head of a long column of men. They were decked out in Kildare livery, more like a victorious army home from battle than the retinue of an earl under suspicion of misbehaviour. It only needed a couple of carts full of treasure and a straggling line of prisoners in chains to complete the illusion. Gerald sat high on his horse, acknowledging loud cheers from the crowds lining the streets, looking every inch the noblest and most powerful man in the kingdom, which of course he was not and I hoped he remembered that fact. I forbore to point out that Londoners would cheer anyone, especially a richly dressed lord accompanied by a pair of beautiful women.

'Do you not think my father looks magnificent.' Alice had been bursting with excitement from the moment we'd spied the city walls.

'I do,' I agreed, wondering if Gerald's flamboyant ride through the city streets would be reported to Henry. Old man Kildare might have been called "King of Ireland" but for his son to behave in the same way was courting disaster. It was only five years since Buckingham was brought down for setting himself too high and Henry was not one to forget a man's transgressions.

As for me, I had forgotten the sheer size and noise of the city: the vast number of dwellings beyond the old walls where there used to be woods and fields, the churches, the houses, the warehouses, the shops, and the animals; the cacophony of screaming, shouting and yelling; the thousands of people pushing and shoving their way through the streets, the wealth on show, the rich velvets and gleam of jewels and the poverty, the beggars, the urchins in rags and the wounded. Three and a half years was not a lifetime yet I'd become used to the smallness of Dublin and forgotten how huge and noisy London was. And how disgustingly smelly.

Wishing to provide support for his brother-in-law, Thomas had acquired lodgings for us near the river but I took one look and realised my brother had severely underestimated the size of Gerald's retinue. Meg Wooton, dressed in her finery, was waiting to greet us, but as more and more horses rode in under the gatehouse, her face acquired the anxious look I remembered.

Gerald lifted me down and whispered, 'Fit for a very small king.'

I glared at him and walked up to the steps to where Meg and I exchanged friendly greetings.

'I had no idea,' she said, throwing another appalled glance at the overcrowded courtyard.

'My husband is an important man.'

'Of course,' she said, flustered. 'But I thought, well, Thomas thought, I mean, under the circumstances…'

'You thought we would creep in like a family in disgrace.'

'No, of course not, but I'd not thought…' She ran out of words and covered her embarrassment by leading the way into the hall. Compared to Maynooth or indeed any of our Irish houses, the interior of our lodgings was unimpressive and distinctly gloomy.

'That blue you are wearing is very becoming,' Meg said with more than touch of jealousy in her voice. She gave a little laugh. 'I'd imagined you returning in homespun.'

'My husband is extremely generous,' I said with a smile, glad I'd worn the new blue velvet riding habit and matching hat that Gerald had ordered for me.

At that moment my husband came in with his daughter and I watched, amused, as Meg tried to cope with the arrival of elegant young Lady Slane, poised, confident and beautifully dressed with her riding hat tilted at an alarmingly rakish angle.

We managed very well as Meg, overcome by the sophistication of her sister-in-law's new family, showed us around our temporary home, all the while casting puzzled glances in our direction as if a basket of tame field mice had turned out to be a tribe of flamboyant tigers in disguise. With a vague invitation to dine with her and Thomas later in the week, she departed for Greenwich where, she informed me, the queen awaited her return.

'Does she know the queen?' Alice asked.

'She is the Lady Marquess. She has a position at court as one of queen's senior ladies.'

Alice digested this information, then asked, 'Will I meet the queen?'

'Possibly. I shall have to ask.'

'Tomorrow?'

'No, not tomorrow. Tomorrow I must visit my mother. An order has been issued.'

Alice giggled. 'Truly?'

'My mother has always communicated her wishes in the form of orders, even when I was a child and might have expected a little kindness.'

'How odd. It's many years since my own mother died but I remember her as a kind and gentle lady.'

'I'm sure she was,' I said, wishing I'd known my predecessor at Maynooth. 'However, my mother is not like that. When my sister Cecily and I were young we were sick with fright each time our nursemaid took us to see her.'

'Did she not visit the nursery?'

'Not as I recall.'

I knew that Alice's happy childhood at Maynooth bore no resemblance to my time at Astley where fear of my mother's terrifying presence permeated every single moment of the day.

'May I come with you? I should like to meet your mother.'

I smiled. 'Not this time.'

I hesitated, not because I disliked my stepdaughter's company, but because my mother was a difficult woman and I was afraid that the deaths of my stepfather and my brother John would have made her even more querulous. I reminded myself to be charitable because her heart had doubtless been hardened to stone by the loss of my father, whom my sisters said was the love of her life for why else would she refuse to talk about him. Having experienced the deep joy and contentment of marriage, I could imagine how painful it must be to lose a dearly loved husband.

My mother was waiting for me in the smaller of her two

receiving rooms, dressed in a heavy robe of plum-coloured velvet. At first I thought her unchanged but as I moved closer I noticed a darkness beneath her eyes, deep clefts on either side of her painted mouth and strands of white hair caught beneath her Venetian cap. In the years I'd been away she had become an old woman. But her tongue was as sharp and vindictive as ever. Nothing that mattered had changed, only the outer shell.

'Another child, I see,' she said, offering me her cheek to kiss.

'Yes, Lady Mother, in the winter.'

'Well don't go showing your fat belly at court. No-one will thank you for it.'

I planted a swift peck on her wrinkled skin, inhaling the scent of dead roses and times past, wondering what had gone wrong at court. Meg had said nothing but then Meg was not a noticing woman.

'You have failed to follow my advice,' my mother said with a sniff.

'Which advice was that, Lady Mother?'

'I warned you to stay away.'

'My husband was commanded to present himself at court. He could hardly refuse.'

She considered me for a long moment, doubtless costing my outfit from top to toe and arriving at a figure, half of what my husband had laid out. My mother, like my brother, was mean with money and haggled mercilessly with those charged with acquiring her expensive Florentine silks and brocades, always demanding a bargain. She was ruthless with everyone – even the king's councillors were treated like the lowest of menials.

'What has Lord Kildare done to warrant his recall?' she said at last.

'I do not know,' I replied not wanting to talk about my husband's doings.

Her fist crashed onto the arm of her chair.

'Don't lie to me!' she shouted. 'Of course you know. A wife always knows. D'you think I didn't know what your father was about? All his plotting and scheming, thinking himself so clever, so important, so big a man. Every time he betrayed his king, I knew; every time he betrayed me, I knew. So answer me – what has your husband done?'

I took a step backwards, momentarily afraid of her fury but of course there was no escape as I should have known.

I picked my words carefully, unwilling to go into too much detail. I thought the murder of the Sheriff of Dublin and the crucifixion of an archdeacon would hardly impress my mother. She would not understand Gerald's motives because she didn't know Ireland. She had no idea of the difficulties he faced in defending our key marches and protecting his tenants against threats posed by those hostile to the Fitzgeralds, or of the benefit in courting local Gaelic chieftains, promising protection in exchange for tribute money.

'Lord Kildare says the king's demands are impossible. He says Ireland can only be ruled by the Fitzgeralds. No-one else has the strength.'

She leant back in her chair. 'Henry is no fool. He knows Ireland is full of unruly lords. He wishes to curb their power, not increase it. Can your husband not see that?'

'My husband believes the king needs a strong man to keep the peace.'

She laughed. 'So Garret Og still sees himself as King of Ireland.'

I flushed. 'He would not say that.'

She gave a wintery smile and indicated that I should draw up a stool.

'Shall I tell you who Henry is to make King of Ireland?'

I thought quickly – if not Gerald then, please God, let it not be Piers Butler.

'Who?' I asked warily.

'Little Henry Fitzroy, Duke of Richmond and Duke of Somerset, a prince who is his father's worldly jewel.'

I clapped my hand over my mouth. Bessie Blount's bastard! When I'd heard of the child's elevation to a dukedom, my heart had bled for the queen. To have her husband's bastard publicly honoured in that way was to pile humiliation upon humiliation. But to give the child a kingdom to rule would be monstrous.

'What of the queen?' I asked.

'Sick at heart. She's been in low spirits since the emperor abandoned his alliance with England and his betrothal to little Princess Mary. She and the king still share a table but I hear they no longer share a bed. He wants a son and heir and knows she cannot give him one.'

'Men will not accept a king's bastard,' I said firmly, well aware of what my brothers would say.

'Did you hear me make mention of the duke of Richmond becoming the king's heir?'

I waited while my mother indicated to the elderly woman hovering at her shoulder to adjust the cushion at her back, only then did she continue.

'Henry is afraid. Since his jousting accident he is

afraid of what will happen to his kingdom if he should die.'

'Please Lady Mother, to speak of the king's death is treason.'

She sniffed. 'It is a king's duty to secure the throne for his successor – but who does the king have?'

'He has a daughter.'

'Pah! A girl, and a tiny doll of a girl at that. He needs a son, a legitimate son. Before there was hope, now it seems the queen has reconciled herself to failure.'

'It is hardly her fault God has not blessed their marriage with a son,' I protested.

A glimmer of a smile hovered over my mother's lips.

'Yet fault there must be. God's displeasure is not visited upon a man and his wife for no reason, even if they are a royal couple. So you must ask yourself, where does the fault lie?'

Conversations with my mother were like this. I would be pushed and prodded like a goose, driven with a stick until she had me within reach of the goose pen. Hopefully I would then run for home, my wings flapping, sure of my mother's chosen destination.

'The queen is a perfect example of womanhood,' I said primly.

'So the fault must lie with the king?'

'Lady Mother!'

'Why the outrage? The king is a man fashioned like other men and we know men are punished by God for their misdeeds.'

'You think the fault lies with the king?' I could not believe I was saying such a thing.

'No I do not think that. We know the king can father sons.' Her smile became thinner. 'So if not the king and not the queen, where does the defect lie?'

All my mother's talk of defects and faults was making my head spin. I'd not expected a dissection of the royal marriage and was feeling faint for lack of food. I was always hungry these days.

'I do not know,' I said. 'These are questions for scholars and theologians, learned men, not for women like you and me.'

My mother raised an eyebrow at my doubting her worth to debate matters of religion with archbishops.

'Henry believes the defect lies in the marriage itself.'

'That is impossible.'

'Is it? I once knew a woman who believed her marriage sound only to discover it was not and her children were bastards.'

My mother had a fund of these stories from her past but she never elaborated on them so I was unsure how true they were or if she invented them to fit her purpose. The years before I was born and the turmoil she'd lived through were seldom mentioned. It was as if they were subjects best left alone, buried deep in the past, not subjected to the unforgiving light of day.

'The pope gave a dispensation for the king and queen to marry,' I said firmly. 'Their marriage is perfectly sound.'

She began stroking the arms of her chair with her fingertips. 'Tricky things, dispensations.'

'What do you mean? What could possibly be wrong with a papal dispensation?'

She curled her fingers round the little knob at the carved end. 'Open to interpretation, so I've heard.'

'Open to interpretation?' I could hear myself beginning to shout.

My mother carried on smoothly as if I'd not spoken. 'Popes are men and, contrary to what many believe, they are fallible. Especially when they're no longer alive.'

'Lady Mother! I cannot listen to this. The queen is a good woman.'

'Did I say she was not?'

'No, but what are you suggesting?'

'I am merely telling you that Henry feels the need to be free of his wife so that he can remarry.'

'Remarry!' I squeaked. 'How can he remarry? He already has a wife.'

'Nevertheless, it seems he wishes to remarry so that he can sire a legitimate son.'

'And who would he marry?' I demanded.

My mother examined the rings on her left hand as if they had suddenly assumed great importance. 'A French princess? A fresh young damsel?'

There was something in the way she said those particular words. She knew more than she was telling me.

'Who? Who is he planning to marry before he has even set aside his blameless wife?'

She shrugged very slightly and gave me another thin-lipped smile. 'Just a rumour. Nothing more. Just a whisper or two, a flicker in the dark. I've heard he writes her letters; verses.'

'That means nothing. Every man at court writes verses.'

'Not Henry. He dislikes writing. Always has. So why

now? And why her? Still, as you say, probably nothing, just gossip. I hear you have brought a young woman with you. Who is she?'

My mother wrong-footed me, changing the topic of conversation like a ship's captain catching a stray breeze.

'Lady Slane, my stepdaughter. Her husband is Lord Kildare's ward.'

'And has the husband come too?'

'No, he remains in Ireland.'

She narrowed her eyes. 'Your idea or Lord Kildare's?'

'Lord Kildare thought Lady Slane would be company for me.'

'Did he indeed!'

'Yes, he is a very considerate husband.'

'I'm sure he is but ask yourself whose needs he is considering – yours or his. I suspect Lord Kildare has a use in mind for his daughter. Warn him to be careful. Wolsey doesn't like him and Wolsey is all-powerful.'

I was unsure exactly what she meant but clearly she believed there was more to Alice's presence in our household than first appeared. However, my mother saw conspiracies everywhere, a consequence, my sisters said, of living through the chaos when Henry's father took the throne by force and men had to prove their loyalty or risk death on the gallows. It was a time when nobody knew who to trust.

Next morning I sent a message to Greenwich asking if I might call upon Queen Katherine, then settled down to entertain visitors while I waited for a reply

'Why is your sister, Lady Dudley, so rude to you?' Alice asked, after a particularly fraught meeting with Cecily which ended with her bursting into tears and screaming that I understood nothing and why had I come back if only to taunt her.

'I have the finest wardrobe of any of my sisters. Cecily is jealous, that is all.'

'But is she not married to a lord?'

'She is but he's said to be a wastrel.'

'Not a good marriage?'

I shrugged. 'Cecily does nothing but complain. It's sad. She waited so long for him and had such high hopes of the marriage.'

'Is he handsome?'

'Yes.' I smiled at my stepdaughter. 'But you know a smooth skin and rosy cheeks mean little if the flesh inside the apple is rotten.'

Alice nodded sagely. Her own husband was far from handsome but a personable young man. I doubted Alice still harboured ambitions to be a soldier; not with young Slane in her marriage bed.

Two days after Cecily's visit Alice and I took a barge to Greenwich to pay our respects to the queen. Katherine had grown stouter and plainer over the years and had an aura of loneliness about her. She was gracious and regal but there was no warmth in her words, no recognition that I was a welcome friend despite having served her faithfully for more than seven years. Perhaps in her position, I too would be despondent. She'd been deserted by her nephew, bereft of her daughter and abandoned by her husband who, if my mother was to be believed, planned to cast her aside and remarry.

'She is sad,' Alice remarked as we made our way back to our lodgings. Unlike Meg, Alice was perceptive.

'What makes you say that?' I asked, curious how much Alice had understood.

'She smiles and is gracious but her eyes are empty; if you look closely, they're full of pain.'

'She has much to be sad about. She misses her daughter.'

'Is Princess Mary not at court?'

'The king has sent her to Ludlow. It is too far for easy visiting.'

Alice's eyes widened. She looked shocked. 'Is he punishing his daughter?'

I laughed. 'Not at all. Ludlow is where kings send their eldest sons to be educated in what it means to be royal. King Henry has no son so he has sent his daughter. She will be Princess of Wales. It is a great honour.'

'But this has made the queen sad.'

'Yes.'

'And what of the young woman who has caught the king's eye?'

I wondered who had mentioned the king's latest fancy to my stepdaughter. Not Cecily who, so I had discovered, knew nothing.

'I think it would be wise to be circumspect, Alice. It is just gossip.'

'But it is all that anyone is whispering about.'

'And do they whisper a name?'

'Not to me. Perhaps we should ask Lady Dorset. She would surely tell you.'

I had looked carefully at the women gracing the queen's chamber where the most senior lady was Thomas

Howard's stepmother, the dowager duchess of Norfolk. Also in attendance were my sister-in-law, Meg; Lady Gertrude, revelling in her new title of Lady Marquess; Maria Salinas, the widowed Lady Willoughby; the usual huddle of Spanish ladies and both Sir Thomas Boleyn's daughters. Lady Carey flashed a brief smile but Anne Boleyn looked through me as if I did not exist. There was a row of younger women in Spanish hoods, heads bent industriously over their sewing, all with faces hidden. Perhaps one of those had caught Henry's eye. If the rumour had spread as far as my mother's chamber, I thought it must be true.

23

THE ROYAL MARRIAGE
CHRISTMAS 1526

The Christmas festivities at Greenwich were the finest for years, or so I was told. I knew what these celebrations would be like. There'd be continuous feasting, an endless series of masques and tournaments, and finally, a disguising when the king would umask himself and everyone would pretend amazement. The presence of the queen would ensure a certain respectability to the proceedings but when she withdrew early, as I knew she would, the music would grow wilder, the dancing more riotous and men and women would slip away into the shadows to pursue their private dalliances.

Despite the absence at court of Lizzzie Bryan and the delicious Bessie Blount, both now suitably married, there were plenty of young women only too ready to smile at a good-looking man with a title and prospects. From my own experience at Henry's court I knew that men who flirted with a young women, inevitably expected more from the encounter than a few secret kisses, and most young women, it seemed, were happy to oblige.

I lay crossly on my daybed listening to one of my women read verses from a book of uplifting stories, wondering what was happening at Greenwich. I had sent Alice off with her father, telling Gerald to make sure she was chaperoned, though, to be truthful, I was more worried about what my husband might get up to in the easy-going atmosphere of Henry's court. Jealousy was a new emotion, not one I'd experienced in Ireland where Gerald's absences involved endless discussions with his tenants, his sons-in-law or his brothers, more likely to end in a raid than in wild carousing. Here was different. Here there was precious little for him to do while he waited for the council to reconvene. Here there were myriad temptations.

Gerald paid no attention to conventions surrounding childbirth so when he returned very late that evening, singing and making a great deal of noise, he strode into my chamber. My women tutted their disapproval of a man's presence in their domain.

'How are you, my lady?' he asked, his breath reeking of wine and his words slurred.

'Bored.'

He sat down heavily on a stool.

'Dear Jesu! My head is splitting. I've not drunk so much in years.'

'Well I've nothing here to offer you.'

His eyes gleamed. 'Plenty of others who were offering. Pretty ones. Lips like cherries. Luscious. Very tempting they were.'

'Indeed.'

'Yes. Just like the women O'Connor had on hand at his last gathering.'

'Your son-in-law is a rogue.'

He pulled his stool closer. 'Go on. Ask me.'

'Ask you what?'

He grinned. 'How many women I kissed. I see doubt in your eyes, Lady Kildare, so we'd best get this over with.'

'How many?'

He stood up, leant over and placed his mouth on mine. 'Just one. You.'

'Oh Gerald.' Tears welled up in my eyes and unaccountably I began weeping. I should have known my husband was faithful to me; he was a loyal man.

He gathered me against him and kissed my hair, murmuring Gaelic endearments which I only half understood. The familiar cadences were warm and comforting as I buried my face deep into the front of his dark green doublet, the one with silver buttons he'd had especially made for the occasion.

'Why the tears?'

'I miss Maynooth. I miss our children, our family. I miss you. When can we go home?'

He gave a short laugh. 'Not yet, *macushla*. I have to make my representations to the council and you, my lady, have work to do.'

It was a week before my work was done and our new daughter, safely wrapped in a shawl, was presented to her father. The first of my friends to congratulate me was Cousin Mary who had come from Westhorpe for the Christmas festivities and had kindly thought of me. It was five years since I'd last seen her and she looked thinner, her skin less radiant, her hair less luxuriant; only her eyes and her smile remained the same.

We talked of our children and there was the expected ritual of presenting my Bess, who was a beautiful baby with a heart-shaped face, large dark eyes and a wisp of fair hair beneath her cap. I thought her quite perfect in every way from the top of her soft downy head to the soles of her little pink feet and Cousin Mary agreed with me.

'Tell me what is happening,' I said. 'Meg is hopeless and all Lord Kildare does is keep pointing to the disturbed state of affairs at home as conclusive proof of his unique capacity to govern Ireland in the king's name.'

'Is he right? Can no-one else succeed?'

I smiled. 'My husband makes certain it is so.'

Mary looked at me soberly. 'Lord Kildare should be careful.'

'That is what I tell him.'

Mary hesitated, a sure sign she was about to impart some important news.

'Henry is to make an alliance with François, a treaty of perpetual peace.'

'Because of the emperor?'

'Yes. Charles broke his word so Henry must take steps to secure our place in the world. He cannot allow Charles the luxury of thinking us weak and friendless.' She sighed. 'I sometimes wonder how different everything would be if he and I... but no matter. I did as I was bid and what I believed was right. I married Louis.'

I smiled a little sadly. 'You were a good queen.'

We both sat there in silence, remembering those faraway days when we rode in splendour into Abbeville for Mary's wedding: the glamour, the glitter, the endless feasting and dancing – and all that followed.

'Henry requires my presence at the celebrations when

the treaty is signed,' Mary said, sounding none to happy at the prospect.

'You are the dowager queen of France. It is entirely fitting you should be there.'

'An alliance with the French does not please everyone.'

'Katherine?'

Mary sighed. 'She is melancholy. She and Henry are at odds and it's not just the loss of the Spanish marriage or the proposed alliance with the French. She does not wish her daughter to marry a son of François but knows her duty. She presents herself to others as a serene and perfect queen, content with her lot, but in private, beneath the surface, matters are as bad as ever. Worse I fear. Henry is no longer an attentive husband in any way.' She paused. 'He has eyes for someone else.'

The silence stretched out between us as Mary finally admitted the truth of the gossip swirling around the royal court and out into the city streets.

I said quietly, 'My mother hinted as much.'

'Brandon says Henry is besotted. She only has to smile and Henry quivers with desire. He says Henry cannot leave her alone.'

'You know who she is?'

'Thomas Boleyn's daughter.'

'But Lady Carey has…'

'Not Lady Carey, she is quite forgotten. It is Anne, the younger Boleyn girl.'

I blinked in surprise, thinking of cool, calculating Anne Boleyn with her long neck, flat bosom and sparkling black eyes. An ambitious young woman, unlike her frivolous sister who was, apparently, always obliging.

'Anne Boleyn will not lift her skirts for Henry,' I said firmly.

'Not even to be his acknowledged mistress?'

I shook my head. 'Why would she? It leads nowhere. She has the example of her sister. Lady Carey's years in Henry's bed did nothing but put cuckold's horns on Will Carey's head and afterwards, what is more pitiful than a discarded mistress.'

'A king always gets his way with women. She will not be able to hold out.' Mary smiled, doubtless thinking of the young Henry who had been the most handsome prince in Christendom, irresistible to young and old alike. He could have had any woman he wanted. In those days the only one he wanted was Katherine and he had made her his beloved queen. He had been Sir Loyal Heart. But that was long ago. The love-struck young prince had become a mature and powerful man, accustomed to having his wants satisfied.

'I imagine Henry is dazzled by Anne,' I said. 'She is very French in her ways.'

Certainly Anne Boleyn was one of the most elegant young women in the queen's chamber: no great beauty but witty, well educated, an excellent dancer and possessed of a good singing voice. However to attract a man like Henry there had to be more to her than that.

'Brandon says it is love,' Mary said bleakly, her eyes filling with tears.

'Perhaps he means infatuation, one of those sudden passions men get. For a season they want nothing else, then the feeling burns itself out and is gone.'

'Cousin Elizabeth, you and I both know what love is. I respected and admired Louis but I did not love him. He was kind to me and tried as best he could to be a good husband. But Brandon, I love. It is an entirely different feeling, one which glows inside, giving comfort in the darkest of days, one in which you would sacrifice everything for the loved one, even your life.'

'You think Henry would sacrifice everything for Anne Boleyn?' I said astounded at the thought. 'She is not even an earl's daughter.'

'Brandon says he fears what Henry will do if he cannot have her.'

'My mother believes he wishes to put Katherine aside.'

'He cannot. He must not.'

I agreed with her but neither of our opinions would weigh on Henry. Kings did not listen to sisters or to the wives of disobedient lords.

'What if there was some defect in the marriage?'

'Defect?'

'The word was my mother's,' I said hastily.

Mary frowned. 'That is treasonous. The royal marriage is perfectly sound.'

'That is what I said but my mother believes there could be a defect in the dispensation.'

'Ridiculous,' Mary said crossly. 'I'll not listen to any more of this nonsense. The affair, if affair it is, will be over by the end of the summer.'

Except that it wasn't.

No sooner had the French envoys departed, sated with food and good cheer, clutching their Treaty of Perpetual Peace, than Cardinal Wolsey convened what was supposed to be a secret ecclesiastical court to examine the king's doubts about the royal marriage. The queen said nothing but she must have known that her husband of eighteen years, the man she'd loved and supported devotedly, was trying to find a way to be rid of her.

'It was dreadful!' said Meg, who insisted on coming to tell me what was happening at court.

'What was?'

'The king stormed into the queen's private room and told her he was applying for an annulment of their marriage. He said he'd harboured doubts for years and the Bible was quite clear on the matter.'

'The Bible!'

'Yes, yes. Leviticus apparently. "A man shall not marry his brother's wife." He was shouting. We all heard.'

'Did nobody consider Leviticus at the time of the royal marriage?'

Meg stared at me as if I was stupid. 'How should I know! I don't concern myself with such things.'

'Neither did the king, not until he decided he wanted a new marriage.'

Meg glared at me. 'Stop being so self-righteous. Do you wish to hear the rest or shall I leave you to your thoughts?'

'No, please carry on. Tell me everything.'

'Vey well,' she said in a sulky voice. 'After the king left, the queen stayed where she was. She didn't come out of her room and there was not a sound. No one knew what to do. Lady Gertrude thought the queen might have fainted and be lying unattended on the floor. I wondered if the shock had rendered her speechless. Eventually Lady Willoughby knocked quietly on the door and went in.'

Before her marriage to Lord Willoughby, Maria de

Salinas had been Katherine's intimate friend and would be the best person to give her comfort at a time like this.

'Naturally she won't give way,' said Meg as if the decision was hers. 'If the king imagines the queen will oblige him by stepping aside, he doesn't know his wife. She is resolute. She was raised by her mother to be Queen of England and no-one, least of all some little upstart like Anne Boleyn, will change that. It's not as if the Boleyns are a powerful family despite Mistress Anne having caught the king's eye.'

I agreed. 'Only the pope has the power to end the king of England's marriage.'

Meg gaped, staring me as if I'd said something scandalous.

'That is ridiculous.'

'It is a possibility but I cannot see Pope Clement agreeing to offend the emperor by annulling the marriage of his aunt.'

Since early May Pope Clement had been held captive by the emperor after imperial forces had sacked Rome in an orgy of depravity which shocked the whole of Christendom. There were stories of churches desecrated, women raped and babies roasted on spits. Gerald believed the pope would need to pacify the emperor if he wanted to save the Church.

Meg said mournfully, 'Thomas says Wolsey is leaving for France.'

'Any particular reason?'

'To negotiate a marriage for the king. One of the French princesses.'

I recalled my mother's words on the subject.

'I suppose if the king must remarry to get a son, a French marriage is to be preferred.'

'Lady Gertrude says it will come to nothing. She says the king has gone mad and intends making Anne Boleyn his queen.'

I thought of Anne Boleyn on the day we quit Paris, telling me how she had arranged her future, choosing her own path rather than one planned for her by others. Was this the glittering future she'd imagined for herself when she stood perfectly poised at the gates of the Hôtel des Tournelles, unconcerned at the disruption she was causing. A young woman with a focussed mind, a selfish young woman with a determination to have what she wanted. But who would have thought she wanted to be Henry's queen.

24

THE MANOR HOUSE AT NEWINGTON
MAY 1528

It was a year since the king announced his determination to end his marriage, a long and difficult year where the only moment of joy was the birth of our second son. Edward arrived at the tail end of a winter so cold people said the sea had frozen. Bess was entranced by this small newcomer in the nursery while Meg declared him the handsomest baby she'd seen since her own little Johnny was born. I engaged two more nursemaids, wishing Janet was here to relive me of the tedious task of interviewing young women suitable to care for my children. Oddly, I missed my firstborn even more now I had two other children to delight my days but letters from Maynooth told me young Gerry was making good progress, walking and talking well, learning his prayers and able to recognise his letters.

No progress had been made in the council's case against my husband because Henry preferred to spend his time hunting with Anne Boleyn rather than attending to business, refusing to make a ruling on who should govern Ireland in his name. Though his days were spent with Mistress Anne, the formal routines of court meant the king and queen were often in each other's company. Meg informed me in a scandalised whisper that marital relations were as they always had been. There were also rumours that Anne Boleyn had ordered Lady Carey to return to the king's bed.

'Four of my best palfreys,' my husband said happily.

We were walking together by the river enjoying the sunshine and watching the tilt boats skim by on the incoming tide. A half-dozen ducklings bobbed up and down by the waters' edge while their harassed mother attempted to herd them to safety.

'Forgive me, but who is buying?'

'Mistress Anne Boleyn. She has requested four of my palfreys.'

'Can she not have them from the king or from Thomas Wolsey. Everyone says the cardinal has a fine stable.'

'Apparently she wants Irish ones. Only the best for Mistress Anne.'

'As long as her fancy in husbands does not turn in that direction.'

Gerald grinned. 'Not my taste.'

Just then we heard a noise behind us, footsteps running and someone calling Lord Kildare's name. The man flung himself onto the ground at Gerald's feet and held out a letter.

'From m'lady Dorset. She said 'twere urgent.'

Gerald broke the seal and quickly read the contents.

'Where is Lady Dorset?'

'Greenwich m'lord. On her way to Bradgate within the hour, she said.'

'Tell her she has my thanks. Go now. Don't linger.'

The man scrambled to his feet and ran off down the path. Gerald reached for my hand.

'It's the sweat. A dozen dead in the palace. Your sister-in-law says the king has gone to Waltham. He's taken the queen and Mistress Anne.'

The sweat! Alive at breakfast, dead by supper. That was the sweat. The most dreaded disease after the plague, one which struck terror into the heart of every man, woman and child.

For two months while the sweat ravaged the city we sheltered in the peace of Thomas Howard's manor house at Newington. Everyone I knew had fled: Mary to Westhorpe, Meg to Bradgate and my mother to Astley. Cardinal Wolsey had removed himself to Leeds Castle which was, Gerald reckoned, as far as he could go without losing touch with what the king was thinking. Apparently Henry had Francis Bryan sleeping in the royal bedchamber, though I doubted that would prevent the sweat from gaining entry.

We were not completely cut adrift. We heard dribs and drabs of happenings from men who supplied the house with provisions, also occasional news from Ireland when anonymous persons came unannounced and left packages for Gerald at the gatehouse.

'O'Connor has shod his horse on the hill at Tara,' my husband informed me one morning.

'Is that of importance?'

'Ah my little English wife – it is symbolic. Tara is the seat of the High Kings of Ireland. O'Connor was making a point.'

'Is there more to this story?' I asked, wondering what point Brian O'Connor was making.

'It seems my son-in-law had a parley with Henry's new lord deputy, Lord Delvin. Matters did not go well so O'Connor decided to abduct Lord Delvin.'

'Was that not somewhat foolish?'

Gerald sucked his teeth and looked up at the ceiling, as innocent as a babe in arms.

'What have you been doing?' I demanded.

'Nothing that need trouble you.'

'Good. I should be obliged if you would keep it that way. Each time you interfere, each time you chivvy your sons-in-law to make difficulties for whichever lord deputy Henry has chosen to govern Ireland, our position here becomes more precarious.'

'I always listen to my wife, so my dear Lady Fitzgerald, advise me. What do you imagine Henry will do?'

'Be angry?'

'An explosion of Tudor fury?'

'You are fortunate he's not here or he'd have you by the scruff of your neck.'

Gerald smiled. 'But I have done nothing. I sit here in Thomas Howard's house, my days spent in reading books and my nights in enjoying conjugal warmth with my wife.'

'If Henry were here I'd advise against mentioning conjugal warmth.'

This time my husband laughed. 'If I were Henry I would send our friend Piers Butler back to Ireland to restore order. He would make a strong lord deputy. Henry could give him an earldom – Ossary perhaps – to bolster his importance.'

'Is that truly what you want? I thought Piers Butler is the last man you'd want Henry to choose.'

He shrugged and picked up another letter, scrutinising it closely. 'It seems young Lord Slane is missing his wife. Perhaps it's time to send Lady Slane home to her husband.'

I'd become so used to Alice's company during our enforced stay in England that my husband's suggestion came as a shock, and an unwelcome one at that. A sensible wife would have sensed deception but I was careless, distressed at the thought of losing my stepdaughter, whose wit and conversation I'd come to value. Alice was a more stimulating companion than Meg and her quick mind made discussions on subjects as diverse as the education of women and the designing of gardens, a real pleasure. I'd become accustomed to the sound of her voice as she went about her daily duties and the thought of losing her made me tearful. What would I do without her.

Alice, as I should have guessed, was overjoyed at the prospect of returning to Ireland.

'You will be careful,' I said, trying hard not to weep as we stood waiting for her horse to be brought round from the stable yard.

She kissed my cheek. 'We Fitzgeralds always take the greatest of care.'

'Your father says he has made arrangements for your journey so you've no need to worry. He thinks it wisest you travel to Chester. The roads are in good repair at this time of year so there should be no broken bridges.'

She smiled. 'I shall follow my father's instructions to the letter, have no fear.' She gripped my hand, one last time. 'You have been a wonderful mother to me. I shall never forget.'

I demurred, touched by her words. 'I think Janet did more to raise you than I did.'

'Janet made me the girl I was but you have made me the woman I've become. There are no words to tell you how much I treasure you.'

'Not more than your husband, I trust.'

She grinned. 'Here in London I am the daughter of Lord Kildare but in Ireland I am the one and only Lady Slane.'

And with that she was gone, riding off into the pale dawn of a July morning with her escort close around her.

Summer burned itself out and with it the sweat, leaving poor Lady Carey a widow along with hundreds of other women condemned to wear black. As Gerald predicted, Piers Butler was sent back to Ireland as the new lord deputy together with the earldom of Ossary. His remit was to restore peace. I thought he'd be a fortunate man if he could bring peace to Ireland without my husband in harness.

We had no visitors in our Newington refuge until one morning in early October when Thomas Howard arrived. Since his father's death he had inherited the title and with it the swagger of self-importance required of a duke of Norfolk. I watched out of an upstairs window, at first, surprised by the size of his escort and then alarmed at the sight of members of the royal guard. What were they doing here? We were not the enemy.

But it seems I was mistaken – we were.

I touched my husbands arm, needing the reassurance of his physical presence. 'Gerald, why are the royal guard here? Are you to be arrested?'

'I would imagine so.'

'Jesu! What have you done?'

Gerald rubbed the side of his nose. 'Sweetheart, it is of no account. Just a small matter of some unrest for which Henry undoubtedly thinks I am to blame.'

'Are you?'

He prevaricated which meant the accusation was true.

'O'Connor?'

He stroked his beard the way he did when caught doing something of which I disapproved. 'In part.'

'And the other part?'

He gave a huge sigh. 'O'Neil and my brothers.'

'What have they done?'

'Made trouble for our new lord deputy.'

'Did you tell them to?'

When he remained silent, I suddenly understood.

'Alice took a letter for them.'

'No, no. She might have been searched. I would not put my daughter at risk. I gave her no letters.'

'What did you tell her to say to them?'

He sighed. 'Nothing. There was no need.'

'Why not? Why would these men make trouble unless you gave the order?'

He put his arms around me but I refused to melt against him in the way I usually did. I was too angry. I wanted to know exactly what he'd done. After a terse exchange of words in which I left him in no doubt of how I felt, he told me, albeit reluctantly.

'The order was given before we left Ireland.'

'Are you telling me that your brothers and your son-in-law and your various friends start making trouble at a time decided on two years ago.'

'No, they had to wait.'

'Wait? Wait for what?'

'A sign.'

And in that moment I understood how it had been arranged.

'You sent your daughter to them.'

'Yes.'

'Alice was the sign.'

'Yes.'

'That is why you suggested she go home. What did you tell her to do?'

'I told her to ride straightaway to her uncles and to O'Connor. I told her as much as she needed to know and no more. I was careful.'

'Not careful enough, else we'd not have Thomas Howard at the gate.'

I felt humiliated at how stupid I'd been. I'd been wrong since the day the letters from Ireland arrived. When Gerald decided to send his daughter home, I should have been suspicious, I should have listened more carefully to the actual words Alice used – "I shall follow my father's instructions to the letter, have no fear." My husband had played me for a fool right from the moment he'd said Alice should accompany us to England.

My mother had understood. I remembered her words when I told her how considerate my husband was in bringing young Lady Slane with us to London. "I think you can be sure he has a use in mind for his daughter."

He did, but not the kind of use I imagined.

They took him away to the Tower and would not permit me to visit. I wrote to everyone I could think of, asking for help but Gerald's plight was lost amidst the turmoil surrounding the arrival of Cardinal Campeggio, sent by the Pope to investigate the king of England's marriage. His brother cardinal, Thomas Wolsey, was much too busy with the king's business to consider seeing me. My brothers refused to interfere with the wheels of justice, telling me now was not the right time to ask Henry for favours. Queen Katherine, naturally, was meeting Cardinal Campeggio and Mistress Anne had been installed at Durham House on The Strand.

Cousin Mary wrote from Westhorpe telling me she was still weak from her encounter with the sweat but recovering thanks to the ministrations of her stepdaughters. "I hear the Italian cardinal is to ask Katherine to retire to a convent so my brother can remarry. It distresses me Henry cannot see the damage he is causing."

Meg Wooton came to see me, not to give assistance because Thomas had strictly forbidden her to meddle, but to impart the latest gossip.

'We shall be at Greenwich for Christmas,' she confided. 'We are to lodge in the queen's rooms but I've heard The Lady, as we now call her, is to have a fine apartment close to the king. Lady Gertrude is taking bets on whether there's a private stairway so they can meet in secret.'

'They bed together?'

'Lady Carey says not and I suppose she would know.'

'What of Queen Katherine?'

'Downcast.'

'And The Lady herself?'

'Reading a French translation of the epistles of St Paul. Did you know she owns Lutheran books written in English so anyone can read them.'

'Hmm. Not something approved of by either cardinal, I'd imagine.'

Meg chattered on but had nothing more of interest to impart and no news of my husband.

Nightly I prayed for his return, frightened of what might be happening in the Tower. Great men like Gerald were not tortured, that would not be allowed, but there were ways to break a man's spirit other than damaging his body. No-one had inflicted actual violence on Cousin Mary in the mourning chamber at the Hôtel de Cluny in Paris, but by the time I gained access to that dark little room, she was nearly broken. She would have agreed to anything Madame Louise wanted, signed any confession, done whatever the devious François d'Angoulême suggested. It was a miracle she survived. I prayed my husband would also survive. It was all I could do.

One morning a month later when I'd almost given up hope, he returned, looking none the worse for his incarceration.

'It was a farce,' he announced happily. 'They threatened to charge me with treason but when it came to it, had insufficient evidence.'

'So we can go home.' I was scarcely able to believe a return to Maynooth was within our grasp.

'Alas, not yet. I am released into the care of Thomas Howard and must stay here at Newington.'

I tried hard not to show my distress. Two-year-old

Bess had not seen our home at Maynooth or her brother Gerry who was now three and a half. If we were held here for another year, my firstborn son would be nearly five. By the time we returned he'd have forgotten me. My mother had once spoken of the need to keep my eldest son close, for reasons she'd not cared to elaborate, but how could I when we were separated by such a vast distance. Sitting in Thomas Howard's manor house at Newington on that misty day in late November, our island below the horizon seemed further away than ever and *Tir na nÓg* naught but a distant dream.

25

THE MANOR HOUSE AT SHACKELWELL
MAY 1529

To receive a letter from my brother was unexpected as Thomas usually conveyed his wishes obliquely via his wife. I slid my knife under the seal, wondering what was so important to necessitate putting pen to paper.

I read the letter twice.

'It is my mother,' I said to Gerald who was perusing a letter written in some kind of code which had come pressed between pages of an innocent copy of Thomas More's "Utopia".

'The marquess has ordered me to pay her a visit.'

He looked up with great interest.

'I thought only I was permitted to order my wife.'

I smiled at him. 'Naturally obedience to a husband comes first. Shall I write to my brother telling him my husband refuses permission for me to visit my mother?'

He chuckled. 'I've no desire to offend the marquess. I merely wish to remind my wife who is her master.'

I bent down and kissed his cheek. 'As if I could forget.'

He placed his hand on the front of my gown where even to an untutored eye it was obvious that another little Fitzgerald was growing apace. Gerald had not wasted his enforced seclusion at Newington merely in reading.

'Give your mother my humblest good wishes.'

'She likes you.'

He grinned. 'Women do.'

'It's a pity Wolsey doesn't.'

He eased his shoulders and leant back in his chair. 'Wolsey needs to look to his own problems. I hear the king is becoming impatient. He wants Mistress Anne in his bed and expects Wolsey to make it happen.'

'My sisters tell me there's to be a tribunal at Blackfriars which will settle the matter.'

'Then doubtless your lady mother already knows the verdict.'

My mother was staying at the manor house in the nearby village of Shacklewell so it took me no more than half an hour to walk there. It was a lovely sunny morning, barely a cloud in the sky, and on the green were remnants of the villagers' Mayday celebrations. My escort was nervous at my being on foot but I was unconcerned. The path was well-trodden and there were plenty of women about.

The manor house was quiet, almost oppressively so, with little sign of occupation. I was greeted by my mother's steward who began to make apologies for his lack of preparedness and was still apologising when he showed me into my mother's room where two young maidservants were standing by a table, one with a tray of small glass bottles, the other with a basket of strange-looking fruits. My mother was lying in her great curtained bed, propped up on a lace-trimmed pillow looking very regal and not at all well.

At a nod from the steward both the maidservants scuttled out of the room leaving their bounty behind.

I curtsied, murmured a greeting and approached the bed, noting the sound of the closing door which meant my mother and I were now alone.

As was her wont, she wrong-footed me from the start.

'I hear Lord Kildare's been in the Tower.'

'It was a short visit, Lady Mother. He is returned to Newington.'

She nodded at my belly. 'Been busy I see. Did my son send for you?'

'No, he merely suggested I visit.'

'Did he tell you why?'

I shook my head. 'He gave no reason, not that I need one; I know my duty as a daughter.'

'Hah! He thinks I'm dying or rather he hopes I'm dying. Wants my money. Always has. A greedy man just like our sovereign prince.'

I forbore to correct her on either point as I reckoned she was probably right, though I'd not have said such a thing.

'I'm told you know this Boleyn creature.'

My mother's spies kept her well informed so it was unsurprising she'd heard of Henry's continuing interest in Sir Thomas Boleyn's younger daughter.

'She was with me in France when we both served Cousin Mary.'

'What's she like?'

I paused wondering how best to describe Anne Boleyn.

'Clever, somewhat Frenchified, elegant, ambitious and flat-chested.'

My mother nearly choked on her laughter.

'A minx?'

'A schemer. As I said, she's clever.'

'And Henry? How much destruction will he accept in order to have her?'

'Lady Mother, I have no idea. I am not privy to the king's thoughts.'

She sniffed as if she did not believe me.

'From what I hear, Lord Kildare is capable of demolishing castles as well as men's ambitions. Ask him at what point does a man say – this far I will go and no further?'

'My husband is fully aware of what he is doing,' I replied, devoutly hoping I was right.

My mother's eyebrows rose slightly.

'D'you think Henry does?'

'I believe the king is always cognisant of his actions.'

'Is that so. Katherine's stubborn. She'll not give him what he wants. She is convinced of the lawfulness of her marriage. If Henry cannot contain his passion, he will have to destroy her.'

My stomach lurched at the thought of what form Henry's destruction might take.

'Lady Gertrude says he wants a son,' I proffered as if that was sufficient cause.

'All men want sons and Mistress Anne has undoubtedly promised him one. It is the way to assuage Henry's newly pricked conscience. But I ask myself, is our sovereign prince consumed by lust or by his kingdom's need for a male heir? Who's on her side? The Boleyns will see advantages for themselves, being as grasping as the next family. What of our friend, Thomas Howard?'

'Anne Boleyn's mother is a Howard, a sister to the duke.'

'She'll need a cleric. Wolsey won't do it. He may be Henry's man but he's God's man first. Henry cannot make him pope, more's the pity. That would solve the problem.'

She gave a throaty old woman's chuckle at her way of resolving the king's difficulties. Caught between Henry's need for a son, his lust for Anne Boleyn and an intransigent wife backed by the princes of the Church, I could see no solution.

My mother reached for a handkerchief and wiped her eyes. 'What does Lord Kildare think?'

'He has more pressing problems on his mind that arranging the king of England's marriage,' I said smoothly, noticing how my mother's voice was beginning to fade.'

'Do you know why I asked for you?' she said.

'I thought it was my brother's idea.'

She wafted her hand, dismissing Thomas as an irrelevance.

'He does as he's bid. Now listen carefully. The king's Great Matter, as my son pleases to call this fuss, will likely bring danger to men such as your husband. Warn him to tread lightly. Remind him, *Indignatio principis mors est*. You know what that means?'

'The anger of the prince means death.'

She nodded her approval. 'Glad to see your education's not been wasted. You're the only one of my children with an ounce of intelligence. Tell Lord Kildare that sometimes it is necessary to bend the knee to survive. I've seen many a man mistake their ambition for God's will, and a martyr's death serves no-one. When a good man dies it is we women who are left with the pieces of a life.'

I doubted my mother knew any good men as her opinions were usually hostile. Perhaps, to her, all the good men were dead.

She crooked her fingers, beckoning me closer.

'Come, let me give you a blessing.'

I knelt down, wondering if this would be the last time I'd see her. I felt her hand tremble as she laid it on my head; heard the rasp in her voice as she murmured the words of blessing. My brother might lust after his inheritance but I knew my mother's strengths. She would continue to breathe for as long as she was able, if only out of spite.

A few weeks later my sisters informed me our brother was in London. The king and queen were to give evidence in front of the Legantine Court at Blackfriars and Thomas was to support the king. This was no surprise as Thomas was always a man to be at Henry's side. Like Charles Brandon, his prowess in the tiltyard and his unswerving loyalty to Henry, had brought him the king's favour. Whatever Meg might think, the family's rewards: the manors, the valuable offices, military appointments and princely gifts, all flowed form the king's hand

Like my sisters I was not permitted to attend the Legantine Court as I possessed no private information about the royal marriage, nothing which was not freely available to others who'd observed the king and queen over the years. I presumed the evidence of men would weigh more heavily than that of a woman but the queen could not be excluded, however much the cardinals might wish it. I wondered what she would say or if she would refuse to recognise the court.

My curiosity was soon satisfied when a breathless and somewhat disordered Meg arrived with news. As my mother had predicted, Katherine was in no mood to yield.

'On her knees!' Meg was wide-eyed, still overawed by all she had seen and heard at Blackfriars. 'In front of the king and the whole court. Imagine! The king raised her up, I mean, he could hardly do otherwise, but she cast herself down again. She was magnificent!'

I had no doubt Katherine was magnificent. Her royal pedigree was impeccable She'd been raised by her Spanish mother, Queen Isabella, who devised her daughter's destiny in the cradle. No-one cared to mention it, but whichever way you looked at it, Katherine was more royal than Henry.

'Tell me everything. What did the queen say? How did she counter the king's claim that their marriage was not good and lawful because she was his brother's wife?'

This was the central plank in Henry's argument – a man may not marry his brother's wife. It rested on Henry's claim that Katherine had lain with his brother and he had known her, carnally.

'She put it to his conscience. She dared him to say she was not a true maid when he first had her, that no man had touched her. She appealed her case to God.'

'Will she succeed?'

'I tell you this, if it was up to the women of this country, the verdict would be no doubt, but Thomas tells me there is much work afoot to give the king what he wants.'

'Poor Katherine.'

Meg nodded and prattled on, telling me how Katherine had leant on her gentleman usher's arm as she left the chamber without a backward glance and how there'd been men queuing up to recount their version of the events of that night twenty-eight years ago when Prince Arthur was first put to bed with his Spanish bride. The passage of time did not appear to have dimmed their enjoyment of a good story. Their memories were as sharp as if it had been yesterday.

That evening, once we were alone, I asked my husband what he remembered.

'You were Arthur's friend, were you not?'

He gave a sad smile. 'Yes, I was, A good friend. I feared my heart would break when he died. He would have made a wonderful king.'

'You know what is being said?'

'About?'

'About what passed between the couple in their marriage bed.'

He closed his eyes as if trying to equate the Katherine that was then with the stout little queen of today.

'He was nervous. He'd never had a woman. We told him not to worry, the lady, being Spanish, would know what to do. You must understand, we had a very poor opinion of foreigners in those days.'

'And afterwards?'

He laid his hand on mine. 'Sweetheart, I know you women like to believe we men talk about our wives but the truth is we have more important matters to discuss.'

Such as?'

He grinned. 'Horses, gambling, jousting, warfare, dogs.'

'So I am not important.'

'You are to me but not to someone like, say, Thomas Howard.'

'Do men never discuss their wives, not even to ask how the wedding night was?'

'A man might enquire if his friend found his bride to his liking.'

'And the friend? What might the friend reply?'

'That she was greatly to his liking, but that would be all.'

'And Prince Arthur?'

He hesitated for a moment before replying. 'If I remember any words, I do not say them, and nobody but an inquisitive wife has ever asked. Let that be an end to the discussion.'

I knew better than to press him further. I had no wish to embroil him in the increasingly dangerous tensions circulating around The King's Great Matter. My husband was careless in some of his own affairs but not in Henry's.

Giving birth, even to a slip of a child, is an arduous business, something best achieved without the interference of men, so Gerald's first sight of our second daughter was a tranquil affair. I was sitting in a chair, wrapped in my blue velvet nightgown with the baby asleep in her cradle nearby.

'Thank God you are both safe,' he said, kissing me.

I signalled for the nursemaid to give me the baby.

'My lord, your daughter. Mary, greet your father, the mighty Fitzgerald earl of Kildare.'

The baby gave a little yawn but refused to open her eyes.

My husband grimaced. 'I am in disfavour with young Miss Fitzgerald.'

'But not with your wife. The locket is exquisite.'

He squeezed my hand. 'A mere trifle. I have in mind something more splendid for your next gift.'

I handed the baby back to the nursemaid who took her out of the room to be fed. I placed my cheek against the back of my husband's hand, thanking God and my brother for giving me such a generous husband.

'Tell me your news.'

Gerald looked round the room, at the comforts of our life, even here at Newington. 'Wolsey's gone.'

'Gone where?'

'Henry's booted him out. He's no longer chancellor. He's been told to go North.'

'North to where?'

'Anywhere, as long as it's far away and out of Henry's sight.'

I felt a pang of sorrow for Thomas Wolsey, the man who'd risen high from such low beginnings, who'd brokered the deal with Henry which allowed Cousin Mary and Lord Suffolk to return to England, albeit impoverished and in Henry's debt. Nobody much liked Wolsey but he had proved useful.

'Poor man.'

'Henry sent Norfolk and Brandon to take back the Great Seal.'

'That is cruel but I suppose if you wish to humble a man, you send his enemies to rub his nose in the disgrace. Why now?'

'Wolsey couldn't give the king what he wanted so he's had to go.'

'Is there anyone who can?'

'Only the pope, but I doubt he'll agree to an annulment. Henry's caught in a bind.'

26

A PARTING OF THE WAYS
1530

Christmas was drawing near, our fourth spent away from Maynooth, with still no sign of when we might return. If not for a surprise visit from Cousin Mary, I might have descended into despair. I knew she was at Greenwich for the festivities but had not expected to see her before the New Year.

Like a caring godmother, she first asked to see her namesake, little Mary; we then spent an enjoyable hour discussing the joys of daughters. Mary's two, twelve-year-old Frances and ten-year-old Eleanor. were both old enough to be the subject of marriage negotiations.

'Frances is distraught at being separated from Princess Mary. She wanted to go with her to Ludlow but unfortunately that was not possible.'

I wondered which parent had made that decision: Henry, Katherine or Brandon. Although Cousin Mary loved her daughter, she would have relished the chance for her to be with Princess Mary as she formed her first little court at Ludlow. Perhaps Henry was punishing Katherine or his sister or his daughter. Destruction could take many forms, from shoeing your horse on the hill at Tara, to abduction or death.

'Does your husband have anyone in mind for your daughters?'

Cousin Mary laughed. 'Brandon's talking to the marquess. Your brother's heir is the same age as Frances. We both think it a good match and it would bring our families even closer together. Does that please you?'

'More than I can say. Does my mother know? I doubt my brother has told her.'

'It is not my place to mention it.'

'Nor mine.'

We smiled at each other, recognizing our complex feelings about the duty of a woman to yield authority to a man.

Cousin Mary reached out to smooth Bess's fine red-gold strands where they'd escaped from her cap. 'I had forgotten how enchanting they are when they're little.'

'I'm big,' announced my daughter to the embarrassment of her nursemaid who shushed her.

Cousin Mary laughed. 'You are, *ma petitie*, and one day you will be even bigger.'

I signalled for the children to be returned to the nursery which allowed Mary and I some privacy and an opportunity for me to discover what was happening at court.

'It is truly dreadful. Henry allows that woman to take outrageous liberties. Did you hear she sat in the queen's chair.'

I gave a gasp at the thought of Mistress Anne Boleyn having the temerity to do such a thing.'

'Did nobody stop her?'

'If the king says nothing, how would anyone else dare.'

'When was this?'

'At the feast to celebrate Sir Thomas Boleyn being raised to the earldoms of Wiltshire and Ormonde.'

'I presume, Katherine did not attend.'

'Henry has ordered her to leave Greenwich for Richmond.'

The cruelty! To order his loyal wife of twenty years to leave the palace so that his paramour could flaunt herself in front of the court. Was there no end to the savagery Henry would inflict on an innocent woman to get what he wanted. I remembered my mother's musings as to the lengths a sovereign prince might go. She said Henry would have to destroy Katherine.

'Is there nothing anyone can do?'

'I complained, said words which were less than complimentary about that interloper who has turned my brother's head. Henry was angry; told me I could go back to Westhorpe if I could not be civil. Oh Cousin Elizabeth, I hate being at odds with my brother but I cannot bear what he is doing. It is wrong. It is wrong in the eyes of God and wrong in the eyes of all right-thinking people. Brandon says Henry will stop at nothing to have her. It is an obsession.'

'What of the others who witnessed this?'

'The dowager duchess of Norfolk was affronted. Her words, if anything, were more incendiary than mine, not ones I could possibly repeat. I would imagine Mistress Anne will have her uncle reprimand his stepmother, order her to keep her mouth shut in public. Let her rant in private if she must but not in front of the whole court.'

We talked some more about the impossibility of Katherine's situation. She wished to be a good wife and obey her husband but not if his wishes ran counter to her faith.

It was nearly Eastertide. As I came into the room, Master Holbein, who'd visited us the previous week was just leaving, laden as usual with boxes and brushes and the other accoutrements of his trade. He was a strange man, imbued with the unmistakeable smell of paint. His reputation as an artist was the subject of wistful longings by Meg Wooton who'd been trying for months to persuade Thomas to let Master Holbein draw her, not that I thought she'd succeed.

Master Holbein bowed, smiled and said something in his broken English, which I gathered was a polite farewell.

'Has he finished?' I asked Gerald.

He walked over and stood in front of me.

'Close your eyes.'

I did as I was bid. I heard various scuffles and then, 'You may open them.'

At first I saw nothing unusual, but then I moved my gaze beyond my husband's shoulder and there on the wall was a likeness of him, so true to life it might have been Gerald's image in a mirror. Master Holbein had captured the regular features of his face, the fine line of his nose and his well-set eyes, even the sensuous mouth half-hidden by his luxuriant beard. For a moment I was tempted to touch it.

'What d'you think?'

I put my head on one side. 'A truly handsome man. Do I know him?'

He grinned. 'If you don't by now, Lady Kildare, you clearly need reminding. That is why I had it done for you. An Easter gift o remind you of me when I'm not here.'

A ripple of fear, like a gentle breeze, plucked at the

strings of my heart, reminding me of the many unseen dangers which surrounded my husband whether here or in Ireland. I wanted to keep him close in the way I could my children, protect him from those who would harm him. But I knew that was impossible. In England we were subject to the king's will and in Ireland, danger lurked behind every tree, ditch or castle wall. All I could do, all any woman could do, was pray. I thought of Alice wishing to be a soldier and thought I too, would take up arms if it would keep my husband safe.

Like spring, which crept up on me unawares with primroses and violets tucked under the hedgerows and furious nest building in the elms lining the driveway, the visits of two of my brothers and Thomas Howard, were unexpected. They came, closeted themselves with my husband for an hour, and went; then came and went again. When my brothers arrived once more, this time accompanied by our new earl of Wiltshire and Ormonde, Thomas Boleyn, and still Gerald said nothing, I thought I was entitled to be curious.

'I wanted it to be a surprise,' my husband said plaintively.

'I am already surprised, more surprised than you can imagine. What plot are you hatching with Mistress Anne's father?'

He held up his hands in surrender. 'The king is minded to allow me to return to Ireland.'

'Oh!'

My lips began trembling and I had a sudden desire to weep. 'Home?'

'Yes sweetheart, home. To Maynooth.'

I could hardly speak as wave after wave of happiness swept over me. 'When? How?'

Gerald smiled. 'I know you have a poor opinion of the marquess, nevertheless he, your brother Leonard and our friends Thomas Howard and the Boleyns have been working hard on my behalf. They have persuaded the king that in my absence, good rule in Ireland cannot be maintained, thus it is best that I return.'

'You are to be lord deputy?'

He laughed. 'Henry is not that forgiving. Sir William Skeffington is to be lord deputy.'

'I do not know Sir William.'

Gerald grinned. 'An old man. Extremely old.'

I ignored my husband's smirk at the thought of the extremely old Sir William Skeffington trying to control the warring factions in Ireland.

'If Sir William is to be lord deputy, what does the king want of you? I presume promises of good behaviour have been extracted.'

'I am to compel the border chiefs to make peace. Skeffington has been given the thankless task of reconciling Ossary and Desmond to my friendship.'

'Which will be easy,' I said with thinly veiled sarcasm.

'Skeffington must also convene a parliament to secure a subsidy for the king.'

'Pleasing to Henry.'

'Is not all this pleasing to you?'

'Oh yes, yes, a hundred times yes.'

And with that, I reached up and kissed him, forgetting we were in full view of our household and this was not

Maynooth where such reckless behaviour between a lord and his lady would be appreciated and greeted with cheers.

I wrote to Cousin Mary and to my sisters, informing them that shortly I would be returning to Ireland, so was only a little surprised when next day my sister Cecily arrived, demanding an interview.

She had barely entered the room when she began to weep. After all these years, Cecily was still unable to weep elegantly. Most wives quickly master the art of squeezing out a few tears for a husband while looking suitably woebegone. Not Cecily. I was treated to several noisy snuffling sobs which she failed to stifle with the handkerchief she'd pulled out of her sleeve, dabbing ineffectually at her eyes.

'It is our lady mother. She is sick.'

The pathos was spoiled by a great hiccough and another sob.

I cursed myself for postponing my planned visit to Shacklewell. I should have gone as soon as I knew we were leaving.

'She is asking for you,' Cecily mumbled.

'What does she want?'

'How should I know. It's not me she asked for.'

Now I understood. From the moment I was chosen to join Cousin Mary's little household at court, Cecily had nursed a grudge. I was only seven years old and a little tearful but before I left Astley for the last time, my sister had pinched me and whispered, "Don't imagine you're our mother's favourite, 'cos you're not."

That was long ago, yet the resentment still lingered, lurking just below her surface pleasantries.

'Shall we go together?' I suggested.

She looked at me, cheeks tear-stained, her nose decidedly pink.

'Why? It's not me she wants.'

'Cecily, I want you. You're my sister. I'd feel more at ease if we went together. Please, Cecily.'

She looked at me warily as if I was proposing some trick to her disadvantage. 'Oh very well. If you insist.'

Gloom invested the house at Shacklwell, a funereal atmosphere made worse by the presence of our brother, muttering to himself about the debts his mother had accrued and how he'd be ruined. Thomas was standing outside her bedchamber with a sheaf of papers in his hands, looking morose. It was perhaps not acceptable to notice at such a moment, but he did not appear joyful at the prospect of imminent riches. In fact, he looked none to well.

He eyed me. 'You'd best go in '

When Cecily made to follow, he put out his arm to bar her way. 'Not you; just Elizabeth.'

Not waiting to hear Cecily's complaints, I stepped hurriedly into the room and shut the door. This time there was no doubt my mother was nearing the end of her long and troubled life. Her face was ashen and her lips had a blueish tinge. Two elderly maidservants hovered at one side of the bed while on the other, the chaplain, head bowed, was murmuring a litany of prayers. My mother seemed asleep.

As I approached the bed she opened her eyes.

'Elizabeth! Is that you?'

'Yes, Lady Mother. I am come to see how you are.'

'Get rid of them,' she whispered, 'All of them.'

It took some persuasion to get the three to leave their posts, the chaplain, in particular, convinced his presence at a time of imminent death, was necessary. But I was firm. My mother wished for privacy with her daughter. Once the door was finally closed, I returned to the bedside.

She grasped my wrist. Her fingers were thin, her knuckles shiny, and her grip not as strong as it used to be.

'What is it, Lady Mother? Are you in pain?'

She struggled for breath.

'Danger,' she whispered.

'Where?' I said, foolishly looking over my shoulder for some unseen attacker.

'Your grandmother. The Woodville woman.'

'Lady Mother, my Woodville grandmother is dead. She died before I was born.'

She tried to shake her head, dislodging her lace-trimmed night cap in the process. I carefully rearranged the cap and retied the ribbons, noticing how beneath her nightshift, my mother was nothing but skin and bone.

She glared at me. 'Of course she's dead; died poor. Sent to a nunnery by the Tudor. He had to be rid of her; she knew too much.'

She began to cough, little exhalations of greenish phlegm while her chest heaved beneath the bedcovers. She let go of my wrist to clutch at her throat.

I found a cloth and wiped her mouth. 'Lady Mother, please; you are tiring yourself.'

'Meant to tell you before but I forgot. Not enough time.'

'I am here now and we have plenty of time.'

'Her fault she lost them. Greedy she was. Thought she could fool us.'

It was hard to follow these ramblings about my Woodville grandmother, the one I shared with Cousin Mary. Her two marriages had made Mary a princess while I was born just plain Lady Elizabeth Grey.

'What did she lose, Lady Mother?'

She looked at me as if I was stupid. 'Her boys. Went into the Tower. Never saw them again.'

'They were murdered by Richard the Usurper.'

My mother began to laugh, a hideous old woman's cackle. 'Who told you that?'

'Everyone knows Richard the Usurper had the two little princes murdered. It was a tragedy but there's no mystery.'

'Didn't happen like that but no matter. It's in the past. Precious few of us left who remember. Henry's grandmother. She remembered. She knew the truth. Clever woman. Kept her mouth shut.'

I gave a sigh. 'Lady Mother, this is in the past, there is no danger, not now.'

The grip on my wrist tightened.

'I despised her but the fault was not hers. He lied. A single untruth. If he'd not lied none of this would have happened.'

'Lady Mother, I don't understand what you're trying to tell me.'

She stopped, lost in the tangled web of her story. With

a great effort she pulled herself back to the present, to the two of us together in that fetid little room.

'Elizabeth, take care of your sons. I pray you do not lose them. I know you are neither greedy nor careless, but watch your husband for I fear he has become both.'

I tried to speak but she waved my protests away.

'Elizabeth, I'll not see this year's harvest no matter what the doctors say. I am ready to meet my maker but I need to know you will do as I ask. Swear on the Bible.'

I fetched her Bible and laid my hand on the worn cover and vowed I would do as she asked. She put out her hand to take mine.

'You have been a good daughter. Do as I ask and remember what I told you: guard your sons from Henry. Now come closer and let me kiss you.'

She died the next day and two weeks later we buried her, as she had wanted, in the Church of St Mary the Virgin at Astley, beside my father. As she was lowered into the ground my brother was still muttering about the vast cost of providing the tomb she'd requested in her will and the thousand Masses for her soul to be said in as convenient haste as may be.

27

THE CASTLE OF MAYNOOTH
LATE SUMMER 1530

We went home. Sir William Skeffington, looking none to happy with his new appointment, must have been nigh on seventy and as we waited to disembark, he regarded my husband with a sceptical eye. He knew, as we all did, that no matter how well-polished were his two hundred and fifty troops, or what powers Henry had decided to invest in his new lord deputy, Lord Kildare would be seen by most as the true governor of Ireland. As my husband had told me on many occasions, a king of Ireland can never be ousted by an English deputy.

Dublin was full of my husband's supporters who made such a din with their bugles and drums that I was tempted to feel sorry for Sir William who doubtless thought the welcome was for him. All the way to Maynooth we were accompanied by what must have been thousands of Gerald's friends. I spied two of his brothers as well as dozens of Brian O'Connor's men, singing and waving flags. Every so often, someone would leap on top of a rock to give an impromtu rendering of a verse praising the manifold virtues of the earls of Kildare. Each time, the crowd erupted into cheers and shouts for more whereupon we were treated to songs lauding battles of the past. Flagons of ale were passed round and by the time I spied our home, the men were all wildly drunk and the noise so great it must have been heard by Sir William far away in his castle in Dublin.

I could barely breathe for fear I'd not recognise my son. He'd been a child of two when we left and I'd not seen him for four years, but I would have known him anywhere. A lightly built boy with my hair and that very distinctive Fitzgerald look. He was standing on the steps holding Janet's hand.

I dismounted and without waiting for my husband walked up to our welcoming party. Janet curtsied, her face one wide smile.

'Welcome home, m'lady.'

I sensed rather than saw the slight push she gave my son. He looked at me with his father's eyes and gave a little bow.

'Welcome home, my lady,' he whispered.

I smiled at him. 'Do you know who I am, Master Gerald?'

'Lady Mother?'

'Yes, I am your lady mother and I have come home to be with you.'

He looked at me warily. 'Is Mistress Janet going away?'

'I think she will be too busy to go anywhere. I have brought more children for her to look after. Would you like to meet them?'

He was unsure. I was a stranger whereas Janet was familiar but after a little hesitation he let go of her hand and allowed me to take him to where my other children were being lifted down from the cart.

That evening, as Gerald and I sat in our private room, all four children were brought in to say their goodnights to their parents. The nursemaids had managed to remove the grime of travel from the younger three and detach Bess from her newfound brother who was, she told me, more fun than Edward who knew no interesting words.

'What interesting words does Gerry know?' I asked, expecting some Gaelic.

'I'd not ask that, m'lady,' Janet murmured. 'The guards are none to careful with their language when young Master Gerry is about.'

I flashed her a grateful smile, wondering how I had managed all those years without Janet. She was the woman who lifted a hundred burdens from my shoulders, the rock to which I and my children could cling when the cold east winds threatened to engulf us in danger.

My husband and I kissed our children and gave them our blessing for a safe night. As the little procession left on their way to the nursery I saw Edward appropriate Janet's hand. He was a child who needed to feel safe because he was not as brave as his older brother and sister.

After a month it was as if we had never been away. The rhythm of our days settled over me and I began to feel that special contentment I always felt at Maynooth. My husband was not off making trouble and we were surrounded by our children. Perhaps this was my *Tir na nÓg*, my land of everlasting youth where bloom was on every bough and the air was heavy with the sweetness of orchards.

Even news from England failed to disturb my peaceful

existence. Gerald had a letter informing him of the death of my brother, Thomas, followed quickly by a lengthy missive to me from Meg, mainly decrying the paucity of her dower, the meanness of her late husband and the difficulties she was having with her eldest son. Thomas's heir saw no reason why his mother should spend his income and live in what he regarded as his properties.

A month later we heard that Wolsey was no more, hounded to death by a vengeful cabal of Howards and Boleyns. But at the last, the cardinal had cheated his enemies of a public disgrace, dying on his way south to stand trial for his so-called crimes.

Cousin Mary wrote, a litany of complaints about the harsh treatment meted out by her brother to Katherine and reports that Mistress Anne had shocked the court by wishing all Spaniards at the bottom of the sea and how she would rather be hanged than confess that Katherine was her queen and mistress.

'One day Mistress Anne will go too far,' I said to my husband.

'I reckon she will, but not yet. She still has the king in the palm of her hand.'

How far a person might go before incurring the king's wrath worried me, not because of Mistress Anne and her intemperate outbursts, but because of my husband's increasing difficulties with Sir William Skeffington, not to mention those with his cousin, Piers Butler. Henry's grand plan for his kingdom of Ireland depended on goodwill and co-operation, both of which were in increasingly short supply.

By the time we heard that Henry had quit Windsor,

riding off to Woodstock with Mistress Anne and the rest of his court, abandoning Katherine to a palace of empty rooms and bitter memories, my husband had fallen out with Sir William and recommenced his feud with his cousin. We'd been home for less than a year.

In October Gerald told me the Irish parliament in Dublin had thrown out the subsidy bill which meant no money would be forthcoming to fill the king's purse. Throughout the winter I worried what Henry's next move would be, nurturing the wholly unworthy thought that if only Mistress Anne would surrender her long-prized virginity, Henry's temper might improve.

My hopes were in vain. Before Easter Gerald was summoned back to court to explain himself. The only glimmer of brightness was that Piers Butler's son, James, had also been summoned.

'We shall blame Skeffington,' Gerald announced happily.

'Indeed,' I said, wishing I knew someone who could weigh in on my husband's side other than the son of his unreliable cousin.

Our visit to England was mercifully brief, allowing me a short visit to Mary at Westhorpe and my husband time to persuade Henry to return him to the position of lord deputy with Piers Butler as treasurer. Poor Sir William Skeffington's reputation was suitably trashed. He was to be recalled.

That autumn, word from England was of Queen Katherine's continuing humiliation and isolation from her friends.

This was eclipsed by news of the impending visit to France by Henry and the scandal of him taking with him, not his queen, but Anne Boleyn, the newly ennobled Marquess of Pembroke.

'Do you think she has yielded?' I asked my husband.

Gerald looked up from the letter he was reading. From the frown on his face I guessed he'd not been listening. The man who'd brought the message had ridden in less than an hour ago, almost fainting with tiredness and hunger.

'Bad news?' I asked.

'Son-in-law O'Carroll. Problems. He needs help.'

I'd heard words like these often, when one kinsman or another required assistance from the mighty earl of Kildare, when Gerald gathered his galloglass and his followers and rode off to do battle, so there was nothing to account for my sudden stirring of disquiet. There was no reason. The demesne was only a week's ride to the west, wooded country, long held by the eternally squabbling O'Carrolls.

The garden was covered in the slightest of frosts, a breath of silvering on every branch and stone, an eerie silence betraying the absence of birds or small animals. Even my faithful hound, kept close to my skirts as if sensing some impending disaster. As I walked, I thought of the gardens at Greenwich where Gerald had courted me and where we had finally sealed our compact. I smiled, recalling how Francis Bryan had once tried to lure me into the bushes for what he described as a little dalliance. He reminded me of my stepson Tom who had grown into a handsome, reckless, charming young man. I loved him as a son but wholly disapproved of his behaviour. Janet was more forgiving, telling me all young men were the same.

I was about to open the door to the lower garden when I felt the hairs on the back of my neck begin to prickle and a shiver run right down my spine which owed nothing to the frost. That was when I knew.

I turned and fled back across the garden, through the door and up the back stairs. Janet was waiting for me.

I looked at her in horror. 'What is it?'

She put an arm round my shoulder and gently but firmly pushed me down into a chair by the fire.

'One of the lads came. They are bringing him home.'

'Is he dead?'

'No, but he's badly hurt.'

'But not dead?'

'No; he's been shot.'

She told me over and over again that my husband was alive, there was still hope, that I must be brave. The lad had little to tell, only how the lord had taken a shot to his body from a handgun. At first they'd thought him near slain until they noticed he was still breathing. His men had done all they could, then put him on a cart. But the journey would take some days as the driver had no wish to jolt the lord and make the bleeding start again.

I have little memory of the day he was returned to me, a broken man, closer to death than life. In the cart he'd lain on a board which meant the servants could carry him to his room without having to manhandle him – a mercy, Walter said.

The Maynooth doctors, assisted by Janet, worked tirelessly to repair the damage caused to his body. It was like a scene from my worst nightmare. Working by candlelight first they washed the site of the wound with a cloth soaked in vinegar, then used a metal implement to recover the shot.

'How do they know the shot is still inside his body?' I asked, alarmed at what was to be done.

'No exit wound,' murmured Janet.

The most experienced of our three doctors, having satisfied himself that the skin around the wound was clean, dipped the metal probe into a large pot of rose honey, then gently inserted it into the hole made by the wound.

I felt close to fainting and clutched at Janet.

'The sweetness of the honey cleanses the inside of a body,' she explained.

'Light!' murmured the doctor.

Two servants carried the candleholders closer. I was terrified but unable to look away.

And so it went on, hour after hour, a terrible assault on my poor husband's already damaged body.

It took nigh on half a day to finally locate and remove the shot – a vile-looking lump of lead the size of a pebble, yet still the doctor probed.

'What is he doing?'

Janet soothed me. 'There's danger of souring the air inside. Pieces of cloth may have been carried into your husband's body by the shot, so the doctor must search and, once found, try to remove them. It is a skill possessed by few and not one to be rushed.'

Each time the probe was pulled out, it had to be dipped in honey before it could be reinserted. It was a slow and lengthy procedure but eventually the doctor announced he was satisfied all foreign matter had been retrieved and the body fully cleansed.

He then turned his attention to the repair of Gerald's shattered left hand. Bone and flesh were mangled together so splints were of no use. His final verdict was a pithy statement: 'As well 'twas Lord Kildare's left hand. He'll manage fine with his sword arm.'

The doctor must have been exhausted but he smiled at me out of a pair of tired eyes. 'Your husband's recovery now lies in God's hands and in yours, my lady. Mistress Janet knows what to do.'

I wish I could claim credit for Gerald's recovery, slow though it was, but Janet was the one with the skill and the knowledge. I merely followed her instructions as we bathed and bandaged and poulticed his chest and shoulder. The wound had to be cleansed daily with honey lest it should start to smell, a sign dreaded by those with experience of dealing with wounds.

What made our task harder was that Gerald was unable to speak.

'Dinna fret,' Janet said. 'Give him time; 'tis best he lies quiet for now. Just talk to him. Tell him how the children are doing; things that will give him pleasure. No talk of sieges or warfare. Sing to him. Perhaps play your lute or read to him. Say your prayers with him. Tell him about that friend of yours, the one who inherited a fortune.'

In the spring I'd received a letter from Jane Bourchier, happily married to Edmund Knyvett and the mother of a fine brood of children. We'd not seen each other for nigh on eighteen years yet still maintained an occasional correspondence. She wrote to tell me Lord Berners had died in Calais, still surrounded by his books and papers. Athough she was sad to lose a father, she said the inheritance would enable her and her husband to help their children.

At Easter we celebrated Gerald's first intelligible words, as precious to me as those of each of our children. Prior to that we'd been treated to grunts and expletives and the increasing frustration of a man who knew what he wanted to say but was unable to form the words. Most days he sat in a chair, not the most restful of patients. Now that he was out of danger and pronounced likely to live, he wanted to be outside, back in the saddle, leading his men. I feared those days would never return but had not the heart to tell him.

The children treated him as they always had, his inability to answer their questions no bar to conversation. Bess would offer to comb his beard which she pronounced, most tangly, while Edward would sit at his side, clutching his good hand, whispering about fairy men in the churchyard. Gerry was the only one who realised his father was not as he should be.

'Will he be able to take me out on his big horse?' He asked, a puzzled frown on his face.

'Not this summer,' I said, stroking his sleek head.

Not this year, I thought, not ever.

By late July we had news of Archbishop Cranmer's declaration that Henry and Katherine's marriage was invalid, followed swiftly by news of the marriage of Henry and the Lady Anne and of Queen Anne's coronation.

Cousin Mary had not lived to see this final betrayal of everything she held dear. She died at Westhorpe at the height of the summer surrounded by her family. Henry gave her a magnificent funeral, a poor reward for a sister whose devotion he had taken for granted and who had never ceased loving him however much she disapproved of his actions. Of Katherine, I heard nothing, exiled to one of Henry's damp little manors on the edge of the fens, forgotten by everyone except for a few faithful friends.

Gerald's speech was improving but the weakness in his limbs persisted, making him an irritable companion, best left to Tom, who alone seemed able to lift his spirits. I fingered the letter wondering how to tackle this latest upset to my hopes for a peaceful home.

Father and son were laughing when I came into the room.

'That is a pleasing sound,' I said, smiling.

Tom rose and gave me a small bow. 'Would you have me leave, Lady Mother?'

I shook my head. 'Stay, for this concerns you as much as your father.'

He pulled up a stool for me and I passed the letter to Gerald, being careful to offer it to his right hand.

He gave it a glance. 'Thomas Howard.'

'Yes. He warns you that you're to be summoned to court. Henry is not pleased.'

'When is Henry ever pleased.'

'I shall write, say you regret you cannot attend as you are injured.'

Gerald shifted in his chair, wincing in pain as he did so. 'I think I must go.'

'Husband, you cannot. You'd not survive the journey.'

'I doubt a letter will suffice.'

'Then I shall go. As your wife, I shall speak for you.'

'Should I go?' Tom said, doubtfully.

'No,' chorused both Gerald and I.

'As your father's heir, you are needed here, in case of trouble,' I said firmly. 'I shall go. I shall take our daughters. Henry is fond of children and Bess could soften any man's heart.'

'I mislike the plan,' Gerald grumbled.

'Mislike or no, it is the best we have. I shall discover who has Henry's ear and request an audience.'

'You'll have to approach the council.'

I smiled at him. 'Is that supposed to frighten me?'

He gave me a lopsided grin, all he could manage because of the continuing paralysis on the left side of his body.

'Thomas Howard is a ferocious biter.'

'And you doubt your wife's courage, she who ventured into the den of the notorious François d'Angoulême and emerged with her dignity in tact.'

This time he laughed. 'Then go with my blessing. Take advice from your brother, Lord Leonard and tell Henry I am his humble servant in all things.'

28

THOMAS CROMWELL
AUTUMN 1533

When I arrived in London, weary after more than a week of travelling, the city was sunk in a late autumn gloom. Even the shopkeepers were grumbling. Londoners retained a fondness for their Spanish Queen and had no love for the Boleyn woman and the upset she'd caused. Trade was poor and in some parishes, people preferred to walk out of the services rather than pray for Anne Boleyn as queen.

Leonard was nowhere to be found but Meg, luxuriating in her new role of dowager marchioness of Dorset, elected to give me some advice.

'Naturally, as one favoured by the king and queen, I hear things. It seems Lord Leonard is thick with Master Cromwell these days which means your brother has found a use for the man. It's said Cromwell arranges everything for Henry just as Wolsey did.'

'The name is familiar. Who is he?'

'Lady Gertrude says he's from Putney, son of a blacksmith. A low-born upstart.'

'If he has the king's ear, it is of no matter to me if he's a gentleman or a man who cleans the privy pits at Greenwich.'

'Elizabeth!'

'Where will I find him?'

"You intend speaking to Cromwell?'

'Yes. Does he still live in Putney?'

Meg sniffed loudly, keen to show her disapproval of any plan which involved a man like Master Cromwell.

'They say he has a house at Austin Friars. Ask anyone. Apparently there's not a man in the city who doesn't know Master Cromwell's house.'

'Thank you Meg, I do not know what I would do without you.'

She bridled a little and eventually produced a smile, showing I'd been forgiven.

Master Cromwell was not what I expected. His face was fleshy with small eyes and an expression showing neither pleasure nor annoyance. He was dressed in black, the cloth of good quality but nothing extravagant. Not a gentleman but a man with a courtier's manners. A careful man.

In that first moment I knew he had appraised me from head to toe, costed my outfit with a merchant's eye and divined my purpose in coming to see him. This was a man who understood the best and the worst in people.

'Lady Kildare, please sit. Would you care for some refreshment?'

'I thank you, no.'

He settled himself, his large hands resting comfortably at his waist and waited for me to speak.

'Master Cromwell, as you may know, my husband, Lord Kildare has been summoned to court by the king.'

His lips twitched at the corners. 'Lord Kildare is summoned by the king yet it is not the earl who is here but his countess.'

'Master Cromwell, my husband is grievous sick The journey from Ireland is arduous. I fear he would not survive. I wish to petition the king for mercy on his behalf.'

His eyes never left my face as I struggled to describe the extent of my husband's incapacity, his continued wish to be of service to his lord, the king, and his distress at being unable to sit a horse. I stumbled over my words, unnerved by the stillness of the man opposite, knowing Master Cromwell for an extremely clever man.

'Lady Kildare, the king's wish is simple. He desires to see your husband, not you. In this there can be no shades of meaning, no misunderstanding. If your husband had been a more obedient subject, an exception might be made. Alas, your husband has taken advantage of His Majesty's kindness, not once but on several occasions. I'm sure you do not need me to enumerate the injuries your husband has done to His Majesty, the many times when, but for His Majesty's generous nature, a charge of treason might have been brought.'

'If I might see His Majesty. As his cousin...'

'A half-blood kinship I believe.'

I bowed my head and murmured that it was so.

'I regret it is not possible to disturb His Majesty with such a request.'

'Master Cromwell, what must I do?'

He gave a sad smile. 'Have your husband come to court, as bidden.'

'The journey would kill him.'

'That, Lady Kildare, is not His Majesty's problem. And now, if you will forgive me, I have business to attend to.'

I recognized the dismissal and made my farewells,

noting that I was given a courteous lowering of Master Cromwell's head, nothing more.

I wrote to Thomas Howard and received a polite note saying it was not possible for him to challenge a royal request. I petitioned Charles Brandon, citing the friendship between me and his late wife but was told his lordship was unavailable. Meg said Brandon had wasted no time in finding a replacement for Mary, marrying his fourteen-year-old ward. He would be embroiled in the joys of newly married bliss. I even begged favours from friends of my mother but found no-one prepared to speak on my behalf. The only spark of light in the gloom was a note from Master Cromwell informing me that a letter had been sent to my husband, stating His Majesty's permission for the earl to appoint a deputy to act on his behalf while he was in England.

Thoroughly despondent at my failures, I wrote to Gerald, telling him I had done all that I could; a delay while he sorted out Tom's duties was the best we could hope for. I asked for his forgiveness, promising I would wait for him here with our daughters.

By Christmas the city was in seething discontent over news of the king's proposed Act of Succession which would place parliament's seal on Henry's new marriage. With the declaration that Henry and Katherine's marriage was null and void as contrary to divine law, the king's daughter, Mary, would be effectively bastardised and excluded from the line of succession. Until such time as the expected prince was born, Anne Boleyn's daughter was to be recognized as Henry's heir. I thought sourly, that as one of the child's godmothers, Meg would be delighted.

My husband came with the first signs of Spring, a gentle westerly breeze guiding him across the sea and back to my arms. Each night during our separation I had kissed his portrait, placing my lips on his, remembering the touch of him, the smell of him, the feel of his body pressed against mine. I had whispered his name and heard the sound of his voice from those far off days when we'd first met at the Field of the Cloth of gold. "The past is always with us."

The lines of pain etched into his face spoke of a journey which he should not have been forced to make. Despite the prayers of his priests and the care taken by his personal servants to ensure his comfort, nothing could protect him from the mountainous waves, the lurching vessel and the jolting passage by litter. By the time he arrived at the house I'd taken for our stay, he could barely speak let alone stand.

A month of rest and my careful nursing gave him enough strength to face examination by the council, an ordeal he brushed aside with his usual invocations for me not to worry. I observed he had fewer visitors than the last time he was in London which boded ill for the outcome. In private, Leonard told me the amount of evidence proved against Gerald was too great for the council to ignore.

'It is his enemies,' I cried, distressed beyond caring how shrewish I sounded. 'You of all people know what Ireland is like: the feuds, the petty quarrels, how every man looks to his own advantage no matter the allegiance he owes to his lord. Whatever he's accused of, it's not true.'

Leonard coved my hand with his. 'Elizabeth, be calm. There is something else you should know. The council believe your husband may not have long to live.'

'Don't say it. Please, don't say it. He won't die. I shall nurse him back to heath. I've done it before. I can do it again. I could not bear to be without him.'

'I was merely going to tell you that Henry has ordered young Tom, in his position as deputy, to summon the Irish council where the king's pleasure will be known.'

'What pleasure will that be?'

'I'm not privy to the king's thoughts. I only know what the council here are likely to advise.'

'I shall ask Thomas Howard. He will help.'

'Thomas Howard will do nothing. His interest is all turned to ensuring his niece gives Henry a son.'

'What shall I do?' I wailed.

By now I could scarcely see for tears. Leonard pulled out a handkerchief and stuffed it into my hand.

'Tell your husband not to do anything rash.'

I treasured the time Gerald and I spent together through the early days of that summer, when the sun grew hot and we sat in our garden beneath the apple tree. I taught our daughters to make chains from the daisies which grew in the grass. Bess was a quick learner and soon had a chain long enough to loop over he father's head which caused both girls much amusement. We did not speak of the future, perhaps both of us sensing the dangers which lay ahead.

I should have been suspicious when Gerald did not talk about what might be happening in Ireland, when

Maynooth was barely mentioned and the doings of his eldest son seemingly of no interest. We spoke of the joys of *Tir na nÓg*, and of Henry's desire to be the Supreme Head on Earth of the Church of England.

'Next to God,' said my husband, smiling.

I smiled back. 'Naturally. Henry may wish to banish the Bishop of Rome from his earthly kingdom but he has always had a healthy respect for the Almighty.'

It was midsummer when I heard the click of the gate followed by the sound of a man striding along the path. I rose from my seat to see Leonard coming towards me. He was in a great fury.

'I told you not to let him do anything foolish. I warned you both and now it's too bloody late.'

I seized his hands. 'What is it? What's happened?'

'The guards are coming to take him to the Tower.'

'But he's done nothing wrong.'

'You think not?'

'Why would you think him guilty? What is he accused of?'

'Fomenting rebellion.'

I covered my mouth with my hands as my eyes widened in horror.

'Who?' I whispered.

'That hot-headed idiot son of your husband.'

'Tom? What has he done?'

Leonard's hands were balled into fists as he struggled to control his temper. I'd never seen him look so angry.

'The fool has publicly renounced his allegiance to the king.'

'That cannot be true.'

'I told you he'd been ordered to convene a meeting of the Irish council. That was where he did it. In front of everyone. The chancellor tried to make him see sense but the young hothead flung down his sword of state and stormed out. To make matters worse, he had with him a hundred and fifty men, all heavily armed.'

His galloglass, I thought. For protection. But why? Why would Tom do something so rash?

Gerald was dressed and ready. His calmness in the face of disaster told me he'd known they would come for him.

'Please, tell me what you did.'

'Who says I did anything?'

'My love, I am your wife. Please tell me.'

He put his good arm round my waist. 'I sent my son a pair of black dice.'

'A privy token?'

'A warning.'

'Of what?'

He sighed. 'Not to trust the Irish council for they'd send him to England where he'd most likely lose his life. I also sent him my little hart of silver gilt, the one you admired when you saw it lying on the table.'

'Why?'

'It was an agreement between us. If I sensed danger, I'd send him the hart. He would know to keep out of the way.'

'To hide.'

'If needs be.'

'Oh Gerald. how could you be so…'

'…careful of my son.'

It was only then that I understood. What he'd done was not foolish; not the act of a man wishing to foment rebellion against his overlord. He had sacrificed himself for his son, his beloved heir. He was old and sick and there was nothing more he could do for himself now he'd been ensnared by Henry, but he needed to keep Tom safe. He thought he could outwit both king and council but in laying his plans he'd forgotten how making grand gestures was part of a young man's nature until age and experience taught him wisdom.

I loved Tom as if he were my own son but I was not blind to his faults, the faults of a young man anxious to prove himself to his followers, to the uncles who watched over him and the brothers-in-law who rode with him. I heard echoes of my mother's last words – "Guard your sons from Henry. Keep them safe." Gerald thought he was keeping his son safe but Tom had ridden straight towards the danger.

They took my husband to the Tower and refused to let me visit. I pleaded with Sir William Kingston, the constable. He was sympathetic but said there was nothing he could do without the king's express permission and that had not been given. There were others, equally as exalted as my husband, under his care and when the order was "no visitors", it meant no visitors. I could send in a change of linen, a warm cover for his bed and some little delicacies if I wished but, no writing materials, and I was not permitted to nurse my husband.

I wrote to everyone I could think of, asking for help but no-one had the king's ear other than Thomas Cromwell.

He was now the king's acknowledged chief advisor with the title of Master Secretary and a number of minions at his command. It was at a meeting with the great man that I abased myself utterly in my attempt to get him to intervene on my behalf. Perhaps in an attempt to get rid of me, he suggested I might try my luck with the queen – a woman might lend a sympathetic ear.

Sly, knowing little Anne Boleyn from twenty years ago, now elevated to the position of most powerful woman in the land. I wondered if she'd remember me or care to be reminded of those months we spent together at the court of the elderly King Louis, serving his English queen. Recalling my foray into danger when I'd approached François d'Angoulême, I knew I must find someone to smooth my way. I considered who I knew at court, then sent a servant with a note to seek out Sir Francis Bryan.

Apart from a dashing eyepatch, he had changed little since the days when he'd tried cozening me in the gardens at Greenwich; a greater display of jewels and a few more lines of dissipation on his face, but in his approach to a woman he remained the same.

'Lady Elizabeth. At last! Tired of your rustic life amongst the peasants?'

'Sir Francis, please, I need your help.'

He grinned. 'I thought you might. I hear your husband no longer basks in Henry's favour.'

'My husband is grievous sick but I am denied entry to the Tower, to nurse him. I need someone who will speak for me to the king.'

He frowned. 'My influence is...'

'Not you, Sir Francis. I would not ask you to beg on my behalf. I thought, your cousin, the queen. If you could get me an audience with Queen Anne, I would be most grateful.'

He came closer and laid the fingers of one hand on my cheek. 'There was a time, Lady Elizabeth, when the exact nature of your gratitude was a matter of debate between us, when dalliance was what we both desired. Now, I fear, your heart is full of thoughts for only one man.'

'He is my husband and I love him.'

'Ah yes love, that fickle mistress.' He gently stroked my cheek with his fingers but I felt nothing. 'You are still a beautiful women, the ravages of age have barely touched you. If only,' He sighed and removed his hand. 'I have a certain *tendresse* for you, Lady Elizabeth, as you must know, so I shall do as you ask. Anne owes me a favour and, although gratitude to a kinsman is not in her nature, I will ensure you have your audience.'

'I thank you, Sir Francis. You cannot know how much this means to me.'

He gave me a crooked smile. 'Would that it meant more; but no matter.' He bent his head over my hand and kissed it. 'Farewell, sweet lady. I shall send a note.'

The queen's room was lighter and brighter than I remembered, with sunlight streaming in through the windows. Three pretty young men in green tunics, playing lutes, glanced up as I walked the length of the floor to where the queen's ladies were clustered on cushions, half-heartedly stitching, alert to what might be an interesting encounter.

Anne was sitting on a large chair beneath a canopy of white cloth-of-gold. She looked every inch a queen in a deep rose-coloured overgown, its voluminous sleeves turned back almost to her shoulders revealing a luxurious white satin lining. The square neckline, tight across her small breasts, was filled with a pleated silk partlet trimmed with tiny pearls which, paradoxically, made her look more unclothed than if she had naked flesh on display.

She honoured me with a tiny cat-like smile.

'Lady Kildare.'

'Your Grace.' My curtsey was as deep and as humble as I could manage. I was not here to score points but to ask a favour.

'I cannot think why you have come to see me, Lady Kildare. Our paths diverged many years ago. I heard you'd gone to Ireland.' She raised her dark eyebrows.

'Your Grace, I would beg a favour.'

She tilted her head to one side, a habit I remembered from our time in France. 'Indeed! And what is it you want, Lady Kildare?'

'Your Grace, my husband is sick and like to die. He is in the Tower and I am denied entry. I beg of you, as one woman to another, to ask the king to allow me to visit my husband, to nurse him.'

'You would put poor Doctor Butts out of a job?'

'Your Grace, I would not presume to ask for the services of His Majesty's doctor.'

She laughed. 'Just as well. I hear Lord Kildare has caused a great upset. His Majesty is not pleased.'

'Your Grace, I beg you. You would have my undying

gratitude if you could persuade His Majesty to allow me to nurse my husband.'

She regarded me the way a cat does with a mouse, knowing she held my future happiness in her hands.'

'I do not want your undying gratitude, Lady Kildare. What else can you offer me?'

'I do not understand, Your Grace. I possess nothing which you do not possess ten times over.'

'You have a daughter, I believe.'

'Yes, Your Grace. I have two.'

'The elder one – how old is she?'

'Bess is seven.'

'Pretty?'

I smiled. 'She is very pretty.'

'Good! I shall have your daughter and in return I shall do as you ask.'

'I do not understand, Your Grace. Why would you want my daughter?'

She smiled at my ignorance. 'The king's daughter, the little Princess Elizabeth, has her household at Hatfield. Your daughter will go there. She will learn to serve *my* daughter.'

I was unsure whether to be flattered or horrified. To serve the king's daughter was a great honour but I would miss Bess keenly. But this might allow me to be with Gerald.'

'You Grace, I do not know what to say.'

'I do not recall you being at a loss for words, Lady Kildare. In France I seem to remember you being somewhat forward with your opinions. Perhaps your years in Ireland have tamed your rebellious spirit.'

I was about to refute the allegation but luckily remembered why I was here.

'Come back tomorrow, Lady Kildare, and bring your daughter with you. In the meantime I shall speak to the king. Now, you may go.'

I dropped down into another curtsey. Then moved backwards until I was far enough away from the royal presence to turn my back and hurry out.

Bess, naturally, was thrilled at the idea of joining the princess's household. She chattered away to her sister about the new wardrobe she was to have, the duties she imagined performing, the friends she would make.. Mary smiled and said not a word. It was Janet who first noticed my second daughter's impediment, patiently explaining her belief that the child could not hear. She was deaf. She made noises so nothing was wrong with her mouth or her throat, she simply was unable to hear so didn't know the words to say. She was not unintelligent. We drew pictures for her and in that way taught her simple written words. But she would never speak, never find a husband, never go out into the world like Bess. In one way it was a comfort, knowing I would always keep her by my side but I grieved for the life she was denied.

Anne was as good as her word. Once Bess was pronounced suitable to attend a royal princess, I was given a letter of permission to show to the constable at the Tower.

29

THE TOWER OF LONDON
LATE SUMMER 1534

I was escorted by Sir William Kingston himself, a rare honour accorded to only the most respected of visitors. We walked across the green and through a stout door held open for us by one of the guards. Part of The Tower might be set aside as a royal palace for Henry's enjoyment but the Beauchamp Tower was reserved as a prison for those who had crossed the king. Everywhere I looked there were locked gates, high walls and armed men.

With Sir William leading the way and a silent warder at my heels, followed by my maid carrying a basket and a bundle of my clothing, we began our ascent of a seemingly endless set of stone steps. The thickness of the walls kept out the stifling heat and muffled the sounds from outside, leaving me wondering what sort of place I was entering. There were occasional brackets with lanterns giving just enough light to see where to put our feet but I had to hold up my skirts to prevent myself stumbling.

Eventually we stopped outside a sold door with a small grille at eye height. The warder produced a set of keys on a ring from his belt, selected one and unlocked the padlock on the chain. He shot back the bolt and opened the door to allow us to enter. The room was a reasonable size, but gloomy with just a single window. The arched alcoves gave the appearance of grand lodgings but the room needed hangings or carpets to disguise the bare stone walls. Despite the heat of the day there was a chill in the air, a damp chill; and an unpleasant odour of decay.

'I have brought your wife, my lord,' Sir William said politely. He turned to me. 'Your maidservant may not remain here but the warder will be outside the door, m'lady. Ask him if you need anything.' He nodded at Gerald, then spoke to me in an undertone. 'Send word when you need Lord Kildare's chaplain or his confessor.'

In my heart I knew he was only trying to be kind but I felt like scratching out his eyes and screaming, 'He is not going to die!'

Gerald lay in a narrow cot with covers pulled up to his chin. At first I thought him asleep but when I eased myself onto a stool by the bed, he opened his eyes.

'Welcome, wife.'

I leant over and kissed his forehead. It felt hot and I did not care for the unhealthy pallor of his skin.

'My love.'

'I see you come bearing gifts.' His smile was shaky and the words slightly slurred. He still suffered from the paralysis which had plagued him since his accident and no amount of careful nursing or potions improved matters.

I lifted up my basket. 'See! I come as an apothecary: herbs, ginger and honey for the fever; willow-bark for the pain. And a special surprise: a jar of your favourite beef broth and some cinnamon comfits from your daughters.'

He tried to chuckle but ended up choking. All the while I was assessing his state. He looked dreadfully weak, as if at any moment he might slip from this world. No wonder the council thought him near death. But the Kildare Fitzgeralds did not accept defeat easily. He gripped the sides of the cot and tried to pull himself up but failed, collapsing back against the pillow.

'Forgive me, Lady Kildare. Your husband is unable to muster a proper welcome. Perhaps come back tomorrow.'

'Lord Kildare, If you think I am going anywhere, you are greatly mistaken. Here I am and here I stay.'

He closed his eyes, a slight smile hovering on his lips.

'Then I surrender myself to your care.'

By the end of the day I had exhausted the poor warder, ordering pitchers of water, another table, a pallet bed for myself and a note to be delivered to my lodgings.

'My maidservant will bring blankets and linen and my lute.'

'A lute, m'lady?'

'Yes. You know what a lute is?'

The man looked discomforted. 'Yes, m'lady. But is it permitted?'

'You'd best ask the constable. And you can tell him I shall need a fire.'

'A fire?'

'Yes. I require hot water.'

He nodded. 'Is there anything else, m'lady?'

'I have arranged for my manservant to come to the outer gate each day with cooked meals and something for the earl and myself to drink. The dishes will be covered and the flagons stoppered, so I expect them to arrive in this room intact with no pilfering by your lads.'

He was counting on his fingers, repeating the words. 'Lute, basket of logs, food, hot water. drink.' He looked up. 'Be it wine or ale, m'lady – in case the constable asks?'

I smiled at him. 'I doubt it matters but if Sir William wants to know, tell him he is welcome to join us for a meal.'

Within two days I had the room well organised. My jars of herbs and medicines were arranged neatly on one of the tables together with a basin, a spoon, a ladle and a knife. Underneath the table was a large pitcher of water covered by a cloth and a basket of soap and salves. A small pan for boiling water for infusions sat on a trivet beside the fire. A large chest, positioned well away from the window, contained changes of clothing, an extra blanket and a large quantity of linen for washing and drying my husband.

Each morning, once I had attended to Gerald's personal needs and seen that he ate some breakfast, I would entertain him by playing my lute, or singing. I did not speak of Maynooth or our absent sons or of what might be happening in Ireland; instead, I told him stories of my childhood at Astley and little anecdotes of my time in France with Cousin Mary. These always amused him. Each evening before I went to bed, I would kneel beside him and say my prayers, remembering each one of his children. Sometimes I noticed a tear in his eye, sometimes he seemed already asleep.

During the day while Gerald slept, I inspected his accommodation. On one of the walls there were carvings: names and occasional dates; images of flowers and a dog, or it might have been a lion. Carving the intricate images into the stone must have taken a long time but time was something every prisoner had. I wondered which poor souls were desperate enough to spend their lonely hours etching the stone and what had happened to them. Some, I suspected, ended their lives outside on the green at the hands of a Tudor executioner. My sisters said our Nevill grandmother's second husband, Lord Hastings, had died there, his death ordered by Richard the Usurper.

Towards the end of the month Sir William agreed with me that Gerald showed signs of improvement; his skin was a better colour and he talked more easily. Sir William explained, with some embarrassment, that he was bound by his orders to pass on the good news to the council; regular updates on his important prisoner were required. He was kind enough not to mention what would happen next. I dared not imagine what the council might do once Gerald was deemed fit and able to stand. Would there be more accusations, further punishment?

I would never know. Two days later, he was unable to sit up and in a great deal of pain. I mixed him a potion of willow bark but it did nothing to ease his agony. He asked for his confessor, saying it was time to make his peace with God and I must be brave.

I watched him slip away from me, his eyes closed, his breathing barely disturbing the air. His chaplain came, and Sir William. Prayers were said and absolution given. I held his hand to let him know he was not alone in this his final journey. At the end, my beloved husband opened his eyes, tried to smile and whispered softly, *'Tir na nÓg'* – a promise that we would meet again in a paradise beyond our earthly existence.

Later, I allowed myself to be led away by Sir William's wife. Lady Kingston took me to small room where she gave me a cup of wine and some words of comfort. She was very kind. After a while Sir William reappeared. He too was most solicitous.

'I have to ask you, my lady, what did Lord Kildare say – at the end? I did not catch his words.'

'He said, *Tir na nÓg*, Sir William.'

'That is what I thought, though it makes no sense to me. Here in the Tower, I have housed Italians and Germans, but those words I do not recognise. What do they mean?'

'It is a place, Sir William.'

'Ah! A place. Is that so. Well, naturally the council will need to know. A prisoner's final words can often prove vital in the search for truth.'

I almost smiled at the thought of the council chasing around trying to find the mysterious *Tir na nÓg*. Perhaps they'd think it a clue to the whereabouts of Lord Kildare's rebel son and heir.

On a blustery day with ragged white clouds scudding across a pale blue sky, they buried my husband within the precincts of the Tower. Here in the Church of St Peter ad Vincula, far from the land he loved, his bones would lie for eternity next to others destroyed by the vengeful Tudor kings.

My cousin Mary once told me a woman can live on very little provided she has the crumbs of a great love to nourish her inner self. Brandon had been Mary's great love, the man for whom she'd sacrificed her position as a royal princess and a queen. But the life she'd imagined in those halcyon days in Paris, was cruelly denied her. Henry took everything: her treasured Mirror of Naples, the rest of her jewels, her plate, half her dowry, the profits from her lands in France and, most importantly, her husband. Through necessity and royal command, Lord Suffolk was obliged to stay by Henry's side, thus depriving Mary of her husband's company. Desperately short of money and deeply in debt, she retired to Westthorpe where she lived a small life while her husband hunted and roistered with the king. Her occasional visits to court were strictly at Henry's invitation, when he found it useful to parade his sister, the French queen, in front of foreign dignitaries.

All I had left of my great love were our four children and memories of the years we'd spent together. Gerald believed he had left me well provided for; our children safe, his heir and the rest of his family on hand to protect us from harm. In England I had my kinship with the king and my Grey family to give me succour.

Instead I was to be hounded by Henry, deprived of my freedom, my title, my lands and my income, and my sons were to be hunted down as if they were traitors.

30

BEAUMANOR HALL
SUMMER 1536

Six weeks after the event and the servants were still speculating about the young lady the king had taken as his third wife. My maid was particularly intrigued, happily chattering away while she combed my hair.

'They say she's from Wiltshire, m'lady; a god-fearing young woman. Did ye know her when ye were at court? I pray she gives the king a son. Poor wight, he's had his fair share of troubles, what with that hussy and what she got up to. Don't seem right to me, not right at all.'

None of it was right. Not the accusations laid against Queen Anne which were utterly despicable and could not have been true; not the trial, presided over by her uncle, Thomas Howard, Lord Norfolk, a charade designed to find her guilty no matter lack of evidence. And most certainly not the verdict and the king's decision to have her executed. I heard a swordsman was brought over from France to deliver the final coup de grace, a fact which would have amused Anne if the person kneeling on the straw of the scaffold had not been her.

Henry, in his rage, had destroyed another blameless woman whose only offence was her failure to give him a son. I, too, prayed Jane Seymour would quickly give Henry a son. Then we might stop this ruthless culling of English queens.

I'd spent almost two years at Beaumanor, Leonard's house near Leicester. As a place of exile it was wonderfully peaceful. The buildings lay in a slight depression amid gentle rolling countryside, surrounded by woods and fields. The house was ancient and rambling, one my mother would have enjoyed rebuilding. Leonard had never married so the house lacked a woman's touch but otherwise was comfortable enough. Outside the gate was the tiny village of Woodhouse and at the end of the village street, the parish church of St Mary in the Elms.

Naturally there were restrictions on my activities which Master Cromwell's man, who had accompanied me on my journey from London, made abundantly clear: no correspondence with anyone in Ireland, or with my brother Lord Leonard; or with anyone at court. I might write to Master Cromwell if I had any requests. No visitors were permitted and straying beyond the immediate vicinity of Beaumanor and its village was forbidden. If I wished exercise, I might ride in the park or walk through the woodland.

By the time he left I was glad to be rid of his unwelcome presence, preferring my own company or that of my younger daughter, even if she could not speak.

Almost a year after coming to Beaumanor, with still no word of my sons, I had another visit from one of Master Cromwell's minions. This time the young man was plainly dressed but exquisitely polite. Laying a document on the table, he explained that under the Act of Supremacy recently enacted by parliament, everyone was required to sign the oath of supremacy, recognizing King Henry as Supreme Head on Earth of the Church of England.

He said nothing about what would happen if I refused but as I dipped my quill in the ink pot, I thought I would happily sign a pact with the devil if it helped my children. Once my name was added to the list of those who had bowed to Henry's greater will, the document was returned to the young man's satchel. He then produced a letter addressed to me from Master Cromwell.

I was informed that as an obedient subject of the king, I was permitted to write to my elder daughter at Hatfield and receive letters in return. But I should be aware that any correspondence would be read by those in authority.

'What of my sons?' I enquired.

The young man's face was inscrutable. 'I know nothing of your sons, my lady.'

Naturally he didn't. Nobody did. Not a single soul. No sightings, no mentions, no letters, no privy words: my sons had disappeared without trace from the face of the earth.

Since his dramatic speech to the Irish council in Dublin, two months before his father died, Tom had been at large in Ireland, harrying Henry's army together with his supporters. For all their determination, it was an unequal struggle so news that Henry had at last got his hands on my stepson, did not come as a surprise. Neither did I blame Leonard for Tom's capture.

It was another of Master Cromwell's men who told me how the young earl of Kildare had failed in his bid to get help from England's enemies and, facing defeat, had written to the king's commander of the army in Ireland, Lord Leonard Grey, soliciting a pardon for his lands and his life. The pardon was given and the young man escorted to court by Lord Leonard where the he now awaited the king's pleasure. If I wished, Master Cromwell's man suggested almost as an afterthought, I might write to my stepson.

Sensing a trap, I declined. I had no wish to incriminate myself and Tom was in no position to pass on what I wanted to know: the whereabouts of my two young sons. Tom had been given a pardon but I knew Henry would kill him. It was what Tudor king's did – destroy their enemies. It was what he would do to my boys if he got hold of them. Everybody said Henry loved children but that would not stop him from killing my sons. If they were still alive and I was beginning to doubt they were.

I was close to despair. I'd seen Leonard once, shortly before he returned to Ireland after delivering Tom into Henry's hands. The meeting had been brief and Leonard nervous, as he was not supposed to be at Beaumanor, but at Leicester. He was not hopeful.

'Neither were at Maynooth when Skeffington razed the walls to the ground and hanged the garrison. It may be your elder boy is with the Irish but I truly do not know. They'll want to keep him out of Skeffington's clutches but none of my contacts has heard anything.'

'And Edward?'

Leonard shook his head. 'Nothing. But take heart, Elizabeth. Be patient.'

Patience in a woman is considered a virtue and over the months that followed every ounce of my being was tested. My life was dominated by being patient from the moment

I opened my eyes until the moment I went to sleep. I waited patiently for others to tell me what they'd heard; for a letter from Thomas Cromwell; for passing strangers who might know something; for scraps of news, however small. I waited patiently for visits to church in case a parishioner might have heard from a cousin in Dublin or an acquaintance with an interest. But Ireland remained stubbornly below the horizon: unseen, unknown, unimportant.

Mary and I walked slowly down the village street, nodding and smiling to those who cared to acknowledge our presence. To them I was the lady at the big house. I guessed most of them did not know why I was there and why I did not entertain like high-born ladies were supposed to do. Mary would have worried them. Like all poor people, they did not like children who were different, not normal, touched by the devil.

I was undecided whether we should take our daily walk as far as Muclklin Wood, a favourite place in springtime to enjoy the bluebells, or circle round the side of the park and visit the ponds to see if we could spy a kingfisher. At some time in the past, streams were diverted to create a network of weirs and fishponds, a source food for the house and of endless delight for Mary. As we passed the church, my daughter tugged on my arm, so I decided we should go first to light a candle for my sons. The interior was cool and we were the only people walking down the nave. This was not a grand place like Westminster Abbey, just a little country church, built to serve the villagers and used by the Beaumonts, the original owners of Beaumanor.

Watching the candle flame flicker, I wondered if I was a fool to imagine my sons were still alive. It had been two years since I'd last had news of them. Since then – nothing. I thought of my grandmother, the one I shared with Cousin Mary: Queen Elizabeth who, in her youth, had married Sir John Grey, my grandfather. She too had lost her young sons, the royal princes. They disappeared from The Tower one summer, never to be seen again. As a child, I was told they'd been murdered by their uncle, the Usurper, but my mother said that was a fiction. The truth was secret and would never be known. Would that be my fate – never to know if my boys were alive or dead. And if they were dead, who killed them.

After a lengthy afternoon searching for dragonflies, we walked back, hot and weary, to the house, ready for something cool to drink. As we approached the door, the steward came running down the steps.

'A man, m'lady!'

'A man?'

'Yes m'lady.'

'His name?'

'Didn't say m'lady but when I told him you weren't at home, he rode off. Said he couldn't stay. Left his boy here with a note for you.'

I wondered who the man was and whether he had news. I concluded that if he lacked the manners to wait, his visit was of no importance.

'Very well, you'd best bring the boy to me.'

The steward looked embarrassed.

'Is there a problem?'

'He won't move, m'lady.'

'What do you mean, he won't move?'

'It's like this, m'lady. The man told the boy to sit on the bench and not move till you came. So he won't.'

'And you, a grown man, are unable to make this boy get up.'

'It's not that, m'lady. It's best you come and see for yourself.'

Shaking my head at the ridiculousness of servants, I followed the steward through the hall and out to the yard by the kitchen door. There, sitting on a bench was a young boy dressed in a jerkin, breeches and a none-too-clean shirt. On his feet were a pair of scuffed shoes and on his head, a cap pulled down low over his forehead, covering his hair.

'Alright, lad,' said the steward, keen to be seen exerting his authority, 'Get to your feet. This be Lady Fitzgerald, the lady of the house. You'd best say what you've come to say.'

The boy raised his head and looked at me. His face was filthy and tear-stained. He was about eight years old, appeared exhausted, but possessed of a pair of eyes, so hauntingly familiar, I nearly fainted. I'd seen those eyes before, in another life, a life I'd thought gone forever.

I knelt down in the dirt, not caring of the damage to my skirts or how I must look to the servants.

'Edward?' I said tentatively.

The child put out a hand. His fingers were curled tightly as if fearing otherwise he might drop whatever it was he held. His arm shook a little and the narrowness of his wrist was heartbreaking. The end of his shirt sleeve was torn and his fingernails black with dirt. Slowly, with great deliberation, one at a time, he straightened his fingers. In the palm of his hand lay a screwed-up piece of paper. It was unsealed.

Gently, so as not to frighten him, I took the note and unfolded it, hardly daring to look at what was written. The message was brief – just a few short words.

"This one is yours. The other one is safe."

Author's Note

In July 1536 Elizabeth Fitzgerald wrote to Thomas Cromwell, informing him that her son, Edward, had been deposited at Beaumanor by persons unknown while she was absent from home. No action was taken against the boy or his mother.

In 1536, the Irish parliament passed a Bill of Attainder against Thomas Fitzgerald, depriving him of his lands and title. In February 1537, Thomas and his five Fitzgerald uncles were executed by Henry VIII.

Elizabeth's elder son, Gerald, was spirited out of Ireland in May 1540, probably with the connivance of his maternal uncle, Leonard Grey. He remained overseas until after Henry VIII died in 1547. He then petitioned for permission to return to England.

Two days after his long-time supporter, Thomas Cromwell was sent to the Tower, Leonard Grey was arraigned on a charge of treason. He had long been suspected of trying to effect a return of the Fitzgerald earls of Kildare. He was executed at Tower Hill in June 1541.

The Mirror of Naples

Descriptions of the "Mirror of Naples" are tantalisingly vague and its ultimate fate is unknown. After the jewel was sent to Henry VIII by his sister, Mary, the king most likely wore it openly and may have been painted wearing it. After Henry refused to sell the jewel back to the French, disputing their valuation of thirty thousand crowns, it disappears from the historical record.

There are suggestions the "Mirror of Naples" is the jewel worn by Mary I in one of her portraits and that it was noted in the inventory of Elizabeth I's jewels after her death. Another theory is that Queen Henrietta-Maria sold it to pay for supplies during the English Civil War. At some point this fabulous jewel was probably broken up and the huge diamond re-cut into smaller diamonds to make it easier to sell.

Acknowledgements

There are so many books, articles, websites, plays and television programmes about the Tudors and particularly about Henry VIII and his wives, it is hard to know where to begin.

Early on in my research I came across Walter C Richardson's book "Mary Tudor: The White Queen" which contains wonderful descriptions of her time in France when Elizabeth Grey was part of her household.

Antonia Fraser's "The Six Queens of Henry VIII" and Alison Weir's "Henry VIII: King and Court" furnished many details of life at Henry VIII's Court.

"The Kildare Ascendency" by Mary Ann Lyons in "Aspects of Irish Aristocratic Life" edited by Patrick Cosgrove, Terence Dooley and Karol Mullaney-Dignam, introduced me to the Fitzgerald Earls of Kildare who, until 1534, ranked amongst the wealthiest and most powerful magnates in the entire Tudor realm.

As always, I want to thank my friends and family for their help, particularly my husband Richard, an unfailing supporter in all my trials and tribulations.

Coming Soon

MAIDS OF DISHONOUR

It is 1540 and Henry VIII has just acquired a fourth wife. New to court is Agnes Leigh, a young woman with a shameful secret who has connections to the powerful Howard family. When Henry discards his queen to marry Katherine Howard, Agnes sees opportunities for advancement.

Henry is besotted with his young wife but when Katherine's past indiscretions are uncovered, those close to her are in danger. With the king swearing vengeance, there is little hope for the queen, but for Agnes, could salvation come in the shape of an unlikely proposal of marriage?

From the peaceful Wiltshire countryside to Norwich and the scene of an armed rebellion, *Maids of Dishonour* navigates Agnes through fourteen years of turbulent Tudor rule until an attempt to subvert the lawful succession of Henry's daughter forces her to face her fears and choose a side.

About the Author

Caroline Newark was born in Northern Ireland and as a child she wanted to be a farmer's wife, have twelve children and live in a cottage with roses round the door. Instead she became a teacher, a lawyer, a dairy farmer and cheesemaker. Other remnants of that early dream survive – she has two daughters, five grandchildren and lives with her husband, Richard, in a house in a village in the West Country with roses growing round the door.

In 1997 after her mother died, Caroline found a small, red leather-bound book lying in a drawer in a bureau. Inside were details of twenty-one generations of her mother's family starting in 1299 with a marriage between the Royal Houses of England and France. With one book for each generation, Caroline has imagined the lives of these women who lived in our past.

The Mirror of Naples is the ninth book in the series.

Website:	www.carolinenewark.com
Contact:	caroline@carolinenewark.com
Follow:	Caroline Newark on Facebook